WHAT READERS ARE SAYING ABOUT
I MADE A MISTAKE

'**Excellent book** . . . I would read more from this author without hesitation' ★★★★★

'This is **one of Jane Corry's best**' ★★★★★

'**Wow wow wow. Absolutely loved** this book' ★★★★★

'Another **emotional rollercoaster** from Jane Corry' ★★★★★

'**Thrilling** and **enthralling**, this is a **must-read** for any thriller fan' ★★★★★

'Well worth **5 humongous stars**!' ★★★★★

'**Thought-provoking, moving** and a **fantastic** read' ★★★★★

'**I absolutely loved** this book . . . an **addictive** read' ★★★★★

'**I cannot wait** for the next Jane Corry novel' ★★★★★

'The characters were **fascinating** . . . A **great, enthralling** read' ★★★★★

'The ending is **stunning**' ★★★★★

'What a **clever plot**! What a **good read**!' ★★★★★

'**Fabulously** written and such a **twisty tale**' ★★★★★

'Kept me on the **edge of my seat**!' ★★★★★

'A **must-read** book. If you haven't read a Jane Corry book then you are missing out' ★★★★★

'**Oh my word**, another **masterpiece** from Jane Corry!' ★★★★★

Jane Corry is a former magazine journalist who spent three years working as the writer-in-residence of a high security prison for men. This often hair-raising experience helped inspire her *Sunday Times*-bestselling psychological thrillers, *My Husband's Wife*, *Blood Sisters*, *The Dead Ex* and *I Looked Away*, which have been published in more than 35 countries. Jane was a tutor in creative writing at Oxford University and is a regular contributor to the *Daily Telegraph* and *My Weekly* magazine.

I Made a Mistake

JANE CORRY

PENGUIN BOOKS

PENGUIN BOOKS

UK | USA | Canada | Ireland | Australia
India | New Zealand | South Africa

Penguin Books is part of the Penguin Random House group of companies
whose addresses can be found at global.penguinrandomhouse.com.

First published 2020
003

Copyright © Jane Corry 2020

The moral right of the author has been asserted

This novel is a work of fiction. Names and characters are the product of the author's
imagination and any resemblance to actual persons, living or dead, is entirely coincidental.
The Association of Supporting Artistes and Agents is a fictional organization, as are the
Poppy Page Extra Agency and Sally's Agency, and there is not and has never been,
as far as I know, any such drama as *Peter's Paradise*.

Set in 12.5/14.75 pt Garamond MT Std by Integra Software Services Pvt. Ltd, Pondicherry
Printed and bound in Great Britain by Clays Ltd, Elcograf S.p.A.

A CIP catalogue record for this book is available from the British Library

ISBN: 978-0-241-98465-9

www.greenpenguin.co.uk

This book is dedicated to my ever-supportive husband,
my children and my grandchildren.
They help me to keep life in perspective.
Always remembering my mother.

Waterloo Underground Station, Platform 3 – January; early evening

MIND THE GAP scream the yellow capital letters on the edge of the platform. But not everyone can see the writing on the danger zone. Only the passengers at the very front who are being pushed by those at the back, centimetre by centimetre, further and further towards the empty track. It's a bit like one of those coin machines in an amusement arcade, where you just need to shove a few more pennies in to send the whole lot tumbling.

At least there's a Help button on the wall. But how fast can you get to it in an emergency, surrounded by a crowd like this? Maybe not fast enough.

It is 6.30 p.m. Rush hour. Platform 3 for the Bakerloo Line from Waterloo to Queen's Park is teeming. Commuters, taut and grey after a day in the office, gaze yearningly at the white-sand poster for Mauritius on the other side of the line. (GO ON! TAKE A SPRING BREAK!) A woman with flamingo-pink acrylic nails opens her briefcase as if to check something and then snaps it shut. A man whips off his yellow tie before stuffing it in the right-hand pocket of his jacket. A couple in black are in fervent discussion about 'the deceased' and the 'court case'. Lawyers or funeral mourners? Tricky to tell. Either way, neither will forget this day.

A musician with a cello is humming quietly. She does not know it but a piece of chewing gum has stuck to her shoe. Only when she returns home that night – shocked and barely able to speak – will she find it. By then, it will seem irrelevant compared with the tragedy she will have witnessed.

A middle-aged Japanese couple, almost dwarfed by their giant silver metallic suitcases, observe their surroundings with confusion. The man is rifling through his shoulder bag as if looking for something. If only they had been somewhere else, there might have been a very different ending to their holiday.

A bleary-eyed student nurses a Starbucks cup. And amidst them all, a young woman is holding up a plastic-wrapped cream wedding dress as if to keep it creaseless from the mob around her.

The stale air tastes of booze, frustration, routine and expectation.

A message flashes up on the board. *Train approaching.*

Where will the doors open? Here there are no sliding glass panels for safety, as on the Jubilee Line. The favoured few who had found respite on the metallic rows of seats lining the walls leap up, upset to find themselves trapped at the back of the throng. Later they will count their blessings.

'*Mind the gap, please!*' exhorts the pre-recorded announcement. The male voice, with its emphasis on the last word, carries just the right balance of courtesy and warning.

No excuse now.

There is a rush of air as the train nears the station. More last-minute arrivals from the back surge forward, hoping to grab a spot even though they should, by rights, wait for the next. Greed can kill. They will learn that soon enough.

The train is in sight now. Speeding closer. Minds are set on the preparation to pounce, jostle shoulders, squeeze through somehow. How on earth will the Japanese couple manage with those enormous cases?

Apprehension is tight. Knuckles clench. Everyone is determined to board, whatever it takes. There are children to meet. Partners. Cats. Lovers. First dates. Work shifts. Flights that can't be missed. Brace for the race.

Then it happens.

Did the victim cry out? Hard to know with the thunder of the train and the screech of its brakes as it tries to stop in time. '*Mind the gap, please,*' repeats the disembodied announcement in oblivious irony. There's a split-second of horrified silence. Then a woman screams.

PART ONE

I

Six weeks earlier

Poppy

'Poppy! How are you?'

My heart fills with love and pride as an enormous orange-and-black striped tiger bounds up and flings her arms around me.

'Jennifer!' I say, hugging her back. I know that as an agent I shouldn't have favourite clients but there's something so warm and endearing about this one that I simply can't help it.

'Isn't this party AMAZING!' she says, finally letting me go from her Tigger hug and wiping the trickle of sweat running down her face; the only part of her that isn't camouflaged by costume. Everyone else is in evening dress but Jennifer is a one-off.

She also has a habit of speaking in capital letters to convey her infectious enthusiasm, which I find rather sweet. 'Talk about a posh hotel!' she purrs, gazing around, her eyes wide. 'I've never been in a ballroom before! And those prawn canapés are to DIE for.'

This place *is* pretty swanky with its rose silk curtains, glittering chandeliers and ceiling frescos, even if it is a bit further out from London than the previous parties. Everyone who is anyone is here; either because they are 'supporting artistes' (also known as extras) who hope to

3

be noticed or because they're connected to the industry like me and need to network. Reputation, recognition and reliability are the three big Rs in this business. And I try very hard to tick all the boxes. My job is to supply casting directors with the ordinary man in the news-agent queue in front of the lead actor; the woman who pushes an empty pram down a street just before an explosion; the child who cycles past a robbery on his bike and carries on without mishap. The sort of person you might not even notice when you're glued to the screen but who makes the action seem normal. It's quite a challenge. But I love it!

I almost didn't get here tonight after that disagreement with the girls over their homework. Melissa and Daisy – aged seventeen and fourteen respectively – used to adore each other but they're currently going through a tricky argumentative stage. Perhaps it's because they're so different, inside and out. Melissa has my husband's glossy raven hair from his father's side with the lofty height to go with it. Daisy, with her auburn curls, is more like the old me: small and slightly dumpy with a shy smile that hides the feistiness underneath. She still believes in magic. When she wants something, she turns her pillow over three times 'for luck'.

I try hard to reason with them like you're meant to, according to my well-thumbed *How to Bring Up a Teenager* book, but they just don't seem to listen. At times, it breaks my heart. I'd have given anything to have had a sister for company at their age. As the years go by, I find that longing growing even stronger. It would be so good just to confide in someone . . .

If it wasn't for my mother-in-law, helping me to 'steer the ship', as she puts it, I don't know what I'd do. Betty is warm, loving, a brilliant gran and wonderfully eccentric, with her passion for one hobby after another. One moment it's making jewellery out of tin lids; the next it's tap dancing. She's also stylish, with a sweet, heart-shaped face that suits her trademark purple berets, which she often wears inside the house as well as out of it. (I suspect she does so to hide her thinning hair, which, according to family photos, used to be light brown until she dyed it blonde in her twenties. Now it's silver.) Betty adores the girls and the feeling is mutual. She's the mother I never had. At least for as long as I care to remember.

It was Betty's idea that I set up the Poppy Page Extra Agency from home after Melissa was born, using my married surname because the alliteration made it sound memorable. For some time back then, I'd been to countless auditions for all kinds of minor roles but hadn't been recalled to any. Not even one. I had to face facts. My career as an actress was over before it had even begun.

'Women like you need something else as well as looking after a family,' Betty told me. 'Trust me. I can tell.'

She was right. How lucky I am to have a mother-in-law like her! I sometimes think she's the glue that holds us all together. Yet on darker days, I fear that without her we might just fall apart.

'And LOOK!' continues Jennifer, bouncing up and down next to me. 'There's that Doris Day lookalike who was in the shampoo ad. Isn't she one of your clients too?'

'Yes,' I say proudly. 'She is.' I wave across the room to a stunning seventy-five-year-old former supermarket cashier who used to be teased mercilessly for looking like the original Doris until she spotted a magazine article about being an extra. Then she made a note of the 'useful numbers' at the end and rang me. 'Do you think I'm too old?' she'd asked.

'You're just beginning,' I'd told her. Now she's actually changed her name by deed poll to Doris Days. 'I know the real one didn't have an "s",' she said. 'But I didn't want to mislead people.'

Age is no boundary in this business, as I am always assuring clients. You don't need an Equity card, even if you have a speaking role. It's possible to earn a steady income if you get a good name simply by being available at short notice, turning up on time at the right place in the right clothes, not pestering the stars for an autograph or – as one of my clients kept doing until I was forced to take her off my books – constantly walking in front of big-name stars to hog the camera! But it's not really about the money. It's the thrill of being onscreen, even if it's for a blink-and-you-miss-it second.

'You know,' says Jennifer chummily, threading a velvet paw through my arm. 'If it wasn't for you, none of us would be here.'

I flush with pleasure. I wasn't born with a silver spoon in my mouth. Nor did I inherit my business from Mummy or Daddy, like one or two of the agents here. I've had to work long and hard to get where I am but it's been worth it. My agency is doing pretty well, financially speaking, and we've really built a name for ourselves. Recently, one of the industry magazines did a two-page 'Casting Agency of the Month' profile on me.

'Very nice,' was all Stuart said when I showed him. He'd been engrossed in some dental article about mandibular jaws at the time, so was probably only half listening.

It's OK. I'm used to it. Stuart lives for his work. Besides, the real reward is helping my clients, many of whom have become good friends, to fulfil their dreams. But every now and then, I can't help feeling a teeny bit jealous that I never made it as an actress myself. I could have done it. I know I could. If only things had been different.

Meanwhile, my clients' successes have now made me a 'name' in the business. It might not be what I had in mind all those years ago. But it's a pretty good second-best.

'I couldn't do it without you and the others,' I say, giving Jennifer's paw a pat.

'Actually,' she replies, lowering her voice just a fraction, 'I've been dying to ask if there was any news on you-know-what.'

She is referring to a zoo film that's about to be made by a certain production company. (They want to use actors in costume rather than special effects or real animals.) I've already put Jennifer up for it but am still waiting to hear back.

'Not yet,' I say. 'But I'm sure it won't be long.'

'Oh well,' she says. 'I'll just have to keep my fingers crossed – or should I say claws!' She guffaws out loud at her own joke, slapping my back. 'Sorry,' she says, wincing. 'When I'm dressed up like this, I can't help getting into character. By the way, is it true that that actor is here? You know, the one who played the gorgeous vicar in that show?'

'Which show?' I ask while noticing another client across the room. Jennifer has a truly remarkable memory and is forever bringing up actors who nobody else remembers, as though they were A-list stars.

'Oh you know, what was it called . . . THAT'S IT! *Peter's Paradise.* And the actor was Matthew Gordon.'

I start. My skin goosebumps. 'Matthew Gordon?' I repeat, incredulous.

Jennifer is looking at me with an odd expression, Swiftly, I try to pass off my shock. 'Wow! That was years ago, wasn't it?'

'Yes.' She seems, thank goodness, to accept the reason for my reaction. 'Well, apparently Ronnie . . .'

She stops, cut off by a sharp tap on my shoulder that makes me turn round.

'Poppy! Don't you look wonderful.' Sharon is one of my rivals who has never particularly liked me since a male client of mine got a plum walk-on role that she'd been after for someone on her own books. 'Black leather trousers. Very cool.'

'Actually, they're my eldest daughter's,' I say. 'I was rather pleased they fitted me.' Too late I wish I'd kept my mouth shut. Sharon isn't exactly svelte. From the look on her face, she's taken my comment as a dig at her own ample figure whereas in fact I was simply admitting the truth. I couldn't decide what to wear tonight until Melissa really surprised me by offering to lend me the new trousers I had recently bought for her. They were a bit long as my daughter is taller than I am, so I had to fold them back into turn-ups. Luckily, these were hidden inside my black suede boots. 'Wow, Mum,' she'd said, leading me to the mirror. 'They look amazing on you.'

This hadn't always been the case. At the time when I still had hopes of the stage, one of the directors I'd auditioned with had described me as 'Little Miss Dumpy' to my agent. (I'd found this out through another girl on her books who had taken great delight in telling me.) It has to be said that my optimism for an acting career had been prompted by encouragement from my parents and school, rather than my five foot two and a half inches of average looks. My main assets, looks-wise, or so I've been told, were and are my glossy auburn hair, which curls naturally on the nape of my neck, plus my permanent smile, whatever the weather. 'Poppy,' Mum used to say to me when I was growing up. 'You were born with a naturally sunny disposition like me. That's a gift. Make the most of it.'

She certainly had. *But you're not her*, I remind myself. *You're you*.

If my mother were here now, she'd see that, by a stroke of luck, I've turned into one of those women who look better in their forties than they did in their twenties. My once podgy looks in the acting world have slimmed into a 'sexily curvy body', according to one roving-eyed casting producer who made it clear that he was interested in me from a very non-platonic point of view. Naturally, I'd brushed him off.

'Your daughter's trousers?' repeats Sharon now in a sarcastic tone. 'I'd have thought you could afford your own clothes.'

Bitch. I don't normally use that word but trust me, this woman is one.

'Very funny,' I say. Then I gesticulate at Sharon's shapeless navy silk shift; an expensive designer tent, contrived to hide bulges. 'You look extraordinary.'

I'm not lying. She does. And yes I know that my choice of words could be taken either way. Guess which one she seems to have gone for, from the look on her face? To be fair, she wouldn't be wrong. The problem with being in this business is that you can say or do some pretty awful things just to stay ahead of the game – even if you kid yourself that you're really a nice person.

'Sorry,' I blurt out, spying Ronnie, another of my clients, in the corner and seeing an escape route. 'There's someone I have to talk to over there.'

'Me too,' she retorts in a cold, clipped voice. 'Catch you later.'

'Another drink, madam?' asks a passing waiter.

'Thanks.' I stop to have my sparkling water topped up. I can't drink because I'm driving home tonight. I only hope the weather isn't too bad. It was freezing on the way over and there were warnings of snow.

But just before I can reach Ronnie, my mobile flashes. *Home*.

'Everything all right?' I ask.

'No,' sobs a small voice.

I can only just hear my younger daughter with the loud party music around us.

'Melissa has taken my sketchpad and won't give it back.'

Daisy has lived and breathed art from the moment she picked up a pencil. No one knows where this particular skill comes from. Betty tries to be arty with her various hobbies, but although we praise her efforts, she's not a natural. Obviously, I'd never say so for fear of hurting her feelings.

'Can't Gran sort it out?' I ask.

'She's meditating in her room.'

'What about Dad?'

'He's going to be late again.'

I swallow my irritation. Stuart had promised to be back early from the surgery because of this party. Although Betty is brilliant at dealing with the girls, she's not getting any younger and I don't want to impose on her.

'Give me that!'

It's Melissa. 'I only took it off her because she wouldn't let me watch *I Want to Be a Star*.'

It should be said here that my eldest daughter's entire aim in life is to get onto the stage. I don't know how many times I've tried to talk her out of it, but the conversations always end so badly that I've given up now. 'Just because *you* failed, doesn't mean I will,' Melissa had snapped the last time. Ouch!

'Please, girls,' I say down the line. 'Can you get Gran to come downstairs?'

'She says she will in a minute but that we've got to sort out our own arguments because it's good for us.'

That's all very well, but right now I'd rather Betty intervened.

'And where have you put my leotard? I need it for dance class tomorrow.'

I try to think. 'In the linen cupboard.'

'I've looked and it's not there.'

Maybe that's because it's a right old mess. I never seem to have time to fold everything so I just chuck it in. I can't ask my mother-in-law to do everything.

'In the dirty laundry bin?' I suggest.

'Nope.'

Then it comes to me. The gusset had torn and needed mending. So it was by my bed, waiting for me to ask Betty if she'd mind. I know my stuff when it comes to running an agency, but sewing is not one of my skills. 'I remember now—'

Damn! My mobile's just cut out. I meant to recharge it in the car on the way here but forgot to bring my lead. Now I'll have to go and see if they have a spare at reception. If not, I'll ask if I can use their phone to ring the children back.

'Poppy,' says a plaintive voice at my side.

It's Ronnie. My heart instantly softens. He reminds me a bit of my dad with that combination of anxiety and determination on his face.

'I heard that vicar chap from *Peter's Paradise* is here. The really good-looking one. You don't think . . .'

I know what he is going to say. Matthew's success came from his role as a vicar. Vicars are Ronnie's speciality. In fact he was a vicar himself until he got defrocked (he's rather vague on the details) and now he specializes in pretend ones. Clearly Ronnie worries his toes are about to be trodden on.

'Ronnie, I'd be amazed . . .' But before I can say any more, Jennifer comes lolloping over to us.

'Poppy, it's true. He's HERE!'

The music stops just as she yells the last part. Suddenly, the whole room goes silent.

Everyone is looking at the man who has just entered the ballroom. He's wearing a black dinner suit but has made it look different from everyone else's by artfully tucking that scarlet bow tie into his jacket pocket so it is just peeping out; rather like a nosegay. It's the sort of thing that someone might do halfway through a party but it takes a certain confidence to arrive like that.

The crisp white shirt is open at the neck, revealing a mass of curly brown chest hair. On his feet, he's wearing winkle pickers. In our day, they might have been considered old-fashioned but now they look cool. His dark hair is swept back from his face, revealing a strong forehead and a nose that isn't afraid to stand out, rather like his dress sense.

He takes the glass of champagne offered by an admiring waitress. Downs it in one and accepts another. 'Cheers,' he says in a deep rich voice, as if he is talking to the cameras. Deeply. Intimately. You can't help feeling that this is a man who enjoys an audience. He scans the crowd, resting momentarily on Doris Days and a few selected others as though each is the only person in the world who matters.

Then his eyes settle on my face.

I cannot breathe. Matthew Gordon is making his way straight towards me.

'Pops,' he says, now standing so close that I can smell his minty breath. No one has called me that for years.

I am aware of several jaws dropping around me and the unspoken 'please introduce me' expressions. This is a man whose name would mean nothing to my children. It might not mean much to my generation either unless they have encyclopaedic memories like Jennifer. But it doesn't really matter. People would be staring anyway. This man is objectively drop-dead handsome in a fifty-plus way and he has presence. In spades.

Matthew puts out his hand to shake mine. His skin feels warm. Just as it had twenty-three years and three months ago when it had last pressed against mine in my little Kilburn bedsit with its one-bar electric fire. 'What a lovely surprise!'

Central Criminal Court, London – Summer

Court No. 1 is large and modern, with white walls and an RAF-blue carpet more suited to an office. There is a series of long tables laid out before the judge's bench, almost like a classroom. The prosecution and the defence barristers in their wigs and black gowns with flapping crow-like wings are seated in separate tiers. Behind them are their respective teams in their sharp suits who lean forward at times to pass a note or whisper in their barristers' ears. There are computer screens on all the desks, including the judge's, and even on the wall.

And, of course, there's the jury. When the jurors first filed in at the beginning of this murder trial, they looked rather stunned and out of their comfort zone. But now, two days in, some are becoming more assured. Others are still twitchy, like the man fiddling with his anorak zip as though there was something wrong with it.

He stops, however, when a woman is called to take the stand. Instantly a deafening silence sweeps across the courtroom. All eyes are fixed on her. She is wearing a loose emerald-green dress with a bright white collar, which she keeps smoothing down as though nervous. The colour suits her auburn hair. Her face is devoid of make-up. She is not wearing earrings, although if you look closely you might see that her ears have been pierced.

Her eyes dart from one place to another, resting fleetingly on all the heads turned towards her.

'Poppy Page,' says the prosecution counsel in her crisp clear voice. 'Can you tell me precisely what happened when you met Matthew Gordon, the deceased, at the Association of Supporting Artistes and Agents' Christmas party?'

The woman starts to answer, but the words appear stuck in her throat. Her fingers are twisted awkwardly as if she is threading one through the other like a child's game.

'We talked,' she says finally.

'About what?' says the prosecutor sharply.

The woman looks up to the public gallery. There are quite a few there. It's a popular place, not just for the family and friends of those on the stand but also for those seeking free entertainment and shelter from the rain. Right now, it's actually nearly thirty degrees outside. We are, according to the forecasters, set for a heatwave. Both in court and out.

'About the industry,' she says. Each word that she utters appears to be a huge effort.

'Did you talk about anything personal?'

Her eyes meet those of the prosecution barrister who has just spoken. 'Why would we do that?'

'That's for you to tell me, I believe, Mrs Page. Let me ask you another question. Is it true that you used to know the deceased in a . . . non-professional capacity?'

The woman looks down at the ground. She nods her head in a quick, awkward jerking motion, rather like a puppet on a string.

'Please use verbal responses only.'

'Yes,' she whispers.

'Louder, please. I'm afraid the court might not have caught that.'

'Yes.'

'How did you originally meet?'

There is silence. The barrister glances at the judge, who wears a pair of thick-rimmed glasses. They appear almost anachronistic, set just below the wig, which looks like it belongs to a different age. He leans forward disapprovingly.

'Mrs Page,' he says. 'Would you like the question repeated?'

She shakes her head and then visibly swallows hard. It almost seems that something is stuck in her throat. She takes a sip of water. After that she looks down at her hands – now perfectly still – as if they are not her own.

And then she speaks.

2

Betty

Dear Poppy . . .

'How can any of this have happened? You've been like a daughter to me and now . . . well, what can I say? I'd like to talk to you, face to face. But as you've discovered, you poor thing, it's not private enough during visiting hours. So I'm writing to you instead. You might not like all of it. I'm not even sure where to begin. But I'm going to start with my own adult life. You'll understand why, later on.

When I got married back in 1970, I was twenty and life was all very different. In our part of the East End, it wasn't on for a couple to live together without a wedding ring. 'Only a slut would do that,' my mum used to say. 'Don't you ever go getting yourself into trouble, girl, or your dad and me will sling you out faster than you can say "sorry".'

'It's "your dad and *I*",' I wanted to say. But I didn't dare or she'd have clipped me one for being cheeky. We used to have neighbours whose daughter had 'got into trouble'. She had to get married, of course, but they couldn't deal with the scandal and moved away. 'That girl ruined her parents' lives,' my mother muttered every time we went past their block of flats.

It's incredible how attitudes to these things have changed in what isn't such a very long period of time. Then again, maybe all generations feel the same. Who knows what life will be like when Melissa and Daisy are my age? It's both scary and exciting to think about it.

I'd never had a boyfriend before Jock. It wasn't for the wanting. I'd have given anything for one! But I was painfully shy. Once a boy at school started to chat me up on the bus but I didn't know what to say. It might have been different if I'd had a brother but men, to me, seemed like an alien species.

Besides, the opportunities for finding love were few and far between. My parents wouldn't let me go to the dances that my friends did. 'Plenty of time for that sort of thing when you're older,' my father used to say. I was fifteen at the time. Dead strict, he was.

My mother persuaded him to let me go to the church youth club but there were mainly girls there. Then a group of skinheads came in one night and brought bottles of beer with them. They smashed up the place and the youth club closed because it couldn't afford to repair the damage. My parents wouldn't let me go out at night after that – they said it wasn't safe. So that was the end of my social life for a while apart from spending my pocket money on a fizzy lemonade at the local Wimpy bar on Saturday lunchtimes with girls from school. Of course, we always eyed up any of the blokes who came in. But none of them showed us much interest. So instead, we just talked about Davy Jones from the Monkees. Fancied him rotten, we all did! I had a poster of him on my bedroom wall that had come free with *Jackie* magazine. Every night I prayed that Davy would somehow find me and whisk me away. Of course, I knew it wouldn't really happen but we all need our dreams, don't we?

I wasn't very bright at school. English, maths, geography . . . That kind of stuff never made sense in my head. Maybe it was because my school was so rowdy. It was hard to concentrate in class. I'd actually got a place at the Grammar when I was eleven but my parents wouldn't let me take it because they couldn't afford the uniform. So I went to the local comprehensive instead, which had quite a name, for the wrong reason.

But I liked art and needlework. 'Your Betty has a real skill,' the teacher told my parents. 'She could go on to art college or teach domestic science if she stays on.'

There was no way my parents would allow that. They didn't believe in further education. In their view, students were 'layabouts' and 'spongers' with long hair. I believed them, not knowing then that their narrow-minded attitude came from fear of the unknown. They could still remember the war. All they wanted now was safety and a sensible occupation for me. My mother had worked in a light-bulb factory until she'd had me. My father was still there. It was the way it had been when they were young in the late forties and early fifties and they didn't see why it had to change now.

'I've made inquiries, Betty,' Dad told me with pride on my sixteenth birthday. 'Spoke to my boss, I did and got you a place on the factory line. You're a very lucky young lady. There's people would kill to get a steady job like this.'

'Why can't I go to college to do dressmaking?' I protested. I'd always been a good girl and done what I'd been told, partly because I was an only child. There was no one else to fight my battles for me. But the thought of working in the same factory as my dad, just round the corner from our council estate, filled me with dread.

'Arty crafty stuff and nonsense, you mean,' snorted my dad. 'That's not going to help us put bread on the table. You need to start earning your keep if you're going to carry on living here.'

I know that sounds hard. I can't ever imagine you saying something similar to the girls, Poppy. But it was the way that many working-class families thought at the time. They believed it was good for us. Maybe it was.

Then, just before I was due to start work, I caught the 38 bus to Tottenham Court Road and went window shopping in Carnaby Street with some of my old schoolfriends. None of us could afford much but I liked to look at the clothes and work out how they were made. Afterwards, I'd browse round the local market and buy some material from saved-up birthday and Christmas money. I'd make my own pattern and run up outfits using Mum's sewing machine.

Then I saw the vacancy on the door of a boutique. (It was really 'cool', as Melissa and Daisy might say, although we used the term 'groovy'.) It had blacked-out windows and dim lighting inside so you could hardly see the clothes. They also played music, which in those days was really different. WANTED, said the advert, SHOP ASSISTANT. PERMANENT POSITION.

Almost without knowing what I was doing, I went in and filled out a form. 'We want someone who can advise our customers on fashion,' the manageress told me.

'Well,' I said, smoothing down my jacket. 'I made this and the skirt I'm wearing.'

'Did you now?' she said thoughtfully.

When I got home, my dad was livid. 'What's this about working in some clothes shop?' he'd demanded. The manageress had already rung our home number (which I'd put on the form) and told my parents that the job was mine if I was still interested! I expected Mum to be furious too but the funny thing was that she was quite impressed. 'Don't you worry. I'll talk your dad round.'

She did as well, partly because the pay was higher at the shop than the factory. Oh, how I loved it there! I got to know lots of the customers who kept coming back because I'd show them what suited them and what didn't. They seemed to appreciate my honesty. Often, I'd explain how to wear something in a slightly different way – like a jumper off the shoulder or with a chain belt from our new range.

Sometimes they'd ask where I got the clothes I was wearing. I explained I made them myself. 'Can you come up with something for me like that?' customers would inquire. I asked the manageress for permission. 'No,' she said. 'But you can make a couple of outfits for us and we'll sell them, keeping half the profits. Does that sound all right for you?'

It sounded more than all right. I was able to save enough to buy Mum her favourite perfume – Blue Grass – for her birthday. But the other girls in the shop got jealous because I was making more money than they were with my on-the-side earnings. They started whispering about me and kept asking me why I didn't have a boyfriend. It made me feel that there was something wrong with me. In those days, people still talked about being 'left on the shelf'. The worst thing that could happen to you, apart from getting pregnant before being married, was not finding someone who wanted to marry you.

By now, Mum had persuaded Dad to allow me to go to discos with my friends. I was seventeen then. But they were so noisy and full of confident girls who danced with their arms raised above their heads. When the quiet music came on – the signal for boys to come up and ask for a 'slow' dance – no one ever came near me. So I'd just go home early and sew instead.

Then two really big things happened, both of which changed my life in their own way. The first was that I got a new job in the hat section of a department store nearer home. The staff were older than the last lot in the boutique, and much nicer. It feels rather awful to admit it, but looking back on it, that might have been the happiest time of my life. After a while, they asked if I could do a bit of modelling at shows for regular customers. Apparently I had 'just the right kind of face', as the department manager put it.

Even in my wildest dreams, I'd never thought of being a model! That sort of thing happened to other girls – pretty ones. I was just ordinary-looking, wasn't I, with mousy-coloured hair and freckles. At least, that's what I'd been brought up to think. On the other hand, Twiggy had been living proof that a working-class girl could get on to the front cover of *Vogue*. Of course, I couldn't do the same. But wearing hats on a catwalk would be so exciting, wouldn't it? They might also cover part of my face so people wouldn't see I was nervous.

Once again, my parents weren't keen. 'Modelling isn't the kind of thing that a nice girl does,' said my mother. But she changed her mind when I told her about the store discount I could pass on to them. It's easy to think they were mercenary, but you've got to imagine what it had been like for them to have been brought up in the war years. Money was tight. Rationing went on until 1954. Every penny counted. Not like now, when many people 'max out' their credit cards.

You might be wondering, Poppy, why I'm telling you so much about my early life. But it's important for both of us. Trust me.

The second big thing was that I finally got my first boyfriend.

I met Jock through the choir at our local church in Hackney. It was a Saturday, and we'd all been asked to sing at a wedding. Got paid 2s 6d each, we did! 'Blimey,' said one of my friends, elbowing me in the ribs. 'He's new, isn't he? Bit of a looker, don't you think?'

Yes he was, even though I could only see his back. But I liked his dark glossy hair which came down to his collar. He was also tall – at least six foot! Then we started to sing the hymn 'Love Divine', and from the minute he opened his mouth, I was lost. I'd never heard such a deep, powerful voice. When he sang 'All loves excelling', I got shivers of excitement running down my spine!

Then when the service had finished and we all filed out, he caught my eye and actually gave me a wink! Of course, he was just being friendly.

'I heard that his parents moved down from Scotland a few years ago and that he came with them,' whispered one of my friends.

Yet Jock's warm, friendly accent was as strong as if he had just crossed the border, as I found out when we all met up in the choirmaster's little office to get paid. Of course there was no reason why he would give me a second glance. There were lots of other girls in the choir who were much better lookers with bigger busts and prettier faces. So I couldn't believe it when Jock and I found ourselves walking back along the high street together.

'I turn off here,' I said when we got to my road.

He seemed disappointed. 'Fancy a drink next Saturday night?'

I'd never been asked out on a date before, let alone gone into a pub.

'I'll have to ask my dad,' I said, feeling myself go red. It was the truth. I couldn't go out without permission. Jock would think that was so childish! He'd be bound to lose interest now.

But he surprised me. 'Tell you what,' he offered. 'Ask me round for a cuppa and I'll ask your dad myself.'

I can't tell you how nervous I was! From the stuff you read nowadays, it's easy to think that the late sixties and early seventies were all sex and drugs. But that was just for a small group of people. There were still lots of repressed teenagers with strict, old-fashioned parents who were scared of the way the world was changing. Sometimes I think it's why there are so many rebellious grannies around now. We're fighting for what we should have fought for back then.

'I've invited a friend from the choir back here,' I said that evening.

'What?' said Mum. We weren't the kind of family who had guests.

'He only wants a cup of tea,' I said quickly. 'You don't have to make him a proper meal.'

'He?' said Dad sharply.

'Jock sings in the church choir. He works in your factory too. His surname is Page.'

My dad's eyes narrowed. 'That young man with the Scottish accent?'

I nodded.

'He's OK,' said my dad slowly. 'All right. He can come round if you want.'

So he did. Mum even asked him to stay on for a bite to eat. 'It's not much,' she said. 'Just bangers and mash.'

'That's my favourite,' Jock had declared, and my mother beamed at him. 'By the way, would you mind if I took your wee Betty out for a drink up in the West End next Saturday?'

My mother raised her eyebrows. 'Very fancy.' Then she looked at my dad questioningly.

'Only if you get her back here by ten p.m.,' he said.

'Not a minute later,' promised Jock.

Can you imagine, Poppy, what Melissa would say if we imposed a curfew like that!

I shook all week with nerves at the thought of my first proper date. Supposing I ran out of things to say? What should I wear? What if I didn't know what to order and he suddenly thought I was too young for him? (He was twenty!) Maybe he'd see sense and cancel me. All week, I expected the phone to ring and for him to make some excuse. When that didn't happen, I convinced myself he'd stand me up.

But instead he arrived dead on time.

'You look lovely,' he said, as if he really meant it and wasn't just being polite. 'What a pretty dress.'

'Thanks,' I said nervously, smoothing down the blue-and-pink Viyella fabric. 'Actually, I made it myself.'

'Did you now? I like a woman with style and talent.'

Woman? The word sounded so strange to me. I'd always thought of myself as a girl. As for the style and talent bit, I thought he was having me on. A flash of panic struck me. What if he was just a 'charmer'? I wasn't exactly sure what a charmer was but I remembered hearing it on the radio in a way that suggested it wasn't a good thing for a man to be.

But Jock was a perfect gentleman. He insisted on buying my Tube ticket and found me the only empty seat in the carriage, which was stuffed full of people going out for the evening. He already knew London 'like the back of my hand' and took me to a pub in Argyll Street, near Oxford Circus. 'I like it here,' he told me. 'It's not rough but it's got atmosphere.' He ordered me a second glass of sherry without asking. We didn't run out of things to say. Far from it, in fact. He asked me about my work and friends. Then he told me about himself and how he'd missed Scotland at first but really liked it down here now. He was also saving up to rent a flat of his own. How grown up!

On the way home, he actually put his arm around me. Every single bone in my body was on fire. When we reached the corner of my road, he stopped under the lamppost. 'You're very special, Betty. Do you know that?'

My heart stopped as his face drew closer. Then his lips closed in on mine. I'd read about snogging in magazines and about how magical your first kiss is, but honestly I had always thought that it sounded rather disgusting with tongues touching. It felt a bit odd when Jock's lips came down on mine. Not weird odd. Just different odd. But I was sure I'd get used to it.

'You're beautiful, Betty,' he told me. 'When can I see you again?'

We went out every Saturday night for the next year. He began to call me his 'wee hen', which I found rather strange at first until he explained it was a Scotsman's way of 'addressing his lady'. Then it made me feel special. On my eighteenth birthday, he took me to the local Berni Inn! I'd often walked past it and admired the smart couples going in and out with their flash cars. Never had I thought I'd go into it myself.

'Don't mind if I order for us both, do you?' he asked.

Thank goodness! I wouldn't have known what to choose. We had steak (I'd never had it before!) and chips, followed by apple crumble.

As I dug my spoon in, I felt it hit something hard. I didn't like to say anything in case it was part of the dessert. Then I gasped. It was a beautiful small diamond ring. When I wiped off the custard, it sparkled in the candlelight.

Jock got down on his knees. Everyone in the restaurant was looking.

'Betty,' he said. 'Will you do me the honour of being my wife?'

I could feel my heart pounding. What should I say?

'I don't know if my dad will let me,' I whispered.

'It's all right,' he replied. 'I've already got his permission.'

When I said yes, everyone around us clapped like we were on stage. Part of me was on cloud nine. I was going to get married! Of course I'd done the right thing in accepting. Yet at the same time, something didn't feel quite right – though I couldn't have said what, exactly.

'You'll have to wait until you're twenty to get married,' said my father when we returned home that night with the diamond sitting proudly on my left hand.

'And no hanky panky until then,' my mother added in front of my new fiancé. I'd blushed like a beetroot.

'Two years is a long time to wait, sir,' said Jock smartly.

Just what I'd been thinking. But I wouldn't dare say so.

My dad's eyes went hard. 'My daughter's still young. Marriage is for life. If you can't be bothered to hang around, that's your decision.'

I wanted to cry. 'Please, Dad,' I said.

But Jock placed a hand on my arm. 'It's all right, Betty. Your father's right.' Then he took his hand away and reached out to shake my dad's. 'You have my word. Love is worth waiting for. And meanwhile, I promise to treat your daughter with the respect she deserves.'

My parents believed him.

And so did I.

3
Poppy

Matthew Gordon is here? I can't believe it, and yet there he is, standing right in front of me.

What do I say? Shock makes the inside of my mouth go dry and sponges up all the words that might otherwise have come out. I can smell the curiosity in the air. Everyone is looking at us. As I've just said, it's not because they recognize him, since the younger ones probably wouldn't even have heard of him. That TV drama which had afforded him a short burst of fame had been years ago, when I'd been in my twenties. Since then, he hadn't appeared in anything major, as far as I knew. The acting profession can be like that. Loves you one minute; turns its back on you the next.

No. People are staring because Matthew has all the presence of a Hollywood star. That assured, easy stance and penetrating stare can make you feel like the most important person in the world. As I know all too well. The spotlight is also on him as a new face in a room where nearly everyone is acquainted with everyone else in this industry. And unless I'm careful, people will want to know exactly why this distinguished-looking man has headed straight for me and – more importantly – why I am standing here like a complete goof, unable to talk. In fact, why am I? He is the one who should be nervous about meeting me again.

'Hi,' I squeak, finally finding my voice. 'I didn't expect to see you here.'

'Actually . . .' he starts to say, but before he can finish, Jennifer rushes up, followed by Doris.

'I loved you in *Peter's Paradise*,' she gushes. 'I used to cut your face out of the *Radio Times* and stick it on my bedroom wall. I wept buckets when my mother tore it down and your forehead got ripped. I looked everywhere for you after that.'

'Me too,' Doris says breathlessly. 'I wanted you for my toy boy! All the checkout girls had the hots for you. Where did you go? Hollywood?'

Matthew laughs. He used to have several versions but I remember this one. It's a laugh designed to conceal embarrassment. That had been part of his charm. When I first saw Matthew, I thought he was far too good-looking and confident to talk to me. But when we got to know each other better, I discovered how touchingly vulnerable he was underneath. At least it seemed touching, back then.

'Actually, I did audition for some roles in LA,' he says, 'but I didn't want to leave the UK.' He glances at me. 'My wife was keen to stay over here and family has to come first.'

'Ah,' coos Doris. 'That's so nice. But what have you been *doing*?'

I want to take her to one side and gently explain that she can't ask these kind of questions. But Matthew doesn't seem to mind. Perhaps he likes being recognized again.

'This and that,' he says airily. 'A few small roles here and there. A bit of teaching too at drama school. These young actors need all the help they can get nowadays.'

He manages to sound almost philanthropic. I remember now how adroit he was at being nice to others while at the same time putting himself in a good light. I also recall how he would encourage me to do something for 'my' benefit when it was really for his. So why, when I know what this man is like, am I feeling so ridiculously jittery?

'How good of you,' gulps Jennifer, brushing against him, no doubt in the hope of catching some of his magic stardust. 'I'm always saying that diction simply isn't what it was!'

Matthew puts his head to one side as if considering this. 'That is sometimes true.'

'I heard,' adds Jennifer eagerly, as if encouraged by his partial agreement, 'that you're looking for a vicar role! I must say that I can see you as that dishy priest if they remade something like *The Thorn Birds*! SO sexy!'

I want to sink into the ground in embarrassment but Matthew appears flattered. 'That's very kind. Actually, you heard wrong. I'm not really the vicar type.'

You can say that again.

'So why are you here?' demands Doris, who usually comes straight to the point where men are concerned.

Matthew fiddles with his open collar for a second and then stuffs his hands in his pockets. Both are acting techniques for delaying replies on stage and in real life, as I'm well aware. 'A casting director friend suggested I came along to network. In fact, I'm thinking of becoming an agent myself.' He pats my bare shoulder. (I'm wearing an emerald-green halter-neck top, tucked into my borrowed trousers. The colour, or so I was once told, goes well with my hair.) My skin burns at the touch. 'And who do I find here? My old friend Poppy.'

'You know each other?' gasps Jennifer. 'What a small world. There's me, who used to go to bed under your picture every night, and now I'm an extra myself with an agent who actually knew Matthew Gordon back in the day. How incredible is that?'

They're all looking at me. I have to say something. 'You're right,' I blurt out. 'It is a small world. Great to see you, Matthew. Sorry I can't stay longer to chat but I've just got to ring my kids.'

For a minute, I enjoy the brief moment of surprise on his face. Yes, that's right, Matthew Gordon. I have a family of my own now. I survived without you.

'Did you know that Poppy has found me a role in a really great advert?' I hear Doris telling Matthew.

'That reminds me. I need you to sign the contract for that,' I say. 'It's quite urgent.'

'I could pop round to your place if you like,' she offers.

Doris lives near me and we shop at the same local deli. Although we know each other's address, neither of us has been to the other's house. Despite working from home, I don't usually invite clients round. I want to keep the two separate. It's more professional and besides, it wouldn't be fair on the family. Luckily, nearly all my work is done online or on the phone. Signed contracts are scanned and emailed through. But Doris is old school and can't do it that way, so we usually meet in public places like coffee shops. This is an exception because of the urgency.

'Monday morning, first thing?' I suggest.

'Perfect.'

Then, desperate to get away from Matthew, who's still hanging around, I start to thread my way through the crowds towards reception.

I'm in need of a phone charger so that I can ring home and sort out the latest domestic upset. But I also need some headspace to get over the shock. Matthew Gordon doesn't belong here. I had packed him firmly away in a box labelled *To Be Forgotten*. Sometimes over the years, I'd wondered uneasily if we might bump into each other at some point. Maybe on set when I went along to support my clients. But we never have. Until now.

'Would you like a drink, madam?' asks a passing waiter. Without thinking of my drive home, I take a glass of bubbly and swig it down, followed ten or so minutes later by another. I need something after the shock.

It takes time for the young things on reception to find me a charger that fits my three-year-old phone but eventually one of the girls comes up trumps. She produces it with a triumphant flourish – as if she's just discovered it in the archives – and offers to plug it in so I can speak immediately. 'Everyone all right?' I ask when Betty answers. Clearly, she must have finished her meditation session now, or perhaps my daughters have interrupted her.

'Fine, dear,' she trills. 'I've found Melissa's leotard and mended it. We've also been playing this really clever game called Articulate. So good for the brain, you know!'

I can't help feeling a bit hurt. The last time I suggested Snakes and Ladders to the girls, my older daughter declared she wasn't a 'kid any more'. But they don't have any problems playing games with Betty. 'Thanks,' I said. 'Is Stuart back?'

'Not yet. He had to take an emergency, poor man.'

'I'll try not to be long,' I say. 'Just got to talk to a few more contacts.'

'No rush, dear. But keep an eye on the weather. According to one of my yoga friends, Storm Tanya is heading over from the Caribbean. The bad ones never seem to have male names, do they? Talk about sexist! Now come on, Daisy, it's Melissa's turn. See you later!'

I head back into the ballroom, keeping my distance from Matthew, who looks as though he hasn't been able to escape from Jennifer and Doris's barrage of questions. Part of me would like to join them and ask him a few myself. Maybe even mention Sandra. But I know that's a really, really bad idea. I need to let bygones be bygones.

'Hi! It's Poppy, isn't it?' says a voice behind me.

I swivel round. It's one of the new casting directors I've been trying to network with. They're the ones who read the scripts and see that the storyline requires a couple snogging in a coffee bar in the background, behind the main characters. Or a grandfather feeding the ducks in the park with his grandchildren just before a body is discovered. Usually extras aren't required to speak or have experience but directors can't just go out and find anyone to play these parts. There are too many rules and regulations. So they use agencies like mine.

'Yes,' I say, 'it is.'

'Who was that man you were with just now?' he asks. 'The rather striking middle-aged bloke with the scarlet bow tie?'

'Oh,' I say lightly, 'just someone I trained with at drama school.'

'Is he on your books?'

I almost laugh at the thought. 'No.'

He strokes his trim goatee beard. 'I need to find out if he's available. I'm looking for some middle-aged men for a comedy that might be coming up.'

'Really?' I say, mentally running over my client list. 'I think I might be able to help you with that.'

Then I reel off a list of names – including 'Vicar' Ronnie's – and launch into my pitch. Frankly, it's a relief to distract myself. But as I talk, fragments of memory come floating back. The pain when my mother left home to 'find herself' soon after I'd started my first year at drama school. And the unexpected comfort that had come from the stunningly handsome fellow student whose own mother had also 'bolted' when he was only twelve years old at boarding school.

'I understand your pain,' he'd told me, giving me a hug in the kitchen of my college halls of residence where I had broken down.

I can see it now as if it was yesterday. I am inside the body of the dumpy, completely overawed young girl, lying next to Matthew Gordon in bed.

'Why me?' I'd asked.

He'd stroked the outline of my breasts and then bent down to kiss my nipples. 'Because you don't know how beautiful you are.'

'I'm not beautiful,' I'd laughed, embarrassed.

'Yes you are. Well, you're pretty on the outside and beautiful underneath.'

I wasn't sure whether to take this as a compliment or not.

'But the most wonderful thing about you,' he continued, 'is that you're different from the others. You wouldn't kill someone to get a role. And you understand. You know what it's like when your whole family falls apart.'

That was certainly true. My poor dad was in bits after being abandoned. He was in no state to help me. As for Mum, I refused either to take her calls on the college payphone or to open her letters.

'My mother married again,' said Matthew. 'And again and again. I don't even know where she is now and I don't care.' His face had darkened with anger. For a minute, I had almost felt afraid. 'What is it with women that makes them such sluts?'

Matthew must have felt me stiffen beneath him at his words because he quickly added: 'Now come here. I want to show you how much I love you.'

Love me? I couldn't believe it. Nor could anyone else when it became general knowledge that Matthew and that dumpy little Poppy with the wild auburn curls were going out. Sandra, who'd been in our group and had never liked me for some unknown reason, was particularly vociferous in her disapproval. 'I can't think what he sees in her,' I overheard her telling another student.

And then, almost three years later, she and Matthew had got together . . .

The two of them had broken my heart. And although Matthew had said he was sorry and that he felt terrible and so on, Sandra had acted as if she hadn't done anything wrong.

Of course, that was only part of it. I'd never told Stuart the full story. I wasn't sure he'd understand. I'm not even certain that I do myself.

'Now, while we're on the subject,' continues the casting director, bringing me abruptly back to the present, 'I was rather impressed by your profile in that write-up. I'm involved with a new production that's going to be filmed in the south-west. It's a sort of *Mamma Mia* meets *Les Mis*. Devon and Cornwall are becoming *the* hot spots. We're looking for some extras – accommodation will be provided – and I was wondering if you might be able to help.'

He leads me to a corner and calls the waiter to give us each a glass of bubbly. I knock it back, partly out of politeness and partly because I'm still in shock from seeing Matthew. I've had far too much to drink now to drive home. I'll have to take a taxi, even though it will cost a fortune.

'Great,' he says, when we've finished running through some of my clients. 'Put it all in an email, would you? We'll talk on Monday.'

He stands up. I'm aware that the room has emptied. 'Looks like everyone's left early because of the weather,' he says, pointing at the window. I suddenly realize it's white outside. The threatened snowfall has arrived.

There's no sign of Matthew now. I'm both relieved and disappointed. Part of me was pleased that he'd seen the new me: the slimmer one who can get away with wearing her daughter's black leather trousers. The woman whose ginger hair is now described as 'Titian' by her hairdresser. The new Poppy who runs a successful business.

The wife whose husband isn't interested in making love to her any more.

I press Stuart's number, to tell him I'm on my way home. There's no signal. 'Try the foyer,' suggests one of the waitresses.

I make my way down to the bright, tinselled area with its glittery HAPPY CHRISTMAS banners and a giant snowman bobbing in the middle. Stuart's phone goes straight to his messaging service. Thanks to the landscape lights outside, I can see that the snow has settled thickly. I ring one of our local taxi companies. Even though it's not in their area, they might come out. As a family, we've used them a few times. 'Sorry,' says the man. 'We're up to our eyes cos of the weather.'

I google for more options but the answer is the same. If I were the swearing type, I'd make my feelings clearer out loud. But when you're the mother of two teenage girls, you have to set an example. I've become used to holding it all in. Not to mention keeping my balls in the air. Doctors' appointments; washing machines flashing on overload; client contracts; making sure Melissa and Daisy are on top of school coursework deadlines; turning up at photographic shoots to reassure nervous clients . . . It never stops! And now this.

A couple of other guests are talking about getting rooms for the night here. The thought of having space of my own to mull over the shock of seeing Matthew again and get my thoughts straight is tempting. Then I'll be able to go home and continue acting out the part of wife and mother just as I've been doing for years. I make my way over to the young man on the desk with a sparkly red-and-green SEASON'S GREETINGS sign suspended, Damocles-like, above his head. 'Sure – we can help.'

He quotes an eye-watering price, inflated, no doubt, by the weather and season.

'I'll take it,' I say, telling myself I'll put the cost down on my company expenses sheet. There are also, I notice, toothbrushes and paste on the counter for sale. I didn't bring any clean underwear but what the hell. I'll just get up early in the morning and go straight home. Armed with my purchases, I head for the stairs. I always prefer walking to using a lift. So much healthier! But as I take the first step, I hear a voice. I look over the bannisters and see a sofa in the space below. Matthew is sitting there, his head bowed over a phone. His voice is low but clear.

'I'm so sorry, Sandra. Like I said, it's snowing. There aren't any cabs and . . . you know I'd come home if it were possible. You've got someone with you. No. Don't say that . . .'

I draw back. The voice sounds like Matthew's. Yet at the same time, it doesn't. This is a Matthew I've never heard before. It carries a desperate, humble, wrung-out-through-the-mangle timbre.

I stand still. Not sure what to do. Then curiosity gets the better of me and I peer over the staircase again at the figure beneath. Matthew is no longer speaking into his mobile. He is crying. I've only once seen him do that. I'd been crying too then – in fact, my sobs had drowned his, proving, or so I'd thought at the time, that my grief was bigger. I shiver and blank the memory from my head as I'd taught myself to do all those years ago.

I must have made a noise because he now looks up at me. I walk down to join him. It seems the right thing to do.

'Poppy!' Instantly an 'everything's fine' expression replaces the one of horror on his face. 'I'm sorry we didn't get a chance to speak more earlier on.'

'It's fine,' I say. 'You were clearly in demand.'

He looks at me questioningly, as if wondering whether I'm being sarcastic or understanding. I don't know myself. There's a distinct air of tension between us. I'm suddenly reminded of how hard it was to read Matthew's mind when we were younger.

'I would suggest we chat now,' he says. His tone is light. Almost deliberately so. 'But I've been trying to get a taxi home. Seems there aren't any.'

'I had the same problem so I've decided to stay.'

'Really? That's a good idea.' He looks as though he's going to touch my arm in a friendly way but stops. I'm both relieved and disappointed. 'Listen – why don't we meet in the bar?'

No, I think to myself. *Absolutely not*. 'Actually, I'm a bit tired.'

'Come on, Pops.'

Once more I freeze at the use of Matthew's old name for me. Stuart had called me that in the early days of our relationship and I'd stopped him.

'We've got so much to catch up on and . . .'

There's a choking quality to his voice.

'. . . and I could really use some company right now to talk about something that's going on in my life.'

I hesitate.

'Please, Pops.'

His hand does touch my arm this time, squeezing it lightly. His eyes are pleading.

'One drink,' I find myself saying, despite that *Are you crazy?* voice in my head. But those tears of his had shaken me. What was wrong? I have to admit that I was curious.

His face relaxes. 'Thank you. Let's find somewhere to sit and I'll tell you.'

Matthew orders a couple of glasses of our old favourite white. Is that intentional? Either way, I don't need any persuasion. There are times when one needs some Dutch courage, as my father would say. That reminds me. I quickly check my mobile but there's no message from him. Is that good or bad? I should have rung him earlier but it's a bit late now. He'll be in bed.

'It's Sandra,' he says, as soon as we sit down.

They're getting divorced, I tell myself. Of course, it's irrelevant to my own life. I'm married with two lovely daughters. This man means nothing to me. But I can't help feeling a wicked frisson of karma shooting through me.

'The thing is,' he says slowly, watching my face as if he's not sure whether to tell me that . . .

'The two of you are splitting up?' I suggest.

'No!' His face is horrified. Instantly I realize I've made one big mistake. 'God, no.'

I don't know where to look.

'Maybe I shouldn't mention it ,' he says quietly.

I'm still mortified by my gaffe. 'No,' I say. 'Please do.'

He seems unsure. 'It would help to tell an old friend. I've lost touch with all the others but . . .'

'I'm a good listener,' I say.

He nods. 'I remember.'

There it is again. The reminder that this man knew me long before my husband and girls.

'The thing is that Sandra has got MS. Multiple sclerosis. We've both tried to keep it quiet because she doesn't want anyone else to know. But it's got worse and now . . . well, now she's in a wheelchair.'

I might not have liked Sandra. But I wouldn't wish this on anyone.

'I'm so sorry,' I say.

He puts his head in his hands, rubs his eyes and then looks up at me. 'Life can be so cruel sometimes. It's why I haven't been working much, to be honest. I've been her main carer. Of course, I don't mind. How could I? I'd do anything for my wife. I promised to love her in sickness and health, after all.'

I brush away that pang in my chest. 'It's what marriage is all about,' I say firmly. 'But it can't be easy for either of you.'

He nods. 'I knew you'd understand.'

Then his eyes go soft.

'What about you?' he asks. When he'd been younger, Matthew had been the kind of man who talked at you rather than to you. But now he seems genuinely interested. 'You're doing really well.'

I'm upset now. Not just with him but with myself. With the past that he's brought back to me. But I can't tell him that. 'The agency is doing great, thanks.'

'It's funny, Pops. I thought you'd make it one day as an actress.'

Me too. But I'm not telling him that. 'Well, you know,' I say lightly, 'one has to be realistic. We can't all be as successful as you.'

'I only hit the big time once. Fame doesn't always last.' His voice cracks. 'Besides, you have a family. I'd have given anything for that.'

That small ball of pain in my chest that had formed when I first saw him this evening is growing bigger by the moment.

'You know,' he says, his eyes suddenly glistening, 'Sandra and I tried really hard to have children. But she couldn't.'

I'm so lucky to have Melissa and Daisy. I know that. Sometimes I wonder if I deserve them.

'Anyway, tell me more about your husband,' he says, waving a hand as if to shrug off the last topic. 'Is he in the profession too?'

I detect a note of curiosity on his part, just as there had been earlier on mine. It gives me a sense of worth. *That's right, Matthew*, I think. *You might not have wanted me at the end but someone else did.*

Again, my mind wanders back to those wilderness years after Matthew had dumped me, when Stuart and I met at a restaurant. I'd finished drama school by then and been working as a waitress. Stuart had been there on a stag do with one of his mates. The drunken groom-to-be had tried to grope my bottom ('I like a woman with a decent arse') and Stuart told his friend not to be so rude and apologized on his behalf. He'd then waited for me after I had finished work and asked if he could walk me home.

'No thanks,' I'd said, thinking that he might be trying it on too. Since Matthew, I hadn't been interested in dating again.

'Please,' he said. 'There are a lot of boozy louts out there. I don't like to think of a young woman going back on her own.'

'How do you know I'm on my own?' I'd said.

He'd made a 'you're right' gesture. 'I'm sorry. It was a huge assumption on my part.'

Then another vodka-up-to-the-eyeballs stag party had lumbered past us. The week before, one of the waitresses had been attacked after work. The thought of walking through the dark streets to my lonely bedsit had seemed even less appealing. 'It's kind of you. Thanks. I would like the company.'

'Stuart is a dentist,' I say now, in answer to Matthew's question.

'Pretty different from acting, then.'

'Yes,' I say, trying to keep the exasperation out of my voice. At the time, Stuart's job had been part of the attraction. Dentistry was a solid profession. Even though it has its own stresses, they are totally different from the insecurities of the acting world. Besides, I had also fallen in love with Betty and Jock, his parents. They seemed the embodiment of the stability I had never had. My mother was now in Australia with her second husband. Dad had remained resolutely single in Worthing.

When we'd started dating, I'd known at once that Stuart was a very different man from Matthew. But he was kind. What the older generation might have called 'a real gentleman'. He brought me an armful of daffodils on

St David's Day, partly because I'm half-Welsh through my mother and also because I'd let slip that they were my favourite flowers. He always rang when he said he would. He was never late for dates. If I expressed interest in a certain play or film, he bought tickets as a surprise. And although he was different in bed from Matthew, I grew to love his more thoughtful and slightly hesitant technique. *This was the man to have children with*, I told myself.

And I was right. Stuart was, at least initially, a dedicated father. But his work, with its long hours, inevitably got in the way, as did mine when I started the agency. Like many young couples, we found that children and the pressures of everyday family life changed us. Almost without noticing, we began to snap at each other and then, as our businesses grew, to lead almost separate lives under one roof. Just when exactly did Stuart start to sleep on the far side of the bed? Or stop kissing me properly? I can't put a date on it. All I know is that I am only just managing to keep on top of work and be a more-or-less good-enough mum. If it wasn't for Betty, who had moved in with us after Jock had died, I don't know how we'd manage.

On top of that, my father is getting older and more forgetful. I go down to Worthing to see him as often as I can, but I'm aware it's not enough. I'm not alone. Lots of my friends are in the same position. The media call us the 'sandwich generation': middle-aged men and women who are feeling the squeeze of children on one side and elderly parents on the other.

'Coming up to your twentieth wedding anniversary, aren't you?' asks Matthew, interrupting my thoughts.

I stiffen. 'How do you know?'

'It was in that profile piece,' he says. 'I still try to keep up with industry news.'

There hadn't been much about Stuart in the interview. I'd deliberately steered clear of him in my answers, although the journalist had asked how long I'd been married for.

I take a swig of Chardonnay. 'Actually,' I say, leaning forward. 'I've never told anyone else this but . . .'

Don't! says my brain. Yet the words are almost there. *Stuart and I are more like a brother and sister now. In fact, we haven't had sex for three years.*

It would be so easy to tell him. It's not as though I have time for friends to share this with. Matthew is part of my past. He would understand. There's something about someone who used to know you so well that can make you reveal secrets you'd never tell anyone else. Yes, Matthew treated me badly, but I'd only been a bit older than Melissa. And like I said, I can't hold him to blame entirely.

'But what?' prompts Matthew.

Think of something, I tell myself urgently. *Something that doesn't give it all away.* 'But there are never enough hours in the day to get everything done,' I say lamely. 'There are moments when I'm only just holding it all together, juggling marriage with motherhood and working . . .'

He nods. 'I imagine that must put a strain on your marriage.'

No. I don't want to imply that. I bat his comment away in the air. 'Actually, we're fine. In fact, we're really good. Great. I'm just a bit tired, that's all, trying to be superwoman.'

Phew. That's better. For a minute there, I'd almost dropped my guard. It must be the shock of having the once love-of-my-life sitting beside me. Matthew reminds me all too clearly of the passion I'd once known. I'd almost forgotten how thoughtless he'd been. My mind had repainted the picture. Made him into the man I'd wanted him to be.

But I've saved myself just in time.

'I know.' Matthew is taking my hand. 'I'm tired too. Yet the thing is that, unlike yours, my marriage hasn't been good. I'm desperately sorry for Sandra but things began to go wrong before she got ill. Then when she did, I couldn't leave her. It would have been cruel.'

'What about me?' I can't help blurting out. 'You left me when –'

I stop. There is no point in going on. What is done is done.

'Do you ever wonder,' he now says dreamily, 'what life might have been like if you and I had stayed together?'

'Yes,' I say crossly. 'But you were the one who ended it.'

'And don't you think I regretted it enough times? You were the only person who understood me.'

I laugh hoarsely. 'Do you realize what a cliché that is?'

'That's the thing about clichés though, isn't it, Pops? They work because they're basically true. You know the real reason I'm here? I read your profile in that trade magazine that said you were going to this party and felt I had to see you.'

'Why, Matthew? What good could possibly come from it. I have Stuart and you have Sandra.'

For the first time, I see him blush. 'No, Pops I didn't mean . . . I just wanted to catch up, you know. Talk to you.'

Instantly I feel utterly stupid at mistaking his need for friendship for something else. Actually, it wouldn't be the first time that a married man had made a pass at me. One of the dads on the school run had cornered me outside at a PTA party three years ago and complimented me on my dress. 'That's so sweet of you,' I'd said, thinking he was just being chummy. Then he'd leaned towards me and tried to give me a kiss. Shocked, I'd pushed him away and then withdrawn from the PTA. I felt responsible and agonized over the episode for weeks. Maybe he'd misread my 'so sweet of you' as an invitation for more. Maybe I'd been staring at him without being aware of it.

Perhaps after that incident I'd been on the lookout for similar 'come-ons', even when there weren't any. I'm suddenly aware of a young man hovering by our table. 'Excuse me, but I'm afraid we're closing the bar early because of the snow. The staff need to get home.'

'Of course.' Matthew's face changes in an instant to one of a composed confident companion. The inveterate actor. I take a bit longer.

'I should have rung my wife again,' Matthew says, standing up. 'But it's too late now.'

'Who is looking after her?'

'I paid extra for an overnight carer in case I was late.'

So that explains what he'd meant by 'you've got someone with you'. His face is racked with concern. Poor man. Then he touches my arm again. *It's nothing*, I tell myself. Actors are renowned for being touchy-feely. 'How about a coffee in the lounge? I see that's still open and there's so much more I want to talk about.'

I hesitate. 'I'm not sure.'

'Please, Pops. We might not have this chance again.'

I realize that, despite myself, I don't want him to disappear; maybe for ever. There's a sort of dangerous fascination about him. Besides, the thought of going to my room alone and turning over the events of the evening endlessly in my mind isn't that appealing.

'Good,' he says. 'Wait for me. That snow really has settled, hasn't it? I'm just going to see if I've left it too late to get a room.'

I both hope he has – and that he hasn't. Already I'm deeply regretting my confidences just now. And yet it's so amazing to see him again, even though I should, by rights, tell Matthew Gordon to get right out of my life after what he did. But that's my trouble. I'm too forgiving. Apart, that is, towards one person thousands of miles away.

Guiltily, I ring Stuart's number but it goes through to voicemail. So I send a text instead:

> Had to stay overnight because of
> weather. Betty knows. Hope you
> had a good day.

Then, unusually for me, I add a kiss.

Matthew comes back.

'Just texting my husband,' I say pointedly.

'Is he all right about you staying away for the night?' he asks.

'He probably won't even notice. He's married to his work too. To be honest, we lead pretty separate lives.'

Why did I say that? Hadn't I just made myself hold back a few minutes ago? Now look what I've done.

'I'm sorry,' he said. 'I didn't realize things were difficult.'

'They're not,' I say quickly, trying to redeem myself.

His eyebrows rise questioningly.

'It's just that . . . well, things change after you've been together a while.'

He nods. 'Tell me about it.' He drains his drink. 'Anyway,' he says, 'the good news is that I was lucky. I got one of the last rooms.'

But our conversation has made me feel awkward. 'Actually,' I say, 'I'm feeling pretty tired, to be honest. Think I'll leave that coffee and turn in. Maybe we'll see each other before I leave tomorrow.'

It's a brush-off and we both know it. He looks disappointed but I feel relieved. I've done the right thing even if I did open my big mouth just now. Still, no harm done.

'I'm bushed too,' he says. 'I often have to get up during the night for Sandra. She needs help with the bathroom and . . . sorry. You don't need to hear about this.'

I feel a flash of sympathy. 'It can't be easy,' I say.

He gives a tight nod. 'It's not, but it's much harder on her. She's the one who is ill. I don't want to complain.'

'You're not,' I say quickly. 'We all need to offload sometimes. By the way, I was only joking when I said Stuart wouldn't notice me being away for the night.'

'Of course you were. In fact, I've forgotten it already.'

I might not have believed the old Matthew, but this new one is different. More responsible. His attitude towards his wife surely shows that.

We walk together to the lift.

'Which floor are you on?' he asks.

'Four.'

'Me too.'

We go up in silence and then walk along the corridor, which has a rather tasteful grey patterned carpet. I can't help wondering how many people have trodden here before. Married couples on weekend breaks from the children; lovers on secret assignations; professionals on stale business trips. I've suggested a hotel getaway to Stuart several times but he always says he's 'too busy'. Yet again, one more rejection.

'Looks like this is my room,' I say, checking the number on my key card.

'What a coincidence,' says Matthew. 'Mine is just opposite. Perhaps they kept this part of the hotel clear for the latecomers.'

'You could be right,' I say. Then I remembered that he'd gone to the reception on his own to ask for a room. Supposing he'd asked where mine was? No. The receptionist wouldn't be indiscreet enough to tell him. Once again, I'm letting my imagination run away with me.

'See you in the morning, hopefully,' he says.

'Yes.'

I need to get into the room quickly. Shut the door behind me. But as soon as I do, I sink onto the bed, my face buried in the pillow. Tears stream down my face.

Seeing Matthew has brought back the pain that I'd been bottling up for all these years.

My old boyfriend might look different, but I can still see glimpses of the handsome young drama student he used to be; the one who dried my tears through my parents' divorce and who stirred up a fire that no one has ever been able to do since. *You still love Stuart*, I tell myself. But I feel ignored by my husband. Rejected. Maybe he feels the same.

Then there's a knock on the door. Rubbing my eyes, I go to it. It's Matthew! My heart both leaps with excitement and also thuds with terror. *Don't let me be tempted. Don't.*

'Just in case we miss each other at breakfast, could I take your number?' he says. 'I'd hate to think we'd lose contact again.'

He's holding out one of those notepads that you get in hotels, and a pen. He doesn't come inside. I don't ask him to. Instead, I stand at the doorway and write it down. Then he gives me his. I rather like his old-fashioned approach instead of simply punching in my number on his phone.

'Thanks,' he says. 'Are you all right?'

'Yes,' I say. 'Why?'

'It's just that, well, you look as though you've been crying.'

'No,' I say. 'It's just my eyes. They get like that when they're tired.'

'Ah yes,' he says. 'I remember. Try cotton-wool pads soaked in cold water. I do that for Sandra if she hasn't slept.'

This really is a new Matthew, I realize. A kinder one. A man I'm beginning to warm to – but not, of course, I tell myself firmly, in *that* way. I'm a married woman and I love my family.

'Night, then,' he says. 'It was wonderful to see you again.'

Then he steps forward and brushes his cheek against mine. It's the sort of thing people do all the time in my working world but this feels different. My face is on fire. So is the rest of me.

'Night,' I say, stepping back quickly.

He walks away but just as he reaches his door opposite, he turns. 'Do you still do that thing when you go to sleep?'

No one else knows that I turn my pillow over three times for luck, apart from my husband, as well as Melissa and Daisy, of course, whom I've taught to do the same. It's a tradition – or silly habit, whichever way you look at it – that I learned as a child but which has stuck.

'Yes,' I say.

'Good,' he replies. 'I always used to find that really sweet. Goodnight, Pops. Sleep well.'

He gives me a lingering look. I've a feeling I might be doing the same. I shut the door firmly, lock it and lean against it for some minutes before taking a shower and going to bed. Alone.

It is nearly 4 a.m. before I finally nod off.

4

Betty

Of course, Jock and I desperately wanted to 'do it'. When he kissed me, I felt all tingly below, like nothing I'd ever felt before. 'I'll be careful if you let me,' he said to me. I wasn't exactly sure what he meant by that and didn't like to ask in case it made me look stupid.

What I did know was that I was too scared to go all the way in case I got into trouble. Like I said before, my parents would have thrown me out on my ear if I'd got pregnant before there was a wedding ring on my finger. So Jock and I waited, frustrating as it was.

Every Saturday night we'd go to the local pub, where I would have a bitter lemon and he'd have a pint. Afterwards, he'd walk me home through a little park near my home in Hackney, past the tramps on the benches with their bottles, and I'd be holding my breath with anticipation. Then at last we'd stop and he'd take my face in his hands to gently kiss me. The first time he slid his hands up my jumper, I felt I ought to brush him away. What if he thought I was cheap?

But the truth was that I couldn't. I ached for him to touch me there. 'You're gorgeous,' he panted, even though he couldn't actually see me in the dark.

Then he tried to slide his hand below my waist, but I wasn't having any of that. 'No,' I said in a voice that I hoped was as firm as the longing inside me.

He seemed to respect that. Instantly he stepped backwards. 'I'm sorry,' he said in a small, boyish voice.

'Don't be,' I replied, taking his hand in mine. 'I want to, but it wouldn't be right.'

'I know,' he said, and then he went back to kissing me. Snogging was safe. It was also wonderful. Sometimes I think that it would be so much nicer if people simply kissed instead of doing the other. It's just as intimate.

Soon after we got engaged, Jock got me to write down exactly what I earned in the shop and how much I had to pay my parents every week so he could 'do the figures'. He didn't tell me what he earned and I didn't think to ask. I'm aware, Poppy, that all this sounds very naive. The late sixties were a time of change for some. But for others like me and my family, our morals and attitudes hadn't moved on from the previous decade, or even the one before that.

'It's going to take us eighteen months to save up for the deposit and the first few months' rent on a flat,' he declared. 'We've got to allow enough for bills too, and the reception.'

That was a sticking point. My parents had said that, although they were very happy for us, they couldn't afford a slap-up wedding. We'd have to make do with a cold buffet for 'close family only' in the Labour hall. I'd set my heart on a 'do' at a local hotel. Some of my friends were beginning to get married and they all held theirs there.

Jock saw my disappointed face and immediately declared that he would make up the balance so I could have my wish. But 'making up the balance' meant us scrimping and saving, without any honeymoon. 'I don't mind the hall,' I said when he told me this. 'Really.'

His mouth was set in a grim line. 'But I do. I'm going places, Betty. I'm already in line for another promotion in the factory. I'm not having anyone saying that I made do with a cheap wedding for family only. There are people I need to invite. Influential blokes at work who will then remember me.'

Jock was a man who knew exactly what he wanted. Back then, I was impressed by that.

I spent those eighteen months poring over old bridal magazines that Julie, the girl next door (who was going to get married soon), lent me. I made my own wedding dress out of silk I bought from Petticoat Lane. Then Jock's boss offered to lend us his holiday caravan in Devon for our honeymoon. I was so excited that I floated through the rest of our engagement.

'You look wonderful,' said our department manager. 'Love obviously suits you, dear. I wonder whether you would like to take part in our annual fashion show, modelling the new season's hats?'

I loved every second! The show was a great success. Everyone clapped me when I walked down the catwalk, but that was because Mum had got all her friends in the audience. (Now I'd got a pay rise, she'd started to be proud of me.) The local paper was there too – the journalist seemed quite excited when I told him I was getting married soon, saying it would it a 'nice angle', and they ran a big picture of me on the front page under the headline 'Bride-to-be Wows Audience at Fashion Show'. All the staff, including me, went out for a roller-skating evening – paid for by the manager – to celebrate. Such fun! But I noticed that Jock was a bit quiet the following weekend. He hadn't called me his 'wee hen' for some time either, I realized with a pang. 'What's wrong?' I asked.

'Nothing,' he said, running his finger round the rim of his beer glass, something I noticed that he did when he was nervous.

I could tell that something was up but I didn't want to push him. Please don't say he was getting cold feet! Julie, who had lent me the bridal magazines, had been jilted at the altar. She hadn't been out of the house for weeks because of the shame. I would die if that happened to me. I just knew I would. Maybe I shouldn't have borrowed from her. Perhaps it had transferred her bad luck.

I did my best to cheer Jock up as the month of our wedding approached, pretending to ignore his moodiness and those awful silences between us. One night, when we were walking back from the pub, he stopped in the park as usual and took my face in his hands. But instead of kissing me, he looked straight into my eyes. 'What if we're making a mistake?' he said. 'It's a big thing, marriage, isn't it?'

My heart felt all fluttery, as though it was falling out of my body.

'Yes,' I said. 'But we love each other, Jock. We'll be all right.'

He let go of my face. 'I hope so.'

My legs felt weak and I feared they might give way. 'What do you mean?' I said in a small voice. 'Have you found someone else?'

'No,' he said firmly. 'Of course not.'

A huge wave of relief swept through me.

'It's just that . . . well, my lads have been saying at work that the divorce laws have changed.' He shifted from one foot to the other nervously. 'It's going to be much more difficult financially for a bloke if a marriage breaks up.'

In fact, Jock was only partly right. The new rules meant that neither partner had to prove 'fault' (like infidelity) in order to end a marriage. However, this didn't necessarily mean it was going to be 'more difficult financially for a bloke', as my fiancé had declared. Yet it was typical that he and his mates had interpreted the change as something that helped women more than men.

In those days, I didn't know much about the law. But I did know that I loved Jock. And I couldn't bear the humiliation of a broken engagement. One of the women who worked in the lingerie department still wore her diamond ring, but on her right hand. 'He said I could keep it,' she said one evening when we all went out together. I couldn't help thinking that if it was me, I'd have given it back. Having it on full view like that was like telling the whole world about being let down.

'But our marriage won't break up, Jock,' I cried. 'It's going to be wonderful. We'll have lots of children. A whole football team!'

He laughed then. 'That might be rather a lot of bairns to cope with.'

'Why are you even thinking of divorce?' I pressed him.

In those days, it wasn't as common as it is now. I only knew of one girl from school whose mum and dad had split up and they'd always been a 'bit odd', as my parents said. Marriages were still meant to last for ever. There was no expiry date. It wasn't allowed.

'I suppose it will be all right if . . .' said Jock. Then he stopped.

'If what?' I asked.

'If you give up work at the department store.'

I stopped. My breath seemed to freeze, despite the warm summer air. 'Why would I do that?'

I'd heard my mother talking about how, in her day, some husbands didn't like their wives working because it looked as though they couldn't afford to 'keep them'. So old-fashioned!

'But Jock,' I said quietly, 'I love my job.'

'Well, I don't like the way that men look at you,' said Jock. His voice was colder now.

'What do you mean?'

'Come on. You must have noticed. It all started after that piece about you in the paper after the fashion show. My mates have been ribbing me ever since, telling me that you'd be off to sign up with some fancy agency before I know it and be jet-setting all over the world.'

What? 'I'd never even thought of that. You've got the wrong idea. Honestly. And it's nonsense that people are looking at me.'

'Really? The other night when I came to pick you up from work, I saw that old man with the hat and smart suit. He was leering at you.'

'You mean Mr Goddard?' I burst out laughing. 'He wasn't leering. His wife is one of my regular customers. He comes along to tell her which hat he likes best.'

Jock took another step away from me as if he didn't want to be close any more. 'Don't you laugh at me. He *was* leering. I saw him. And he's not the only one. That fashion show really opened my eyes.'

I could hardly believe he was saying these things. 'But I thought you'd enjoyed it. You said I looked beautiful.'

'You did. But all the other men in the audience clearly thought so too. And I don't like the idea of my wife being ogled by other blokes.'

'So what are you saying?' I asked. My head was beginning to throb with confusion and anxiety.

'If you resign from your job, I'll still marry you.'

He said it as though he was doing me a favour. I thought of the beautiful silk wedding dress I'd finished, which was now hanging in the wardrobe. Of the bridesmaids' outfits for my cousins (all three of them!), which I was making now. Of the hot buffet with mushroom vol-au-vents, which had been paid for in advance, and the hotel, which had been booked along with a band after all that scrimping and saving. The silver-and-white invitations that had been sent out. The landlord's deposit for our future home, which was due soon.

'But how will we manage without the money?' I asked. 'We need it for the flat.'

'I'm not agin you working,' said Jock as though I was being stupid. 'I just said you'd have to resign from the department store. My boss said he can find you a job at the factory instead.'

He spoke quickly, as if he had it all sorted. 'You'll like the girls on the line. They're a friendly crowd. Not stuck up like that lot in the store. And we'll be able to meet up at lunchtime. We can go to work together and come back together.' He cupped my face in his hands again. 'Won't that be nice?'

I'm aware that this might sound controlling to you, Poppy. But in those days, most women wanted a man to be in charge. It made us feel safe and loved. Of course, I didn't want to change jobs. But a dutiful wife did what her husband told her. Or so I'd been brought up to believe.

'Yes,' I said, swallowing back my doubts. 'It would be nice.'

'Good.' Jock slid his hand up my jumper. 'I can't wait for us to get married.'

But that feeling of lightness and excitement had gone from my heart. It didn't return for a few more years. And when it did, it turned my life upside down.

Now, as I read though this letter to you, I want to laugh at my old self. How stupid I was! How naive. Yet at the same time it taught me three lessons that I'm determined to pass down to you, Poppy, as well as to my precious granddaughters. The first is to value yourself. The second is to follow your gut. And the third is to understand right from wrong.

But I know what you're thinking. It's too late for that. For all of us.

5

Poppy

I wake bolt upright the next morning, sensing that something isn't quite right but not knowing what. Then I take in the peacock-blue brocade curtains, so different from our creamy plantation shutters at home, and the modern dressing table at the foot of the bed instead of my old Victorian bureau in front of our lovely bay window with the view out to the park. And it all comes flooding back to me.

I'm in a hotel. I was here for the Association of Supporting Artistes and Agents' Christmas party. And I saw Matthew Gordon. More than that, I spent hours talking to him about things I shouldn't have done. I'd told him that Stuart probably wouldn't notice I'd been gone for the night and that we led pretty separate lives. My skin crawls with embarrassment. Maybe the taste of last night's booze – still in my mouth – is a clue, but that's no real excuse. What if he tells someone that my marriage is shaky? A casting director, perhaps? Gossip is rife in this business. It's unlikely it would get back to Stuart. Isn't it? But any suggestion that someone is going through a rocky personal time can affect other people's confidence in you. I saw it happen a few years ago to a rival who had a breakdown after her divorce. Her clients left in droves and she closed her agency.

But no. Why would Matthew do that? He'd said he'd forget it, hadn't he? Besides, he'd divulged confidences too. Sandra had MS and was in a wheelchair. He'd actually cried. And then there was that whole conversation about children . . .

Enough, I tell myself firmly. This is why it's not a good idea to go backwards in life. *The past should stay in the past.* Betty is always saying that and she's right. You have to work your way forward. And right now that means getting back to my family. I have a sudden strong yearning to race home and slip into bed beside my husband, snuggle up to his back (Stuart rarely sleeps facing me), and then, when the alarm goes, get up to make breakfast for the girls. They'll no doubt squabble and tease each other; Betty will be meditating upstairs, with incense wafting out of her room; Stuart will talk about cross-bites and how he needs to take the rubbish to the tip. Right now I yearn for the safe mundanity of it all. Even though the man I used to love more than my own husband is, right now, sleeping just across the corridor.

Stop right there. I glance at the neon hotel clock next to the bed: 5.30 a.m. Worry must have made me wake up early. If I'm quick, I can be out of here without bumping into Matthew outside the door. It'll mean skipping breakfast, despite the fact that it's included in the extortionate price I paid for the room. But so what?

The shower helps. The water gushes over my head, washing away all those confused thoughts. *That's all they are*, I tell myself. Thoughts about what might have been. Not actual deeds. I haven't done anything wrong. OK, so I was a bit indiscreet about my personal life, but if it does

64

come out, I'll just deny it. Even though, after Mum, I've always prided myself on telling the truth. But I feel uneasy. For some reason, it takes me back to the fact that I'd never told Stuart about Matthew when we met, because it still hurt. Then again, omitting information doesn't count as a lie. Does it?

I blast my hair with the hotel dryer. It looks a bit of a mess without my air brush, which curls the ends and gives a good impression of a blow dry. I don't have my usual foundation and blusher either. I wasn't expecting to stay the night. What will my old love think if I do bump into him and he sees me looking like this? *Not that you care*, I tell myself. I just feel odd because Matthew had once played a big role in my life. It doesn't mean anything now.

Slipping into yesterday's clothes (turning the knickers inside out to make up for the lack of a spare pair), I grab my phone, glance at Matthew's closed door and scuttle towards the lift so I can drop off the borrowed phone charger at reception. Then I remember. The weather! It's still too dark to see properly through the window. What if I can't drive back or get a taxi? I'd have to have breakfast here and I'd probably see Matthew. We might even share a table. Or would he be as embarrassed as me about those late-night confidences and pretend he hadn't seen me in the cold light of day?

'Looks like the snow didn't settle for long after all,' says the receptionist chattily.

A quick flash of disappointment zips through me followed by relief. *This is a good thing*, I tell myself. OK. I'm unsettled by bumping into Matthew after all these years, but that was just because he'd played such a big role in my life. My old life. Not this one.

'Am I the first to check out?' I ask, handing over my key.

As I speak, I know I shouldn't ask. It probably contravenes some confidentiality law. But the girl shakes her head. 'There've been a couple of others before you.'

My heart skips a beat. 'Any good-looking middle-aged men with dark hair swept back from the forehead and a nose that isn't afraid to stand out?' I want to ask. But, of course, I can't. Instead, I settle my bill before venturing out into the car park, bracing myself against the cold, which seems to pierce right through to my bones. Then I try to clear the ice off my windscreen with my credit card because that de-icing scraper I bought the other month appears to have vanished from the boot. Why does that always happen?

I'm a summer person, but Stuart loves the winter. Matthew and I had once splashed out on a cheap package holiday to Corfu during our second year. We'd made love on the beach at night. Stuart would never do that. He'd go on about the sand getting into our 'crevices'. Dentists can be very fussy.

Stop, I tell myself again, starting the engine and carefully making my way out of the car park and onto the main road. OK, our sex life isn't perfect. It's non-existent at the moment actually. But there's more to marriage than that, isn't there? Stuart is a good man. The father of my children. Yes, it would help if he was at home more, but he's only trying to provide for us all, just as I am. Of course, he's ambitious too. But then again so am I!

I turn right at the end of the road, following the satnav directions, but my mind isn't keeping up. I'm not just being mentally disloyal to my husband; I'm doing the same to the girls. If I hadn't married their father, Melissa and Daisy wouldn't be here. The very idea is impossible. What would I do without them? And then the same question that keeps coming up in my mind, even after all this time, emerges once more. Had my mother had any regrets about leaving me? Clearly, she'd decided that, in the end, I wasn't worth the pain of staying.

Suddenly the car in front of me stops dead. Talk about not giving me any notice! I slam on my brakes but it's too late. The roads are still icy and I slide into the back of a black BMW.

'What did you do that for?' I say, getting out. Only then do I see there are traffic lights, which I should have spotted if I hadn't been thinking about the what-might-have-beens in my life.

Luckily, no one is hurt. The other car has a small scratch but mine has a substantial dent in the front. We swap numbers and insurance details. All the time, I keep saying, 'Sorry, sorry,' which isn't what you're meant to do. But I mean it. I should have been concentrating. I shouldn't have been letting my imagination play games.

'It's not just the cost – it's the inconvenience,' snaps the driver, a sharp-looking woman who (judging from the flash of pink silk I see between the buttons) is wearing an evening dress under her coat. I wonder from her distress if she'd been somewhere she shouldn't. Maybe I'm just projecting my guilt about being in a bar with Matthew. Not that I should have any. It wasn't as if I'd actually done anything. *But you could have done*, suggests a small voice in my head. Nonsense. I'm not that kind of woman.

'I'm sorry,' I say again, examining my car more carefully. The damage is even worse than I'd thought. The front is all buckled. In the old days, when I was just starting up my business and Stuart was growing his practice, the cost of the insurance excess would have been a real problem. At least we can afford little annoyances like this now. The main thing is that no one was injured. But someone might have been. And it would have been all my fault. I've also got to explain this to Stuart. I'm a careful driver. If I admit I was distracted and made a mistake, he might wonder why . . .

Sombrely, I drive back, taking extra care on the treacherous roads, which are now beginning to thaw. Amazingly, there is a parking space outside our house. Even though the average price in our road is around the £1 million mark, none of us (in common with many London homeowners in a similar price bracket) has a designated spot for a car unless you choose to pave the front garden – something I refuse to do because I love the magnolia tree too much. Stuart thinks I'm being sentimental but luckily Betty agrees with me. 'You can't cut down a living thing,' she'd said, appalled, when the subject was raised. 'It's no better than murder.'

Quietly I slip my key in the lock. Our beautiful hall with the dawn light streaming in through the pink-and-green stained-glass panel above the front door, stretches out before me. When I think of the small bungalow I'd grown up in and then all the poky student bedsits followed by the tiny apartment that Stuart and I had started off in, I can still hardly believe that we live in such a stunning house. But when Betty had moved in with us, she'd insisted on putting in the savings she and Jock had accumulated – a surprising amount, thanks to some canny investing by my father-in-law – and we'd then bought this house cheaply. The couple who owned it at the time were divorcing and needed to liquidate their assets fast.

'We'll have to get rid of the negative vibes,' Betty had said. 'Houses retain good and bad experiences. Don't worry. I'll sort it out with some blessings. I've got a book on it.'

Now, as I tiptoe past her bedroom – it's only just gone 7 a.m. and everyone is still asleep because it's a Saturday – the thought occurs to me that I could confide in my mother-in-law. 'I met someone last night who I used to love,' I might say. That's ridiculous. It might sound like regret that I'd married her son instead. And, of course, I don't wish that. It's just that seeing Matthew after all these years has stirred up feelings I'd long put to rest. Or so I'd thought.

I open our bedroom door, preparing to slide into bed next to Stuart. But the curtains are open. The bed is empty. Where is he? There's a note on the dressing table. *Gone to conference. Hope you had a good time.*

I'd forgotten! Stuart had mentioned some meeting a few weeks ago but it had slipped my mind. Where was it again? Leicester or somewhere like that. Is he driving or taking the train? He must have only just left because his pyjamas, neatly folded on his side of the bed, are still warm. I hold them to me, breathing in their familiarity. Matthew used to sleep naked. Does he still do that, I wonder.

Stop!

I lie down on my side of the bed, exhausted from the shock of it all. Matthew. The car. Before I know it, I've dozed off only to find that someone is leaping onto the empty side next to me.

'Gran said we shouldn't bother you and that you need to rest after the party.' Daisy is shaking me awake. 'But tell me about it. Was it fun?'

My youngest daughter might be fourteen but I still see her as my baby. She has that youthful exuberance that Melissa, borne down by the weight of impending A levels, is already beginning to lose. 'Sort of,' I say sleepily. 'But I was really there to make contacts.'

'What kind of contacts?' she asks, twirling a strand of my hair.

Matthew's face comes into my head.

'Just people who can help my business.'

'Remember I've got to get new shoes today,' says Daisy excitedly. 'I know just the kind I want.'

My heart sinks. How I dread shoe shopping! Melissa now buys her own with the allowance we give her, thank goodness, but I still have to go through the 'I know you want them but they're not sensible/don't fit' routine with her younger sister.

'And don't forget you promised us all a lift to the party tonight,' says my eldest from the doorway.

'Did I?' I ask, taking in Melissa's tousled hair and smudged mascara, which she hadn't taken off last night. I've told her how important that is – and how she'll regret it when she's older – yet she doesn't take any notice. But who am I to talk? Unremoved make-up comes very low down the 'fault' list of life right now.

'I need to get the car looked at first,' I continue, trying to sound normal. I can feel Melissa's eyes X-raying me as if she knows what I've done. Or haven't done. 'I had a bit of a bump on the way home.'

'Are you all right, love? What happened?'

It's Betty. They're all here now in my bedroom.

'I didn't stop in time because of the ice and the dark.' It's at least partly true.

'But you can still drive it?' This is Melissa. 'We've got to get to that party and none of my friends' parents can take us.'

Why are teenagers so selfish at times and so loving at others?

Her eyes narrow. 'Where were you, anyway?'

I take in this beautiful, tall, raven-haired young woman and marvel once more, as I often do a) that she is my daughter and b) that she can treat me like I am the adolescent. I would never have dared do that to my parents. I sometimes wonder whether I should have been tougher with her. But Melissa has such a strong character. Betty says it's important to keep 'lines of communication open with teenagers' and I think she's right. Even though it looks as though I'm giving in at times.

'I told you I had a work party to go to,' I remind her.

'And I told you, young lady,' adds Betty, 'that your mother couldn't get back so she stayed the night because of the snow.'

'But it's all gone now,' says Melissa, staring at me. This is ridiculous. I feel as if I am on a witness stand. Then again, her best friend's dad has just gone off with another man and half her class's parents are divorced.

71

'It was heavy last night where the party was,' I say. 'But then it cleared in the morning. By the way, did Dad tell you when he was going to be back?'

'No.' Betty is giving me an odd look. 'Are you all right, dear?'

I try to sound like a woman might if she hadn't just unexpectedly bumped into the man who had once broken her heart and changed her life for ever. 'Just a bit upset about the car.'

'Well, don't worry about it. I can drive Melissa and her friends to that party.'

Really? Betty had only learned to drive after Jock had died. She'd 'never got round to it' before, but actually took to it like a duck to water.

'That would be great.'

I am suddenly flooded with love for my amazing family. *How lucky I am*, I think, cuddling my two girls (Melissa has instantly stopped being cross now the party situation had been sorted). 'Tell you what,' I say. 'How about we go bowling after Daisy and I finish shoe shopping?'

Melissa wrinkles her nose. 'Boring.'

'You always used to love it,' points out Betty.

'Well, I'm older now. And I've got coursework to do otherwise Mum will nag me.'

I've got work to do too, I remind myself. Saturday is my day for catching up with admin that I haven't got round to during the week. But the children have to come first. So off we head for Brent Cross.

The shoe-shopping expedition does indeed turn out to be everything I'd feared. 'I hate this style,' protests Daisy, pushing away a sensible pair of lace-ups.

72

I groan. 'It's the only pair that fits! We've already been to seven shops. Just have them. Please.'

The young assistant, whose complexion looks as though it was applied with a builder's pasting brush, throws me a disapproving look. When you have teenagers, I want to tell her, you'll end up pleading too.

Stuart sends me a text:

> Conference going well. How are
> you?

> Nightmare.

I reply.

> Shoe shopping with Daisy.

> Lucky you!

he fires back.

It's all right for him. He's well out of it with his erudite lectures about crowns and molars and root canals.

When we get back, Melissa is stomping up and down. 'Where are my black leather trousers? The ones I lent you?'

'Sorry. In my room.' I run up and bring them down.

'You've torn the hem on the left leg.'

'Have I?'

'How did that happen?'

I honestly don't know but I feel my colour rising. 'No idea.'

'It's OK,' says Betty. 'I'll sew it up. And don't speak to your mother like that, love. She's not a slave, you know.'

Melissa rolls her eyes. 'If she was, I'd sack her.'

'Now that's not very polite . . .'

73

I ought to agree but I don't feel strong enough for a teenage argument. Not after the shock of last night. So I'm afraid I leave them to it, heading up to the sanctity of my office, where I sink down on the squashy yellow chesterfield that's positioned close to the door to hide a patch of worn carpet. If it wasn't for 'my space', I might go mad. On the far side is my desk, piled high with papers. It's not a big room but there's just enough space, even though the drawers are stuffed with things that I really ought to clear out. But there are just never sufficient hours in the day, and besides, there are some sentimental bits and bobs I can't bring myself to get rid of.

Despite the fact it's the weekend, my inbox has already acquired several new messages. There's a furious email from a casting director because one of my extras didn't turn up for an ad shoot yesterday. It's not the first time. I won't be using that person again. If someone lets you down in this industry, it reflects badly on you. Mud sticks.

Then the phone rings. It's Sally, the assistant I took on last year. She's a sixty-something divorcee who wanted 'something to do', and although I really needed someone with more experience in the acting world, I took her on because I felt sorry for her. Since then, she's proved to be worth more than her weight in gold. Sally's great with people and is really organized. Like me, she works from home so we can keep our costs down.

'We have a problem,' she says. 'Karen has got herself a tattoo.'

Karen is one of our new extras. She was due to be in an historical drama today. Filming often carries on over weekends. 'As far as I know,' she says, 'they didn't have tattoos in the time of Henry VIII. Says she didn't realize it would be an issue.'

I groan. 'We'll need to find someone else.'

'Don't worry,' says Sally. 'I'm onto it.'

'Thanks.'

No sooner do we finish talking than there's a musical ripple from my phone, indicating a text. I glance at it. Then freeze.

> Lovely to see you last night.
> How about a coffee some time?
>
> M

Yes, is my first thought. *Yes, I want to see you again too.* A coffee to talk about the what-might-have-beens. No more than that, of course, because it wouldn't be right.

But if I did see Matthew, I'd need to tell Stuart. I'd have to say that there'd been someone before him who broke my heart. Or would I? I could fudge it, tell him part of the truth. But then I'd be lying. I'd be no better than my mother had been. And what about the children? What would I say to them? 'Hey, I'm just off to have a coffee with a former lover?' Or, 'I'm meeting up with a friend who did things to my body that your father has never been able to?'

Big lies begin with small ones.

> It was good to see you too

I message back, adding:

> Thanks for the offer of coffee but
> I'm pretty busy at the moment.

My finger hovers over the Send arrow. I hesitate.

'Mum? Where are you?' yells Melissa from downstairs. 'I can't find my black ankle boots.'

And I press it.

I've done the right thing. I know it.

So why, I ask myself as I go down to sort out the boots and wonder what I can rustle up for everyone's dinner (given that I haven't been food shopping), do I feel so flat?

6

Betty

'I'm so sorry you're leaving us,' the department manager had said when I'd reluctantly handed in my notice. 'We were going to offer you a promotion as a hat buyer. There'd be another rise in salary, of course. And obviously we'd want you to continue modelling for us.'

But Jock wouldn't be moved, even though the pay at the factory was lower. 'You'll be with other women of your own sort,' he said firmly. 'You'll like it there.' He squeezed my bottom. 'I've got big plans for us, Betty. We're going to get ahead in life, you and I. One day, we'll be able to buy our ain place and not have to rent. Just do what I say and we'll be all right.'

I was beginning to learn a lot about my fiancé that I hadn't appreciated at the beginning. As long as I agreed with him on decisions, it was OK. He would be in a good mood like he was now. There was no more 'cold feet' talk about the wedding. Instead, he kept asking me who had replied so far to the invitations. 'Has the big gaffer accepted?' he asked, meaning his boss's boss.

'Yes,' I replied checking my list.

Jock punched the air. 'Good. That means he likes me. There's talk of another opening in management two positions above me now old Brown is retiring.'

Occasionally, I felt a little quiver of doubt inside me. Was I doing the right thing in marrying a man who didn't listen to what I had to say and was only interested in his own voice? But it would be even worse if I broke it off than if he had done so. Girls got themselves a bad name that way round here. Besides, I wanted a husband and a home of my own; and children. It was what we all aspired to, unless you were what Mum called a bluestocking, like the teacher who lived next door to us and had never 'found herself a man'.

It rained cats and dogs on our wedding day. Some might have taken that as an omen. But not me. I'd managed to quash those doubts and now all I wanted was to walk down the aisle. 'You look beautiful,' said Dad when I came down the stairs of our council house wearing the white silk A-line dress I had made myself with little beads round the sweetheart neckline.

Beautiful? He'd never once called me that before.

Mum's eyes were brimming with tears. I'd never seen her so emotional. 'My little girl. You're about to be a woman now.'

Then she took me into the kitchen. 'I probably should have said this to you earlier but, well, on your wedding night, you need to be prepared for . . .'

She stopped.

'It's all right, Mum,' I said, trying to save her from the embarrassment. 'I know about that sort of thing.'

Her face turned dark. 'You haven't *done* it?'

'No,' I reassured her hastily. 'Of course not. But I've read *Cosmo*. One of the girls in Lingerie gave it to me as a leaving present. There was a big piece on . . .'

I faltered, unable to say the 'sex' word to my own mother.

Her face cleared. 'You daft brush. Don't believe what you read in magazines. Marriage belongs to the real world.' She gave me a brief hug. Then she stood and looked at me as if for the last time. 'You'll find out soon enough.'

I didn't pay much attention to her words at the time. All I wanted to do was step into the big shiny blue second-hand Rover that belonged to one of Dad's mates and get to the church. Jock had told me not to be late, 'even if it is fashionable', because he didn't want people thinking I'd changed my mind.

'You're marrying a good man,' said my dad gruffly to me in the back. 'That Jock of yours is going far.'

'He's got a mouth on him at work, sure enough,' said Dad's pal from the driving seat.

But from the way he spoke, it didn't sound like a compliment.

As I walked down the aisle, I could feel all eyes on me. *Those funny thuds in your chest are just butterflies*, I told myself. It was normal to have doubts. *Cosmo* said so. All I had to do was remember that I was getting married to a decent, strong man who wanted to look after me. And there he was now! My handsome fiancé waiting for me at the altar in his hired Moss Bros suit. He'd had his hair cut and slicked back. And he smelled reassuringly of Brut, just as he always did.

'Hello, princess,' he said to me as I took my place next to him. Then he put his arm around me. I wasn't sure that was allowed from the way the priest frowned. Jock said his vows loudly and clearly. No one listening to him would ever have suspected that he'd had doubts not so very long ago.

Even so, the service didn't go according to plan. No one objected, thank goodness (there was no reason why they should, although my heart was still in my mouth at this bit), but the organist got the hymns wrong, playing the one about saving us from troubled times instead of 'All Things Bright and Beautiful'. Nor was there a choir, because they'd all been struck down with flu.

'I'm going to get a refund,' said Jock tightly when we posed for the photographs. 'It's not on. No one tries to pull one on me like that. I paid good money.'

And as he spoke, I could feel his fingers dig a little deeper into my arm.

The speeches at the reception seemed to go down well. Dad talked about me in a way that I almost didn't recognize myself, calling me his 'precious only daughter'. Jock's best man made lots of smutty jokes that made everyone laugh, including the big gaffer, although his wife looked a bit shocked. When my new husband and I had the first dance to 'All I Have to Do Is Dream', by Bobbie Gentry and Glen Campbell, he placed his cheek next to mine. *It's going to be all right*, I told myself. *He loves me. And I love him.*

Then we drove to the caravan in Devon that Jock's boss had lent us for the honeymoon. All the way there, I was a bundle of nerves – not because of the night ahead but because of the way my new husband was driving. He'd been taught by a friend because he couldn't afford formal lessons and had been cock-a-hoop when he'd passed last month.

'Please,' I begged when he overtook yet another car, which hooted him in disapproval. 'Don't go so fast.'

Immediately he screeched into a lay-by. His eyes were black with rage and his breath stank of beer. The government had not long ago introduced a limit to drinking and driving – Dad had been moaning about it – so I only hoped my new husband wasn't over the limit. 'Don't criticize my driving,' he snapped. 'You don't know what you're talking about anyway. It's not like you've passed your test.'

'I'd like to one day,' I said, trying to calm him down.

'We've got more important things to pay for first.'

'Sorry, Jock,' I said. 'I didn't mean it. It's just that I get travel sick sometimes.'

'Really?' His voice was calmer now. 'I didn't know that.' He patted my arm. 'Just you sit back and close your eyes. We'll be there before you know it. The caravan has got its own little kitchen. You'll be able to make us some tea before we settle down for the night.' Then he gave me a wink. 'We've waited long enough for this.'

I don't want to talk too much about the first time, but let's just say, it wasn't the way *Cosmo* had described with its 'show him how to please you' suggestions.

Forgive me for being so blunt, Poppy, but I wince even now, all these years later, as I remember how he shoved himself into me, heedless of my cries of pain.

After what seemed like hours, it was all over and Jock rolled off me onto his side. I was praying that in the darkness he wouldn't see the tears streaming down my face.

'Where's the blood?' he said suddenly.

'It's all right. You didn't hurt me that much.'

'The blood,' he said again, heaving himself onto his elbows. 'There should be blood if you're a virgin.'

'Of course I am,' I protested.

He turned the light on to look at the sheets. 'Then where is it? A woman is meant to bleed when she has sex for the first time.'

'I didn't know that,' I said, shaking.

Jock was squatting, still naked, facing me now. 'Have you had sex with anyone else?'

'You know I haven't.'

'Do I? What about those old men leering at you when you modelled your hats.'

'Don't be daft –' I began.

'And don't you call me daft.' His voice rose in the darkness. 'Have you been making a fool out of me with all your prissiness about not having sex before marriage? Turn the light on. I want to see properly.'

I stumbled across the cold, uneven, rocking caravan floor and did as I was told. 'Aye, there it is,' said Jock. His voice was kinder now. 'See?'

There was indeed a smear of blood on the sheet.

'That proves it, then.' Jock was looking very pleased with himself. 'Congratulations, Mrs Page. You're officially mine now.'

Just as in the car, he'd changed from being angry to loving in seconds. 'You'd better go and wash,' he told me. 'You'll have to find the toilets outside.'

As I scrubbed myself clean, going over my legs again and again, I noticed a cut on my arm from where Jock had held me down with his hands and nails. It was still bleeding. Maybe that's where the blood had come from.

I'd need to find a plaster for that. But something told me it would be wise not to tell my new husband.

I couldn't wait to leave. Devon was beautiful enough, but I just wanted to move into our new home and make it ours. Maybe Jock would go back to his old self then. It never occurred to me, you see, that his up-and-down temper *was* his old self.

Our one-bedroom flat was on the fifth floor in a block that had been built soon after the war. No one told us, when we looked around, that the lift was frequently out of order. There was no central heating and we made do with electric bar fires, which I almost hugged in the freezing evenings. The damp, which came through the peeling brown wallpaper in big patches, made me cough and the landlord ignored our requests to have it looked at. The boiler didn't work properly and the water was always lukewarm.

We were only minutes away from the factory and you could smell it from our tiny balcony where I hung the washing because we didn't have a garden. *If you're in love*, I told myself, *it doesn't matter where you live.* The problem was that I didn't know if I was in love any more.

My doubts had started during the honeymoon but they increased afterwards when I went straight to work on the factory assembly line. The girls were standoffish, and the job (fixing light bulbs into their metal bases without breaking them) was boring and repetitive. How I missed my lovely customers from the department store and those fashionable hats! I couldn't help feeling resentful towards my new husband – and I also blamed myself for going along with his wishes.

Jock no longer tried to make me laugh or be kind or look after me, as he had done during most of our engagement. If supper wasn't ready within a few minutes of us getting home, he'd ask me why I wasn't more organized. He started to object to my eyeliner, which made me 'look like a tart', and my clothes. The polyester navy-blue jumpsuit my mother had bought me as a birthday present was 'too revealing'. Goodness knows what he'd have said about some of the things that Melissa and Daisy wear!

We had constant rows about money, too. One day, one of the heels from the only pair of shoes I owned came off. The mender said he couldn't do any more for it so I had to buy a new pair. 'What?' thundered Jock when I told him how much they'd cost. 'How do you think we can afford that?'

'It was the cheapest I could find,' I protested.

'Well, you'll have to do without meat for a month. And the electric fire as well.'

He put his coat on. 'Where are you going?' I asked, alarmed.

'To the pub.'

'But we don't have any money.'

'*You* don't. I'll do what I like with my wages. I'm not the one who spent half a week's pay packet on shoes.'

Nowadays, girls wouldn't stand for this. At least not many. But in our day, women like me were less certain of ourselves. I didn't want to tell my mother that things weren't good between Jock and me. It made me feel that I was a failure. But one day, when we were asked over for Sunday lunch, and Jock made a great show of putting his arm around me and calling me his 'lovely wife' (affection

84

he never displayed at home), I burst into tears in the kitchen.

My mother instantly shut the door so I couldn't be heard. 'What's wrong?' she said.

I told her between sobs. 'There are some men,' she said slowly, 'who need to be in charge. It comes from the war. Women had more independence then, and when their menfolk came back, they didn't always like it.'

'But that was years ago,' I said.

My mother gave a hoarse laugh. 'Attitudes stick. They get passed from one generation to the other. Sounds to me like Jock takes after his father.'

She stopped. I didn't care for my father-in-law, although, of course, I'd never actually said so. He was a gruff man who thought nothing of spitting on the ground, even if he was in the house. Maybe that's why Jock had discouraged me from going too often round to his place when we were engaged. He also expected his wife to wait on him, just as Jock now expected me to do.

'Does he beat you?'

My mother said this in such a casual manner that I was shocked.

'No. Of course not.'

'That's something, then.'

'How can you say that?' I cried. 'I'm not happy. What shall I do?'

My mother shrugged. 'You do what countless women over the centuries have done. Just get on with it.'

'But I don't know if I can.'

'You can't get divorced.' My mother's voice was low and sharp. 'What would people think of us? Anyway, you have to work at a marriage. It's normal to have ups and downs at first. It will be better when you have a baby.'

'But we can barely afford to eat, let alone have a child.'

My mother shook her head. 'You lot don't know when you're well off. I didn't even see an orange during the war years when I was a kid. Where's your spirit, Betty? I'd have thought more of you than this. Besides, you were desperate to marry Jock.'

'Yes, but he was different then.'

'They all are.' My mother sounded wistful for a minute. Then her voice turned tough again. 'You girls with your modern ways! You think you know it all, don't you? Well, you don't. It might sound hard, but you've made your bed and now you'll have to lie in it. There's no way you're bringing disgrace on this family by leaving.'

So I soldiered on. I became a different me to make the new Jock happy. I wore cheap baggy clothes from the market. I gave him the best cuts of meat, telling myself I wasn't hungry. I pretended not to care when the girls at work ignored me because I didn't smoke during breaks or cuss like a trooper.

And when Jock made love to me, I pretended he was someone else. An actor in the series we were watching on television. Anyone. Just so long as I could get through it.

This went on for two years. Then Jock got promoted at the factory. His wages doubled. 'See?' he said. 'I told you we'd be all right. The boss says I'll go far.' He preened. 'Reckons I've got what it takes to get right to the top.'

'That's wonderful,' I said. I'd learned that the best way to make Jock happy (apart from providing regular food and sex) was to praise him.

'We'll be able to afford a baby soon.'

'Really?' My heart thudded. Of course, I wanted a child. But that would also mean I'd have to stay in the marriage. There'd be no way out. Although I'd told myself my mother was right about not leaving Jock, I also took heart from the fact that I could still do it one day if things became unbearable. But if there was a child, I couldn't. Single mothers, you see, were still disapproved of in those days.

The night after his pay rise, Jock refused to wear what he referred to as a French letter. I'd been using a Dutch cap too, just to be sure, but he took it out of its box and threw it away. 'There,' he said, beaming at me. 'We don't need that either.'

I tried to reassure myself. No one got pregnant first time without contraception. I'd learned that from gossip amongst the girls on the assembly line. Some of them had been trying for months.

But four weeks later, my period didn't come.

I said nothing for another four weeks just in case. Then I began to be sick every morning.

'It's a bug that's going around,' I told Jock. But my mouth tasted metallic. Again, I knew from assembly-line chat that this was a sign of early pregnancy.

Still I said nothing and waited. If I told Jock I was pregnant and I wasn't, he might blame me for 'getting it wrong'. But my third period didn't start, I went to the doctor. The receptionist rang two days later. 'I'm delighted to tell you, Mrs Page, that you're pregnant.'

At last I'd done something he'd be pleased with. And he was. 'I've done it,' he said, punching the air. 'That'll show the boys.'

'What do you mean?'

He looked slightly abashed. 'They kept asking when I was going to be a father, as if there was something wrong with me. But now we're going to be a real family.'

That night, he made love to me so hard that I cried.

The following morning there was blood on the sheet and the cramps in my stomach were so bad that I was doubled over with the pain. Jock rang my mum, who came racing round.

'Get the doctor,' she said.

I was terrified. We'd never got the doctor out in our lives.

'What's happening?' I cried. 'Am I going to be all right?'

But my mother didn't answer.

7

Poppy

The doorbell goes straight after supper. 'Expecting any-one?' asks Betty as we're clearing up together.

'No,' I say, finding myself going red as I rush to answer it.

It's Doris! Looking quite the part in a natty little lime green 1950s-style suit and high heels. I breathe a sigh of relief, although it's not really necessary. I mean it's not as though Matthew is actually going to turn up on my door-step. He doesn't have my address and, besides, why should he visit me?

'I know we'd arranged Monday for me to sign the con-tract,' she trills, 'but I was passing on my way out to meet friends and thought I'd call in on the off chance. I hope it's not too inconvenient.'

'No,' I say. 'Please. Come up to my study. The paper-work is there.'

'What a pretty house,' she says, following me.

'Thanks.'

'I love your office,' she says, looking around. 'To think that all your magic happens here!'

I glow with the compliment. 'None of this would work without brilliant people like you on the books,' I tell her, giving her the contract to sign.

'You know,' says Doris, 'today's my birthday. That's why I'm celebrating with friends. But my life has only come into its own since I met you. You really have made all my dreams come true!'

'That's so nice of you,' I say, giving her a hug.

'Mum!' calls out Daisy from downstairs.

'I must leave you to your little family,' says Doris, heading for the door. 'OH!'

To my horror, she falls to the floor. 'I tripped on the carpet,' she groans.

Her right high heel is still entangled in the worn section that the chesterfield usually hides. Betty must have pushed it a bit further over when vacuuming. 'Are you all right?' I ask, worried.

She gets up and rubs her right shoulder. 'This hurts quite a bit.'

'Would you like an ice pack?'

'No, thanks.' Doris carries on down the stairs, still holding her shoulder. 'I don't want to be late for my friends.'

'Are you sure?'

She nods. Doris is a real trooper. She's from the generation that never complains. Once she told me that, just after the war, they were so poor that her mother had pulled out one of Doris's teeth with a pair of pliers because they couldn't afford a dentist. I hadn't realized it was her birthday. Maybe I'll send her some flowers.

After she's gone, I order a lovely bouquet of roses and lilies through an online site and do a bit more work on my computer. Then Betty, Daisy and I snuggle up on the sofa to watch a soppy box-set romance. I'm not entirely sure if it's suitable for a fourteen-year-old but, as my mother-in-law says while she hands round a plate of home-made honey-and-sultana flapjacks, times have changed.

I try to concentrate but I've got a blinding tension headache. The trauma of seeing Matthew again – and then turning down what might or might not have been an innocuous invitation to coffee – has taken its toll. Every now and then I can't help checking my mobile but he hasn't responded. Of course he hasn't. My polite rebuff had been more than enough. There is, however, a text from Stuart to say he's been delayed at the conference and will be back 'late'. He doesn't specify a time.

'Ooh,' squeals Daisy, grabbing my arm as the film hots up. 'Look! He's going to ask her out.'

How sweet! I do hope my youngest daughter doesn't grow up too fast. May she be blessed with an uncompli-cated (if old-fashioned) married life like my mother-in-law had had. As for Melissa, I've got a feeling that she might always be looking for something that doesn't quite exist. At the moment, she seems quite sweet (as my father would put it) on a boy called Jonnie from school. 'He's just a friend,' she told me tartly when I inquired. I'm not sure I believe her but I don't want to push.

When the programme finishes, Daisy goes up without demur to bed. 'Think I'll turn in now,' says my mother-in-law, yawning. She's looking tired, I notice with a pang. Betty usually seems much younger than her age. Since Jock died, she's started to wear a touch more make-up and buys well-cut trousers instead of what she refers to as 'slacks'. She's also so much in tune with the rest of us that I forget that she's actually seventy, according to the paper-work we helped her with after Jock's death. (Betty herself has always been a bit hazy about her age. I suspect it's because she doesn't like getting older.)

'Sleep well,' I say, giving her a big hug. Once more, I honestly don't know what I'd do without her. Other women I know are always moaning about their mothers-in-law. Mine is the mother I never had . . .

'What about you?' she says, holding me out with her arms as though inspecting me. 'You must be exhausted after that work do of yours last night.'

Is it my imagination or can she sense all the emotions churning inside me?

No. Of course not. Betty, with the experience of her steady, traditional marriage with Jock, would be shocked if I told her about the imaginary scenes that had been playing in my head since I'd seen Matthew again.

'I'm fine, thanks,' I tell her. 'Now, you go off to bed. I'll wait up for Melissa.'

One of the other parents is bringing her back from the party but it's nearly 1 a.m. by the time I hear my eldest daughter's key in the lock. By then I'm out of my mind with worry, imagining all kinds of disasters.

'Sorry,' she slurs. 'Jonnie's mum got lost trying to find the house.'

'I tried to ring you,' I said. 'Why didn't you pick up?'

'Out of battery.'

How often have I heard that one? 'Have you been drinking?' I say, following her up the stairs. It's a stupid question. Of course she has.

'No. And stop nagging.'

She goes into her room and shuts the door in my face. For a minute I wonder whether to go in after her but then decide to have a calmer discussion in the morning. Instead, I have a long lovely hot steamy bath in which I close my eyes and imagine that . . .

No, I tell myself. *This isn't right*. So I get out and check my mobile. Nothing from Stuart. Or anyone else.

At some point in the night, I'm aware of my husband climbing into bed next to me. 'You're back,' I mumble.

'Sorry I'm late,' he says. He doesn't exactly smell but I can tell that he hasn't washed either. I take this as a re-assuring sign. Men are meant to have power showers or deep baths as soon as they get back if they have affairs, aren't they? At least, they are according to the odd magazine article I've read. Anyway, Stuart simply isn't the kind of man who would cheat. Isn't that one of the reasons I'd married him? Besides, he only has eyes for his work.

Then he starts to snore gently. I've always envied my husband's ability to fall asleep the minute his head hits the pillow. I, by contrast, am now wide awake.

I lean over and try to kiss him.

He turns away. 'Don't wake me up,' he murmurs, before starting to snore again.

'*When* are we going to show each other some affection then?' I want to say. I almost want to tell him that if he's not interested, there are others who are. I don't want to cause a row. It's more a question of self-esteem. But he's out like a light now.

Or at least pretending to be.

In the morning, I wake to find an empty space beside me. I wander downstairs, feeling better after a night's rest. It's already 10 a.m. I haven't slept this long for ages.

Stuart is in the kitchen, washing up everything I'd put in the dishwasher the night before. This is an ongoing area of tension between us. My husband prefers to do it all himself by hand, carefully cleaning each little fork prong or knife edge. 'It's a dentist thing,' he'd once told me. 'When you see what's inside people's mouths, you realize the importance of sterilizing anything that enters it.'

'Sorry if I woke you up last night when I came to bed,' he says now, dropping a light kiss on my forehead.

If he remembers his rebuff, he isn't going to apologize. Why should he? It's not as though it was the first time.

'How was your work party on Friday night?' he continues. 'We haven't had a chance to discuss it. Did you have a good time?'

My husband isn't being sarcastic. Stuart and I are used to going our own ways when it comes to work. He has his out-of-hours appointments for patients while I often have shoots that go on into the evening or interviews with possible clients and also 'wraps' to enjoy the success and make more contacts. Part of a casting agent's responsibilities is to make sure that clients are happy and doing what they should be. Even at the weekend, one of us might well be working. We each accept this is part of our respective jobs. Yet today I feel I've broken the rules. Which I have. Even if it's only in my head.

'It was all right,' I say, trying not to sound nervous. But inside, I feel as though I am a different woman from the one before the party. I almost expect the kitchen to have changed; for its gleaming range, the expensive vintage-look kitchen table, the honey-pine floorboards and the view out of the French windows to our long (if thin) garden to have been somehow transformed. We are particularly proud of the latter, given that in this part of north-west London each square centimetre costs a small fortune. How can everything still be the same when I drifted off to sleep last night thinking of Matthew Gordon and doing things to my own body that I wish he had done? Some might say I am overreacting. Maybe I am. But it still feels wrong.

'I tried to get back from the party,' I say, 'but I had a couple of drinks and then couldn't get a taxi because of the weather.'

I'd already told him all this in a text during the day yesterday but Stuart doesn't seem to think it's odd or that I'm babbling nervously.

'We had a lovely family evening last night,' I add, deciding to skip the various earlier domestic dramas. 'Your mum, Daisy and I watched a film. Melissa was out partying. How are you? How was your conference?'

'Really interesting, actually. There was this new paper on . . .'

He then launches into a lengthy monologue about the pros and cons of a certain filling mixture. Is this really the man who, on our first date, had recited the whole of the 'Shall I compare thee to a summer's day?' sonnet by Shakespeare. (Later, he told me that he'd learned it off pat in order to impress me because he thought I'd like that, as an actress.) Now I pretend to listen to his dental talk, nodding at the right bits, or so I hope, while making toast on the Aga.

'Are the girls still asleep?' I ask when he's finished.

'No. Melissa's having her driving lesson.'

It had completely slipped my mind. 'But she had too much to drink last night. She'll be over the limit.'

Stuart looks concerned. 'Really? She seemed all right to me this morning.'

'What about Daisy?'

'At her painting class.'

Our youngest always goes to the Sunday-morning session at the local arts centre. What's happened to my brain?

'Don't worry,' he says kindly. 'None of us wanted to wake you so Mum said she'd collect her after her class. They'll be back soon. Mind you, they had a bit of an argument about something before they left. Daisy found an old photograph album of Mum's and she seemed to get really upset.'

'Who? Daisy?'

'No. Mum. I told Daisy she shouldn't have been in her grandmother's room in the first place.'

As if on cue, Betty bounces in wearing one of her purple berets. She has a collection of them in different shades, hanging on a row of hooks in her bedroom. This one is pale lilac. As well as the beret, Betty has her yoga outfit on. This ensemble of a pale pink leotard under a cream floaty tunic top plus loose trousers teamed up with ballet pumps might seem incongruous on anyone else, but my mother-in-law can get away with almost any combination of clothes and still look stylish. In her younger days, apparently, she modelled hats for a department store. She has an old faded newspaper cutting showing her in a fashion show, which she brings out every now and then. Sometimes I wonder if she needs to reassure herself of her worth as a person in her own right, rather than 'just' as a mother and grandmother. I get that. Isn't it what my own work is about? There's certainly no signs of an earlier argument over those photographs Stuart had referred to, so I decide not to mention it.

Daisy follows her in, carrying a canvas.

'Look what your youngest daughter has done!' beams Betty. 'Go on, show them, love.'

It's pretty amazing, I have to say. A wonderful mélange of pink, green and blue hills. Where does she get it from?

'Such a clever girl.' Betty holds Daisy close to her and once more I feel so lucky that my kids have had the opportunity of living with their grandmother. They will have a close bond that many families don't have. A bond that needs to be kept safe.

Then Melissa marches in.

'You should have cancelled your driving lesson after drinking last night,' I say, trying to get close to smell her breath.

'Get off me, Mum,' she snaps, shaking me off. 'I was fine this morning. Ask my instructor. He thinks I'm nearly ready to take my test. When's lunch? I didn't have time for breakfast.'

'Blast,' I say. 'I meant to go food shopping.' That's the thing about working from home. You get glued to the computer and forget to do normal things like dust or cook. Or you stay overnight at Christmas parties and find yourself talking to a man you once loved . . .

'Tell you what,' says Betty brightly. 'Why don't you and Stuart go out on your own for a change. The girls and I will do our own thing.'

My husband and I look at each other. 'We could,' he says doubtfully.

'Maybe it would be nicer if we had a family lunch together with the children,' I retort, hurt by his lack of enthusiasm.

'Come off it,' snaps Melissa. 'We're not babies any more. Just go. It will be nice to have time with Gran and not be nagged all the time.'

I wince. Why is it that you always get told off for trying to do your best?

'Now now,' says Betty, 'that's not the way to speak to your mother.' I see her giving Stuart a pointed look. He takes the hint.

'Mum's right. Let's have some time on our own. We could go to that new bistro on the other side of town and then have a family evening in tonight.'

'Great,' I say, trying to sound as though I mean it. Haven't I been wishing that my husband would spend more time with me? I need to try too. It might make up for the guilt I feel after seeing Matthew. Not, of course, I remind myself for the umpteenth time, that I did anything wrong.

'Everything all right?' asks my husband as we drive in his car. I've told him about my collision and he was surprisingly unfazed, saying it was 'one of those things'. He seems just as distracted as I feel, in fact.

'Fine,' I say. But the truth is that I can barely string a sentence together, with all the emotions whizzing round in my head. Then again, Stuart and I aren't great talkers. We can sit for hours in the car without saying anything. It's not a problem. Neither of us takes offence. But I do sometimes wonder if it's because we have little in common apart from the family. Then again, isn't that enough? I didn't realize, until I had children, just how full-on parenting is. How does anyone manage it on their own? It's hard enough with the two of us – and we are particularly lucky to have Betty to help.

My phone bleeps. Another domestic drama already? But it's an urgent call-out message from a production manager seeking extras who are five months pregnant. No more or they might go into labour early and then claim it was the stress of the shoot. (You have to be so careful with health and safety.) And no less or they won't show.

I've got the perfect woman! 'Sorry,' I say. 'Just got to send some emails.'

Stuart is used to this. Business doesn't stop, even on a Sunday.

Then an incoming call flashes up on the screen. It's Sally. Her voice sounds odd.

'Doris has just rung me. She tried to get through to you but you were busy. Apparently she fractured her shoulder when she visited your house last night to sign a contract.'

Fractured?

'She fell in my study,' I say, my mouth going dry. 'She was wearing heels and one caught in the carpet. But she said she was fine.'

'Caught in the carpet?' repeats Sally. 'Do you have public liability insurance?'

'No,' I say, feeling nervous. 'I didn't think I needed it.'

'You might if people visit your premises for business purposes.' Sally's voice is crisp. 'Doris's shoulder got worse after she left and she went to A&E. She doesn't need an operation, thank goodness. But she's got to wear a sling and she's also in a great deal of pain – which means she can't work for at least six weeks.'

That's awful. But something else is also worrying me. 'Is she blaming us?' I ask with a lump in my throat.

'No. And we hope she doesn't think of it. You've got home insurance, I presume?'

Sally doesn't normally sound so headmistressy, but she has a right, this time. I never even thought about the safety implications of inviting Doris round to the house. She feels more like a friend than a client.

'Yes. Of course I do.'

'That should cover you,' she says, sounding slightly less strained. 'Can you check the small print?'

'Sure.'

'Meanwhile, we'll have to find a substitute for that ad shoot that Doris was meant to be in.'

That's all I need right now. Another job to do. But I feel dreadful about poor Doris's shoulder – and on her birthday too. I'd been meaning to replace that carpet for ages. It just came low down on my list of priorities. What bad luck that Betty had moved the sofa.

'Oh and I've got the perfect vicar part for Ronnie,' continues Sally, sounding brighter. 'It's only small but it might lead to something.'

'Great! Tell me about it . . .'

When Stuart and I reach the bistro, I tell myself I ought to turn off the phone. But I can't relax. We've been put at a corner table close to the kitchen doors, which keep opening and closing. After we order – chunky vegetable soup for us both as starters, followed by tofu salad for me and asparagus tart for him – we sit there, quietly. I wait for him to ask me more about the party but he doesn't. I'm both relieved and offended. It would be nice if he showed a bit more interest in my work. Sally – who's become the nearest that my schedule allows to a friend – said once that this is probably because it's so far removed from his own that he doesn't want to show his ignorance.

'He could ask questions though, couldn't he?' I had said.

'In my experience,' said Sally, 'men don't like doing that. They think it makes them look weak.'

'One of my retired vicars has been picked for an extra in a new crime series,' I now tell Stuart.

He finishes his soup before replying. 'Really? That's nice.'

I could tell him about Doris and the carpet but I don't want to put a dampener on our lunch. Besides, I keep telling myself, we have home insurance, don't we?

'So did you see anyone you knew at the conference?' I ask as we wait for the mains to come.

'Quite a few,' he says. 'The keynote speaker was pretty great. He was talking about this new technique for . . .'

He then goes into dental-speak, which, as usual, and despite myself, I zone out of until realizing he's stopped.

'Sounds fascinating,' I say.

He seems pleased. 'I thought so too.'

There's silence.

'Actually, I've come across something else that's rather interesting,' he then says.

My heart pounds. For one moment, I fear this is his way of saying he knows I ran into Matthew. But how could he?

'I've been using a different painkiller in certain cases,' says Stuart. 'Some of the patients find it really helps. There was a piece on it in one of my dental magazines. Seems to work quite well.'

I breathe a sigh of relief. 'Sounds fascinating.'

He frowns. 'You said that just now.'

'Did I? Well, it is. Both bits, I mean.'

Frankly, I'm beginning to wish I was back at my desk or with the kids.

I look across at the next table, where an older-looking couple are leaning across to coo at each other. Their legs are entwined underneath. Both are wearing wedding rings. I feel a flash of envy. Then doubt. Maybe they're married to other people. Perhaps they think they're safe from prying eyes. But all it takes is for one person to spot them. I shiver.

They clink glasses. Giggle. Then the waitress comes over carrying a gateau with a mini-firework candle in the middle. On it is written 'Happy 10th Anniversary', in swirling icing.

So they *are* married! Mind you, ten years isn't that long, considering they're hardly spring chickens. Is this their second marriage? Or did they wait until they found the right person? Had they been brave – or selfish – enough to cast their first family aside (if indeed there had been one) and take a chance with someone different?

If only I could ask. Then again, their choice is not a blueprint, I remind myself. We all have to make our own decisions. And I have made mine. Haven't I? And it doesn't – it can't – involve Matthew Gordon, even if he wanted me. Which, of course, he doesn't because he is married. To a disabled wife.

The main courses arrive, much to my relief. It saves me having to think. My husband tucks in. Maybe he feels the same. We attempt some more conversation, mainly about the children.

'Melissa will be hearing from her choices soon,' Stuart says.

Inwardly, I groan. It had cost us blood, sweat and tears to help fill in her personal statement. I had felt a bit guilty about this until I realized loads of parents do the same. Yet now Melissa wants to go to drama school instead of reading drama at university. I agree with her, but Stuart favours the latter. Then my phone rings from the bag next to me. I jump.

'Thought we said no phones over lunch,' Stuart says with a hint of reproach.

'I forgot,' I lie. The truth is that I'd found myself unable to put it on silent or turn it off in case Matthew rang. Even though we are only friends, it would feel awkward to have a conversation with Stuart here with me. But I'm also scared of missing Matthew's call and then wondering what he'd been going to say. Could this be him? I can barely breathe. 'Sorry. I'll leave it until later.'

The screen flashes to indicate that someone has left a voice message. There's no contact name. Just a number I don't recognize. I'd not yet keyed in Matthew's details to my phone. So it might be him.

'Better check it in case it's the kids,' says Stuart noticing.

I should have played safe and switched the wretched thing off at the beginning. Now there's no getting out of it. Turning away so my husband can't hear, I listen to it.

'*In a spot of bother,*' says a familiar voice with an air of desperation. '*Ring me, can you?*'

'It's Dad,' I say. 'But it isn't his usual number.'

Stuart rolls his eyes. I know what he means, but his unsympathetic reaction also annoys me. My father is as traditional as Betty is eccentric. Or at least he used to be. After Mum left, he'd soldiered on, resisting the advances of divorcees and widows who flocked to get his attention. And no wonder! He's a handsome man, my father. But then the forgetfulness set in. Once when I made it down to Worthing – I found that the oven was piping hot with a charred cottage pie inside.

'How long have you had this on?' I'd asked.

'Oh, I don't know,' he'd replied, batting the question away. 'I can't quite remember.'

Alarm bells started ringing in my head. After all, dementia is a subject very much on the mind of anyone with elderly relatives or friends.

Since then there have been other things. My father has begun to look rather unkempt. Last month when I visited, he had egg stains down his shirt. 'I can't seem to work the washing machine,' he told me.

When I investigated, there was a tin of baked beans inside. Open. On another visit, I smelt burning and found the iron standing face-down on the board. 'I only left it there for a few minutes,' said my dad defensively.

My suggestion that he should see his doctor about memory loss went down like a lead balloon. So I contacted the practice manager myself to say I was concerned about him. The GP paid a visit and gently suggested a routine 'overall check'. 'No way,' he said. 'Nothing wrong with me.'

What can you do?

But now he is actually asking for my help.

I ring back the number.

'Not at the table,' Stuart says.

'This is an emergency,' I retort. 'You'd be worried if this was your mother.'

My father picks up immediately. 'Eileen?'

That was my mother's name.

'No. It's Poppy,' I say gently. 'What's wrong, Dad?'

'Nothing. Why should it be?'

'But you just sent me a message saying you were in some kind of trouble.'

'Did I? I don't remember. I'm fine.'

I picture him in the bungalow he'd stayed in after Mum had left. Anything could be going on there. The iron might be face down again. The washing machine could be churning with baked beans. Not for the first time, I wished there was a kindly neighbour I could ring. But my father had hacked them off through either his romantic rebuttals or his eccentric behaviour.

'Why've you got a different number?'

'I broke the last phone. So Reggie got me another with one of those new simmy things.'

'How?'

'From a shop, of course. What do you think?'

'How did you break it, I mean.'

'Dropped it in the lav, didn't I? Bloody thing fell out of my pocket.'

'Look, Dad,' I say, glancing across at Stuart, 'I'll come down.'

My husband pulls a 'What?' face.

'I'll be there before the evening,' I say, glancing at my watch and mentally working out the train times. It's easier to go that way because I can work while travelling, which I obviously can't do in the car. 'Do you want me to bring anything?'

'Milk,' he says quickly. 'You can never have enough, can you? But make sure it's the green lid stuff.'

We have this conversation every time. I always arrive with the promised two pints of green only to find that the fridge door is already stacked with them.

'Thanks, Poppy.'

His voice is soft now. Almost like a child's.

'But I thought we were going to have a family night in,' says Stuart, when I finish the call. There's a reproving tone to his voice that irritates me. We have his mother living with us, don't we? And although we couldn't manage without her, Betty needs us too. Just as Dad needs me. It's not as though I have any brothers or sisters to help out.

'I have to look after my father,' I say. 'You could come down with me if you want.'

He shakes his head as though the suggestion is ridiculous. 'I'm on call tomorrow morning.'

'Aren't you worried about him too?' I demand.

'Of course I'm concerned. But if he got some proper help, he'd be all right.'

I put down my knife and fork. 'He might have dementia, Stuart. People aren't in the right frame of mind to make decisions when that happens.'

'Or he might just be stubborn.'

Stuart had never cared for my father after he'd over-heard Dad telling me, soon after I'd introduced them, that 'this new boyfriend of yours isn't as much fun as that other chap'.

'What other chap?' Stuart had demanded and I'd brushed off his jealousy with a 'someone I dated briefly' remark instead of mentioning Matthew by name. I didn't feel strong enough to go into our relationship right then. And there hasn't seemed a good time to mention it since.

That was years ago, but Stuart is the kind of man who takes umbrage if he feels slighted. Betty had warned me about that in the early days. 'He's a bit like his dad was, in that respect,' she said quietly. I'd never noticed that. Then again, Jock had died when the girls were quite young, before I'd got to know him. I sensed he was a private kind of person.

'How can you talk about him like that?' I say now to my husband. 'I wouldn't speak like that about your mother.'

'That's because she's kind and does so much with the children. Your father has never been very interested in them.'

I'd put that down to the fact that my father was scared of getting close to anyone after Mum had left. Stuart has no right to criticize Dad. He has no idea what it was like to come from a broken family. He doesn't realize how lucky he was to have parents like his. I couldn't manage without Betty. Not just because she helps us so much, but also because I really love her.

We drive home in silence. *Matthew would understand*, I tell myself. He'd been the one who had comforted me when my parents had split. He'd come down with me to see Dad and even took him out to the pub to 'cheer him up'. They'd got on really well.

I try to book a room at the hotel I normally use in Worthing, but it's full – there's a conference, apparently – as are two others I try.

I go to the bathroom. Get out my phone again. *Don't do this*, I tell myself. But I can't help it.

> How are things with you?

I text.

> It's pretty manic here. My dad's in
> some sort of trouble and I need to
> go down tonight to see him. I can't
> stay with him because you can't
> even get into the spare room with
> all the stuff he's hoarded over the
> years! Now I've got to try and find
> a hotel in Worthing that isn't
> booked up. Never stops, does it?

Then, in an attempt to sound like the kind of casual 'just-wanted-to-share-this' message to a friend, I add a rolling-eyes emoji.

The reply comes back almost immediately.

> Poor you. Actually I stayed down
> there once. I can still remember
> the name of the hotel. Would you

like me to check it out for you? I've
got a few minutes to spare.
Sandra is having a nap, bless her.

How thoughtful. I feel relieved (and a teeny bit jealous, for some ridiculous reason) that he mentioned Sandra. It makes our 'chat' seem open and honest. Which, of course, it is. Especially as we're not actually talking. Texting is more casual. Nowadays, it seems a phone conversation is reserved for serious matters. And this isn't. Is it?

It's OK, thanks

I text back.

I don't want to bother you.

There's nothing for a minute. Then the reply pops up.

I've got it! Here are the details. It
says online that they still have
limited availability. Hope that helps.

He follows this with a link to the hotel's website.

That's so nice of you!

I type.

No probs.

There's a hammering on the door. 'Mum!' It's Melissa. 'I need the loo and Gran's in the other. How long are you going to be?'

'Nearly finished,' I say, hastily saving Matthew's number to my contacts and putting the phone in my pocket. I'll have to book later.

Then I come out. Telling myself that I haven't done anything wrong. I've simply been chatting to a friend who has helped me out.

8

Betty

There was so much blood that the doctor called an ambulance. They carried me out on a stretcher and all the neighbours came out onto the street to gawp. It felt unreal, as if this was happening to someone else.

'I want to come as well,' said Jock, trying to clamber in after me.

'There's no room, I'm afraid, sir.'

Jock's face went red with fury. 'I'll do what I want. I'm her husband.'

'Rules is rules, sir.' The driver was actually barring his way. No one did that to Jock in his book. 'I'll let them know at the hospital that you'll be coming.'

The doors shut. 'Now don't you worry,' said the kind ambulance man sitting next to me, taking my pulse. 'We'll soon get you sorted out.'

When we got there, the huge sanitary pad they'd given me had soaked right through. 'It looks to me, love,' said one of the nurses, 'that you might be having a threatened miscarriage.'

'No,' I gasped. 'I can't lose my baby. I just can't.'

One of the girls on the factory line had miscarried. She was three months gone too. That was last year and she still hadn't got pregnant again.

The nurse squeezed my hand comfortingly. 'And you might not. "Threatened" doesn't mean "definitely". I've seen others who've lost more blood than you have and the pregnancy ended up as right as rain. We'll soon find out when the doctor examines you.'

I began to feel a ray of hope.

'Are you on any medication?' she continued.

'No.'

'Did you and your husband have sex recently?'

I nodded, my mouth dry, as I watched her write something down. 'Could that have done it?' I asked, feeling sick.

She avoided my eyes. 'There's one school of thought that says it's a good idea to avoid intercourse around the time when you would have had a period. It's been twelve weeks, you say. That would bring it to the third missed monthly.'

'So it *might* have brought it on,' I said.

'It's possible. But not definite.'

'What about if . . . if my husband was quite rough?'

The nurse gave me a strange look. 'Is he violent?'

'No,' I said quickly. 'It's . . . it's just his way when we . . . when we make love. I suppose it was just . . .'

I stopped, trying to think of the right word. It wasn't passion. More like him wanting to assert his ownership over me. But I was too embarrassed to say so. So I let the sentence tail away.

Again, she wrote on my file.

Hot tears ran down my cheeks. 'I just want everything to be all right.'

She took my hand. 'Look, Betty – I can call you that, can I? Let's just wait and see what the doctor says, shall we? Ah, here he is.'

I steeled myself. The 'internal', as they called it, really hurt.

The doctor's face was serious when he finished. Just as he was about to speak, Jock came rushing in. 'Is my bairn all right?' he panted. He was flushed and sweating, as if he'd been running.

'I'm so sorry.' The doctor looked me in the eyes. 'But it looks like you have lost the baby.'

The tears came instantly, thick and choking. Jock's eyes were moist too. 'It's all right, love,' he said, taking my hand. 'We'll have another.'

'Miscarriages are very common,' added the lady in the white coat. 'They do say it can be nature's way of . . . well, weeding out the babes who aren't meant for this world.'

But I sensed, deep down, that my baby would have been all right if it hadn't been for Jock. And I hated him for that.

When we got home, I pushed him away when he tried to put his arm around me. 'This is all your fault,' I yelled at him. 'The nurse said that sex can bring it on and you were rough with me.'

'Don't be so bloody stupid,' he said. 'That's typical, isn't it, blaming me.'

I never dared to criticize him usually but losing the baby had changed everything. I burst into tears.

'Look,' he said, holding me. This time he sounded kind and almost sorry. 'You're upset. It's understandable. But we'll have another. I promise.'

'They said we have to wait three months,' I sobbed. In those days, that was the advice they gave. But I gather it's different now.

'Then we'll wait. Now don't you worry. It will be OK. Meanwhile, we have to get you feeling stronger.'

Jock was as good as his word. It was almost like having another husband. He was thoughtfulness itself, bringing me cups of sweet tea and then telling me not to 'overdo it' when I went back to work.

When the first three months were up, he started to make love to me again, but differently. He wasn't rough. In fact, he was tender. I began to see flashes of the man I thought I'd married. But I couldn't relax. What if I didn't get pregnant again, like that girl on the assembly line? Would Jock still be as gentle then?

The following month my period didn't come. 'See,' said Jock, 'I said we'd hit the jackpot, didn't I?'

Yet when the doctor's receptionist rang to say that yes, my pregnancy test was positive, I couldn't allow myself to become excited about it. Supposing I lost this one as well?

'No,' I said to Jock when he tried to make love to me. 'You might hurt the baby.'

'That's rubbish,' he said.

'How do you know? I just want to wait a bit.'

As the next month went past and the next and the next, I kept putting him off until he no longer asked for it. Perhaps, I thought, he realized it was best for our child. It was what some people thought in those days.

Meanwhile, I was getting bigger and bigger. I started making my own maternity clothes to save money. Already I was worried about how we'd manage when I gave up work. Jock had insisted that I should do that. 'I'm not having anyone saying I can't support my family on my own. We'll just have to watch the pennies.'

And while I knew that this 'I'm not letting my wife work' view was old-fashioned, I wasn't all that sorry. If I was honest with myself, I couldn't wait to give up my boring factory job. Besides, who else would look after the baby? 'Don't expect me to be much help,' Mum had said when I'd told her I was pregnant. 'At my age, I need time to myself.'

This sounds hard, but it was only later that I realized how much my parents had been through as children in the war. My mother had lost her little brother to a direct hit during an air raid, although she hardly ever spoke about it.

Even so, I couldn't help wondering how Jock and I would make ends meet. We'd been living on tinned spaghetti and toast since the last electricity bill. Then, when I got to five months pregnant, Jock was promoted at the factory again. Looked like Dad had been right when he'd said my husband was 'going far'.

A month or so later, I signed up for the free course of antenatal classes being run by the midwife at the surgery. I went along, feeling very shy and scared. The baby was really kicking away now. It felt both weird and amazing!

'I felt the same way with my first,' whispered the pretty blonde girl who sat next to me on the floor, each of us on our mats with a large diagram of a lady's insides in front of us on a screen. 'But you'll soon get used to it.'

'Thank you,' I whispered gratefully.

'What's your name?'

'Betty.'

'I'm Jane.'

She had a gentle voice. She sounded quite posh, but not in a stuck-up way.

'I had a miscarriage before this one,' I said, without really knowing why I was confessing this.

'Poor you.' She put her hand on my arm. 'I had one too. I know what it feels like. But we're all right now. It usually happens in the first three months.' She patted her stomach tenderly. 'And we're well past that, aren't we?'

The 'we' made me feel really warm and happy.

This woman who was so kind, became my first – and only – real close friend. Before long, she asked me round for coffee and I met her four-year-old daughter. Alice was a beautiful child with long blonde hair swept back with a velvet hairband. She chatted away incessantly. 'You're big like Mummy! Have you got a baby hiding in your tummy too?'

How I longed for a little girl like her! It was almost painful. Deep down, I'd always wanted a daughter. I would be so much kinder to her than my mother was to me.

'Why don't we do that spin-the-ring test?' suggested Jane. 'You take off your wedding ring, thread a piece of cotton through and get someone to hold it over your stomach. If it goes round in a circle, you're having a girl. If it goes back and forth, it's a boy.'

'Does it work?' I ask.

'It did for me last time!'

We tried it on each other. Mine showed I was having a girl. Jane's a boy.

'Perfect!' said my friend, giving me a hug.

A tingle of excitement shot through me. Not just because I was (if the test was to be believed) going to have a daughter, but also because I had a friend to do things with. Most of the girls from school I used to meet up with at the Wimpy bar had moved.

Jane only lived about fifteen minutes away (in a better part of town), so we often went for walks together or took Alice to the local playground. It seemed a miracle, I thought, as we took turns to push the swing for this happy, smiley little girl, that I was growing a baby who might be just like her. I simply couldn't wait.

My natural shyness, especially after leaving school, meant I'd never clicked with anyone from the factory either. I didn't mind too much then – most of the girls on the assembly line were all so rowdy and confident and different from me – but now I was pregnant it was nice to have someone like Jane around. Because she'd already had a child, she was able to reassure me about all the questions I had – such as whether one should really go for a 'natural birth' as the midwife suggested or whether it was 'cheating' to have all the drugs on offer.

'I didn't have time when Alice was born,' Jane had already told me. 'It all happened so fast. I just made do with gas and air, which seemed to work for me. Don't worry. You'll be all right when it happens.'

Then she patted my hand. 'I'm so glad we've met,' she said. 'I got a bit unhappy after Alice and . . . well, I don't have any of my old friends any more because they didn't really understand.'

'Why were you unhappy?' I asked. 'Weren't you excited at having a baby?'

'Yes. I was. But . . . oh it's difficult to explain. Anyway it probably won't happen again.' Then she linked her arm through mine. 'We're going to have such fun bringing up our babies together, Betty. I just know it!'

Oh, Poppy. If only I'd walked away right then and never seen her again.

Central Criminal Court, London

'You had "simply been chatting to a friend" who had helped you out,' said the barrister.

Poppy Page goes a deep red, which clashes with her auburn hair. 'Yes,' she says. 'I was at the end of my tether and Matthew's suggestion of a hotel meant there was one less job for me to do.'

'And did you arrange to meet him there at this hotel?'

'No.' She says this firmly and loudly.

The expressions on the jurors' faces are mixed. Many appear to be sceptical. One or two look sympathetic. But all are expectant. Poppy Page's fingers are fiddling with the chignon knot at her nape. Tendrils of hair are escaping onto her crisp white collar.

'This wasn't the first time you'd been at a hotel together, was it? As we've already heard, the witness Jennifer Lewis saw the two of you going up to the fourth floor of a hotel after a Christmas party held by the Association of Supporting Artistes and Agents?'

The barrister says the name in a slightly disparaging way, as if the association is not to be taken seriously. The law can be very good at looking down its nose at others.

'Yes. But that was totally innocent. We'd both had to stay the night because of the weather. And we were in separate rooms.'

'You *booked* separate rooms, certainly,' says the barrister. 'It doesn't mean that you stayed in them.'

'But we did.'

'Can you prove it?'

'What relevance does any of this have?' she blurts out.

'I'm coming to that in a moment.'

Poppy Page is really hot and bothered now. Interestingly, the defence counsel is sullenly silent, as if she accepts that Poppy has to endure this line of questioning. Either that or she isn't doing her job properly. (It happens. People assume the law is above reproach. But there are incompetent barristers as well as untrustworthy clients.)

The prosecution barrister, on the other hand, is positively glowing. She has the court in her hand and she knows it.

'So can you tell me, Mrs Page,' she continues in a voice that might seem almost chatty if it were not for the underlying insinuation, 'is it true that the deceased was indeed waiting for you at this second hotel – this time in Worthing – after you had visited your father on the Sunday after the Christmas party?'

There is a taut silence.

'Please answer the question, Mrs Page,' repeats the barrister.

When Poppy Page finally speaks, she sounds as if she is being slowly strangled.

'Yes. But I didn't arrange it.' Her face goes hard. Her eyes flash. She is spitting out the words as if they were poison. 'And afterwards, all I wanted was to get that man out of my life for ever.'

9

Poppy

I have checked the train times. If I rush now, I can work in the carriage, get to Worthing early evening and then make Dad a meal. I throw a few things into an overnight bag and scribble down the phone number of the hotel on the kitchen noticeboard in case of emergency.

'You can reach me there,' I tell Betty. 'It's a different one from usual.'

'Hope it's all right,' she says. 'I've just been reading about some of these places without proper fire regulations.'

'I'm sure it's fine. A friend recommended it to me.'

Immediately I wish I hadn't said that.

'Which one?'

Is she being suspicious or am I imagining it? If I tell her about Matthew she might jump to the wrong conclusions. 'Sally,' I say. Instantly I regret this. But it's too late now. 'I've got to dash.'

I give both girls a long cuddle, breathing them in. 'Why have you got to stay away for another night?' says Daisy.

'Because Grandad is going gaga, stupid,' says Melissa.

'It's not quite like that,' I say. Then I look around for Stuart, who had come straight in after our bistro lunch before disappearing again. 'Have you seen Dad? I need to say goodbye to him too.'

'I think he's in his study,' says Betty, her back to me as she gets something out of the Aga.

Stuart has a little room on the ground floor where he has a desk and shelves for his own private research work. My hand is on the door handle to open it when I hear his voice.

'That sounds good.' His tone is different from usual. Perkier. More upbeat. 'Nine p.m.? Look forward to it.' Then it drops slightly. 'Yes. You too.'

I go in. He appears to jump at the interruption and slides the phone into his trouser pocket.

'I'm off now,' I say and then, with an air of nonchalance that I don't feel, add: 'Who was that?'

We never ask questions like this. It's an unspoken agreement between us that we trust each other. Just like it's a 'given' that we each work crazy hours.

'Just a colleague.'

'From the practice?'

Why am I interrogating him like this?

'No. It's a woman I used to work with. I bumped into her again at the conference and it turns out that she's interested in the painkiller research I was telling you about.'

Normally this is where I tune out, but the word 'woman', along with that earlier snatch of conversation I'd overheard, makes me feel . . . well, uneasy. So too does the way my husband isn't meeting my eyes. I think back to how he'd got back late; how he hadn't responded (yet again) to my suggestions in bed.

'You're meeting up at nine p.m.? Tonight? On a Sunday?'

He gives me a challenging look. 'Yes. You heard correctly. She's writing a paper and wants to know more about my findings.'

'I wasn't eavesdropping,' I say sharply. 'I was just coming to say goodbye before I go to Dad's.'

He brushes my cheek. 'Hope you have a good trip. Give my best to him.'

'Will do.' I turn to leave and then, before I can stop, I find myself asking it. 'So when did you work with this woman?'

'About three years ago. She was a locum at the practice.'

Three years ago? Round about the time when Stuart stopped making love to me.

'What's her name?'

'Janine.' He answers without meeting my eye.

I go back and give the kids one more kiss before going. But my mind is running riot. Is it possible that my husband is having an affair? *No*, I tell myself, walking briskly to the station. As I've always believed, he's just not the type. No more than I am. Yet as I clamber onto the train – making it by the skin of my teeth – I can't explain the sense of unease in the pit of my stomach.

Then another email comes through. It's from the twenty-four-hour claims team at our home insurance company. I read it through twice. And then text Sally.

Dad lives in a 1970s honey-brick bungalow that had been quite cutting edge when he and Mum had moved in soon after it was built. I'd been a kid then. When I tell people that I grew up by the sea, they usually say how wonderful it must have been. When I go back now, I have to admit it seems pretty idyllic. But as I was growing up, all I could think of was getting away to London.

Dad loved living here. Long ago, he'd told me how he'd 'done the London bit' when he'd been young (he's about ten years older than Mum), and that when she'd got pregnant, he'd wanted me to have the fresh air that they hadn't. I suppose each generation tries to give their offspring the chances that they didn't have. Isn't that why Stuart and I cut costs on other things so we can afford 'luxuries' for the girls like acting classes, drawing courses, driving lessons (for Melissa) and nice clothes? All these would have been out of the question when I was young. I still remember having to make do with only one pair of non-school shoes, unlike some of my friends whose parents were better off.

I never yearned for a brother or sister. The three of us were happy as we were. Of course, with hindsight, I realize that Mum – who'd been an only child like Dad – must have been putting on a great show. We did things together at weekends. We looked for shells on the beach. Once, Mum found a beautiful one with a mother-of-pearl sheen inside which she gave me for my special 'treasure box'. Dad built me kites from balsa wood and wrapping paper. We did jigsaws – one of his passions, although Mum always said they bored her to death. We took long nature walks along the coast. Mum would often tell me stories about her own childhood in Wales. 'How I miss the valleys,' she'd say wistfully. When I went to secondary school and got the role of Nancy in the Christmas production of *Oliver!*, Mum and Dad filled the front ten rows with all their friends. 'Reckon you get this acting lark from my mother,' she told me proudly. 'She'd have adored you. In all the am-dram groups, she was. Wanted to be a proper actress but then she had me.'

My grandmother had died before I was born but I loved the idea of carrying on the tradition. Except that I was going to go one further. This was no hobby. I set my sights on being a proper actress. Even so, I might not have done it without the encouragement of our English teacher, who organized the annual musical.

'It's a tough world but I don't see why you can't try,' he told me when I was in the sixth form. 'Someone's got to make it big, so why not you?'

Maybe it was his faith – and my parents' – which meant I wasn't as surprised as perhaps I should have been when I was accepted by one of the well-respected drama schools. I was on my way! I couldn't wait to be off, packing my bags with such haste that I put the tension between Mum and Dad down to the fact that they were going to miss me. 'Don't worry,' I announced cheerily. 'I'll be back at Christmas.'

What I hadn't banked on was that Mum would no longer be there.

Dad broke the news in a phone call just before I was about to audition for Portia in *The Merchant of Venice*, our first student production. Stunned, I poured all my grief and anger into my feisty character. 'You were amazing,' said one of the other students when I came offstage. 'So realistic!'

Only then did I burst into tears. He held me while I sobbed bitterly and then took me to the pub for a drink. His name was Matthew. He was a mature student, nine years older than me. (He'd spent time in America, travelling, which sounded very grown-up to me.) But most important of all, he understood my grief. After his own parents' divorce, he'd spent his teenage years being handed over from one to another. 'That must have been awful,' I said.

His eyes had glistened with tears. 'It was.' Then he cupped my face in his hands, looking straight into my eyes. 'You'll learn to get used to it. I'll help you.'

The porch of Dad's bungalow, I notice now as I stand inside, waiting for him to answer the bell, is dirty with boot marks on the tiles and there's a spider's web in the corner. I'd often suggested to Dad that he might like to get a cleaner in, but he always got so defensive. 'I'm more than capable of looking after myself, thank you very much.'

These phrases have become more regular over the years. 'Waste of good money.' 'I can do it myself.'

In vain, I pointed out that I was happy to pay. 'Very good of you, but I'd rather you kept it for the kids. 'Sides, I don't want strangers poking around my private papers.'

But a cleaner might keep an eye on him. His arthritis had got worse in the last few years and he was distinctly unsteady on his feet. What if he fell? I'd contacted the council with my fears – surely they could send someone in to help with housework and so on? It turned out that he was just above the level needed to qualify. Besides, even if he hadn't been, I was pretty sure that Dad would have turned it down rather than have strangers in the house.

Through the glass door panel, I can see a shape making its way towards me. He's lifting the letter box on the other side. 'Who is it?'

'Me – Poppy.'

'Poppy?' There's the sound of bolts being undone until the door finally opens. 'What a lovely surprise!' He puts his arms around me and gives me a big bear hug.

I hug him back but inside I'm really worried. Is his memory getting worse? 'It's not a surprise, Dad. I told you I'd be here. I even gave you the time of the train I was getting.'

'No you didn't.' I can hear anger in his voice now. These changes of mood make me desperately sad. He used to be so different.

'You said you were in a spot of bother,' I say firmly but gently, stepping inside. There's a smell of burning. Then a high-pitched whine. Looks like I've come just in time. 'Dad,' I say, 'your smoke alarm is going off.'

'Oh, that.' He bats away the smoke coming out of the kitchen. 'It's just the cooker. Needs fixing.'

I head for the source. 'It's because you're frying cornflakes!'

'Of course I'm not.'

'Look, Dad.'

His voice is cross, as if I am responsible. 'Well, I don't know how that happened.'

The top of the cooker is covered with congealed food (not just the cornflakes). Ugh! Heaven knows when it was last cleaned. The oven is just as bad. 'No wonder it doesn't work, Dad. The vents are blocked up. You're lucky there hasn't been a fire.'

But my father isn't really listening and I decide it's best not to press the point. 'Give me a few minutes to clear this lot up and then I'll cook you something else.'

His voice is impatient and cross. 'I'm not hungry now. Lost my appetite, I have.'

I give him another hug. 'It's all right, Dad.'

'I know it is. I just wish you wouldn't treat me like a child.'

He goes back to his chair in a strop and turns the television up loud. I put the muck from the oven in the bin, which is, of course, overflowing. I go out of the back door – unlocked! – and that's when I hear the voice from over the fence.

'Everything all right there?'

It's dark by now but in the light from the back door I can still make out the face of Dad's neighbour, the one he doesn't talk to any more.

'Fine, thanks,' I say, leaning over to remove the lid of the dustbin. 'Just the smoke alarm.'

'I didn't mean that, love. I was talking about the police turning up this morning.'

I straighten up. 'What do you mean?'

Her voice sounds smugly excited, the way it does when someone is conveying bad news and relishing every minute of doing so. 'Didn't your dad tell you? He forgot to pay for petrol when he filled up that car of his. Drove straight off from the garage, he did. Luckily they got his registration number and the police paid him a visit. Did they press charges? You can get a criminal record for that, you know.'

Is that what Dad had meant when he'd told me he was in a spot of bother? I wish I could wipe that look off this woman's face. She might mean well but I don't like the way she's talking about Dad. 'How do you know all this?'

She has the grace to look abashed, but only slightly. 'My daughter-in-law works in the garage. Your dad needs someone to keep an eye on him. The other night, he went to bed with the back door wide open. I had to go round and wake him.'

'Thank you,' I said curtly.

'The thing is,' she continues, 'where's it all going to end? If you're not careful, he could do something that harms himself or someone else.'

The implication is clear. I am not being a good daughter. I don't answer her for fear of losing my temper. This woman doesn't know anything about the things I have to deal with in my life. How dare she judge me like that?

Going back inside, I find Dad bashing the remote control against the arm of his chair. 'Bloody thing. Why won't it work? In my day, you just had an on/off switch.'

'Dad,' I say, trying to sound calm. 'Did the police press charges when you didn't pay for your fuel this morning?'

I expect him to deny it. Instead, he rubs his eyes as if suddenly exhausted. 'It was just some stupid mistake on my part. I forgot. It's their fault. They ought to have someone to put the petrol in for you like they did in the old days.'

'Things have changed, Dad,' I say softly.

'Too damn true.' He begins thumping the remote again. 'And I don't like it. Anyway, in answer to your question, they're not going to press charges. But they gave me a "verbal warning", like I was a bloody schoolkid.'

I say nothing and, leaving him to the television, head into the kitchen to sort him out with something to eat. It's really dark outside now.

I ring home to check everything's all right. 'Fine, love,' Betty assures me.

But she sounds hesitant.

'You're sure?'

'Absolutely. The girls are doing their homework.'

'Can I speak to Stuart?'

'He's gone out to some meeting.'

But that wasn't meant to be until later.

I ring my husband. It goes straight through to answerphone.

Then I see I've had a text. From Matthew.

> How's it going with your dad?
> BTW, I'm in the area tonight.
> Fancy a drink at the hotel?

In the area? Really? Did he honestly expect me to believe that?

On the other hand, says a little voice inside me, it would be nice to have some company after everything with Dad, and now this new confirmation of my suspicions about Stuart. Once more I wish I had a best friend to talk to. I don't want to confide in Sally. Although I have let her in on the odd gripe about my husband or the girls, this feels too personal. It would mean explaining my history with Matthew . . .

I text back.

> Bit of a coincidence, isn't it?

The reply comes instantly.

> I'm not stalking you if that's what
> you mean! It just happened that
> I've been called down for a
> voiceover audition in Eastbourne
> tomorrow morning. It's an early
> start so I thought I'd stay locally for
> the night. Sandra's with one of the
> carers we use when I'm working.
> It's not a million miles away from
> you so thought I could drive over.
> But no worries if you don't feel like it.

I feel stupid. He thinks that I think he's after me.

> Sounds like a good idea

I text back.

> I could do with someone to talk to.

> Great. How about an hour from now?

It's just a drink between friends, I tell myself. My husband is out too, isn't he? But it still doesn't feel totally right.

'Would you like me to stay over with you?' I ask Dad. 'I've got a hotel room but I could cancel and sleep on your sofa instead.'

'We've been through this before, Poppy.' Dad can be quite gruff when he wants to. 'I wander round the house if I can't sleep and switch on the telly. I'm best off on my own.'

'If you're sure.'

'I am.' He yawns. 'Why don't you get going? Tell the truth, I could do with an early night. I didn't have my usual afternoon nap.'

'I'll be back in the morning,' I promise, kissing his rough cheek.

He hugs me back, warm and loving again. 'Don't bother, love. I'm going to bingo with Reg down the road. And I've got my jigsaws to keep me busy. You go back to those girls of yours. They need you more than me.'

I'm not sure that's true, I think to myself as I take the taxi I've already ordered from Dad's house to the hotel. One minute he seems so independent and the next he's so confused he's got the police after him. What am I going to do?

As soon as I walk into the hotel foyer with its huge Christmas tree in the centre and squashy sofas, I see Matthew. It's as if he is waiting for me.

'Great timing,' he says. 'I only just got here myself.'

I'd been wondering on the way what we would do when we met. Will we go for the cheek-to-cheek air kiss? Shaking hands would be strangely formal, wouldn't it?

But instead he simply gives me a sympathetic look. 'How did it go with your dad?'

'Pretty awful,' I say.

'Poor you. Let's have a drink and you can tell me all about it.'

We walk, with a space between us, towards the bar. It's all very proper and correct. Yet as we sit down and I start telling him about how Dad could have set the house on fire, I am amazed at how natural I feel with Matthew. It's so easy to talk to him, despite – or maybe because of – our past. Why don't I feel like this with Stuart? I think of the awkward silence that had stretched out between us at our lunch earlier today.

Then I think about Sandra, and how Matthew had fallen for her, and the way the two of them had treated me. We were so young then. We've all changed.

Here I am now, a mother of two with a husband who no longer wants her. And here's Matthew, no longer a TV star, devoted to his sick wife in a wheelchair. Matthew orders two glasses of Chardonnay.

'How is Sandra?' I ask.

Instantly, a strained look crosses his face. 'Not good. I felt awful leaving her for this audition but, as I mentioned, we've got this amazing carer who she gets on with. It's not like that with all of them. The pain can make Sandra understandably cross with people at times.'

His voice trails away as if he's said too much.

'Of course,' he adds, 'we have to pay for some of this help, especially if I've got a last-minute job. The social care side only goes so far.'

'That must be difficult,' I say.

He leans forward towards me, but not too close. 'That's why it's so good to talk to you, Poppy. You knew me from the days when our lives were so different. You knew Sandra too. I'm aware I behaved badly but . . .'

'It's OK.' I can't help it. I touch his shoulder in recognition of what he's saying. 'We were just kids.'

'I know.' His tone sounds a bit brisk now. 'But that's all in the past now. Talking of kids, you haven't told me much about them. You've got two, you said. Boy and girl, wasn't it?'

'Two girls,' I correct him. I'm sure I'd told him that before. If I hadn't, I should have done. 'Melissa and Daisy.'

'Pretty names.'

'Thanks.' I glow inside. 'They mean the world to me.'

'I can imagine.'

'Would you like to see some pictures?' I'm already scrolling down my phone to show him.

'The little one is so like you were!' he exclaims.

I blush. 'I was plump too.'

'Nonsense. We all loved your curvy look.'

I blush again.

'Melissa takes after Stuart,' I say quickly, to hide my embarrassment and bring us back to safer ground.

'Have you got a picture of him too?'

I scroll back to find a family shot. My husband has his arms around the girls. He is at the far end of our little group from me.

'He must be so proud of you,' says Matthew.

'I'm not sure.'

I didn't mean that to slip out but immediately he picks up on it. 'But he must be,' Matthew insists. 'You're beautiful . . .'

I flush, batting the compliment away with my hand.

'Yes you are! You've evolved into a gorgeous, sophisticated woman. Not only that but you have your own agency.'

'It's hard work,' I interrupt.

'Of course. I can imagine.' He makes a sympathetic face. 'Is your husband supportive, though?'

I remember how I'd been stupid enough to tell him that Stuart and I lead separate lives. I don't want to sound disloyal so I fudge it.

'Yes. Sort of. It's just that we don't really "get" each other's work.' I try to put on a front by making a joke out of it. 'Cross-bites and fillings aren't my field any more than extras are his.'

He shrugs. 'Personally, I'm terrified of the dentist.'

'Me too!' I say. 'I mean, Stuart being an exception, of course.' And we both laugh.

'Doesn't Stuart come down to see your dad with you?'

I take a sip of my wine.

'Well, they're not that close really.'

Again, I don't mean that to slip out. I can't even blame the drink this time. After Friday night, I'm just sticking to this one glass. Mind you, I hadn't expected a large one.

'That's a pity. I really got on with him.'

'He liked you too.'

'Did he?' Matthew looks wistful for a moment. 'In those days, the future looked so bright, didn't it? Especially when I got that major role. I thought I was going places. But then it all went pear-shaped.'

'What exactly happened?' I ask.

'Who knows? There was talk of another series but the casting director left and the new one didn't like my face so much. Then the demand came for a different kind of look in the industry.' He spreads out his hands. 'But hey, I get by on small parts and making contacts.'

Then the phone bleeps with a text. It's Sally.

> Still trying to find a substitute for
> Doris.

I groan.

'Anything wrong?' asks Matthew.

I put down my glass. 'One of our extras has fractured her shoulder.' I pause, wondering whether to go into details. Maybe not. 'I feel so sorry for her, but we've also got to find a replacement.'

Matthew shakes his head. 'These things happen.'

While I'm looking at my phone, I check to see if there's been a reply to my 'How's it going?' text to Stuart. There hasn't.

'Mind if I make a call?' I ask him.

'Be my guest.'

I go outside to the hall and dial my husband's number. He picks up. At least, I presume it's him. I hear a snatch of laughter. Then the phone goes dead. I try again. It goes through to voicemail.

I feel sick as I walk slowly back to the bar.

'What's wrong?' asks Matthew. 'You look as if you've just had bad news.'

I want to cry. It's all too much. That laughter on the other end of the phone. Stuart 'bumping into' this Janine woman again. Dad. The girls and the struggle to keep work and home life balanced. Doris's shoulder and the stress of finding a last-minute replacement. But most of all, that aching emptiness inside. All I want is someone to cuddle me. A pair of arms to make me feel desirable instead of a husband who turns his back on me at night.

I can't help it. I tell Matthew everything. By the time I've finished, there are tears streaming down my face.

'It sounds,' he says, handing me a proper linen hand-kerchief from his pocket, 'as though you've got a lot to carry. I know what that feels like.'

Then he leans over and gives me a hug. 'It will be all right, Pops,' he whispers. 'I'm here for you.'

10

Betty

'You must come round to dinner soon,' said Jane one day out of the blue.

'That would be lovely,' I said. Although we'd been to the park several times, we'd never actually visited each other's houses. But as soon as I'd agreed to it, I began to worry. If I went to hers, I'd need to return the favour. I couldn't imagine anything more embarrassing! It wasn't just that our poky little flat was cold, or that the paper was peeling off the walls with damp, even though we'd complained to the landlord enough times.

It was also because of Jock. How would he behave? I knew he'd think Jane was posh, with her accent and the way she pronounced words like 'party' properly with a clear 't'. I also knew he could take against people easily. When we'd bumped into a girl who'd been in my class at school, he'd been distinctly frosty. 'She disnae like me,' he'd insisted.

I was astounded. My friend had been perfectly friendly. In fact, she'd been one of the ones who had asked me to tea at her place even though Jock hadn't allowed me to have her back here. 'Why do you say that?' I'd asked.

'I could just tell.'

I was beginning to learn that my husband had a chip on his shoulder. He'd worked his way up in life from a family of manual labourers. Even though my parents had been so enthusiastic about him, and despite the fact that Jock was rising up the management ladder faster than anyone else we knew, I sensed he thought that my dad, as a factory supervisor, looked down on him a bit.

'Where does this new friend of yours live?' he asked when I told him about Jane's invitation.

I named the road.

'The new modern semis? Posh, are they? What will they think of our rented flat, then?'

'They won't think anything,' I said, more firmly than I felt. 'It's our company they want.'

Eventually, I persuaded him to go. I wore the smartest of my maternity smocks that I'd made myself, copying a style I'd seen in the fashion pages of the *Daily Mail*. But when I suggested to Jock that he might wear his Sunday best trousers and polyester jacket from C&A, he flatly refused. 'Anyone would think we're going to visit the bleeding Queen.'

Instead, he wore his black football-match anorak and jeans.

When we arrived, a sandy-haired man in beige trousers with shiny leather shoes – so different from Jock's trainers! – opened the door. He wasn't a big man like my husband but I soon found out that what he lacked in height, he made up for with charm and good manners. 'I'm Gary,' he said warmly, putting out his hand. 'Come on in. It's lovely to meet you, Betty. Jane's talked so much about her new friend.'

'Good to meet you too,' I said shyly, taking his hand. I noticed Jock's were firmly in his pockets, and when Gary turned to him, he just nodded curtly by way of a greeting.

'May I take your coats?' Gary asked once we had stepped into the hallway.

'No thanks.' Jock kept his hands in the pockets as if to indicate there was no way he was parting with his old football jacket. 'I'll hang on to it, if you don't mind.'

I tried to take off mine but struggled a bit with the sleeves. I looked to Jock for help but he was ogling a painting on the wall. 'Let me give you a hand with that,' said Gary.

'Thank you,' I flushed, embarrassed by my husband's lack of manners. Then again, Jock wasn't the type to walk on the outside of the pavement or let me go through a door first.

'I'll put it in the coat cupboard,' said Gary. We didn't have any storage space in our place. Just cheap plastic temporary wardrobes that looked a bit like tents.

'Nice stuff you have here,' said Jock, picking up a china figure of a shepherdess from the hall table.

'Thanks.' Gary was looking a bit embarrassed. 'That came from Jane's grandmother.'

I watched nervously as my husband continued to examine it. 'You don't go round picking other people's things up,' I wanted to say to him. He'd go mad if someone did that in our flat.

'Let's go through, shall we?' said Gary. 'Jane's in the kitchen, putting the final touches to dinner. I'll fix you a drink in the sitting room.'

'The "sitting room"!' Jock muttered to himself, just loudly enough to make my heart sink in case Gary might have heard him. 'Is that a fancy way of saying "front room"?'

'What can I get you?' Gary was standing by a trolley with all sorts of bottles on it. He gave me a kind smile. 'I expect you want something soft, like Jane prefers. We've got orange juice, lemonade or lime.'

What a choice! I made do with water at home. 'Lemonade please.'

He hands it to me in a beautiful glass with a pretty pattern on it. 'It's nice that you're both expecting at the same time. How are you doing?'

I flush. In my family, none of the men talked about pregnancy. Jock certainly didn't ask how I was feeling. He just took my growing stomach for granted. 'Very well, thanks.'

'That's good.' Gary turned to Jock. 'Now, what would you like?'

'How about a real ale?' said my husband, without so much as a 'please'.

Gary looked uncomfortable. 'We don't have any, I'm afraid. There's lager, if you fancy that. Or a whisky? I've got Glenfiddich, which is really good.'

'Go on then,' said Jock, as if he was doing Gary a favour in accepting it. I could feel my face grow hot with horror at his bad manners.

'How much water would you like with it?' Gary asked, picking up a bottle from the trolley and pouring some into a glass.

'I'll take it as it is. No point in ruining it.'

Gary handed it over silently. 'So, Betty.' His voice was gentle, as if to reassure me in the face of Jock's rudeness. 'Jane mentioned –'

'Did I hear my name?' said a cheery voice, as my friend came in. She was still wearing her pinny, but underneath I could see she had a pretty blue-and-white maternity dress and was wearing eyeliner and lipstick, which she didn't normally do.

'It's so lovely to see you,' she said, kissing me on both cheeks. I flushed with pleasure. Then she turned to Jock. 'How do you do?' she said, putting out her hand.

He ignored it. 'Pretty well, thanks.'

'Ask her how she is,' I wanted to hiss, but there was no opportunity to do so without being heard. Jane, to her credit, started chatting to Jock about how excited he must be about the baby and whether he'd got the nursery ready.

'We haven't got a nursery,' Jock's voice was cold. 'Our flat only has one bedroom so the bairn's going to have to sleep in a cot by Betty's side of the bed.'

'I'd like the baby to sleep in our room,' said Jane quickly. 'It would mean we could keep an eye on it.'

'But we've got a baby monitor, darling,' said Gary.

'That's true. We've had to get a second because we still use the original one for Alice. Which make are you going for? Ours is from Mothercare. I can really recommend it.'

Jock drained his glass of whisky. 'We can't afford anything pricey like that. Our bairn's going to have to yell loud enough so we can hear it.'

Jane gave a small laugh. 'Very amusing.'

'I mean it.' Jock got up and strode towards the drinks trolley. 'This is good stuff. Mind if I help myself to more?'

'Please,' said Gary stiffly. 'Be my guest.'

There was a moment's silence as we all watched my husband fill his glass halfway up. *He's going to get drunk*, I told myself. *And there's nothing I can do about it.*

In embarrassment, I excused myself to go to the bathroom.

'Do you know where it is?' asked Gary kindly.

'Probably needs a map to get there in a house like this.' Jock laughed as he spoke and slapped his thighs as if pleased with his weak joke. But Jane and Gary had both turned crimson. 'Don't be getting any ideas about us getting a mansion, will you, Bets?'

He knew I hated it when he called me that. It made me feel like a barmaid. Besides, Betty had been my grandmother's name. I'd never known her, so it made me feel special.

If Gary and Jane thought he was being rude, they were polite enough to hide their expressions. Personally, I wanted to sink into the ground. I had to escape, if only for a few minutes. Besides, the baby's weight was pressing down on my bladder. 'Excuse me,' I said. 'I really do need to go . . .'

'Of course,' said Jane warmly. 'No rush. Dinner can wait.'

Shutting the toilet door behind me and locking it, I took in the spare paper roll on the window sill with its frilly blue lace cover. I prayed Jock wouldn't need to come in here. I could just see him taking the mickey out of it to our hosts. Next to it was an air freshener spray. I wouldn't mind one of those at home, but we could only afford essentials. Instead, we had to light a match to get rid of smells.

'Dinner's ready now,' said Jane when I came out. 'Shall we go through to the dining room? Gary, darling, could you possibly bring the avocado mousse through?'

I'd never had avocado before! It was what Mum called 'one of those expensive new-fangled things'.

'So how many rooms have you got here?' asked Jock as we took our seats round the table, which had a glass top and really nice comfortable chairs. It was all so different from the rickety plastic table in our kitchen, where we ate all our meals.

'Two receptions and three bedrooms,' replied Gary quietly.

'Reception now, is it?' chipped in Jock. 'Thought it was a sitting room a few minutes ago.'

He was like a dog with a bone. I wanted to curl up with embarrassment.

Jane was handing the dishes round with a neat little green mound inside. 'We could never have afforded it if my grandmother hadn't helped us.' Then she added, almost apologetically: 'I know how lucky we are.'

Almost as if we weren't there, she reached out to take Gary's hand over the table. I couldn't help feeling a pang of envy. They clearly loved each other so much!

Jock looked as though he was about to say something. I could just imagine some sharp comment about it 'being all right for some'. I needed to change the conversation fast. 'This looks so clever,' I said, eying my plate. But inside, I couldn't help wondering what avocado tasted like and how exactly you ate it. There were so many knives, forks and spoons on either side of my place mat that I didn't know where to start.

Jane looked pleased. 'Thanks. I got the recipe from *My Weekly* magazine.'

I waited for everyone else to be served, but to my horror, Jock started tucking in as soon as his was in front of him. He swallowed it in three mouthfuls and made a big show of pushing the empty plate away and then draining his glass. I could see Jane looking at him.

'Jock,' she said, 'may I get you another drink or anything?'

'I'll go,' Gary said sharply, before she could get up. 'You need to rest. Another whisky, Jock?'

'Cheers,' Jock said curtly. I wanted to tell him that he shouldn't have any more. But I knew that would be a disastrous move.

'I'm always telling Bets here to take the weight off her feet,' Jock said, suddenly conversational. 'She's put on enough.'

I wanted to sink into the ground.

'It's normal to get bigger,' said Gary. 'Jane did the same with Alice, didn't you, darling?'

'I did,' she chirped. 'And I lost it all really fast. Breast-feeding helps.'

Jock said nothing to that. Instead he grabbed the whisky Gary handed to him and took a big swig.

I couldn't stand any more. 'Excuse me,' I said, getting up. 'I'm just going to the toilet.'

'Again?' sneered Jock.

For a few minutes, I sat on the closed lid, shutting my eyes and wishing with all my heart that I'd never accepted Jane's invitation. What would she think of me? Hot tears rolled down my face. A deep shame knotted itself in the pit of my stomach. How could I have married a man like this?

When I came out, having dried my eyes, Jane was waiting for me. 'Are you all right?' she asked.

I bit my lip. 'Not really. I'm so sorry, I don't know what to say.'

She seemed to understand exactly what I meant. 'I expect it's just because he's nervous, and maybe a little drunk.'

I hugged her. Jane always knew how to make me feel better.

I'm still not sure how I made it through the rest of that dinner. When Gary politely asked Jock about his job, my husband talked loudly and at length about the factory and how much responsibility he had. He didn't ask Gary anything about his work as a teacher.

I could barely bring myself to speak to Jock as we walked home. But when we reached our block of flats, it all came blurting out. 'How could you?' I asked him tearfully as we climbed the stairs to our front door. (The lift was broken again.) 'How could you be so rude to them when they were so nice?'

Jock didn't answer me until we were inside. Then, in a tone more quiet and threatening than I'd ever heard before, he said: 'You won't be seeing them again. Stick to your own kind. Then we'll both be much happier. Got it?'

11

Poppy

'I mean it,' says Matthew in a throaty voice, looking straight at me amidst the clatter of the glasses and the laughter and the Christmas cheer of the bar. 'I really am here for you. It's what old friends are for.'

'Yes,' I say doubtfully. 'Although we haven't seen each other for years.'

'Doesn't matter, Pops.' He puts down his drink and leans across the table. 'We've always had a connection, haven't we? And life doesn't go on for ever, you know.'

He runs the last two sentences together as though one is the natural conclusion of the other. But they're very different things. I try to make sense of it, but I can't. I'm too confused. Right now, I don't see the middle-aged man who had come back into my life after all these years. I see the young Matthew who had comforted the eighteen-year-old me when my mother had run off. The Matthew who had told me that I would always be the only girl for him.

A man who makes me feel wanted. Still. A man who is making my body respond without even touching me. What the hell is going on?

I find myself standing up.

'Are you going?' asks Matthew, alarmed.

'I'm not,' I say. 'And I don't need the Ladies either.'

'I don't understand,' he says slowly.

'The old Matthew would have done,' I find myself replying. 'Shall we go upstairs?'

Then I hold out my hand to him and we walk towards the lift. It's as though another woman has taken over my mind. I know this is wrong. More than that. It's crazy. But I simply can't stop. And now Matthew realizes my intentions, he is walking as fast as I am.

Ironically, my room is on the fourth floor again. Is this meant to be? It's almost like the last time we were in a hotel together – could that just have been last Friday? – except that now it is different. Now we know what we are doing and where we are going. I'm me. A braver, more honest me than I've been for years.

We walk along the soft-carpeted corridor to Room 404, his arm now firmly around me. I take the key card out from my handbag. I drop it. We both bend to pick it up at the same time. Our hands brush. My skin is on fire. I put it in the wrong way. He takes it and places the magnetic strip the other way round so the door finally clicks open. There is a king-size bed in front of us.

I stop for a minute, remembering. 'They only had a double left by the time I rang,' I say, embarrassed.

'Perfect,' he murmurs.

Suddenly his hands are on me. Tracing my curves on the outside of my cashmere jumper. His face is drawing closer. His lips are on mine. His kiss is meaningful. Loving. Familiar, as if this is twenty-three years ago, when he was mine and not Sandra's. I feel a flash of guilt for the poor woman in a wheelchair. But I am also overcome by something else – grief for what I lost all those years before; for what had been taken from me so unnecessarily.

Tears begin to roll down my face. All the hurt and pain from that time comes roaring back.

'It's all right,' he soothes, kissing them away. 'I'm here now.'

I think of Stuart and almost instinctively I feel myself pull back slightly. I am a married woman. We have children together, for pity's sake. I should stop this now.

But my body won't let me break away. I am under a spell.

Now his tongue is in my mouth, probing. His hands are gently easing my jumper off over my head. He undoes my bra and nuzzles my breasts, kissing each nipple in turn. Then he kneels down and unzips my trousers. 'God, I've missed you,' he breathes.

And I know I've missed him too. Missed the longing for another willing body. Missed the feeling of being wanted.

I'm undressing him now. Urgently. Hungrily. There is no point in pretending otherwise. I am on top of him. Then the other way round. The relief when he enters me makes us both gasp out loud.

How could I ever have told myself that life would go on after Matthew? My body hasn't felt this alive since the last time he touched me. He is doing things I had forgotten were even possible.

'I love you, Pops,' he breathes. 'I always have. Not a day has gone by that I haven't thought of you.'

And even though what he's saying is absurd. Even though I have a husband I love, and children I adore, I find myself agreeing.

'I love you too.'

'Good morning.'

I can feel warm breath in my ear and a finger softly tracing the contours of my face.

'You're so beautiful when you're asleep.'

That doesn't sound like Stuart. I sit bolt upright.

'Almost as beautiful as you are when you're awake.' Matthew props himself up next to me.

It all comes screaming back to me. The hotel, Matthew, the wine. The sex.

I've been unfaithful. No. NO! How did this happen? How have I become a completely different person? A wave of nausea hits me, so strong that for one horrible moment I think I might be sick there and then. I groan.

'Feeling a bit the worse for wear? Me too.' Matthew laughs and puts an arm around me.

But I'd only had one drink, albeit a large one. Besides, I'd been the one who'd led him on. I had suggested going upstairs, hadn't I? I have only myself to blame. I stagger towards the bathroom, stunned by what I've done. 'You'll feel better after some breakfast,' he calls after me.

Shutting the door, I close the lid of the loo and sit down, trying to think through the thickening fog of panic. This can't be real. I lean across to the sink and splash my face with cold water. I can hear Matthew calling to me from the bedroom.

'I was saying we should talk about what to do,' he repeats when I emerge.

I survey the rumpled sheets and his naked body. I can still smell our sex. We didn't, I suddenly realize with a ghastly flash, even use a condom.

'What to do about what?'

He looks at me, surprised.

'About us.'

Us? I stare at him.

'What do you mean? There's no "us", Matthew. You have Sandra. She needs you. And I'm married, I have a family.' I can feel I'm about to cry and I'm suddenly very aware that I'm naked. Gathering up my clothes that are heaped on the floor, I hold them against my body as if he hasn't already seen me in the flesh.

'Shhhh, don't cry.' Matthew is out of bed in a flash and crossing the room to where I'm standing. He pulls me towards his chest. He's stroking my hair. I'd forgotten how he used to do that.

I'm weeping copiously now. 'How could we both have behaved so badly?'

Matthew doesn't say anything for a moment. I can hear the rise and fall of his breath. 'I know, I feel awful too. But if we love each other . . .'

'Love?' I repeat. Love is a word for my children. For Stuart, despite everything. For the life that we all live together.

'Yes.' There's a tightness to Matthew's voice now. 'That's what you said last night. I told you that I loved you and then you said – quite clearly – "I love you too."'

I did. I know I did. And I had meant it then. But now, in the cold daylight, I don't.

Suddenly Betty flashes into my head. My wonderful, kind, supportive mother-in-law. What is she going to think of me? I can see it now. Stuart will divorce me. Melissa and Daisy will despise me. I will be estranged from my beautiful daughters. And what about my father? What will he say? I have done exactly what my mother did. I have inherited her bad blood.

The woman who so willingly took her lover up to Room 404 last night seems like a stranger to me now. I am not her. *Nor*, I tell myself fiercely, *am I the type to be the 'other woman'; the sort who has an affair with someone else's husband.* I have to leave. I have to fix this.

I free myself from Matthew's grasp and put on my underwear.

'What are you doing?'

'This was a mistake, Matthew.' I can barely look at him. 'A terrible mistake. I love my husband.'

As I say it, I realize with a horrible pang of certainty that it's true. I don't want to be with anyone but Stuart. It's almost as if I had to cross that line and have sex with someone else in order to see that, amazing as it was, the only thing that really counts is the solidity of the family life that my husband and I have built around us.

'And you love Sandra,' I add.

When he says nothing I force myself to look at him. He is staring at the floor.

'I don't,' he says quietly. 'There's been nothing between us for years. She has never forgiven me since she worked it out. Realized that I've never been able to get over you.'

What? I vaguely remember Matthew saying something like '*Not a day has gone by that I haven't thought of you*' last night. But this revelation about Sandra is something else. I wonder if he's gone mad. But he seems deadly serious.

Shock is now followed by anger, which fires out of me. 'Then why did you leave me in the first place? Why has it taken you more than twenty years to get in touch?'

When he replies, it sounds like he's choking. 'Because I heard you'd got married and didn't want to mess up the life you'd created. I thought you wouldn't want anything to do with me anyway. But meeting you again, Pops . . . well it's made me reassess my life. Last night was amazing! I just can't lose what we found. I thought about leaving Sandra years ago. I almost did, but then she got MS and it wouldn't have been right.'

'Exactly,' I say. 'And it wouldn't be right now.' I reach for my bag from the chair and make for the door.

'Don't,' he says, grabbing my arm. 'We can work this out, Poppy. It'll be hard, but we can't let this go. It's too precious.'

'Stop it!' I say, trying to pull away. 'You're hurting me.'

But he doesn't seem to hear. 'I can't go on like this. I'm so unhappy.' He is sobbing like a child.

'Matthew . . .' I finally manage to free myself from his grip. 'I will not leave my husband. I will not destroy my family for this.'

He lets me go then. I'm already out of the door. Running towards the lift. Pausing briefly at reception to pay my bill only to find out from the young girl at the desk that it 'has already been covered by the gentleman'.

I rush out of the doors. A voice shouts my name, but I don't look back. See a passing taxi. Hail it and then fall into the back seat. My arm is throbbing from where Matthew had grabbed me. Then my phone shows I've got a voicemail message. From Melissa, half an hour ago. 'Where are you, Mum?' her voice pleads. 'You're not picking up? Daisy can't find her French file and Gran says I should have told you that I've got detention tonight. Don't be mad.'

Mad? How can I ever be angry with them again after what I've done?

I cover my face with my hands as if I can erase the events of last night this way. What will they do if they find out?

A small, dangerous voice answers me.

'You'll just have to make sure that they never do.'

12

Betty

For weeks after our dinner at Jane and Gary's, Jock barely spoke to me. When he did, there was so much anger and disdain in his voice that I came to prefer the stony silences and the long empty evenings when he was out drinking at the pub. By accepting the invitation, I'd made him look stupid as well as inferior. And that, in my husband's book, was unforgivable. It had, I suddenly thought, been months since he'd called me his 'wee hen'. He'd stopped for a time before when he hadn't liked me working in the department store. I was slowly beginning to realize that the real Jock wasn't the charmer I'd thought I'd married, but a bullying, moody man who was only happy if everything was going his way.

'What's up with your Jock?' Mum demanded when I went round one day. 'Dad says he's been storming through the factory, throwing his weight about and giving the men a right talking to for the smallest thing.'

I sat down heavily on the sofa. The new colour TV Mum had just had delivered – after years of saving up her Green Shield stamps – was blaring out but she showed no signs of turning it down and I didn't like to ask.

'A friend of mine from antenatal class invited us to dinner,' I said. 'They live in one of those new semis on Mill Street and Jock got it into his head that they were up themselves.'

Mum sniffed. 'Maybe he was right. You need to stick with your own kind.'

Exactly Jock's words.

'If you ask me,' she continued, 'all that hat modelling stuff turned your head a bit. Still, when that baby of yours is born, you won't be going out anywhere.' She gave me a warning look. 'You won't know what's hit you. Kids take all your sleep and all your time. Life will never be the same again.'

She sat down next to me on the sofa, one eye on the telly and the other on me. 'I'll give you one piece of advice for nothing. Your dad says that Jock of yours is very popular in the factory with the girls. So make sure you keep him satisfied. If you ask me, he's the sort who'll look around if you don't.'

You see, Poppy, in those days, the only thing worse than not getting married, or having a baby before marriage, was having a husband who went to prison or walked out on you. You didn't get the state handouts that you get now. I'd probably have had to move in with my parents – that's if they were prepared to have me.

So I couldn't afford to upset Jock. But without Jane, I was desperately lonely. And with my due date drawing ever closer, I turned over my mum's words about the baby again and again until I felt sick with fear.

A week or so later there was a knock on my door. To my amazement, it was Jane, looking, as usual, immaculate, with her make-up in place and her baby bump neatly centred.

I have to tell you, Poppy, that Jane was really lovely. Not just in looks but in spirit too. I have a picture of her and little Alice from one of our picnics in the park. Jane actually had a camera and gave me the print. It's one of my most precious possessions. I'm afraid I had a bit of an argument with Daisy when she found it in my bedroom not long before the accident. She asked me who the woman in the photograph was, but she caught me so off guard that I pretended I'd forgotten. Then I grabbed it back from her before it got creased.

'Jane!' I said when I opened the door. 'What are you doing here?'

I didn't mean to be rude but Jane had never been to our place before. Like I told you earlier, I hadn't asked her over because I'd been too ashamed.

'I haven't seen you in the park and I wanted to make sure you were all right,' she said. 'Our antenatal midwife gave me your address. I hope you don't mind.'

Alice was standing by her, tugging at her mother's navy-blue maternity dress. I recognized it from the window of a pricey boutique in town.

'I'm OK,' I said, almost pulling her in before someone could see her on the doorstep and tell Jock I'd had a visitor. People were like that round here.

I watched Jane's eyes widen as she took in the dark lounge with my husband's cheap polyester shirts in a pile on the shabby brown velour sofa, waiting for me to iron them. I took a deep breath. 'It's just that, well, Jock says I can't see you any more. He says that –'

She interrupted me gently. 'I know I only met him once, but I get the feeling that your husband is rather insecure.'

I flush. 'He has a bit of a chip on his shoulder,' I admitted.

Jane gave my hand an understanding squeeze. 'I'm sorry.' Then she glanced at the stained carpet, which we couldn't afford to replace. 'It can't be easy.'

'It's not,' I said, embarrassed. 'This place is a tip compared with yours.'

She flushed. 'I wasn't talking about your home. I meant that it can't be easy having a husband you have to tiptoe round all the time.'

I could feel that I was close to tears.

'But look,' she said suddenly. 'It's you and I who are friends. We don't need to involve the men. In fact, I'd say it's none of their business. Let's just meet up in the park like we used to. Jock doesn't need to know.'

I shook my head. 'Someone might mention to him that they'd seen us.'

It was almost like arranging an affair, I thought. How ridiculous that I couldn't even see my friend.

'OK,' said Jane thoughtfully. 'Then let's go out of town.'

'But I can't drive!'

I'd expressed interest in lessons but, as Jock said, where were we going to afford the money for that? When I suggested he taught me like his mate had taught him, he said he didn't have time. I got the feeling he liked being the only driver in the family.

'I've got a car,' said Jane. 'I'll take you. We can go on some little trips, can't we, Alice? Your favourite is the zoo, isn't it, poppet?'

Her lovely daughter nodded solemnly. There was something almost doll-like about her, and yet also adult, as if she had witnessed things that other children hadn't. I don't know why I thought that. I just did. Sometimes I get these strange thoughts. My mum's mum used to be what they call 'fey' and see things. I don't do that. But I have found that I can sense things in other people that others might not see. That's why I knew Jane was a good woman. If only I'd had the same intuition about my husband before we got married. But it doesn't work with everyone.

That reminded me. I glanced at the clock. Jock wasn't due to get back for ages but Mum could well pop round and then she might mention Jane's visit to my husband.

'Don't take this the wrong way, but I think you ought to go,' I said.

'Do we have to walk down all those stairs, Mummy?' asked Alice. 'They smell of wee-wee.'

I felt even more embarrassed than before. 'I'm afraid the lift is out of order again.'

'That's fine, darling,' said Jane brightly to her daughter. 'It's good exercise.' Then she reached out and touched my hand once more. 'I'll ring you to arrange our trip.'

But after that dinner with Jane and her husband, Jock had had the phone disconnected. (Of course, we didn't have mobiles then.) He said we needed to 'cut down on costs'. He also told me I had to wait until next month until I bought myself another pair of shoes. I didn't understand. After all, he was earning decent money now. When I told him this, he pointed out that we needed to save 'every penny' for when I gave up work to have the baby. But I couldn't help thinking he wanted to be in control of the purse strings and I didn't dare argue about it.

'Actually, there's a problem with our line at the moment,' I said, not wanting to tell her the truth. 'And you can't just call round because Jock might be here. It's a good thing he's not around now.'

'You really are scared of him, aren't you?' My friend looked at me worriedly. 'He doesn't . . .'

But I wasn't listening to her. A trickle of water was running down my legs.

I reddened with shame. I'd wet my knickers a couple of times in the last few weeks – something we'd been assured in antenatal classes was normal because of the pressure of the baby on the bladder. 'Oh dear. I think I've had a bit of an accident.'

My friend's eyes widened. 'It looks to me as though your waters might be breaking.'

'Are you sure?' They'd talked about this too at class, but somehow I expected there to be more of it. This felt more like I was just weeing myself again. Then almost immediately I felt a spasm of pain across my stomach and grimaced.

'I think we'd better get you to hospital,' said Jane, zipping up Alice's coat.

'But I'm two weeks early.'

'Ready or not, you're going into labour. You need to get hold of Jock.'

'He's at work.'

'Just as well I've got the car outside, then.'

I began to panic. 'But he'll know we met up!'

'Stuff it.' I'd never heard Jane use that expression before. 'This is an emergency.'

By the time Jane helped me in through the doors of the maternity wing, the pain had increased. It was as though huge waves had seized my body, churning it up, stopping to give me a quick breather and then starting all over again. What was happening to me? It was far worse than the midwife had described a 'typical' labour to be.

The pain brought back memories of my miscarriage. 'I don't want to lose it like the other one,' I cried out to Jane.

'You won't,' she said, gripping my hand and holding a wide-eyed Alice with the other. She rushed up to the desk. 'Can someone help us please? My friend's having her baby.'

'I've got a terrible headache, too,' I groaned, feeling my knees buckle under me.

'Let's get you in a side-room, love,' said a nurse.

'Jock!' I called out. Part of me knew he'd be furious not to be here. But I was also relieved because I knew he'd try to take over.

'Don't worry about your husband, love,' said the nurse. 'We've got his work number on your file. We'll call him for you.'

'You need to go,' I blurted out to Jane.

'I can't!' she cried. 'I want to stay here for you.'

'You mustn't. Jock will be cross.'

'What about your mum? What's her number?'

'It's . . .'

But I couldn't remember it. The panic was engulfing me. It was just like last time, except that now I was far more advanced. I'd felt the baby moving inside me for months. I had to save it. I just had to.

A band tightened round my upper arm. 'Betty? Can you hear me, love? We're taking your blood pressure.'

I could barely focus on what was going on around me. Instead, I heard snatches that included the words 'high' and 'caesarean'.

And after that, it all went blank.

13

Poppy

I can't help looking behind me as the taxi makes its way slowly through the traffic. What if Matthew is following me in his own car? Could he have got it out of the hotel car park fast enough to do so? Might he have hailed a cab and be just behind?

I want to be sick. Instead, I force myself to text my daughter back. I would ring as she had done (a real sign of desperation in a teenager), but I don't trust myself not to break down.

> Daisy's French file is drying out in
> the laundry room after she spilt
> water on it

I write. And then, just because the old me – the one who hadn't just slept with another man – would have asked this, I add

> What did you get detention for?

There is no reply. Either she hasn't seen my message, which is unlikely because my eldest daughter's phone is more or less surgically attached to her hand. Or else she doesn't want to give me details.

Not that I'm in any position to criticize.

I think about Melissa's moods, Daisy's soggy French file. I remember an article I read once about a woman who had been on the brink of leaving her husband for a man at work. She'd even started packing for herself and the children. But then she went to get some clothes from the linen cupboard and realized that she couldn't do it. There were so many odd socks; so many badly folded school shirts; pillow cases; sheets and even a stack of old baby blankets, smelling of happier times. The very thought of sorting it all out into things they had to take and things that could be left behind was simply too much. So she'd stayed.

It didn't make sense to me at the time. But it does now. The linen cupboard is a symbol. Dismembering a home, let alone a family, is all too complicated. Too painful. I still remember the agony of coming back from my first year at drama school to comfort my father and finding my mother's empty wardrobe, the spaces where her shoes used to sit, the gaps on the bookcases where her favourite novels had been.

'That'll be seven pounds fifty, madam,' says the taxi driver, pulling up at the side of the station.

As I hand him a ten-pound note, I wonder when I became a 'madam'. I was always a 'miss' or a 'love'. 'Madam' had seemed reserved for an older generation. For women like Betty. What, I ask myself as I tell the driver to keep the change so I can race into the safety of the station, would my mother-in-law think of me after this? She would, quite rightly, be shocked. Appalled. She'd tell her son to leave me.

For some reason, that hurts almost more than the thought of Stuart's reaction.

But that's not going to happen, is it? Because I'm not going to tell them. I've made it quite clear to Matthew. I am not leaving my family. He will have to accept that I made a mistake. I was emotionally vulnerable and he took advantage of me.

Yet he didn't, I recall as I race through the barrier, flashing my ticket, just in time (miraculously) to catch the train for London. I'm the one who had suggested we went upstairs. I had willingly allowed him to take my hand as we'd headed for the lift. I had let him pull my cashmere jumper over my head in Room 404. I had gasped with pleasure as he . . .

Stop! I have to put this out of my head. I have to forget it.

My phone bleeps. Melissa again? Stuart? Please no. I can't face his voice yet. Matthew? That would be even worse. But it's a message from Sally.

> Sorry – couldn't find another
> Doris. The casting director has
> gone for another agency. Hope
> today's meetings go well.

Meetings? I check my online diary only to remember I'm seeing two different lots of film companies this afternoon to 'nurture contacts'. It's the last thing I need. But Sally and I set up these appointments ages ago and I can't cancel.

All my emotions are spent. I lean back in my seat, feeling utterly overwhelmed as the train flies past green fields

165

and through the odd town where other people – sensible people – are living calm, faithful lives.

There's a woman across the aisle with two little girls. One is reading quietly. The other has her head bent over a colouring book. I am suddenly reminded of Melissa and Daisy when they were small, except that they were always squabbling and I was constantly knackered, trying to keep my work going and be a good mother at the same time. Somewhere along the line, I'd forgotten to be a wife as well. But how is it possible to do it all?

Other women manage, whispers a little voice in my head. *They don't all sleep with men because they're tired or disillusioned with their lives.*

The seaside jingle on my mobile suddenly bursts into song. It's Betty. Should I answer it? Will she be able to tell there's something wrong? But then again, maybe she'll be more suspicious if I don't.

'Hello?'

'Sorry to bother you, love. Just wanted to tell you that the girls went off to school fine after one or two little hiccups. I also wondered how your dad was.'

I realize with a shock that I haven't rung him this morning to see how he is. It's taken my kind, sweet mother-in-law to remind me of my very purpose for going down to Worthing in the first place.

'He's um, not great, actually. But I can't really talk now. I'll tell you all when I get back.'

I'm aware as I speak that the woman with the children is looking pointedly at the sign that declares this to be a quiet carriage.

I say goodbye to Betty after thanking her for holding the fort, hang up and then slip out into the space by the nearest door. The phone rings several times before my father answers.

'Dad? Are you OK?'

'Why shouldn't I be?'

I'm aware that we have short conversations like this almost every day. But the truth is that I do need to know he's all right because of his age – even if he doesn't like me being on his case. I also sense that his reply is particularly defensive today because I'd caught him out over the police calling about the petrol incident.

'Just wanted to check, that's all.'

'I can't hear you.'

'I just wanted to check . . .'

'I can't hear.'

I'm pretty sure he's pretending. But there's no point in going on when he's in a mood like this. Sombrely I hang up and return to my seat. Still nothing from Stuart, not even to ask how Dad is.

I want to put my head in my hands and weep. There are, it has to be said, lots of things wrong with my marriage. But it had provided something that I hadn't appreciated before. Security. And now it's not there, I realize how important it was.

Almost as soon as I return to my seat, my phone rings out again. The mother shoots me another look. It's from a withheld number. 'Hello?' I say tentatively.

'Pops!'

I freeze. Only one person calls me that.

'What do you want, Matthew?'

'Look, I don't know where you are, but come back. Please. I'm still at the hotel. We can talk.'

I cut in. 'Stop. I've told you before. I made a mistake. I am not leaving my husband for you. If you and Sandra can't work it out that's your problem, but I will not be held responsible for that.'

I pause, suddenly horribly aware of what I have said, out loud for everyone to hear. Several heads turn in my direction. The mother I'd observed earlier stands up, issues whispered instructions to her little girls and hustles them out of the carriage; her arms protectively around them as she mutters about 'people who make noises and say things they shouldn't in front of innocent children'.

Mortified, I cut Matthew off. I put the phone belatedly on silent and wish with all my heart that I could go back to the morning of the Association of Supporting Artistes and Agents' Christmas party, when life had still been normal. Then I begin to panic. Supposing someone in the carriage knows me from home? What if there's an extra or a director or another agent who recognizes me from the business? Coincidences happen. I try to scan the faces but don't recognize anyone.

Furious with myself for being so indiscreet, I spend the rest of my journey constantly checking my screen in case Matthew has tried to contact me again. Nothing. Thank heavens. Maybe he's finally got the message. Perhaps he realizes that what he was suggesting is crazy and not an answer to the troubles we're both facing in our marriages.

When I reach Victoria, I head straight for Boots to buy some wipes and then try to clean myself in one of the cubicles in the Ladies. I feel dirty. Wrong. I want to scrub every last speck of last night from my skin. Then I touch up my make-up, pull myself together and head for those meetings. The second one goes on for much longer than I'd anticipated, but it's hard work like this that keeps us going. Stuart and I might look well-off on paper, but most of our money is tied up in the house. Everything else we're putting aside for the girls' future. Last time I checked, we had around £50,000. I know this is so much more than most people have, but with house prices as they are and university tuition fees looming, we can't really afford to rest on our laurels.

There's still nothing more from Matthew, which is a relief. On the other hand, there's nothing from Stuart either. I call his receptionist, who says he's with patients all afternoon and can she take a message? I ask her to tell him I called but not to worry about ringing back.

He doesn't.

It's almost evening when I get out at our local Tube station. It's such a relief to get home. To walk down the path leading to our Edwardian three-storey, red-brick semi in this leafy part of north London. To open the door with its pretty pink-and-green stained-glass art-nouveau panel above; to be greeted with the smell of Betty's fish pie wafting from the kitchen and to have Melissa's arms around me. 'I'm sorry about the detention, Mum, but it was only because I spoke out in class last week when I'd been told not to. Besides, it really wasn't my fault because I knew the answer and the teacher doesn't like me. It's so unfair!'

'Welcome to the real world,' I nearly tell her. But I stop myself. 'It's all part of the learning curve,' I say instead, almost as if I am trying to reassure myself.

'Where's Daisy?' I add, sensing that Melissa is about to continue her tirade at the injustice of her punishment. I just can't deal with it right now.

'At French,' says Melissa, slipping away now I've sort of forgiven her. 'Gran's collecting her.'

I often think I need a spreadsheet like some of the other mums at school to remember our various commitments. I had completely forgotten about Daisy's extra French lessons. They're quite expensive, but Daisy was falling behind at school so we didn't have much of a choice. The tutor came highly recommended by another mother. Such is her demand that we had to wait eighteen months before getting a slot.

As if on cue, I hear the front door opening. 'Coo-ee! It's only us!'

In comes my mother-in-law in her purple beret and black Lycra leggings with silver ankle boots. She presses her warm cheek against mine in the hall. 'Stuart rang to say he won't be late tonight.' Then she steps back to look at me. 'You look exhausted, love. Now what's been going on with your dad?'

Still standing in the hall, I tell her about the petrol and the police.

'Poor man,' she tuts. 'It must be terrible when your mind goes like that.'

I want to tell her that mine has gone too. I'm so racked with guilt and worry that I've been on autopilot all day. But I know that's out of the question. I also know I need a bath. I'm still worried I must smell of Matthew. That quick wipe-down in the station loo hadn't felt enough.

'Just going to freshen up after my journey,' I say, breaking away from her hug. Then I realize. 'Where's Daisy?'

'Outside.' Betty is looking a bit shifty. 'She's just taking care of our visitor.'

My skin goes cold. Not Matthew. He couldn't just up turn up, could he? Or Sandra? My stomach plunges as I imagine her wheeling herself down the garden path, tear-stained and furious, admonishing me from her chair. But just as my imagination can't get any wilder, a small white ball of fluff comes flying in through the front door followed by my younger daughter.

'Isn't she wonderful?' Daisy's eyes are shining. 'Madame Blanche asked if we could look after her new puppy. So Granny said yes. She's called Coco. Isn't that the sweetest name?'

I shoot a 'How could you?' look at my mother-in-law. Daisy has been asking for a dog for ages, but both Stuart and I have agreed we can't take on any more responsibility. Daisy's French teacher has been over-presumptuous here.

'It's only until tomorrow,' says Betty. 'The poor woman needed to go somewhere – she seemed frightfully harassed – and didn't have anywhere to leave it.' Then she lowered her voice. 'Daisy was a bit upset about her lesson. It didn't go that well. Those irregular verbs can be pigs.'

My heart goes out to my youngest daughter. Unlike Melissa, who'd been predicted to get top grades at A level, Daisy has never been the academic type. And although she definitely has a talent for sketching, she's going to need some basic subjects under her belt. 'OK,' I say weakly. 'But please don't let the puppy go on the sofa.'

'Ah,' says Betty as we run after Coco who is heading straight for the sitting room. 'Looks like it's a bit too late for that.'

The paw marks are all over my lovely duck-egg blue Colefax & Fowler fabric. Dirt on a clean canvas. Just like my transgression.

'That's a nasty bruise on your arm, dear,' says my mother-in-law. 'How did you get that?'

I'd almost forgotten Matthew's desperate lunge when I'd left. It's stopped hurting by now but Betty's right. There's a big red-and-blue mark.

'I bumped it getting out of a taxi door,' I say quickly.

'Poor you. These's a new tube of arnica cream in the bathroom cupboard. Make sure you put some on.'

'Granny,' calls out Daisy from the kitchen. 'Come and play with Coco! Isn't she cute?'

That dog is getting everywhere! I need a break or my head is going to explode. So I leave them to it and go upstairs to run a bath. I add a generous measure of an expensive lavender and lemon verbena bath oil (a freebie from a shoot) and sink in. Then – bliss! – I lie back and close my eyes for a luxurious few moments, stretching out my legs. My phone is on the side in case there are any more work problems or worse . . .

I submerge my head and try to wash last night out of my mind. That feels a bit better. But when I come up, there's a ping. Hastily, I reach for a towel to dry my hands and swipe the notification. A picture flashes up.

I freeze. It's me. Lying in Matthew's arms.

> Took this selfie when you were
> asleep last night

says Matthew's text below.

> We make a rather good couple,
> don't you think?

What is he doing? Suddenly I feel so angry I could throw the phone at the wall. Supposing I'd been next to the children when the picture had popped up. Or Stuart. They might have seen . . . It didn't bear thinking about.

> Delete it. I am serious, Matthew.

I consider for a moment and then I continue texting.

> I am married for heaven's sake.
> And so are you. What are you
> playing at?

The reply is instant.

> Pops

it reads. I can hear the rich depth of his voice in the message.

I'm not playing at anything. I'm
deadly serious. When two people
like us find each other again after
all these years, we can't let each
other go . . .

I'm about to type a reply but the three dots at his end
suggest he hasn't finished yet. I'm right.

I admit I made mistakes when we
were young but there's still time to
put things right. You want me still.
I know it. You're simply scared
and that's understandable. But
there's no need. Like I said, I'm
here for you. I'll ring tomorrow.
Sweet dreams.

14

Betty

When I woke up – with a tube in my hand attached to a drip at the side – it was to the sight of a terrified Jock. 'I thought you were dead,' he whispered.

Tears poured down his cheeks. 'It was touch and go. They had to cut you open to get the bairn out.'

A sharp shock of panic along with a wave of nausea swept through me. 'My baby!' I cried out. 'Where's my baby?'

He jerked his head towards a plastic cot at my side, which I hadn't taken in before. 'It's all right. But we might have lost you. I was so scared. I don't know what I'd have done. Just me and the wee one.'

My eyes were focused on the cot where there was a small white bundle inside. 'Did we have a boy or girl?' I whispered.

His face softened. 'A lad. He'll be playing for Scotland one day. I'll be signing him up for Celtic.'

I'd never seen Jock like this before. So caring. So loving. It was as if he was a different man. But I couldn't help feeling a flash of disappointment as I thought of Alice with her blonde hair and gap-toothed smile.

'We'll call him Stuart,' said my husband firmly. 'It sounds professional. He could be a doctor or a lawyer with a name like that.'

It was on the tip of my tongue to point out that my husband had always been very scathing of the educated classes. But now didn't seem the time to have an argument. As for the name, 'Stuart' seemed too grown up for a baby. I tried to reach out towards the white blanket where a small head poked out but a stabbing pain in my stomach stopped me.

'Ouch!'

'You can't do that yet, I'm afraid,' said a nurse, marching in. 'No lifting for a bit after a caesarean. And don't worry about the pain. You often feel it in the incision site after the op. Here, let me.'

She placed him in my arms. I stared down. Our antenatal class leader had warned us that our babies might look like 'crinkled little monkeys'. But my son – how strange it felt to say this! – was smooth skinned, peering up at me with bright blue eyes as if memorizing every feature on my face. 'Hello,' he seemed to say. 'I know you really wanted a little girl but you'll learn to love me. Just as I love you.'

Learn to? I already did. Instinctively, I bent down to kiss his forehead. His smell drew me in. And the dark downy hair on his head was so soft.

'We had to sponge him down,' said the nurse, checking my blood pressure and catheter. 'Usually we encourage the mothers to do that but you were still out for the count. Gave us a bit of a fright but you're all right now. I'll leave the three of you alone for some family time.'

I couldn't take my eyes off my beautiful little boy. I was going to give him everything I never had myself. Love. Understanding. A real future.

'He's a good-looking lad, isn't he?' said Jock, putting his arm around me. 'Look at us now. A proper family, my wee hen, aren't we?'

I leant my head against his shoulder, overcome with relief and gratitude. There had been times before this when I'd really wondered if I'd done the right thing in getting married. But now we had a baby, I knew everything would be fine. It was as if our son – such wonderful words! – had brought us together again.

'By the way,' said Jock, moving slightly away to look at me. 'How did you get here? They told me someone brought you in.'

'One of the women from the flats had called round to see if I wanted an old carrycot that her daughter didn't need any more,' I said, crossing my fingers.

'That's good. We need all the free stuff we can get.'

I waited for him to ask me which woman. I didn't like telling lies and felt shocked at how easily this one had come. But to my relief, he didn't.

'How are we doing?' asked another nurse, bustling in. 'Started feeding yet? Looks like little one is rooting for you.'

I remember the term from our antenatal classes. My baby was indeed 'homing in' to my chest. I began to undo my nightdress but Jock cut in. 'My wife's not doing any of that stuff. I've heard about saggy boobs. She's keeping her beautiful figure.'

I flushed at the compliment. I didn't get many of those any more! Surely this was another sign that my husband was changing for the better.

The nurse put her hands on her hips. 'Mr Page. If you want your wife to do that, you're better off letting her feed naturally. It actually helps to get the shape back. It's also free. You don't want to spend all that money on baby milk and bottles and sterilizers, do you?'

Inside, I was impressed. She knew how to influence him!

Jock looked taken aback. 'I don't know. I never thought about it.'

'Well, I suggest that you do. Breast is best. Not just for baby but for the pocket.'

Jock shrugged. 'If you put it that way . . .'

'I do.'

I opened my nightdress again. Stuart immediately made a dive for my right breast as if he'd been waiting.

'See?' said the nurse in a satisfied way. 'Baby's latched on immediately.'

'Thank you,' I said to her when Jock left soon afterwards to 'get my tea at your mum's'.

She shrugged. 'No problem. I see a lot of husbands in here and many think they know everything. The trick is to let them think that a good idea is theirs in the first place. Takes some practice. But it's worth it.'

Then she patted me on the arm. 'Good luck. And well done for that lovely baby boy of yours. You'd never know he was two weeks early. Got everything he should have. A real beauty. Oh – I almost forgot – you've got a visitor waiting. I told her you'd had a boy.'

Jane! My friend was here with a huge bunch of flowers and a lovely warm hug. Thank goodness Jock had gone.

'Don't worry,' she said. 'I rang first to check that no one else was here.'

'But did you see him on the way out?'

'Jock? No.' Then she gasped at the sight of Stuart. 'Isn't he perfectly divine! I'd forgotten how tiny a baby's fingers are.'

Tears were actually running down her face. 'I'm so relieved everything was all right for you. I was really terrified when you passed out like that. And now look. You have a son. I do hope that I have one. I know Gary feels the same.'

'I'm sure you will,' I said, realizing as I spoke that this was silly. No one could tell. After all, that spin-the-ring game to tell the sex hadn't worked for me. Not that it mattered now. It reminded me of something that one of the girls in the factory had said: 'You might think you know what you want when it comes to babies, but you want what you get.'

Yet Jane looked as though she was somewhere else. 'Still, like Gary says, it really doesn't matter just as long as I don't . . .'

Then she stopped.

'Just as long as you don't what?' I asked.

She gave a little shiver. 'It doesn't matter. Now, as soon as you're up and about, you'll have to come round to me with your gorgeous baby. I'll help you. And don't you worry about your Jock. We'll find a way round his disapproval, won't we, little one?'

She stroked my son's cheek with her finger. 'Better go now. Gary is looking after Alice and I like to be there for her bedtime.' She brushed my cheek with hers. 'Well done! See you soon!'

After she left, I stared at the fancy bouquet tied up with pink ribbon she'd brought. No one had ever given me flowers before. White roses! They must have cost a fortune. There was a card inside. *Congratulations from us all! Love Jane, Gary and Alice.*

Quickly, I tore it up. I'd have liked to keep it safe. But I didn't want anything to upset the new, kinder Jock.

In those days, they kept you in hospital after the birth for much longer than they do now (I couldn't believe it, Poppy, when you were in and out within eight hours for both Melissa and Daisy). But after the caesarean and the amount of blood I'd lost, they said I needed to stay in for a week before they allowed me home. But I didn't care, I was too besotted with Stuart. I kept gazing down at his tiny face, his little hands, barely able to believe that God had granted me this miracle. 'I'll do anything for you to make sure you have a happy life,' I kept telling him. 'Anything.'

In fact, even though I was in such discomfort with the stitches, I rather liked being in hospital. It was so nice having people fussing over me and bringing me meals in bed! I also enjoyed the company of the other mums in the ward, despite the noise at night with all the babies yelling.

Jock, of course, wasn't too thrilled about me not being at home. There was no one to get him his tea (unless my mother asked him round), and in those days some men expected that, even if a woman was poorly. But he visited every evening after work, I'll say that for him.

'By the way,' said my husband one day. It was almost the end of visiting time but he'd been held up at the factory. (He said this in a way that indicated his presence had been vital.) 'Your mate Jane's in hospital too. She's not so good. Bumped into that up-his-own arse husband of hers on my way in.'

'Jane?' I repeated. 'What's wrong? Is the baby all right?'

'As far as I know. But your mate won't have anything to do with it. Postnatal depression, according to that Gary geezer. I told you she wasn't a good friend for you. What kind of woman won't even look at her own child?'

This didn't sound like Jane. Where had they put her? I looked around. By now they'd moved me from a side-room to the general postnatal ward but I couldn't see her. I tried to get out of bed. 'I need to find her. Ow!'

The stitches were still sore.

'You're not going anywhere,' said Jock, ringing the bell. 'Where are those bloody nurses?'

'They're busy,' I said.

'That's not good enough.' He dropped a kiss on top of my head. 'You've had a rough time. They should be here for you.'

It took a while for a nurse to arrive but when she did, she backed him up, much to my disappointment.

'Your husband's right. A caesarean's a big thing. You won't be able to do much for a few weeks.'

But how could I look after Stuart? And what about Jane? I felt so desperately useless not being there for her when she had done so much for me.

'Just as well your mother's around to help,' said Jock. 'I can't take time off work.' He was right, of course, but I wish he hadn't said this in such a sharp tone. The kinder Jock was still there, every now and then. But not as kind as when I'd come round from the caesarean.

As soon as my husband had left, I managed to find out that Jane had been put in a private room down the corridor. So I hobbled round on the walking frame they lent me, but when I got there, there was a notice on the door: NO VISITORS.

'She doesn't want to see anyone, I'm afraid,' said one of the other nurses. 'She'll be going home tomorrow anyway.'

Then maybe she was getting better!

I was finally discharged, but because of 'post-caesarean vaginal bleeding', as the district nurse called it (really scary, with big clots at times), I was advised to stay inside for a few days until it stopped. How I yearned to see Jane! But I couldn't go anywhere. And I couldn't call her because Jock had had us disconnected.

'I really need the phone back on,' I told my husband. 'What if Stuart got ill and we needed the doctor?'

'You're right,' he said, stroking our son's head. 'But don't use it too often, mind. We've got to be careful, with another mouth to feed and extra clothes for the bairn.'

It took a few weeks for the phone people to sort it out, but when they did I rang Jane while Jock was at work.

'Hello?' said a flat voice at the other end.

At first I thought I had the wrong number.

'It's me,' I said.

'Who?'

'Me! Betty.'

'Oh.'

I wasn't sure what to say. If I told her I knew she was depressed, she might be even more upset. They'd talked about that at antenatal class. The baby blues, they'd called it. If it got really bad, you had to have medical help.

'How can anyone be miserable after having a baby?' I'd asked Jane at the time. But she'd gone very quiet and changed the subject.

'What did you call your little one?' I asked now instead, realizing I didn't even know if it was a boy or girl.

'Violet.'

'Another daughter! How wonderful.'

'Yes.' Her voice was dull and flat, without her usual chirpiness.

I tried again. 'Such a lovely name.'

'I'm sorry, Poppy, but I have to go now. I'll speak to you soon.' She put down the phone without even asking me about Stuart.

This wasn't right. I knew it. So I got out the second-hand pram with the stained mattress that mum had 'treated' us to and somehow managed to walk all the way round to Jane's, stopping now and then because the stitches were sore and I felt so tired.

Gary answered the door. There were big dark circles under his eyes. 'I'm sorry to call in like this . . .' I began. But he seemed really relieved to see me.

'No. I'm glad you're here. Please come in.'

Jane was sitting in a chair by the patio doors leading out to the terrace in their lovely garden. She barely looked at me. Her hair was limp; unwashed and unstyled. She was still in her nightie and her feet were bare. Next to her was a Moses basket with little pink frills. Even though I loved Stuart with all my heart, I still felt a jolt of envy. How I had wanted a daughter! It's one of the reasons, Poppy, why I warmed to you so much.

'I don't know what to do with her,' said Gary quietly next to me. 'She won't let me help her dress and she won't talk or eat. She was a bit like this with Alice but nowhere near as bad. Thank goodness I'm on school holidays so I can look after her.'

Briefly I couldn't help thinking that since I'd come out of hospital, Jock had just left me to it. I was the one who got up at night, despite the fact that my stitches hadn't healed yet. And although my mother helped every now and then, she seemed to take a certain pleasure in telling me that she had her own life to lead as well. She couldn't just 'drop everything'. After all, I was the one who had 'chosen to have a kid'.

'I'm so sorry,' I said.

Gary's eyes were wet as he gesticulated towards the kitchen, where we could talk more privately. 'It's like she's turned into someone else. I hoped it would be better when we got home. But it's not. The midwife says it should pass but I can't help feeling afraid.' He lowered his voice even more so I could barely hear it. 'Her mother was the same after Jane was born. Depression runs in the family.'

'I'd never have guessed,' I said quietly.

'Well, it comes in bouts. Most of the time, she's fine. And even when she was a bit down she was always good at putting on a cheerful front, especially if she could help others.'

We looked back at the patio doors, where Jane sat stiffly, and I was suddenly overcome with affection and sorrow for my friend. Well, now it was my turn. Caesarean or not, I would help Jane. I owed it to her.

Just then Violet began crying and I made my way as fast as possible back into the lounge, after Gary. Jane was still sitting there, staring at the garden. Alice, who'd been playing with a puzzle, was standing over the Moses basket.

'She needs feeding,' said Gary in a bright voice. 'Do you want to do it, Jane?'

She didn't answer.

Gary looked at me with a 'See?' expression. 'We've had to bottle-feed because she won't do the other.'

He looked embarrassed and I sensed he didn't want to say the word 'breast'.

'Let me help,' I said. Stuart was fast asleep in his pram in the hall.

'Would you?' Gary's face brightened. 'It would mean that I could have some time with Alice. Poor little thing is feeling really confused.'

'Of course.' The truth was that I couldn't wait to scoop little Violet up and hold her in my arms. (I was allowed to pick up a baby now.)

How lovely it was to put my cheek against hers. As I bottle-fed her on my lap, I could pretend that she was mine. That I had a baby girl. A sister for Stuart.

After that, I went round every day. It was always the same. Jane would either be sitting in her chair overlooking the garden or else she'd be listening to *The Archers* or something else on the smart portable silver Roberts transistor radio that Gary had bought her. Whenever I tried to talk to her, she'd continue staring into blank space, without saying a word, as if she was in a world of her own. I'd feed Violet or sing her nursery rhymes to soothe her while Gary would take Alice to the park. Sometimes we changed over. I was able to do more now after the caesarean, thank goodness.

'I don't know what I'd do without you,' he would often say.

To be honest, I loved it. It got me out of the flat, which seemed even smaller now with Stuart's nappies hanging up to dry (disposables were too expensive) and his playpen and high chair taking up the remaining space. It also felt nice to be appreciated. Something I didn't get much of at home.

That's right. After our 'honeymoon' period following Stuart's birth, Jock had gone back to his old self. He criticized me for the smell of the nappies soaking in buckets. He told me off if supper was late, even though I tried to explain that I'd been busy with our baby. And he got particularly cross one morning when there wasn't an ironed shirt ready for him to wear to work.

'My mother managed with seven of us,' he snorted. 'You can't seem to cope with one.'

Naturally, I couldn't tell Jock that I was spending my days at Jane's house or he would have been furious at me disobeying his order not to see her again. He'd also have accused me of neglecting my own 'duties' at home. By now, my stitches were healing and my body was more like its old self. So I used to tidy up before I went to Jane's pretty regularly and then race back to make sure that I was there by the time he walked in from the factory.

Poor Gary was finding it all a struggle. Although it was the school summer holidays, he still had to go in every now and then for meetings and to prepare the next term's lessons. 'I'm happy to look after the girls when you're not there,' I assured him.

By then, Jane had been put on antidepressants. They made her sleepy. Once when I was there, she woke up with a start and put her arms out for Violet. But the poor little thing screamed as if her own mother was a complete stranger. In a way, she was.

Jane had handed her back to me without a word and closed her eyes.

I felt obliged to tell Gary when he got back that night. He shook his head. 'As I said, she was like this with Alice – it's why she lost her friends. They couldn't understand. But then she cheered up a bit and, even though she was never quite the same as she was before, I thought things were getting better. That it was just a matter of time.' He sighed. 'But now she's worse than ever. I can't give up work to look after her full-time.'

He started to cry then. Poor man! Spontaneously, without thinking, I put my arms around him. For a moment he stiffened, as if unsure how to react. But then he relaxed. 'It will be all right,' I said, stepping away.

'I hope so,' he said quietly. 'I miss her so much.'

So did I.

That night, when Stuart woke in the small hours as he always did, Jock lost his temper. 'Can't you keep that bairn quiet?' he roared. 'How do you expect me to do a day's work without any sleep?'

'You could doss on the sofa,' I suggested.

'I've got a better idea. You can do that. What's more,' he added, using more Scottish words than usual as he sometimes did when he was cross, 'y'can damn well tak the bairn with you.'

I thought about arguing back but I knew from experience that I wouldn't win.

At least I could escape to Jane's house to get away. As I walked there the next day, pushing Stuart up the hill from our horrible flat, I couldn't help wishing that I'd found a man like Gary. That I had never married Jock. How different my life might have been.

One of my mother's friends had recently lost her husband to an early death through drink and she seemed so much happier. 'Got a new lease of life, she has,' said Mum darkly.

And though it made me sick to the core to admit it, I occasionally began to wonder if I'd also be happier if something happened to Jock . . .

Central Criminal Court, London

'Poppy Page, I'd like to take you back to the time when you were a young drama student, in a relationship with Matthew Gordon. Is it true that he left you for another student, then known as Sandra Wright?'

The woman on the stand visibly stiffens. 'Yes.'

'And is it also true that you were deeply upset by this at the time?'

'I was only twenty-one,' she says haltingly. 'He was my first love. So, yes. I *was* upset.'

Every member of the jury appears to be paying close attention now. There's nothing that a court loves more than a touch of romance. It helps to lighten the darker issues. Or make them even deadlier.

The barrister is consulting a document. Her manner suggests it contains facts of vital importance. This could, of course, be a ruse. Maybe it's a lawyer's trick to flourish a sheet of paper (the opposition wouldn't know that the content is irrelevant). This might then unsettle the person in the witness box and make them more likely to tell the truth.

'Before he ended the relationship, you had been chosen to play the prestigious lead role in the third-year showcase student production opposite Matthew Gordon, hadn't you?'

'Yes.'

Poppy Page says this quietly. You can almost see the jury wondering what this has to do with the case. The barrister appears, from her expression and tone of voice, to be almost enjoying the suspense.

'And is it correct that Sandra Wright, your understudy, was substituted for you?'

She nods.

'Please answer verbally, Mrs Page.'

'Yes.'

It's as if she has to force the word out of her mouth.

'Perhaps you can explain to the court why that was?'

Poppy Page is gripping the front of the stand. 'I'd had to have a minor procedure in hospital the previous day and stayed in because there were complications,' she says.

'What kind of "minor procedure"?'

Then something happens. And despite the tension in the room, it appears from the faces that no one is expecting what comes next.

Poppy Page starts to weep. Not just shed a few tears. But to cry as if her very insides are spilling out. Several of the jurors lean forward in their seats. Some with sympathy. Others with naked curiosity.

'I had a termination,' she sobs.

There is a gasp from the public gallery. A young girl runs out, followed by an older woman.

'Whose child did you abort?'

'Matthew's, of course!' The tears are still spilling but her eyes are flashing now as the words pour out in a furious torrent. 'I didn't mean to get pregnant. It was an accident. I wanted to keep it but Matthew said it wasn't "the right time". I can remember his exact words.'

There's a sharp intake of breath from a member of the jury, a young man with a pained expression on his face. Is it possible that he might have experienced such a situation? That maybe it was his girlfriend who had decided to abort his child? That's the thing about juries. There is generally at least one person who identifies with the case for personal reasons. This can be useful for the defence. Or it could be a killer.

Right now, Poppy Page's words ring clearly in the air as if she is on stage, determined to project right to the very back row of the audience. '"We're too young to have a child at this stage of our lives," he said to me.' She extracts a tissue from her sleeve and wipes her eyes. 'We have our careers to think of. What if you got picked for a big role, Pops, as I'm sure you will? How could you be an actress with a small baby? We can always think of having a family later on when we are more established.'

'"Pops",' repeats the barrister softly. 'Was that his nickname for you?'

'Yes.' She has her head in her hands now.

'But the two of you *didn't* have a family later on, did you?'

'No.'

'Can you tell us why?'

She looks up. Her face is tear streaked but she's not crying any more. Her expression is one of pure hatred. 'Because he then left me for Sandra.'

'Was he having an affair with her already?'

'He said he wasn't.'

'Did you believe him?'

'Yes. No. I wasn't sure.'

'Yet there's something else too, isn't there? Is it correct that when Sandra stepped into your shoes, she was spotted by a talent scout in the audience? This led to her getting an agent and her first role?'

'Yes. But she never actually made it big.'

'Even so, she got the chance that you might have had. This must have felt very unfair to you, Mrs Page. You terminated your baby for the sake of your career and because of Matthew Gordon's feelings. But you ended up by losing all three.'

Poppy Page holds the barrister's gaze for a moment.

'Yes,' she says tightly. 'You're right. I did.'

'To make it worse, Matthew then married Sandra.'

'Yes.'

'You must have been very upset.'

'I was. But then I met my husband and we had our lovely girls.' She looks up at the gallery. 'I put it all behind me.'

'But did you, Mrs Page? Isn't it true that when you bumped into Matthew Gordon at the Association of Supporting Artistes and Agents' Christmas party, all that "upset" came back?'

'Not really.' She is calmer now. Or at least she appears to be. Maybe she realizes that the previous anger might not have been such a good thing. 'Seeing him revived old memories, but I was wistful, rather than angry.'

'Angry?' The barrister seizes on the word. 'That's rather different from your earlier use of "upset". Is it also true that you slept in a Worthing hotel with Matthew

Gordon shortly after meeting him at the party. In a king-size bed in a double room that you yourself had booked and he had paid for?'

There is a silence.

'Please answer the question.'

Still Poppy Page says nothing.

The barrister's voice is laden with sarcasm. 'Perhaps you would like me to repeat it?'

Poppy Page shakes her head. Whether this is in reply to the barrister or to admonish herself is uncertain. 'I booked the room because I needed somewhere to stay after seeing my father,' she says. 'There was only limited accommodation left, which is why I had to take a double.'

'But did you sleep with Matthew Gordon there?' asks the barrister impatiently.

'Yes!' Her voice comes out almost as a moan. 'But I realized immediately afterwards that it was a mistake.'

The barrister seizes on this with relish. 'You did sleep with him,' she repeats, as if to drum home the point to anyone who might have missed it. 'But he wouldn't leave you alone, would he? He kept pestering you and asking to meet up.'

'That's right. He said we were meant for each other.'

'How did that make you feel?'

She glances up at the gallery again. 'Scared that he might tell my husband.'

The barrister's voice rings out. 'I put it to you, Poppy Page, that you weren't just "upset", as you said earlier. You were indeed angry. In fact, you were furious. Here was a man who had betrayed you. He'd encouraged you to abort your child. The medical complications meant you missed an important career opportunity, which fell into the lap of another student. He callously – some might say – threw you over for this same woman whom he subsequently married. And then he came back, years later, threatening to ruin the life you had built for yourself.'

You could drop a pin and it would be heard as clear as day.

'So please tell the court the truth. Were you furious and bitter enough to want Matthew Gordon dead?'

'No,' she whimpers.

But it is clear from the jurors' faces that no one believes her.

15

Poppy

Just in case I ever need it, I've hidden the phone picture of us in bed using a privacy app I'd read about in one of the Sunday supplements, but I have no reason to hope that Matthew's been as discreet. What if Sandra sees it? She'd be perfectly entitled to turn up at the house and make a scene. She might sue for divorce, citing me as the other woman.

I would, if I were her.

What, I ask myself, had possessed me to go to bed with a man who had hurt me so badly all those years ago? Was it the hankering for what might have been? The fulfilment of a desire that had never gone away? The disappointment in my marriage? Or – and I can barely bring myself to consider this – was it because I wanted to show Matthew Gordon that he'd made one big mistake in breaking up with me all those years ago? Was I punishing him?

Whatever my reason, it's all come back to bite me. Because Matthew Gordon has finally done what I'd yearned for when we were students. He has fallen for me. And now he won't go away.

I'm working from home today without any external appointments. But I've hardly got anything done. I jump every time the phone goes or a text pings, in case it's him. Those words from last night still haunt me. *I'll ring tomorrow. Sweet dreams.*

I've been turning over the events of my relationship with Matthew continuously since yesterday morning. We hadn't even mentioned the abortion, which makes me wonder if Matthew had thought about it at all. At the time, it hadn't, I'm ashamed to say, seemed such a big deal. I knew of at least five people who'd had a termination, including one of my flatmates. It wasn't, I'd told myself back then, as if I was getting rid of a fully grown baby. It was 'simply a seed'.

But years later, when I'd got pregnant with Melissa and felt that first flutter in my tummy, I began to wonder. When she was born and I held her in my arms, I wept both tears of joy but also of grief for the child I'd chosen not to have and who would now have been a person in his or her own right. Perhaps I should have told Stuart right at the beginning when we'd met. But I'd felt too embarrassed – despite my self-justifications – and now it seems way too late.

If I'd had a mother to talk to, it might have helped. But that was out of the question.

That reminds me. Dad! I need to speak to the doctor confidentially. That petrol 'mistake' is one more example that my father's memory isn't right. What if he leaves the gas on? Or the key in the front door? In the last couple of years, there have been three burglaries in his road.

The doctor isn't available so I speak to the same practice manager I'd spoken to before. 'Obviously we can't disclose your father's notes because of confidentiality. But

I can tell you that this is becoming increasingly common; both memory loss and parents not wanting their children to "interfere". I could ask the doctor to pay him a routine call, if you like.'

'But when you did that last time, Dad refused to have any tests.'

'Then I'm afraid there's not much more we can do.'

I call Dad but there's no answer. Perhaps he's putting out his rubbish or sitting in his garden. He loves to watch the birds feed. I catch up on some emails, mainly briefing clients on shoots and chasing payments from production companies (cash flow is always an issue when you're self-employed), and then I try Dad again.

Still no answer. Maybe he's at the social club. He goes to lunch there sometimes. I check my messages again. Nothing from Matthew. Perhaps he's slept on it and seen sense. What a relief that would be! I have certainly, I reflect grimly, learned my lesson. Never again. I'll also go teetotal. It's a big step, but it will be worth it, if only to keep my head clear for the future. Not, of course, that I will ever allow myself to be in such a position again.

I break briefly for lunch. Sometimes I sit down to a bowl of soup or a salad with Betty but she isn't in today. The door of her bedroom is shut and her outdoor shoes have gone. Chances are that she's at one of her meditation or jewellery-making classes. Stuart says that she started all these hobbies after he went to university, but got even more 'into' them after Jock died. I think it's great that she keeps herself busy instead of grieving all the time. I also like to think that, much as she helps us, we help her too by sweeping her into our frenetically busy but loving family life.

Not that you were quite so appreciative of it in the Worthing hotel, says a little voice as I heat up a slice of cheese-and-broccoli quiche Betty had made earlier and take it back to my desk, along with a mug of decaf coffee.

And what about Stuart and this Janine? Or am I making more of this simply to justify my own behaviour? Stuart gave me a kiss on the cheek this morning when he left. He doesn't always do that. Would an unfaithful husband bother with a display of affection?

Well, his unfaithful wife had kissed him back.

Still no answer from Dad.

So then I ring Reg, his mate who lives down the road. My father won't be happy. He only gave me Reg's number because I'd virtually twisted his arm the other year, telling him I needed it for emergencies. 'What if something happened to us and you didn't pick up your phone but we had to get in touch with you?' I'd pointed out, hoping this might carry more weight with my proud dad than the real reason for my concern: that I needed to have a way of checking *he* was all right.

Reluctantly – and to my relief – he'd given in.

'Hi, lass,' says a voice. My name must be in his phone. 'How are you doing?'

Reg lives four roads away from my father. Dad and he go way back. Mum, I remember, hadn't cared for him very much, partly because he smokes like a chimney. I make a quick courteous inquiry into his chilblains – putting him on speaker phone as I often do, so I can also check my emails at the same time – and then cut to the chase. 'Really sorry to bother you, Reg, but would you mind going round to Dad's to see if he's all right? He's not picking up.'

'OK, lass. But it will have to be after I've dropped off the newspaper to a neighbour of mine. She's waiting for me.'

I bet she is. Reg is one of those men who was very shy until his wife died and then he seemed to find a new lease of life. But right now I need to stress the urgency of the situation. 'I'm really worried about him, Reg. I went down to see him at the weekend and found out about the . . .'

I stop, suddenly realizing I might have dropped Dad in it.

'You mean the police and the petrol?' he cuts in. Then he laughs. 'That was just a silly mistake. We all do it. By the way, lass, I saw you coming out of a hotel on Monday morning – having one of my early walks, I was – and spotted you running like a bat out of hell. I called out after you but then you got into a taxi. Everything all right?'

Reg had spotted me? Supposing Matthew had come after me? Reg would have seen him too. He might have told Dad – *would* have told Dad – and then he might have told Stuart and then . . .

'Fine,' I say quickly. 'I was just trying to catch an early train home to the family.'

PING! It's an email from my assistant Sally with a photo attachment.

We need to pitch for this new film. Look!!!! They need a man with a really long beard. Perfect for Ronnie the vicar, don't you think? Can you ring him to check on availability? I've got that shoot to go to.

I try to reply at the same time as talking to Reg. 'Can you let me know when you get hold of Dad?'

'Will do. Is he coming up to you for Christmas?'

'No. He says he wants to be on his own as usual.'

I feel awful about this but it's the same every year. He likes his 'peace and quiet', even though he gets that every day. Secretly I think it's because he still misses Mum.

'Don't you worry. I'll keep an eye on him. And I'll ring you later on today. He's probably having a little doze.'

That's the sensible answer. But my mind spins into all the 'what-ifs'. What if he's fallen and is lying there unconscious? What if he's set fire to the house? Downstairs I can hear the dog barking for a walk. As if there isn't enough to do! Honestly, that French teacher has got a cheek. But when I take Coco to the park after wrapping myself up in the stylish navy jacket that Betty had given me for my last birthday, I begin to see why dog walkers look so happy and healthy. It's actually really nice to get out in the fresh air, even if it is nippy. And Coco is rather sweet. She comes back to me with the ball every time!

'You're meant to pick up,' says a woman walking past, her voice tight with disapproval.

Whoops! I hadn't noticed that Coco had 'performed'. The French teacher had supplied us with poo bags but I've never done this before. Yuck! Then I head straight back home to wash my hands, even though I'm pretty sure I didn't touch anything. Coco has her tongue out, as if she's laughing at me.

'Maybe I'll take you with me to meet Daisy from school,' I tell her. 'She'd like that.'

Then the phone goes. Reg. My heart almost stops. If Dad was all right, he'd have called me himself, berating me for contacting his friend.

'I don't want to worry you,' he says.

'What's happened?' I croak.

'Your dad's all right . . .'

Thank heavens for that.

'But he's in a bit of a pickle. He wasn't picking up the phone because he was trying to sort out his credit card problems.'

'But he doesn't have one. He only has a debit card.'

'That's just it. Apparently he fell for one of those bank invitations to take one out. He's been spending without realizing he has to pay a certain amount back every month. And now they've sent him a warning letter.'

'It shouldn't be allowed,' I say. 'Doesn't the bank realize how old he is?'

'Plenty of people our age are perfectly capable of handling our bills,' says Reg stiffly.

'I'm sorry. Of course you are.'

'Anyway, don't worry. I've been helping him sort it out. He's written a cheque to pay it all off and I've got him to cut up the credit card.'

'Thank you. He'd never have done that for me.'

'That's what friends are for, love. Now you relax and enjoy yourself with those girls of yours.'

Relax and enjoy myself? I'm a working woman. But there are a lot of people like Reg who don't understand the concept of working from home. They think it's an excuse for putting your feet up. Still, at least it allows me some space to do things like meet my younger daughter from school with her on-loan dog.

I'm just about to put the lead back on Coco when my phone buzzes again. It's always like this. Stuart refuses to have his on him unless absolutely necessary. He keeps telling me about research that suggests our brains will all be frazzled with mobile use by the time we're old. 'It's just like smoking in our parents' generation,' he says. 'No one realized how dangerous it was then.'

I glance at the screen. *Matthew*.

I could reject him, but what would be the point? He'd only ring again. Anyway, I'd rather know the score.

'Hello,' I say coolly.

'Pops! I've missed you.'

He's talking as though we're used to seeing each other all the time.

'Please don't say things like that.'

'But I do. Are you free this evening? I've booked one of the carers for Sandra. Don't worry, she doesn't know anything. We could go out to dinner to discuss how you're going to tell Stuart about us. There's this lovely mews flat I've found that we could rent. It's got a Juliet balcony and it's not that far from Kilburn station. There's room for your kids to visit at the weekend . . .'

'Stop,' I say. This is ridiculous! 'I've told you before. I'm not leaving my husband. It was a mistake. I shouldn't have slept with you.'

'But you did, Pops. And it was wonderful. Admit it.'

Coco is whining at my feet as if she knows I am upset. I'm starting to think this man is crazy. Unhinged, perhaps. 'I've got to get my daughter from school,' I say, aware that my voice is shaking with the effort to keep calm. 'Then I'm spending the evening with my family. I am not leaving Stuart or the girls and that's the end of it. Don't try to contact me or any of my family ever again.'

'Not even your mother-in-law with that rather fetching purple beret of hers?'

How does he know about Betty? Facebook again?

'No,' I say.

There's silence. Has he rung off, or have we lost signal?

'Are you still there?' I ask.

'Oh yes, Pops. I'm always here for you. I've told you that before. As for leaving you alone, I don't think I can do that. Sorry.'

Then the line goes dead.

16
Betty

The weeks went by and still Jane showed no signs of improving.

'Mummy still poorly,' Alice would inform me solemnly, gripping her daddy's hand as if she was scared he might get ill too.

'Never mind,' I'd say in a falsely upbeat voice. 'She'll get better soon.'

But she didn't. My friend's once-bright eyes had sunk into her face and there were black shadows around them. Her hair was still lank and flat. 'I try to wash it for her,' said Gary despairingly when Alice was playing, 'but she just pushes me away. At least I persuaded her to get dressed today. There are times when she won't get out of her nightie.'

We spoke in low voices from the next room, not wanting to upset her. Violet was fast asleep in her Moses basket, blissfully unaware of everything going on around her.

Gary was looking worse too. The saggy bags under his eyes were more pronounced than ever. 'It's not me I'm worried about,' he said. 'It's the children. Alice keeps asking questions and Violet isn't putting on as much weight as she should because I don't seem to have much luck getting a bottle down her.'

As if on cue, the baby woke. Soon her mewing sounds turned into desperate screams. Poor little mite was probably starving.

'Let me have a go,' I said. 'Where's the milk powder?'

Gary showed me and I swiftly made some up. For some reason, Violet was more than happy to take it from me, gulping it down so fast that the milk dribbled out of her tiny rosebud mouth. Maybe she'd sensed that her father had been too nervous when he'd tried. Babies like to think an adult knows what he or she is doing, even when that isn't the case. The trick, I'd learned, is to pretend. It gives both of you more confidence. I also knew how to soothe her, using the same methods I did with my Stuart; stroking her little cheek with my finger and then burping her against my shoulder.

'There we are!' I said triumphantly.

'You're amazing,' said Gary and I flushed with pleasure.

Afterwards, I laid her on the yellow-and-green giraffe-patterned play mat which Jane had bought when she was pregnant, and distracted both Violet and my son – whom I'd placed next to her – with one of those lovely little floor-standing mobiles above them. We couldn't afford anything half as fancy as that at home.

Sometimes, if the weather was fine, I'd push the two of them around the garden in the double buggy (a present from Jane's grandmother) to get them to sleep. Then I was able to play with Alice to give Gary a bit of a break. On a few occasions, I fancied I saw Jane standing at the window, watching me in her nightdress with her long blonde hair hanging down. But when I beckoned at her to come out and join us, she turned away.

The doctor prescribed a different type of antidepressant. 'They just seem to knock her out,' said Gary, 'rather than making her any better.' He rubbed his eyes. 'Term starts in a week and I'll have to go back to work. I really don't know what to do. Jane's parents live too far away to help out. They've offered to pay for a nanny but I don't like the idea of a stranger looking after the children. You've been such a help but I can't expect you to carry on full-time.'

'I'm quite happy to do so,' I heard myself saying.

Gary smiled weakly. 'That's so kind of you. But you've got your own little one to look after and your house to run.'

'Flat, you mean,' I corrected him. 'It doesn't take me long to clean it. I haven't got anything else to do apart from looking after Stuart. If I'm doing that for one baby, I might as well look after two. Besides, Alice is going to be at full-time school now isn't she?'

I stopped before I got carried away by my own enthusiasm. 'There's only one problem.' Unable to meet his eyes, I looked down at the ground, embarrassed.

'What's that?' I heard him say.

'My Jock told me I wasn't to see Jane again after you asked us round to dinner.'

Gary nodded. 'I know. Jane told me before she got . . . got ill. But I presumed he'd changed his mind after the baby, otherwise you wouldn't be here.'

'He doesn't know,' I said, raising my eyes to meet his. 'He's at work and he never bothers to ask me how I spend my days.'

Gary bit his lip. 'I see. I don't want to get you into any trouble.'

'And I don't want to leave my best friend in the lurch,' I said. 'I'd like to help out, just as long as you can find someone to take Alice to school and collect her. That way I won't be seen. I'll need to be back before Jock in the evening too.'

'Of course.' He still looked uncertain. 'But I don't like the idea of it causing bad blood with your husband.'

'Don't worry about that,' I said. It was on the tip of my tongue to tell him that there was enough of that already.

'Of course,' he added, 'I'll pay you whatever you want.'

'Pay me?' I took a step back. 'I don't want money. I'm offering because Jane has been a good friend to me and now she needs my help.'

Gary looked like he was going to argue the matter. Then he gave an 'I get it' shrug.

'I'm so sorry. I didn't mean to offend. It's very kind of you. I'm sure Jane will start feeling brighter soon. After Alice was born, it took about six months. So maybe we'll all be back to normal again by Christmas.'

As late summer merged into autumn, I came to love my new routine. It was such a relief to get out of the flat and let Stuart crawl around Jane's lovely home, which had so much more space. Violet had started to crawl too. The two of them looked so cute together. 'Look,' I'd say to Jane as she sat in her chair, staring into space. 'Isn't it amazing to see how they're growing so fast?'

But she didn't say anything. Gary said it was the same in the evening. It was hard to talk to this new surly Jane, who was so different from my old happy friend. Surely something could be done to make her better again? But what? The doctor had already referred her to a specialist who had prescribed other drugs. There was no improvement.

Maybe she needed more of a personal touch. I tried everything to bring that spark back, like turning up Radio One and singing along to The New Seekers, one of my favourite groups, who Jane had liked too. But there was no response. Then I put on the television for the children's programmes when Alice was home from school. That at least seemed to do something. Jane actually stood up and went to the set, leaning forward until her face was in front of the picture. It was almost as if she was trying to get inside the television itself. But she still wouldn't talk to us.

'Why don't you hold your new little daughter instead?' I suggested.

I put the baby in her arms but she pushed us both away. Then Violet screamed and I had to soothe her. 'Shhh, little one,' I whispered, putting my small finger in her mouth so she could suck for comfort.

'Why did Mummy push you?' asked Alice, looking round from the television.

'She didn't mean to,' I said quickly. But inside I was panicking. What if she hurt the children?

'I've never seen Jane do that before,' said Gary worriedly when he came back that night. 'But I have noticed that she perks up when the television is on. She doesn't like it when I'm there, though.'

'Maybe,' I suggested tentatively, 'she wants to be on her own. Don't take that the wrong way. But it's how I feel sometimes when I'm at home. Giving birth is such a big thing and then it's full on with the baby. At times, you need space to yourself.'

Gary nodded. 'I can see that. Actually, I've got an idea.'

He bought Jane a portable TV for the conservatory. This proved a bit of a breakthrough. She'd watch the daytime stuff – mainly schools and adult education programmes in those days – her eyes glued to the screen. When I made lunch for the children and me (Stuart and Violet were on solids now), I'd take her a tray with little delicacies that Gary would leave in the fridge. Smoked salmon! I'd never even tasted it before. Sometimes she would nod at me as if to say thank you and I'd see a glimmer of my old friend. 'You'll be as right as rain before long,' I'd say brightly.

But then her eyes would go dull again and she would look away.

Gary got permission to leave early from school so I could be home to make Jock's tea before he got back. But once I nearly got caught out when the factory closed at midday because of a mechanical problem. 'Where the hell have you been?' he demanded when I returned with Stuart. 'Your mum said she hasn't seen you for weeks.'

'We went for a walk,' I said. It wasn't actually a lie. It was quite a tough walk to Jane's, up a steep hill.

'And where did that fancy buggy come from?'

'That?' I said, playing for time. Gary had given it to me; it was a spare they'd had in the garage and was smarter than the old pram Mum had bought as well as being easier to push now Stuart was getting bigger. 'I found it at the tip. It was going free.'

After that, I was a bit more careful, telling Gary that I was very sorry but I could only do a couple of days a week. So he paid for a girl from an agency to come in for the other three.

That seemed a good solution for a while, but after a fortnight Gary rang me from school – thankfully, Jock had long left for work. 'Dawn's just called to say that Violet won't stop screaming and that Jane is walking up and down in a terrible state, trying to pull her own hair out. We had to keep Alice off school because she has a cold. I'm so sorry to ask but do you think . . .'

I was already reaching for my old anorak and looking for Stuart's (another hand-me-down that Gary had passed on; it looked a bit girly but at least it was warm). 'We'll be there,' I said.

I was shocked when I arrived. Violet's nappy was soaked through – which was probably why she was still crying – and Alice had a runny nose that no one had wiped. Jane's eyes were wild and she caught me by the hands. 'Stay,' she kept saying over and over again. 'Stay.'

It was as if fear had helped her to start talking, even if it was just one word.

Young Dawn, who looked fresh out of school, was at her wits' end. 'It wasn't my fault,' she said defensively. 'I did my best.'

'The children just need someone they know,' I said, trying to reassure her. 'Don't worry. I'll take over now.' I changed Violet's nappy and found her dry clothes in the nursery while strapping Stuart into the bouncing chair so he was safe. I got out Alice's play clay and suggested she made shapes on the kitchen table. Then I settled Jane with a mug of tea (not piping hot, in case she scalded herself) in front of the television.

'It was so kind of you to bail us out,' said Gary when he came back from school. 'I've rung the agency and they're going to try and find someone more experienced.'

'No,' I said. 'Don't. It's not experience that Jane and the children need. It's a familiar face. I'll go back to what I was doing before and come round every day.'

Gary looked concerned. 'But I don't want you to get into trouble with your husband.'

He was so kind. So thoughtful. If only I had a man like him instead of a rough bully who could turn on me if I did something as small as forgetting to polish his shoes. 'I won't,' I lied, knowing that Jock would kill me if he discovered I was going there. I'd just have to make sure that he didn't. 'Now don't worry about me. You've got enough on your plate.'

'I'll tell the agency we don't need Dawn any more then,' he said. 'I must say, I'll feel much happier now the children will be with someone who really loves them.'

My own words were braver than I felt. But as the weeks went by and I wasn't caught out again, I began to feel more assured. If push came to shove, I'd tell Jock that my friend needed me and that was that. Jane couldn't go on being depressed for ever. Then we could all get back to normal again.

But part of me – a terrible part – *wanted* this to carry on for ever. I could almost pretend that Jane's daughters were mine. On a few occasions, Alice even called me 'Mummy' by mistake and little Violet always calmed down when I picked her up. Occasionally – though not often, because I felt sick with guilt afterwards – I imagined when Gary came back at the end of the day that he was my husband returning from work.

I knew it was wrong. I knew I was only thinking that way because Jane's home was such a welcome distraction from Jock's moods and his drinking and the rough way in which he forced himself on me at night. But I couldn't quite get those fantasies out of my head.

17

Poppy

It's the first day of the Christmas holidays so I'm not going to make a fuss about the girls lying in, even though they have revision for January exams. Who am I to tell them to be sensible? I have no right to set boundaries any more. Not after what I've done. I can only hope that Matthew isn't going to do anything stupid with that photograph. What if he sends it to Stuart?

No. Surely he wouldn't do that. But his voice keeps coming back to me. *'As for leaving you alone, I don't think I can do that. Sorry.'*

My mind and body feel as though they are spiralling hopelessly out of control. Not only because of Matthew but also because of Dad. What crazy thing is he going to do next? As for Stuart, I've hardly seen him because he's been working late. Or so he says. I've thought of having a heart-to-heart conversation about this Janine but I'm scared of stirring up a deeper 'what are we going to do about our sexless marriage' talk. Besides, Stuart might be totally innocent. I simply can't imagine him being unfaithful. Yet he might be thinking exactly the same about me.

So many questions. And no reasonable answers.

Maybe it's best to do what previous generations did. Turn a blind eye and hope that it all passes.

But our generation is too honest for that. Aren't we? If we are unfaithful, we move on and destroy our families in the process. My mother was a forerunner of her time. And now, it seems, I have continued the tradition.

My mother-in-law appears to be the most level-headed person in the house at the moment. 'How are your jewellery sales going?' I ask, in an attempt to think of someone else apart from myself.

'Ah,' says Betty. 'Well I've had to give up on the tin can range. Unfortunately, one of my customers from the church bring-and-buy claims she was cut by a necklace she bought from me.'

I'm not surprised. Stuart had told her enough times that her tin can jewellery had sharp edges that might do exactly that. My own bare feet have borne pained witness when treading on the cut-offs. As she tells me this, I can't help thinking that there are some hurts that can be healed. And others that can't.

'I'm making rope bracelets instead,' adds Betty. 'They're proving very popular.'

I have to take my hat off to my mother-in-law. If she faces a little mishap, she simply picks herself up and carries on. Of course, she's never had to deal with anything big apart from Jock's death. Even then, she coped better than we expected, despite his illness being shockingly brief. I hadn't realized you could die in three months from pancreatic cancer. I've since learned it can be less.

I go up to my study and stand at the window, looking down onto our long narrow garden and then the fence that divides us from another garden, the same size, with a house that's similar in design to ours. The symmetry usually soothes me, but not right now. Especially after Doris's fall. My study used to be the guest room until I set up my business but now any visiting friends have to stay on the sofa bed downstairs. Not that we've had any of those for ages. I'm too busy working. So is Stuart.

The girls, when they have sleepovers, have friends on the floor of their rooms. Betty has a room with an en suite, which we squeezed in when she joined us. That's it. Us. Our family unit, which, through one crazy night in a Worthing hotel, I have jeopardized.

Somehow I have to get Matthew off my back. But how?

Maybe if I ring him, I might be able to persuade him to see sense. But if I do that, Sandra might pick up the phone. I can see them now. It's 9 a.m. Perhaps he'll be getting her breakfast or helping her dress. I can't even imagine the intricacies of doing that for someone who is wheelchair bound. Poor woman! I might not have cared for Sandra but MS is something I wouldn't wish on my worst enemy.

Then a terrible thought comes into my head. What if something happened that put Matthew in a wheelchair too; even better, unable to speak; unable to mess up my life again . . .

Stop, I tell myself. *Don't even go there. That's wicked.* What kind of woman am I turning into? Or rather, what kind of woman have I already become? I'd always thought of myself as a fairly kind and reasonable person. The sort who would never cheat. But now I don't know who I am any more. For a start, I should be ringing Dad again to check up on him.

So I do.

'Call back in five minutes, can you?' he says now. 'There's this good programme about wildlife in Borneo on the telly. It's just about to finish.'

At this time of the morning? Still, if you can't please yourself at his age, when can you? At least it means he isn't breaking the law or running up huge bills. At least I hope he isn't.

PING!

A message flashes up on the screen at my desk. I leave the sofa and sit down, my hand poised on the mouse. It's a message from a production company looking for hippy-type sixty-year-olds. I don't even need to check my database. I've got just the wacky-looking bohemian client in mind, with purple hair and a penchant for floaty skirts. She had a small role in the musical *Hair* when she was young and has never been able to match it in her career since. She'd love this! I zip off an email to say I have a possibility and then another to the woman in question. I get a flash of pleasure the way I always do when I'm pretty sure, in my gut, that I've got a hit. Not only that but my *Hair* lady will be thrilled. Then I remember Dad again and pick up the phone.

He doesn't answer.

This has happened before, I tell myself, trying not to panic. He'll have gone to the loo.

I give him another ten minutes. No reply. I begin to panic now. The usual scenarios play out in my head. He's had a stroke. He's cut himself on a kitchen knife. A cold shiver of fear runs through me. Time and time again, I've asked him to come up to London. We'd manage somehow. Maybe build an annexe in the garden or perhaps persuade him to use the money from his house to buy a bigger one that we can all live in.

I ring Dad once more. Still no answer. It's no good. After another twenty minutes of constant ringing, I am forced to call Reg again.

'I'll go round now,' he promises.

'Thanks,' I say. 'I'm so sorry to bother you.'

'No problem,' he says. 'Better safe than sorry.'

By now, I feel sick with fear.

There's another ping. Another production company. They are looking for over-forties for a crowd scene. It's part of a film about the 'sandwich generation' where, says the blurb, *a middle-aged woman is struggling with the demands of her elderly parents and teenage sons*. I want to laugh out loud. It seems so ironic that this should arrive now. Only fools like me would make it even more complicated by tossing an affair into the pot.

Downstairs I can hear the girls arguing. They must be up. Coco is yapping too. She should have gone back to Madame Blanche, the French teacher, ages ago but she texted to ask if we could hang on to 'my darling *chien*' for '*un peu* longer' because she's been delayed in Paris.

I'm used to juggling. But I've never before had a stick of dynamite in my hands that could blow up my family at any moment. Dynamite for which I have lit the fuse myself. Christmas, I remind myself, is a well-known trigger for divorce. It's portrayed as this perfect time when we all love each other. Disappointment is inevitable.

There's a knock on the door. Unlike everyone else in this house, Betty rarely disturbs me when I'm working. It must be important. 'It's your dad,' she says, handing me the landline handset.

'What are you doing ringing Reg?' Dad's voice is furious. 'I've told you before. Makes me look like a complete idiot.'

'But you told me to call back in five minutes and you didn't answer.'

'I was in the lav, wasn't I,' he says, as if I ought to know that. 'Now you get on with your life and leave me to mine.'

He's proud. He doesn't mean to be hard. It started when my mother left and it's got worse over the years. But every now and then, there'll be a caring look or tone of voice that lets me know that my old dad is still there.

I go downstairs to make a coffee and check on the girls. There are odd half-chewed shoes lying on the floor of the kitchen and a ripped *I Love Mum* apron the girls had given me for last Mother's Day. Daisy is sitting by the Aga, cradling the culprit.

'When exactly is that puppy going back?' I say, eyeing this white mop, not to mention the ugly metal dog cage the French teacher had provided. Apparently it gives them security. I could do with one myself. 'It's a real cheek if you ask me.'

Betty and Daisy exchange looks. Immediately, I can see something is up. 'Actually,' says my mother-in-law, 'Madame Blanche has just texted. It seems she's got family issues and wants to know if we can have Coco just for a few more days while she sorts things out.'

What? She clearly thinks Betty is a soft touch. 'Is she joking?' I say.

Daisy promptly bursts into tears.

'Don't be mean, Mum,' says Melissa. 'You know she's always wanted a dog. And it's not like it's for ever.'

'Animals can be a great comfort,' says Betty. 'I've just been reading about how they can help during exam stress.'

I give up. There's too much to deal with right now. 'I'll discuss it with your dad,' I say.

'Thank you!' Daisy leaps up and hugs me, all tears apparently dried.

'That's not a yes,' I warn her.

But she's cuddling Coco as if the decision has already been made.

To my surprise, Stuart comes back at about 6 p.m. from the surgery and suggests some late-night Christmas shopping in town. With everything going on, I haven't even thought about presents yet. Thank heavens for Betty, who sorted out the tree and all the decorations two weeks ago. She's also hung the cards on pretty ribbon. They keep arriving. 'Don't you want this one?' she asked, finding an unopened envelope with an Australian stamp in the bin just before I leave with Stuart.

'No thanks,' I say shortly, avoiding meeting her eye and running upstairs to put on a dab of lip gloss.

This is the second time in a week that we've done something together without the children. It has to be a record. Stuart actually holds my hand – something he hasn't done for ages. I'd have given anything for that until last Sunday night. But now I feel terrible. Not 'just' because of the guilt, but because my husband's grasp is so different from Matthew's. Less meaningful. More like that of a friend than a lover. Where is the passion? Does it matter when you have a family? Yes. No. I'm not sure. But I do know that I will do whatever it takes to keep everyone together so the girls don't have to go through what I did when my mother left. And, of course, I'm aware it's rather like shutting the stable door after the horse has bolted to think like this. But better late than never.

'Cold, isn't it?' he says, taking a pair of black leather gloves out of his pocket.

'They're nice,' I say.

'Yes. I bought them the other day.'

That's odd. Stuart rarely buys anything for himself. He leaves his clothes to me.

We choose some extra little gifts: a small backpack for Daisy with a picture of a dog on it; fluffy pink earmuffs for Melissa and a stripy fun iPad cover for my mother-in-law. Then we go to a cafe for a hot chocolate. To the outside world, we probably look like an ordinary married middle-aged couple. Only I know the truth. And it's killing me.

The stress — and the warmth inside after the cold air — is making me hot. I peel off my jumper, revealing the bruise on my arm where Matthew had grabbed me in the hotel to stop me leaving. 'That's quite a shiner you've got there,' says Stuart.

'I bumped it getting out of a taxi,' I reply lightly. 'You know me. I only have to slightly knock myself to go black and blue.'

I need to change the subject fast. 'How's your research going?'

'Good, thanks.'

'Is your research colleague helpful?' I ask carefully.

I don't want to sound suspicious but I am beginning to feel very uneasy about all the hours Stuart is spending away from home – even more than usual. Then again, it's always people who are unfaithful themselves who are suspicious of their partners. Or so I've read.

'Yes,' he says. 'She is, thanks.'

Then he falls silent. I want to ask more but I am scared of tipping the boat. He might ask me tricky questions in return. I might find myself telling him everything. To distract myself, I stir the frothy bit of my hot chocolate and then lick my teaspoon like a child – exactly the kind of thing I tell the girls off for doing.

'By the way,' says Stuart, watching me carefully. 'A new patient registered with me today. He doesn't live in the area but he had an emergency and his usual NHS dentist was booked up. So he paid to see me privately.'

I nod, trying to look interested. It's not the first time that Stuart has had patients with the same story. Finding a dentist isn't easy nowadays.

'Someone recommended me to him, apparently.' My husband is looking pleased with himself. 'Interesting man, as a matter of fact. He's an actor.' He lowers his voice. 'I told him my wife had been an actress once and runs an agency for extras.'

I wince, wishing he hadn't done that. Even though my work is so successful, my old failure still rankles.

'He seemed very interested,' says Stuart, taking a sip of his own hot chocolate and then dabbing his mouth with a paper napkin with a holly pattern. 'I wouldn't normally mention his name because of patient confidentiality but he specifically asked me to do so. Said he was always keen to keep up with other "thespians", as he put it. Anyway, he's called Matthew Gordon. Do you know him?'

18

Betty

By Christmas, Jane still hadn't got any better. Neither Gary nor I could persuade her to leave the house – not even for a little walk round the garden. 'Not safe,' she kept muttering, looking over her shoulder as if someone was following us.

'What do you mean, darling?' asked Gary. 'Nothing's going to happen to you.'

But she kept repeating the words over and over. 'Not safe. Not safe.'

The doctor arranged for a counsellor to come round but Jane became hysterical. 'Go away,' she screamed, pushing the poor woman out of the room.

I'd agreed with Gary to keep Alice busy in the kitchen with her baking set that included some sweet plastic heart-shaped pastry cutters that her grandparents had given her but she'd heard the noise and come rushing out. 'Why is Mummy so cross?'

'She's not really,' I said carefully, giving Gary a 'what-shall-I-say?' look. 'It's just that she's not very well at the moment.'

The consultant said it was 'disappointing' that Jane's condition had gone on for so long. It didn't 'fit the pattern' of the last bout of postnatal depression. He prescribed more tablets. 'I understand if you want to stop coming,' Gary said to me. 'You must be fed up with us.'

'No,' I said, horrified. 'I love coming here.'

He gave me a strange look. 'Love?'

'What I mean,' I said hastily, 'is that I want to look after Jane and the children. It's company for Stuart too. I am sure Jane would do the same for me if I was in her situation.'

Gary touched me gently on the shoulder. It was only for a second but my skin seemed to burn at his touch. 'You're a good friend. I don't know what we'd do without you. But your husband . . . surely he must be asking questions by now?'

I gave a short laugh. 'No. He doesn't. Jock is totally absorbed in "working his way up". It's all he's ever lived for and dreamed of. He's certainly not interested in anything I do.'

Gary's voice was low. 'Then the man's a fool.'

I felt myself redden. I could feel Gary's eyes on me.

'Now,' I said quickly, 'what shall I cook you all for supper before I go?'

'There's no need. Honestly.'

'I'd like to.'

I didn't really have time to do this before Jock got home but I wanted to do what I could for this poor man whose life had been turned upside down. Escaping to another woman's kitchen would also give me a chance to compose myself before I left.

Even though it was true that Jock never inquired about my day, Mum had started to ask questions. 'You're never in when I call round,' she said. 'What do you do with yourself?'

'Stuart and I go for walks,' I said carefully.

'In this weather?'

'It's warmer outside than it is in our place,' I said.

That wasn't the exaggeration it sounded. Our boiler was always on the blink and Jock said we couldn't afford a new one. ('Not now we only have one lot of wages in this house.') Jane's house was lovely and warm in comparison. It actually had central heating!

Meanwhile, I had started to take risks by staying later so I could spend a little longer with Gary when he came home from work. I lived for the moment when I heard his key turning in the lock! As the hour got closer and closer, my heart would beat faster and faster.

'How were the girls?' was always his first question when he stepped in through the door. There was no point in him asking about Jane because he knew I'd tell him immediately if anything changed. Then I'd ask him about his day. I couldn't help thinking this was the kind of conversation that happily married couples might have.

When I looked in the mirror, I began to see a different woman. One who was more excited about life. A woman with a definite glow.

Jock noticed it too. 'Something's different about you,' he said.

'I've got a new face cream,' I lied.

'Well, I hope it didn't cost much. We've got to be canny with the pennies, you know.'

But by the time Stuart and Violet turned one, I couldn't hide my feelings any more. I began to 'prepare myself' for

Gary's coming back from work, almost like getting ready for a date. I took care to brush my hair and dab lipstick on. Sometimes I added a little spray of perfume from Jane's dressing table. *I'm sure she wouldn't mind*, I told myself, breathing it in. *Go on – have some*, I could almost hear her saying. *You deserve it after everything you're doing for us and I know you don't have any at home.*

Sometimes, in my head, I actually pretended that I was Jane. I'd already consciously adopted some of her gestures and habits, speaking with more rounded vowels and holding my cutlery in the right way when I was at their place. I used the word 'loo' instead of 'toilet', like my friend did. I'd even started to dye my hair blonde like hers with some cheap stuff from Woolworths. (Ironically, Jock approved, saying it 'suited' me.') I continued to imagine that Gary was my own husband. I pictured him kissing me on the cheek. We would eat dinner next to each other, holding hands and then . . .

That's where I stopped. This was a dream I couldn't have. It was wrong. But I couldn't help myself.

Then one evening when he came back from work, Gary shut the door behind him and actually gave me a gentle kiss on the side of my face, just like in my daydreams! It was so unexpected that you could have blown me over.

'I'm sorry,' he said, as if horrified at himself. 'I don't know what came over me.' He rubbed his face with his hands. 'To be honest, it was automatic. It's what I always did to Jane.'

I was so shocked – and excited – that I couldn't say anything.

His eyes were red with grief and exhaustion and shame. 'This can't go on for ever, Betty. What are we going to do?'

Hadn't I been asking myself that question over and over again? 'We just have to carry on as normal. Pretend we're not feeling this way,' I said in a small voice.

He stopped and stared at me. 'I meant what are *we* going to do – Jane and me and the children?'

Instantly I realized my error. 'Sorry,' I said, blushing furiously. 'Yes, that's what I meant too.'

He had the strangest expression on his face. As if we were understanding something for the first time. 'I didn't dare imagine you had feelings for me too,' he whispered.

'Too?' I whispered back, hardly daring to believe it.

He nodded. 'I know it's wrong but . . .'

Alice was watching television before tea, giggling at a cartoon. It was so nice to see her happy. Both Stuart and Violet were having a nap in their pushchairs, breathing steadily. Jane, as usual, was in the conservatory, glued to one of her soap operas. I knew I should not be doing this. Yet every bone in my body was on fire.

Gary led me to the bedroom. *Their* bedroom. 'Quickly,' he whispered. I scarcely remember undressing. All I knew was that now he was lying on top of me. His hands were caressing me more tenderly than Jock's had ever done. His kisses were making my mouth melt. 'You smell so good,' he murmured. Then something made me look up.

Jane was standing in the doorway, watching us. Her face was completely expressionless.

'No!' I gasped, pushing Gary away from me.

'What's wrong?' he groaned. Then he saw my face and looked up too.

'Jane,' he breathed. 'Shit. I'm sorry. I can explain . . . wait.'

But silently, she turned on her heel like a pale ghost. For a minute, Gary and I were both frozen with horror. Then we heard the front door slam.

19
Poppy

It's Christmas Day. Even Melissa is out of bed when it's not quite light, feverishly ripping open her presents under the tree with her sister. It's yet another reminder that the girls might be teenagers but they are still children at heart. Still in need of both parents. Then again, does that ever change? Even at my age, I would give anything to have my mother to confide in. Not the mother who left, but the one I'd trusted in. Just like my children trust me.

My husband's words during our late-night shopping trip keep coming back along with my reply.

'He's called Matthew Gordon,' he'd said. 'Do you know him?'

'No,' I'd replied, with a false brightness that came all too readily with the lie. 'I don't think so. Is he an extra?'

'No, but he said he was thinking about opening an agency specializing in extras, like you. Apparently, he used to be a lead actor in a drama in the nineties. I don't remember it myself.'

Then again, my husband isn't a great one for television. If he's home in the evenings, he'll have his nose buried in dental papers instead.

'Did you tell him my maiden name?' I asked, trying to sound calm. Before I'd married Stuart, I'd been plain Poppy Smith.

'No. I didn't think it was right to give personal details without checking with you first. It was only a brief conversation, anyway.'

Brief? That was something, at least. For a moment there, I'd had a ghastly vision of the two of them nattering away about me.

'How is your painkiller research going?' I continued, in a feverish attempt to divert him.

My husband had taken another sip of hot chocolate, almost as if he was giving himself time to reply. 'Could be quite interesting,' he said. 'In fact, we've decided to write our own paper on it.'

'We?' I questioned, even though I knew perfectly well who he meant.

'Janine,' he said, in a casual way.

I was beginning to really dislike that name now. It made me think of a woman smelling of French flowery scent who flirts with other people's husbands. Of course, that's ridiculous. Names have nothing to do with behaviour. Do they? And if they did, what did 'Poppy' say about me? A tribute to someone who has fallen, perhaps? Or a drug to which someone might become addicted . . .

'So you'll be spending more time with each other, then?' I asked.

He shrugged. 'Probably.'

Then he'd changed the subject to Melissa's university applications. She'd already been offered a place to read English at Durham, which 'she would be crazy to turn down', according to Stuart. But Melissa herself was still holding out for drama school. 'If she's determined to be an actress,' I argued, 'she might be better off there.'

It seemed we couldn't agree on anything. 'Don't shout,' said Stuart at one point, looking around the coffee shop in embarrassment.

Was I shouting?

As soon as we got home that night, I'd taken my mobile into the bathroom with me and fired off an angry text to Matthew.

> How dare you go to see my
> husband like that?

His reply had come back instantly.

> I'll go to whichever dentist I want,
> Pops. It's a free country.

> Come on!

I'd texted back,

> You only did it to tell him you were
> an actor. You knew he might then
> tell you I was an actress too. The
> whole thing was just to try to wind
> me up.

> I told you, Pops. I'm not letting you
> go. You know you want me as much as
> I want you.

Not any more.

No, Matthew, I don't. You've got to
stop this now. Please.

There was no reply.

And now, here we are, playing happy families on
Christmas Day as if I haven't slept with another man at all
and as if my husband's relationship with this Janine is
perfectly above board. What have we done to our children? Supposing they find out about my night in the
Worthing hotel? Teenagers are so judgemental. They
might not want to live with me any more. They will choose
their father and Betty. I've had these fears before but they
are getting louder and louder in my head.

Fear and apprehension make me keep my mobile with
me all day long, even when I am bringing the turkey out
of the Aga along with the nut roast (Betty hasn't eaten
meat for years although she does have fish). I constantly
glance at it to see if Matthew has rung. But he hasn't. Of
course not. He'll be busy looking after Sandra.

As the day goes on, I stop checking the phone so often
and begin to relax. I ring Dad, who sounds decidedly
chipper for a change. 'I'm having a great time,' he says.
'Reg's wife brought over a whopping great plate of duck
with all the trimmings. Now I'm tucking into a box of
Quality Street in front of a good film. Why don't they
have more of those purple ones? That's what I'd like to
know.'

Is Reg's wife aware, I wonder, that I've asked Dad time
and time again to spend Christmas with us? I hope
so. Otherwise it looks as though I'm a neglectful daughter. Fleetingly, I wonder what my mother is doing right

231

now. After I'd ignored her earlier letters to me at drama school, there'd been a long gap. Mobile phones were expensive then and I couldn't afford one. So Mum was unable to reach me that way. Then, when I set up the agency, she'd started to send Christmas and birthday cards to me at our business PO box number. Perhaps she'd tracked me down online. (The details were, after all on our website.) But I always put the envelopes with the Australian stamps straight in the bin.

Too little, too late, I told myself. Besides, if I did open them, all the old hurt would come back and I wasn't sure I could cope with that. I might discover that she had children by the man she'd run off with. Maybe grandchildren. Doesn't she ever stop to think that she might have some over here too? The pain should have got less over the years, but it's become worse as Daisy and Melissa have grown older.

Put it out of your head, I tell myself. *She isn't worth it. Concentrate on the now, such as why Matthew hasn't rung or texted. Is he playing a game with me? Or has he accepted that I don't want any more to do with him?* I cross my fingers. Please let that be the case.

Boxing Day passes with a good family walk in the park. 'Isn't this nice?' says Betty, as Coco runs ahead. Yes. It is. Stuart has actually taken my hand, just as he had done during Christmas shopping. Would he really be doing this if he was having an affair? Or could it be guilt?

Still nothing from Matthew.

It's the same during the rest of the week. Everything is quiet. The emails drop off. The world has – as it always seems to do at this time of year – gone to ground. Stuart,

Daisy, Betty and I watch a feel-good DVD on New Year's Eve after I've taken Melissa to a party. (Another parent is going to bring her back.) I begin to breathe normally again.

Then on 2 January, my mobile rings. My chest pounds for a second until I see it's not Matthew. It's Sally. 'We've got a problem,' she says. Sally is unflappable. It's one of the reasons I took her on. But right now there's an edge to her voice. 'I've just had a legal letter. Doris is suing us for damages owing to lost work resulting from your negligence.'

'What?'

'I've been worried something like this might happen,' she says tightly.

So have I, ever since discovering – and confessing to Sally on the train home from Worthing – that my house insurance only covered me for 'clerical working' and not for visiting clients. But because Doris hadn't been in touch, and because so much else had been going on in my life, I'd pushed it to the back of my mind.

'You didn't tell me you'd sent Doris flowers after the accident.'

I gulp. I'd forgotten about that. 'It was before I knew she'd gone to A&E. They were really for her birthday.'

Sally's voice is tight. 'She's using that card you sent with the flowers as "evidence of our guilt". Apparently the message read: "Happy birthday! Hope your shoulder feels all right now."'

'That's ridiculous. I didn't mean it was our fault.'

'I know. But our lawyers think she might have a case.'

I go cold. 'And we're not insured.'

'Exactly.'

There's a distinct note of criticism in Sally's voice, which I've never heard before. My organized assistant wouldn't have made a mistake like this.

'I'm so sorry,' I gulp. 'I've had a lot of personal stuff going on. I know it's no excuse.'

There's a heavy silence.

'I've got a bad feeling about this,' she says at last.

So have I.

20

Betty

They found Jane's body the next morning, floating in the park pond, near where we used to meet. She must have taken her pills with her because the empty bottle was found on a bench nearby.

I might not have actually had sex with her husband, but I had killed my friend as surely as if I had put a knife into her.

I didn't know what to do during the days after Jane's death. When I plucked up the courage to ring and offer help, Gary sounded like he was in a daze. 'Jane's parents are here,' he said quietly, as if worried he was being over-heard. 'We've had the autopsy. The verdict was suicide by drowning and overdose due to imbalanced mind.'

I sensed the meaning behind his voice. So no one was blaming us, then. But they should.

'The funeral is next Wednesday,' he added.

I couldn't not go, even though I felt like a murderer attending her victim's burial. To my surprise, Jock came with me, although I didn't want him to. 'I must pay my respects too,' he said. 'We went to dinner at their place. People might think ill of me if I don't. I've asked your mother to have Stuart.'

We stood at the back. I felt as though I was going to be sick any minute and had to hold a tissue over my mouth. My body wouldn't stop shaking, as if I was a puppet with some invisible force yanking my strings up and down. I kept my head down. But every now and then I took quick looks up, expecting someone to turn on me, to point a finger in my direction and scream 'It was her. She did it.'

During the service, Jock unexpectedly reached for my hand. I was too numb to take mine away. I watched Alice weeping while Violet wriggled in her father's arms, knowing I had deprived those poor little girls of their mother.

'I'm so sorry,' said one of her neighbours as we left the church. 'You were really good to those kids, coming in every day like that.'

My chest tightened as I watched Jock's expression darken. 'Is that reet?' he said in a menacing voice that made me shiver inside.

'Yes,' said the woman who sometimes used to nod at me over the fence. 'We all used to say that Gary was very lucky to have a friend like you.'

She said the name 'Gary' with a meaningful emphasis. Not 'Gary and Jane'. Just 'Gary'.

My husband dragged me down the church path and out into the street, towards our flat. 'How long has this been going on for?'

'It's not what it sounds like,' I said, crossing my fingers at the lie. 'I just used to go in and help Jane out.'

'But I told you not to see her again.'

'She was my friend! I had to help her.'

'Had to get in there with that namby-pamby husband, more like.'

I had a flash of anger. 'He's more of a man than you are. He loved his wife and he made me feel needed.'

'I'll bet he did. Good in bed, was he?'

Another woman might have denied it; pointed out instead that my 'needed' remark referred to simply being there rather than infidelity. But the grief and guilt of Jane's death was all too much. We were at our door now. I went inside and flung myself on the sofa, weeping. 'It was only the once,' I sobbed. 'Neither of us meant it to happen. But Jane saw and . . . and she went out . . . and that's when she must have done it.'

Jock looked at me as though I was a piece of scum. 'You actually slept with him?' he asked slowly, repeating each word heavily.

My body literally juddered with fear. *Deny everything*, I told myself. But it was too late. Besides, I was tired of lying.

'Not exactly,' I whispered. 'We were just having a cuddle. We didn't . . . you know.'

'How bloody dare you!'

'I'm sorry,' I wept. 'I know it was wrong. Forgive me.'

He advanced towards me, his hands held out. For a minute, I thought he was going to strangle me. Instead, he seized the collar of my blouse.

'You are never,' he said slowly, 'to tell anyone about this, ever. Do you hear me? I'm not going to look like a fool in the eyes of everyone else.'

'Please, Jock, don't,' I begged. 'You're hurting me.'

His eyes bulged with rage but, to my relief, he let go. Then he threw me on the sofa and walked out. Only then did I try to analyse what he'd said. Jock was only worried about what others might say. He didn't seem to care that

I'd been unfaithful to him, partly because I was starved of love and kindness at home.

Later, after I'd picked up Stuart from Mum, I was on tenterhooks, wondering how he'd be when he came home. *If* he came home. I put our little boy to bed early. I made cottage pie for dinner, feeling queasy as I spooned the mashed potato on top, forking it into a criss-cross pattern. Then I sat, biting my nails, with one eye on the clock, and waited for the key to turn in the lock. It was gone 11 p.m. when Jock staggered in, clearly blind drunk.

'Your dinner's in the oven,' I said. 'It's still warm.'

He strode towards me. 'Don't hit me,' I begged, even though he'd never done so before.

'*Hit* you?' he repeated, his breath stinking of beer. 'I'm not that daft. People would see the bruises.'

Then he tore at my dress, which I'd only made the other week, ripping the seams and yanking it off me. 'Please don't,' I whimpered.

'I'll do what I bloody like,' he growled. 'You're mine. No one else's. And don't you ever forget it.'

Then he took me in such a rough, unkind way that it was more like making hate than love. There was nothing else but to grin and bear it. But afterwards, I lay awake all night, silently weeping.

I couldn't go on like this. I really couldn't. Yet in those days, Poppy, a woman was far more reliant on a man for money. How would Stuart and I survive? If it wasn't for my son, life would have had no meaning at all. But even with him, I felt so empty without Gary.

Then, shortly after the funeral, he came round. I was both shocked and – I have to admit this – glad to see his dear face again. 'You shouldn't be here,' I said, pulling him in through the door before one of the neighbours saw him.

'I can't help it,' he said. 'I feel so guilty about Jane . . .'

'So do I!'

'But I also know,' he added, 'that I lost the real Jane when she got ill after Alice. To be honest, she'd never really been the same since. All our friends abandoned us. When you came into our lives, everything changed.'

He took my hands. That same electric thrill as before shot through me. 'I've put the house on the market. The girls and I are going to move away. We're having a new start. Please, Betty, come with us, and bring your little boy. I miss you so much.'

Go with him? Maybe, one day, become Gary's wife? It was everything I had ever dreamed of. For a moment I was seized by the thought of what Jane would have said. But then again, maybe she'd have wanted me to! After all, her girls loved me. I would take care of them, I'd be their substitute mother. It would be my chance to atone for what I did.

But what would my husband say? Or do . . .

'I'll need to talk to Jock,' I gulped.

Gary looked worried. 'He won't hurt you, will he?'

'No,' I said, remembering what he'd said before about people spotting bruises. 'I don't think so.'

Hardly believing what I was doing, I asked Mum to have Stuart overnight and then, when he got in from work, I told Jock I needed to talk to him. I'd had enough of hiding things. I had to tell him the truth. He was late home and had clearly stopped off at the pub on the way.

'You want to leave me?' he hollered. 'With that fancy boy of yours?'

He walked up to me, his eyes glittering with fury, reeking of booze. His fists were raised.

Maybe he *was* going to hit me this time. 'Don't hurt me,' I whimpered.

'Oh I'm going to do that all right,' he snarled, 'but not in the way you think. If you walk out and take our bairn with you, I'll fight you tooth and nail to get my son back. Do you honestly think that any court in this land will give custody to a woman who was unfaithful to her husband and made her so-called friend top herself?'

I began to shake. It had never occurred to me that Jock might fight me for custody, Poppy. It sounds naive, I know, but you have to remember that leaving your husband in those days wasn't as common as it is now. I didn't know much about the law and whether it would be on my side or not.

'If you want to keep our kid, you'll stay here with me,' thundered Jock. 'And like I said before, you won't breathe a word of this to anyone.'

I don't know why but I felt a flash of bravery then. 'Just so you can save face, you mean?' I retorted.

Jock snorted. 'The same goes for you too. How do you think others are going to treat you when you set up home with a man you're not married to. Cos sure as eggs is eggs, I'm not going to give you a divorce without a fight. What's it going to be like for Stuart, growing up without both his mum and dad?'

He was right, I realized. You might not think it after the so-called Swinging Sixties, but some people's lives were still very traditional in the mid-seventies. I couldn't do this to my little boy.

The following day, I called in on Gary, even though I knew I was running a huge risk of being seen by one of the neighbours. But what I had to say was too important for a phone call.

'Betty!' he said, his face lighting up.

'Let me in, quickly, before someone spots us,' I said, heaving the pushchair in through the front door. Then I looked around. 'Where are the children?'

'Both having a nap.'

Stuart was sleeping too.

Gary pulled me towards him but I gently extracted myself.

'I'm sorry,' I said, fighting back my tears. 'I've come round in person to say I can't come with you.'

His face crumpled but at the same time I could see a touch of relief crossing his eyes. 'I understand,' he said. 'To be honest, I'm not sure now that I can either. I feel so guilty about Jane.'

'Me too.' My words came out in one great sob. 'I can't see you ever again. It just wouldn't be right.' Unable to stop myself, I buried my head in his chest. 'I'll never forget you,' I whispered.

His hands stroked my hair. Then he cupped my face with both hands and looked down on me with such love that I thought my very heart would crack with pain. 'And I will never forget you either, Betty.'

'Goodbye,' I said, breaking away. *You've done the right thing*, I told myself as I ran back down his road, my head bowed over the pushchair. Now I could make a fresh start and – somehow – try to get my marriage back on track.

For the next few days and then weeks, I threw myself into being the best wife and mother I could. I took particular care over making Jock's meals. I told him exactly where I'd been that day. I polished and dusted our horrible little flat until it gleamed.

But Jane continued to haunt me. She still does. If it hadn't been for me, she might still be alive. I committed a sin. One day, I vowed to myself, I would find a way to pay for it.

And that, Poppy, is where you come in.

21

Poppy

It's the beginning of a new year and everyone is talking about 'fresh starts', the way they always do in early January. But there's a black cloud hanging over me with Doris's law suit.

It won't be long before everyone knows. This is an industry where people don't hesitate to pass on gossip. And even if Doris doesn't win, our good name will be damaged. I've made a mistake by inviting a client into my home for work purposes without being insured. Our rivals will have a field day. I also feel terribly hurt. Doris had been more than a client. She'd become a friend. Of course, I feel terrible that she had an accident because of me. But I never expected her to sue.

'We're going to have to see a lawyer,' Sally tells me. She's had some experience in this field; it's another of the reasons I hired her.

More expense. And straight on the heels of Christmas, too.

The good news is that I still haven't heard anything from Matthew. I'm pretty sure he's got the message. Never, ever, will I be so stupid again. *Maybe I should spend more time with the girls*, I tell myself, sending one more 'I've got just the right person for you' email to a casting director who is looking for men between twenty and thirty with bald heads. After all, tomorrow they go back to school. Melissa will be leaving home for uni before this year is out. I need to make the most of them.

Meanwhile, Stuart is meeting this Janine again to 'work on' the paper they're writing. He's actually got a locum to cover his patients. He only does this if something really important comes up or – once – when he had acute laryngitis.

I don't want to think about it. Head in sand? Maybe. But also I feel I have no right to pry. Not after Matthew.

I realize I've been staring at my emails for ages while all these thoughts are going round my head. This is no good. I need to concentrate on the parts of my life that really matter. I make my way downstairs.

'How about going roller skating?' I suggest to the girls, who are on their iPads.

I expect them to turn it down like they had done with my bowling idea the other week, but everyone's enthusiastic – especially Betty. 'I used to do that with my workmates when I was young,' she said.

So off we go, leaving Coco with plenty of water and food after having taken her for a walk first.

'Watch out, Gran!' yells Melissa as she skates past.

'Cheeky!' calls back my mother-in-law. 'Just wait until I catch you up!'

I have to hand it to Betty. There aren't many seventy-year-olds who can zip along on rollers without fear of falling over. Then again, she likes to keep active. She does hot yoga once a week and also Pilates. 'It's all part of staying young,' she tells me.

Daisy and I are a bit slower but it gives us time to be together. 'I love Coco so much,' she says. 'Do you think we could keep her?'

'But she belongs to your teacher.'

'Yes, but maybe we could ask if she'll give her to us. She loves me too, Mum. You can see from the way she jumps up at me so she can be on my lap. I'm the only one she wants to be with.'

'Let's think about it, shall we?'

That was parent-speak for 'definitely not'!

Later, in the cafe, I give the girls some money to buy smoothies. 'It's been good to have time together,' says Betty, patting my hand. 'You ought to do the same with Stuart. Why not go down to the caravan together soon? Just the two of you, without the girls. It's your twentieth anniversary coming up, isn't it? You could celebrate it there.'

The caravan is something that she and Jock had bought when Stuart was a teenager and they had a bit more money. It's in a picturesque part of Devon. They'd originally gone there for their honeymoon apparently.

Why not? We certainly weren't going to have a party! We hardly have time for friends any more, apart from Sally, and since she works for me she doesn't really count. Stuart occasionally meets up with an old uni chum for a drink but that's it. It's all we can do to fit in work and children.

Yet the very thought of being alone with my husband on holiday fills me with guilt as well as trepidation. What would we talk about without the girls?

'Think about it,' Betty says, patting my hand. 'You know, marriages take as much work as parenting, if not more. I should know.'

I look up, surprised. Stuart had always made out that his parents had had an idyllic marriage, and they'd certainly seemed a 'together' couple when I knew them, even though Jock had a rough manner about him that was very different from his wife's. But before I can question her, Betty says 'Ah. Here are the girls. Ooh, look. Lovely. Cream on top too!'

I suddenly realize I haven't checked my phone since taking it out of the changing locker. There's the usual stream of emails but nothing that can't wait until I'm back. Sally hasn't left a message, which means she hasn't got through to the lawyer yet to book an appointment. There's nothing more from Matthew (phew!) or any missed calls from Dad. Nothing from Stuart either. It would be nice, I thought, to have a husband who calls at lunchtime to see how we are doing.

'Got to go to the loo,' I say.

But before I can get up, my mobile rings. It's an unknown number. 'Mrs Page?'

'Yes?' Maybe this is the lawyer after all.

'This is the Accident and Emergency department of Worthing Hospital. Your father has asked us to ring you. I'm afraid he's had an accident.'

'What?'

'Nothing too serious. The X-ray shows he's sprained his left ankle. But he's a bit shaky, so he had problems dialling your number.'

'How did he do it?'

'I'll put you on to him, shall I?'

There's an urgent voice in the background ('Doctor needed here!') while she hands the phone over, and then I hear Dad's voice.

'Poppy?'

Dad doesn't sound like his usual grumpy self. He sounds frail. As though he is the child and I am the parent. 'I fell down the step by the front door.'

He says each word slowly and carefully, almost as though he's repeating words from a script.

'How did you do that?'

'I don't know. I suppose I just slipped. It's been a bit icy down here.'

I'd been telling him for ages that he needed a handrail.

'How did you get help?'

His voice falters again. 'A man walking past saw me and called the ambulance.'

Thank heavens for that. The thought of Dad lying in the freezing cold on his doorstep doesn't bear thinking about.

'What's wrong?' mouths Betty.

'Tell you in a minute,' I mouth back.

'I'm on my way down, Dad. Do you mind if I ring Reg so he can pick you up and stay with you at home until I can get there?'

'That's all right.'

Dad must be feeling rough if he isn't objecting.

I fill Betty in. 'I might have to stay the night,' I tell her. 'Dad will just have to put up with me in the bungalow until I can arrange some care. Or maybe I'll find a hotel again.'

'Don't you worry,' she says. 'We'll manage.'

'Is Grandad going to be all right?' asks Daisy.

'He'll be fine,' I say with far more certainty than I feel.

'Do you want me to come too?' asks Melissa.

'Nice try,' I say, in an effort to inject some lightness. 'You've got school tomorrow.'

'We'll all go back to the house together now,' says Betty, gathering our stuff. 'Then your mum can pack a bag and get going.'

I give her a grateful hug. Thank heavens for my family. Whatever would I do without them?

22

Betty

I tried to carry on for Stuart's sake, but Jane gave me no peace. She talked to me in my dreams. Sometimes she screamed at me. Sometimes she said she understood. Then, when I woke up, red and raw from Jock's 'lovemaking' the night before ('Did he kiss you like this? Are you telling me the truth when you say you didn't have sex? Tell me, you bitch. Tell me!'), my husband gave me the silent treatment. He also looked at me as if I was no better than the rubbish in the overflowing dustbins outside.

I could barely eat for grief and guilt. I kept wondering what Jane's body would have looked like when they'd pulled her out of the pond. Suddenly, the very sight of meat made me feel sick. I couldn't touch the stuff. Jock didn't even comment. It was indicative of how little attention he paid me, except in bed, where he constantly told me that I was 'his' and no one else's.

Often I started to dial Gary's number but then stopped. What was the point? One day, however, I couldn't bear it any longer so I let it ring. Someone answered after a while. 'Hello?' she said.

For a minute I thought it was Jane herself. But then I realized – it was her mother. Swiftly, I put the phone down again. To my horror, it started ringing. Maybe she was calling me back. I didn't answer. Then I lived in fear of her doing it again when Jock was in.

Luckily, she didn't.

A few weeks later, when I thought I might be going out of my mind, I took Stuart for a walk up near Jane's house. There was a SOLD sign outside. Removal vans were taking furniture out. I couldn't help myself. I ran up to the open front door. Two men came out carrying a double bed. The one on which Gary and I had had such passionate kisses. The reason for Jane's death.

'Is the owner still here?' I said desperately.

'Sorry, love. You've just missed him.'

Where had he gone? There was no way of knowing. I cried all the way home. Stuart started to cry too, as if he knew I was upset. Maybe he missed his old playmate, Violet.

Then Jock started to come home late, reeking of cheap perfume. It was nothing like the one that Jane had worn and which I, to my shame, had borrowed. This one churned my stomach. 'What's that smell?' I asked.

Part of me thought that maybe it was one of those fancy sprays to take away the stink in a loo. Perhaps the factory had upped its standards. But my husband gave me a cold look. 'What smell?' he said challengingly.

I wrinkled my nose. 'The sickly stench that's coming off you.' I took the polyester brown check jacket he'd bought recently because he needed to look smart now he was 'rising up the management ladder' and sniffed it. 'Ugh.'

Jock whipped it off me. 'Nothing wrong with that! Just because you've got high-and-mighty views on what people should and shouldn't wear. 'Sides, it's my business what I smell like after what you did with that Gary.'

And then I got it. 'You've been with a woman,' I said slowly.

'So what if I have?'

Jock was sitting at the kitchen table now, his hands unwashed, waiting for me to put dinner in front of him. Stuart, who was one and a half then, was in the pyjamas I'd made for him myself. I ought to have put him to bed, especially if an argument was about to break out. But I couldn't help myself. 'Who is she?' I demanded.

He laughed. 'You think you have a right to ask? Just count yourself lucky that I'm still here.'

His old fear that I might leave him now seemed to have gone. Instead he took pleasure in threatening to leave me instead.

As if on cue, Stuart toddled up to him. 'Dad, Dad,' he chanted. He'd got most of his baby teeth through now but there was a big gap between the front two that I couldn't help worrying about.

'If it wasn't for the bairn,' said my husband coldly, 'I'd have gone long ago. But a lad needs two parents.'

'You mean you couldn't look after him yourself,' I found myself retorting.

He shook his head. 'Maybe not. But that's not to say another woman couldn't – or wouldn't.'

A cold feeling snaked through me.

'Think about it, Betty. Supposing this scent did belong to another woman? What if that woman wanted to take me on – and my lad too? Do you really think any court of law would take your side over mine after what you've done?'

'Don't,' I said, collapsing on a chair. I didn't know which was worse – my guilt over Jane's death or the fear that Jock might change his mind and decide he wanted to divorce me after all. What if the judge really did give Stuart to him? I wouldn't want to live any more. Was that what Jane had feared when she'd seen me and Gary? Did it cross her troubled mind that her husband might leave and that the courts would give the children to me and him, declaring her to be an 'unfit' mother? I can't bear to think about it.

'At the moment,' said Jock, setting Stuart down gently, 'I'm prepared to carry on, but only on my terms. And if I come home smelling of someone else, that's my business. Now what's for supper? I'm starving.'

His words brought on a deeper, darker despair– worse than I'd ever felt before. But then a voice popped into my head. '*It's no more than you deserve.*'

Where had that come from? A shiver ran right down my spine. It sounded so like Jane! As you know, Poppy, I've become quite interested in mediumship and meditation therapies as I've got older. Why shouldn't we be able to hear those who have been so important to us after they've passed on? But I'll be honest. Jane's voice freaked me out.

To stop myself going crazy, I tried to follow my mother's advice by gritting my teeth and getting on with life.

I ignored the cheap smells on Jock's clothes. I took no notice of the pink frilly pants I found in the back pocket of his trousers or the packet of condoms in his jacket. I pretended to be flattered by his advances at night.

I didn't hear Jane's voice for a while after that. But she continued to visit me nightly in my dreams. Yet, to my disappointment and shame, she didn't say anything. Just looked at me. And when I said I was sorry, she would turn away.

Central Criminal Court, London

The woman on the stand is looking as if every ounce of strength has been drained from her.

The barrister appears puzzled in an exaggerated way. It's as though she is alerting the jury to a conundrum that she cannot solve herself. A theatrical gesture, perhaps?

Barristers are not dissimilar to actors. They both know how to make their presence swell to fill a stage. They both know how to tell a good tale. But a barrister is meant to do so for the sake of the truth. An actor is expected to elaborate it through mannerisms and voice in order to make the plot more interesting. Sometimes it's hard to tell the difference.

'There's something that is troubling me, Mrs Page,' says the barrister, leaning forward.

The air is tight. Taut. Expectant. Each juror is listening keenly.

'If you wanted to get Matthew Gordon out of your life "for ever" as you've just admitted, why did you agree to meet up with him again?'

23

Poppy

I can drive down to Dad's now that the car has been repaired but the traffic is terrible and I wish, with hindsight, I'd taken the train. I could at least have caught up with emails then. Instead, I'm going to have to find time to do that later on. Right now, it all seems endless. A bit like trying to catch water in a sieve.

Still, at least I'll be able to take him for a run later on this afternoon if he wants one. Poor Dad. It's no fun to have a twisted ankle when you're in your seventies. Despite the law suit, it makes me feel even guiltier about Doris, who is no spring chicken herself. If only I'd had that carpet replaced or Betty hadn't moved the chesterfield in order to vacuum properly . . .

It takes my father an age to open the door and I am shocked by how frail and haggard he has become in the short time since I last saw him. Perhaps it's the pain. 'Thanks for coming,' he says quietly.

I give him a cuddle. 'I'm sorry you're hurt,' I say as he then limps his way over to the sofa.

'It was a silly accident,' he puffs, sitting down heavily. 'If I hadn't fallen over my slippers, it would have been all right.'

Did I hear him right? 'You said you fell on the door-step,' I point out.

He looks embarrassed. 'I did. I landed on it after tripping over my slippers.'

'What were you doing in them outside?'

'Answering the door, of course. What is this? A bloody inquisition?'

He's getting cross now, as if I should know this.

'And who was there?'

'Kids.' He waves his arm dismissively. 'Playing pranks, they were. Ringing the doorbell and then running off. Their parents should be ashamed of themselves.'

'And then someone walking past helped you out?'

'What?'

'That's what you told me,' I say patiently. 'He called the ambulance, you said.'

'That's right. Actually it was a woman.'

I'm sure Dad said it was a man.

'We ought to thank her.'

'Well, I don't know where she lives, do I? Stop going on about it, Poppy. I've sprained my ankle and that's the end of it. It's not like I've broken my neck. But it is a flipping nuisance, I grant you. Are you going to stay down here for a few nights to help me out?'

Dad might be making light of his injury but he's obviously worried. It can't be easy. Yet a 'few nights' is longer than I was envisaging. I'm not sure I can leave my family for that long. Or my business.

'I would if I could,' I say, thinking about the appointment with the lawyer that Sally has now made for the following day. 'But I've got to get back tomorrow.'

Dad's face falls. It reminds me of Daisy's when I say she can't do something. I've more or less given up with Melissa, who does what she pleases. Not surprising, really. She's a young woman now. Almost the same age as I was when I fell hook, line and sinker for Matthew Gordon.

'But I've found a care agency,' I add brightly, to hide my apprehension at his reaction. 'I spoke to this really nice woman who's going to send someone round twice a day to cook you a meal and check you're all right.'

That was something I'd organized when I'd stopped for a break while travelling down. I expected Dad to object but instead he merely nodded. 'OK.'

Things must be bad. Whenever I'd suggested help before, he'd gone ballistic.

'Would you like me to take you out for a little drive?'

'What's the point?' he scoffs. 'I'd rather stay in the warm. Maybe you could just stay and keep me company. I'd like that.'

He keeps glancing at the window as if he's expecting someone.

'Of course. You seem worried about something, Dad.'

'Too bloody true.'

Dad hardly ever swears. 'I've twisted my ankle, haven't I? I'm in pain. And now my only daughter tells me that she can't be bothered to hang around for more than a night to help me.'

My heart sinks. 'The thing is, Dad, I've got a few problems at work that need sorting out.'

He makes a batting motion as if he doesn't want to know the details. 'You can sleep on the sofa tonight if you want, instead of going to a hotel.'

He speaks as though he is doing me a favour. But I can tell it's because he wants me nearby. Though, of course, that's fine.

That night, as Dad and I sit and watch an old film together (he's selected something called *The Scarlet Woman*, which is, in view of the dire mess I've got myself in, rather ironic), my mobile rings. Daisy's name flashes up. What's happened now? My heart thuds so loudly that it's like having a pneumatic drill inside my chest. It's been doing this when my phone goes off ever since the night of the Christmas party.

'How's everything going?' I ask.

Daisy's voice is tight, the way it gets when she's apprehensive. 'There's something I've got to know, Mum.'

I can hardly breathe for fear. She's found out about Matthew. Or maybe she suspects. She wants to know if I could really have done the unthinkable . . .

'Sorry, Dad,' I say, leaping up. 'I've got to take this.'

He frowns. 'Well, don't be long. We're getting to the good bit.'

I slip into the kitchen. 'What is it?' I ask.

'I know you said you wouldn't but . . .'

'What is it, Daisy?' I'm aware that the fear in my voice is sounding like impatience.

I can see my life disintegrating before my eyes. By the time I get back, Stuart will have changed the locks. Tell me I'm no longer welcome there. The girls will look at me through the windows with hate on their faces . . .

'Would you let us keep Coco for ever? Madame Blanche has just called to say she's not coming back because she's getting divorced and she's asked if we can keep the dog. Please say yes!'

The relief is so intense that I almost slump to the floor.

'Mum? Are you there?'

'Yes.'

'Yes you're there or yes we can have Coco?'

All the tension that's been building up has made me irritable. 'Of course we can't. We've got enough to cope with as it is. Ask your father. He'll tell you the same.'

Daisy's voice is desperate. 'But Dad says we can keep Coco if you agree. He's here. Right now. Speak to him. PLEEASE.'

My husband's voice comes on the line. 'Hi. How's it going with your dad?'

'How can you have promised her this without discussing it with me?' I hiss, ignoring his question.

'I didn't.' His voice is calm. Rational. Steady. I want to throttle him. Figuratively speaking, of course. 'I said you needed to agree, Poppy.'

Why is it that when people use your name – especially when it's not actually necessary – you feel as though they are in control of you?

'But the fact that you said she could if *I* agree makes me look like the baddy if I say we can't.'

'I don't see it that way,' he says. 'Anyway, have you considered the fact that a dog might give the girls some comfort during a tricky time.'

My skin starts to break out into goosebumps. What is he talking about? Has he found out about Matthew? Is he about to tell me he's leaving me for Janine?

'What do you mean?' I say. 'What "tricky time"?'

There's a short laugh. 'I know you've been busy at work, Poppy. But surely you haven't forgotten about their exams.'

For the second time I just about manage to keep myself from sighing with relief. 'Of course I haven't.'

'There's been quite a lot of medical research to say that animals can help people deal with pressure.'

'What about me?' I demand. 'A dog will just be adding to my to-do list. I'll be the one who ends up walking it.'

I feel my voice rising, aware that I sound overwrought. My husband, on the other hand, is talking as though he is a doctor in charge of an unstable patient who needs to see reason. 'The girls will do their share. It will teach them responsibility. And Mum says she'll help out.'

'It sounds as though you've got it all sorted, then.'

'There's no need to be sarcastic.'

'Poppy,' Dad calls from the living room. 'Are we watching this film or not?'

'I won't be long,' I call back, putting on a brighter voice. I might not be an actress any more but I've kept some of my tricks.

'I've got to go,' I say down the phone. 'My father needs me.'

'We all do.'

Is there a hint of accusation in his voice?

'I'm doing my best, Stuart.' Tears sting my eyes. 'I'm at my wits' end here.'

'I know.' His voice becomes irritatingly soothing. 'That's why we need that break in Devon. I've booked the time off.'

I'd completely forgotten about that. Forgotten about our twentieth wedding anniversary too, to be honest.

'That's great,' I say, trying to sound as though I had remembered all along. 'I'll try and make sure my diary is clear too.'

'Well, only if it's not too inconvenient,' says Stuart.

If I didn't know my husband better, I might think *he* was being sarcastic as he had accused me earlier. But Stuart says what he thinks. It's another reason I fell for him in the first place. You knew where you were with him. Then I think of his conversations on the phone with Janine and I wonder if this is still true.

'Of course it's not too inconvenient,' I say deliberately. 'I want to go.'

'Good. Mum will look after the girls.'

For the umpteenth time I ask myself how we'd ever manage without Betty.

Meanwhile, Dad's grumbles are getting louder.

'I've got to go now,' I say.

'Of course. Give my best to your dad. How's he doing?'

'Not fantastic,' I say. 'He –'

But then there's a click. Stuart has hung up.

'Hello?' I say blankly, even though I know he's gone. I ring again. It's engaged. It continues that way until I give up. Something doesn't feel right.

I help Dad to bed when the film has ended but I can't help worrying about how he's going to manage when I leave tomorrow. What if he has another fall in between the carer's visits? I decide to ring Reg in the morning and see if he can come round too. There's a blip on my phone. It's a text from Stuart.

Sorry. Reception was bad and
then I had to take a work call.
Sleep well x

After a night tossing and turning on Dad's sofa, I'm woken by the mobile at 6.30 a.m. I swear that if it's Daisy with some nonsense about that dog, I'll . . .

But it's a withheld number.

'Yes?' I say sleepily.

'Pops!'

My chest starts to thump.

'Just wanted to wish you luck.'

'What do you mean?'

His voice is jaunty. Chatty, even, with a low sinister threat. 'Your meeting today. A little bird tells me you're getting legal advice on poor Doris's case.'

This makes no sense. 'How on earth do you know?'

'Ah.' I can almost hear Matthew smiling down the phone. 'You've underestimated me, Pops. People talk in this business. All you have to do is keep your ear to the ground. Then again, you made it so easy for me! After you told me about Doris fracturing her shoulder, I gave her a little ring to offer my condolences. We met briefly at the Christmas party, if you remember. Lovely woman, isn't she? Told me all about your worn carpet. You tripped yourself up there, didn't you Pops, if you'll forgive the pun. Naturally, poor Doris was very upset that she wouldn't be able to work for some time. I suggested that she might have a case against you. After all, your home office was unsafe, wasn't it? So I advised her to go to a lawyer and check out her rights.'

I listen, scarcely able to believe what I'm hearing.

'Of course, Doris said that she'd never sue you. "We're more like friends," she said. So I just set her mind at ease. Told her it wouldn't be you paying out. You'd have insurance that would cover you. In fact, it wouldn't really affect you much at all, apart, perhaps, from raising your premium next time you renew.'

My mind shoots back to that evening in the Worthing hotel when I'd been foolish enough to confide my worries to Matthew, including Doris's accident and other details.

'*Tripped on worn carpet. usually hidden by the chesterfield . . . don't have public liability insurance . . . our home insurance might not cover it . . .*'

How stupid I'd been to tell him all this!

'Who else knows about this?' I thundered.

'I might have mentioned it to another agency I'm dealing with. It's run by a woman called Sharon. She was most interested. Didn't sound as though she liked you very much, actually.'

I close my eyes. I picture Sharon and her shapeless navy dress and our last terse conversation at the Christmas party. The news will have spread like wildfire: *Poppy Page has messed up big time. It doesn't look good.*

'Why are you doing this to me?' I wail.

There is silence for a moment. I can hear Dad calling out. 'Poppy? Are you up? I need to go to the bathroom. Can you help me?'

'Won't be a minute, Dad,' I call out, trying to sound like everything is fine.

'You weren't listening to me, Pops. I had to do something to get your attention. But hopefully now you'll start being sensible and we can talk. I'll text you a time and place.'

And before I can say anything, the line has gone dead.

24

Betty

The only answer was just to get on with life. It's what I'd been brought up to do. So I prepared Jock's meals, cleaned our dingy flat and took care of Stuart, whose chubby arms around my neck were some consolation. But guilt and misery were making me ill. I stopped eating. My scalp began to itch and soon my skin broke out into painful red sores. The doctor diagnosed psoriasis. I woke, sitting up straight with a start, every morning at 4 a.m. Then I'd tiptoe into our son's bedroom to check he was still breathing. For some reason, I became consumed by the fear that he might die. I'd lean over his cot, terrified of what I might find there.

But his little chest always rose and fell steadily.

People began to remark about my thinness. 'You've gone all scrawny,' said Jock when he came on to me. 'It's disgusting.'

'At least you've got your other women to keep you satisfied then,' I almost said. But I bit the comment back. I guessed there must be more than one because the perfumes on his shirt kept changing.

Then one day when Stuart and I were round at my mother's, she declared she wanted a 'little word' with me.

'Don't worry about the lad,' she said, waving her hand at her grandson. 'He's all right in front of the telly for a bit.'

I wondered what she was going to say. Her face was set as she pulled up a kitchen chair to sit down. 'I'm going to come straight out with it. Your Jock has been with another woman.'

'I know,' I said.

Her eyes widened. 'You know? And what are you doing about it?'

'I am getting on with my marriage,' I said curtly. 'Like you told me.'

'I didn't mean you to turn a blind eye to a prostitute.'

I stared at her. 'What?'

'He's been seen coming out of that place in Cross Lane.'

I knew the bar. Everybody did. It was notorious.

She put her hand out and patted mine in a rare display of affection. 'You need to be careful, lass. You might pick up something.'

I thought of how I'd itched after Jock had last touched me. He refused to wear a condom (or a rubber johnnie as we sometimes called them then), insisting that birth control was my problem. Instead, I'd grappled with the Dutch cap. But it was far from foolproof. 'What shall I do?' I asked.

'Better get yourself checked out – but not by our doctor. Go somewhere where no one knows us. There are clinics, aren't there?'

I was surprised my mother was so knowledgeable.

When I got home, I went through the Yellow Pages, barely able to keep my fingers from shaking. There was something called the Brook Advisory Centre in central London, so I picked up the phone and made an appointment, wondering what on earth I was doing. Afterwards, I panicked. I hardly ever went 'up West'. What if one of Jock's friends saw me getting on the 38 bus? So I wore an old hat pulled over my face. Mum had agreed to look after Stuart.

When I got there, I had to walk on round the block to summon up the nerve to go in. Then, when I did, I sat in the reception hiding behind a magazine. By the time I saw the doctor, I was a bag of nerves. To my embarrassment, I found myself bursting into tears on the couch during the examination. 'Is there anything you'd like to tell me?' she asked. 'Don't worry, it's all totally confidential here.'

She seemed so warm and kind and understanding that I found myself telling her everything – including my guilt over Jane, which made me put up with Jock's treatment. 'It sounds like you have a lot on your plate,' she said. 'I can put you in touch with a counsellor if you want.'

But I politely declined. I felt bad enough having told her already.

Then I went back for the test results. 'Good news,' she said. 'You're clear. But I'd advise you to make sure that your husband gets tested too.'

She clearly didn't know Jock. He'd go nuts if I suggested such a thing.

'You know,' said Mum when I told her. 'It's not such a bad idea. Sometimes men like yours act all tough but are more vulnerable than they seem deep down. Tell him he was seen in Cross Lane. Tell him you were itchy and got yourself checked out. Pretend you've got something but that it's treatable. Make sure you say the doctor says it's fairly recent, so he can't blame you.'

'What do you mean?' I said, picking up Stuart to give him a cuddle but really to hide my blushes.

'Don't go all coy with me, girl. People talk. One of the women at bingo is the mother of that girl who worked for your fancy man.'

'Dawn from the agency?'

'That's the one. Wasn't very happy when she was told she wasn't needed no more. Apparently, when she went round to get a jumper she'd left behind, she saw you and that fella Gary through the window. "Standing very close to each other," was how she put it. So she left the jumper and went back another time. "I had my suspicions before they got rid of me," she said.'

My mother gave me one of her looks. 'His wife was a friend of yours before she died, wasn't she?'

I went even redder. 'Then why didn't you say anything?'

'Maybe because I could see you weren't happy with that husband of yours.'

'But you told me I had to keep my marriage together.'

'That was before I realized what kind of a man you'd saddled yourself with.' She sniffed. ''Sides, times are changing. It's different now from my day. But you still don't want to end up raising a kid on your own. It's too bloody tough.'

I could hardly believe her words. Mum was the last person I'd expected to show sympathy.

'And getting involved with a married bloke was just damn stupid. His poor wife.'

I wanted to be sick. 'I don't want to talk about it,' I whispered.

'I'm not surprised. You can't bring the woman back from the dead. But there's still time to fix the mess you're in right now. All you have to do is tell that Jock of yours that the doctor said he needs to get himself tested. He won't like that. But he'll have to. Even if he's clear, it might make him think a bit more carefully about playing away in the future. You might also remind him that if any of this got out, it wouldn't look too good for his reputation.'

I hadn't realized my mother could be so calculating. But she might be on to something here.

For the first time, I felt the power balance in my marriage shift. That night I made one of Jock's favourite dinners – pork chops and chips. I got Stuart into bed before his father came home. Both had been Mum's suggestions.

After Jock had finished his meal, he seemed in a better mood than he had for weeks. I took a deep breath. 'I went to a clinic today,' I told him.

His eyes narrowed. 'What kind of a clinic?'

'It provides contraception.'

'You get the cap from our GP, don't you?'

I tried to steady my voice and hide my nerves. 'The thing is, this clinic also does sexual health tests.'

He leaned forward. 'A VD clinic? Are you trying to tell me that that Gary gave you something? I'll track him down and wring his bleeding neck.'

'I've told you,' I said truthfully. 'We didn't . . . we didn't do it. If you really want to know, I've got thrush. But when I told the doctor what you'd been up to, she strongly advised that you got yourself checked out.'

He rose to his feet, his face contorted with fury. 'What the fuck do you mean?'

'Don't play innocent, Jock. You were seen! You were spotted coming out of that brothel in Cross Lane.'

He looked winded, as if I'd just kneed him in the groin. His face went bright scarlet too.

'Just imagine what the big boss at the factory would say if he knew you'd been visiting prostitutes,' I continued. 'He's a real family man, isn't he? Doesn't look good if his foreman is doing that.'

Now Jock was going pale. I watched fear flash across his face at the thought of all his promotion plans going out of the window. As I knew all too well, the worst thing that could happen to my husband was being criticized or made a fool of.

But now I had the upper hand.

'So here's what's going to happen, Jock,' I said. 'First, you're doing to get tested.'

'There's no bloody way I'm going to the pox doctor,' he scoffed. 'Like I'm going to be humiliated that way.'

'You'll be more humiliated if I decide to tell my dad about what you've been up to. I reckon people at the factory would talk, don't you? I might even get custody of our son if I divorced you for adultery.'

His jaw dropped and his very body seemed to shrink into itself. Suddenly my husband had become a small boy.

'You can go to a clinic where no one knows you, just like I did,' I continue firmly. 'There are things they can do.'

He didn't say anything and I took his silence as agreement.

'And then we're going to have an arrangement, you and I.'

I waited dramatically. He continued to stare at me.

'Play around as much as you like with other women. I'd advise you for your sake to stay well clear of any brothels, although it's your business. But I never, ever, want you touching me again.'

Still he said nothing.

'Is that a "yes", Jock?' I said coolly, though my heart was thudding.

Even though his head was bowed, I saw him nod.

Then I stood up and walked out of the room.

25

Poppy

I've been dreading going down to the caravan in Devon. I simply can't afford the time away from work. There are always emails to answer and people to chase. Then there's the worry about Doris, which is all my fault. The lawyer, whom Sally is liaising with, is still working out 'how we should play it'.

Meanwhile, the thing that's pressing on my mind more than anything is waiting for Matthew to text me with a 'time and place'. So far there's been nothing.

I try to hide all my worries as we drive down. Passing Stonehenge, I glance at the ancient stones, wondering if the people who used to worship there had their own tangled personal lives. My heart begins to thud again. What am I even doing here? I fall silent. Stuart, on the other hand, becomes increasingly talkative as we get nearer.

'Mum and Dad came here for their honeymoon,' he says enthusiastically, as if he hasn't already told me this before. 'It's rather nice that we're celebrating such a special anniversary in the same place, isn't it?'

But what if he wants sex? *The subject probably won't come up*, I tell myself. It's not as though he's been interested for ages. But then again, it is our anniversary. It would be strange if it wasn't on his mind. At times, I cannot believe we've been married twenty years.

Before Matthew, I might have been as excited as Stuart about the holiday. But now I feel so guilty. To make it worse, an old schoolfriend of mine has just been posting on Facebook about her wedding anniversary cruise and what a great time they're having. The pictures of them arm in arm, clearly besotted with each other, makes me feel my life is a complete sham.

Then we round a bend and I gasp at the sea glistening below and the huge rocks rising out of the water. It's been so long since we've been down here that I'd forgotten how stunning it is.

When the girls were small, we came down quite a lot. We used to explore the beach and visit all the local spots like A La Ronde (a stunning octagonal National Trust property) and Paignton Zoo. But as they got bigger, the caravan felt too small, and then Melissa started asking why we couldn't go abroad like all her friends. So somehow the caravan just sat here. Stuart paid for someone to go in every now and then to check it was all right.

Now, as we get out at the caravan site, I breathe in the clean air and marvel at the light dancing off the sea. My body relaxes as if someone has turned off the stress switch. I feel a surprising sense of peace. We unlock the door, open the windows to let out the musty air and put on the kettle. It's really rather cosy.

'How about a walk?' says Stuart. 'I could do with a stretch after that long drive.'

Automatically, we head past the shop, down the slope past the fishermen's nets and straight for the sea. 'Go on,' says my husband, kicking off his shoes. 'Let's have a paddle.'

As the water washes over my feet (freezing, but strangely exhilarating!), I reflect that it's been ages since we did something that was actually fun instead of part of the family curriculum.

'I'll cook some supper, shall I?' I say as we walk back.

'Maybe later,' he replies, putting an arm around my shoulder.

What? Stuart hasn't touched me since he held my hand during Christmas shopping. I feel both guilty because of Matthew and also relieved. Does this mean my husband *does* care for me after all?

His hand is massaging my shoulder, the way it used to in the days when we were closer. I should feel flattered. Isn't this what I'd been wanting for the last three years? But now I'm deeply uncomfortable. We break apart when I open the door and head towards the cooker.

Then I feel his arms around my waist from the back. 'Supper can wait, can't it?'

'What's brought this on?' I say, turning round.

'What do you mean?' he says.

'Come on,' I say. 'It's not as though you show me much affection any more.'

'And nor do you.'

It's true.

His eyes are on mine. It would be so easy to tell him everything. To come clean . . . But then what? Yet I don't know if I can go on living with my guilt. Maybe I should tell him about Matthew after all, explaining that it's all over now.

'Actually . . .' I say, taking a deep breath.

'Maybe . . .' he says at exactly the same time.

'You first,' I say quickly, my courage deserting me.

'Maybe it's because we're here, without any of the stresses that we both have at home.'

He has a point. It's so beautiful and tranquil here; like being in another world, with the sea outside.

'What were you going to say just now?' he asks.

'The same,' I reply swiftly.

He kisses me. Properly. I can hardly remember the last time he did that.

Then he slowly peels off my jumper and leads me to the pull-down bed. He seems nervous. Almost as if he is doing this for the first time.

If only that were true. What I would give to have a clean slate. But it's too late now.

Afterwards, I want to cry with self-loathing. What would my husband say if he knew what I'd done? I also want to weep because – I have to admit this – with Stuart there'd been none of that passion I'd had with Matthew in the Worthing hotel before common sense and morality had taken over.

And there's something else bothering me. Is it possible that Stuart might have made love to me out of guilt? He'd seemed like someone different. Maybe he was compensating for something? Or what if he was used to releasing that passion with Janine. So, without any other outlet down here apart from me, he'd . . .

Stop it, I tell myself. All these 'what ifs' will drive me crazy.

Instead, I kiss the top of Stuart's head. 'I love you,' I murmur.

He puts his cheek against mine. 'And I love you, Poppy Page.'

The next morning, after breakfast, we go to the village shop arm in arm to get the newspapers. I browse around the boxes of fruit and the packets of toffee, choosing a 'thank you for having the kids' box of shortbread for Betty and a ball for the puppy. It feels a relief to do something normal and I try to concentrate on these small actions instead of agonizing over everything else.

Stuart and I have another lovely walk along the clifftops, gazing down at the sparkling sea below. I'm beginning to feel better. Brighter. All this is such a change from London that I can almost pretend I am someone else. 'The air smells so different,' I say.

'Mum always used to say that when I came down as a child.' He squeezes my hand. I squeeze his back. Then he kisses me. It feels safer and more doable than full-blown sex. After an hour or so, we stroll back to the caravan.

'By the way,' says Stuart casually, 'I meant to mention something earlier.'

'What?' I say, not really concentrating as I search for the caravan key in my bag.

His words come out in a rush. 'That new patient of mine came back to the surgery the day before yesterday. Poor chap is in quite a lot of discomfort with those wisdom teeth. Afterwards, he said that he'd looked you up after I'd told him you'd been an actress too.'

My mouth is so dry that I can barely speak. 'Really?'

My husband's voice goes a bit odd.

'The funny thing is that it turns out that the two of you *had* known each other after all.'

I can hardly breathe.

'Then he showed me this picture on his mobile phone.'

I freeze. Unable to speak.

'You won't believe it,' says Stuart, looking me straight in the eye. 'It was of you and him.'

My head starts to ring. My legs shake. My body feels so unsteady with pure, utter terror that I have to hang on to the caravan door handle to stop myself falling.

'I got him to forward me a copy so I could show you. Look.'

He waves his phone in front of my nose. I have no option.

It's me all right. And Matthew. But it's us when we were twenty-one, in rehearsal for the opening night of the show I didn't get to because I was in hospital. Not, thank goodness, the selfie he had taken without my knowledge in the Worthing hotel. I want to weep with relief.

My husband is looking at me carefully. 'Apparently you were at the same drama school together. I'm surprised you don't remember him.'

'There were lots of us there,' I bluster. 'You can't remember everyone. Besides, he's changed . . .'

I stop.

'How do you know?' asks Stuart sharply.

'I *expect* he's changed,' I correct myself quickly. 'A bit like me.'

Stuart shrugs. 'We all have. He seemed quite nice, actually. You ought to get in touch and ask him over for dinner sometime.'

Then he gives me another kiss; this time on my cheek. A cool one, rather like the type you might give to a distant relative. 'Now, how about going out for lunch instead of making it ourselves?'

'I'm not that hungry now,' I say.

He puts his arm around me. 'But it's our wedding anniversary, Poppy! We've got to celebrate. Haven't we?'

Somehow I get through a meal at a rather nice restaurant near Exmouth, although we don't talk a lot. In the afternoon, we drive along the coast and then have an early night. Of course, I can't sleep. Not after Stuart's revelation about Matthew. So I get up just after 5 a.m. and go for a walk along the beach. A fisherman, pulling his boat up over the pebbles, bids me good morning. A young father carries a toddler in a backpack. A seagull swoops overhead. The waves lap against the stones. I bend down to pick up a shell and tuck it in my pocket out of habit from long-ago childhood days.

Everything seems so natural here. So uncomplicated. Why can't my life be the same?

I begin to climb a footpath that runs from the beach up to the top of a hill. Then my mobile reception, which has been dodgy in the caravan, suddenly has a breakthrough. There's a message sent an hour ago from the girls and Betty, telling me what fun they've been having with Coco.

And then one from Matthew.

> Did you like that old photo of us?
> Your husband seemed quite taken
> aback. Took me a fair while to find

it from my stack of old drama
school magazines. Shall we say
the Embankment Gardens on
Tuesday? 2 p.m.? And oh, by the
way, congratulations on your
anniversary. Devon is so beautiful,
isn't it?

My stomach drops. My skin crawls. How on earth does he know where we are? I have never felt such hatred for anyone as I do for Matthew right now. What did I ever see in him?

Then something that Betty told Melissa when a girl at school was being horrid comes back to me: '*Find her vulnerable point, love. Everyone has one. Then go for it. Bullies will always go on unless you throw mud back at them.*'.

It had struck me at the time as being very unlike my mother-in-law, who was such a kind, forgiving person. But now I'm beginning to think she has a point.

Right, I tell myself, deleting Matthew's message and striding up the hill to a bench with a renewed vigour in my step. *That's it. Two of us can play at this game.*

'Poppy Page,' I say firmly. 'It's time to fight back . . .'

But where to begin? Facebook, maybe. In fact, I should have done this sooner. Yet just as I open Matthew's page, I hear a shout. It's Stuart, waving at me from the bottom of the hill. He is coming up. 'Mind if I join you?' he says, getting nearer.

Quickly I change to my weather app. 'Great,' I say. 'Looks like it's going to be a nice day.'

My research is going to have to wait.

26

Betty

'I have to hand it to you,' Mum said when she'd popped round to have a cuppa a few months later. 'You've managed to keep that Jock of yours in check. I haven't heard any more gossip about him being with other women.'

'That's thanks to you,' I said. My relationship with my mother had improved dramatically since her advice about Jock. It was, I realized, the first time we had really understood each other.

She looked pleased. 'Now that's sorted, you can focus on repairing the other cracks in your marriage.' Mum stirred a third teaspoon of sugar into her mug. 'Don't look away and pretend you don't know what I'm talking about. I'm not stupid, love. I've seen the way you two are around each other. Neither of you can stand each other's guts.'

'Frankly,' I said, hoisting Stuart onto my hip and wiping his face, which was all jammy from toast, 'I can't see us ever liking each other again, let alone actually enjoying married life together. Not after everything that's happened. Anyway, I don't want to discuss it in front of this one. He might pick up bad vibes.'

I sat my little boy down on the floor so we could play with a plastic car that Jock had brought back for him the other day from the market. He might not be a good husband but he was a good father. Another reason for staying put.

Mum rolled her eyes. 'I do know what I'm talking about.'

'What do you mean?'

'Don't you think I went through some rough patches with your dad? Granted, I didn't fall for a posh married bloke like you did . . .'

I winced.

'. . . But your dad used to be a heavy drinker and there were times when I felt like walking out of the door with you in my arms.'

I glanced up from Stuart for a minute. 'I never knew that.'

'That's cos I kept it from you. There was this big fight one night at his local and . . . let's just say someone got hurt. Badly. Your dad had to go down to the cop shop for questioning but nothing came of it. There wasn't any proof. But the shock frightened him – just like that shock frightened your Jock when you sent him off to get himself checked out.'

Briefly I thought back to that time. The tests had proved negative, my husband had told me, pretending to be all cocky about it. But I could tell he'd been shaken.

'Anyway, your dad didn't touch a drop after that. It's all history now but the point is this. I could have done what you're doing with Jock now. Given him the cold shoulder and all that. In fact, I did for a bit. You were only two at the time but you started to get all fractious. So I realized that, just as you've said, kids can pick up on a bad atmosphere.'

She put her cup down. 'If you want my advice, love, you need to try a bit harder.'

I shudder. 'I don't ever want to go to bed with that man again.'

She shrugged. 'That's up to you. But you could at least attempt to like him. Otherwise that grandson of mine is going to suffer.'

I didn't want that. But I also didn't care much for Mum's hard-nosed advice. Surely it was hypocritical? I needed to be true to myself.

'Hah,' snorted my mother when I said as much. 'Since when did principles put a roof over a kid's head and give it food to eat? You need to get real, my girl.'

So when Jock came home that night, I sat down with him at the small rickety kitchen table instead of telling him – as I usually did – that his tea was in the oven and then leaving him to eat it on his own.

'How was work?' I asked.

He looked at me suspiciously. 'Why?'

'Just asking,' I said.

It took time, of course, but I started to take more care over making his supper and would wait until he got back to eat my own with him. He began to tell me things about his day like an ordinary husband would. And I'd tell him about mine, which revolved around looking after Stuart and the way he loved putting puzzles together.

I also lifted Jock's banishment and let him back into our bed, even though I took care to stick to the far side. He tried it on a few times at first but I reminded him of our agreement. If I was to stay, I wasn't having any of that.

If Jock did seek solace with other women, he was discreet about it. Or, to put it another way, he never came home reeking of perfume as he had done before. Maybe Mum had been right.

He was also more respectful of me, no longer putting me down or criticizing me. Neither of us ever mentioned Jane or Gary or Cross Lane.

We ploughed our energies into bringing up our son and at weekends we would take him to museums or to the local park together. At times, we actually found ourselves laughing over the same television programme, even though we sat at opposite ends of the sofa.

Yes. Things were definitely better between us. I was content, even if not happy exactly. But then again, I wasn't entitled to that. Not after what I had done to Jane.

I still dreamt about her, but she had at least stopped talking to me, and I became used to her silent presence.

A year or so later, Jock got promoted, and with it came a rise in salary and a move to Milton Keynes. Away from London, we were able to make a fresh start. No one knew us. No one knew I had been friends with a woman called Jane and fallen in love with a married man called Gary.

Stuart went to the local school, which had a good academic reputation. One of his new friends had a mother who was divorced. She confided in me, describing how difficult it was being without a husband and how she and her son had to look for coins down the back of the sofa in order to buy food. It sounds dreadful, but when she was telling me this I felt a flash of relief that I had chosen to stay put. Financially it was so much easier now. And more importantly, Jock seemed to be behaving himself.

Even so, there were times when I couldn't help imagining – as I still do, to be honest – what would have happened if I had followed my heart instead of being practical. I would daydream about the new life I might have built with Gary and those dear little girls who would have loved Stuart like a brother. *Even if I'd gone it alone, I would have survived*, I told myself. I was tougher than I seemed.

But then I'd look at our clever little boy – always top of the class! – and I knew that giving up Gary and staying with Jock was worth it for him. I swore I'd be the best mother I could. And part of this, at least so I believed at the time, was creating a secure and stable family for him. Besides, Stuart worshipped his father. Often they went fishing together – there was this big lake nearby – or they'd go off to a football match. They would return flushed and happy. I would have felt terrible if I had deprived him of that relationship.

On the occasions that I allowed myself to get carried away by a fantasy about Gary, I would try extra hard to be nice to Jock by making him a special meal or suggesting that we went out to the cinema together. It seemed to work because he would do the same to me, even bringing me back a small present every now and then. Never perfume. After Cross Lane, it was as if he knew that was one thing I would never want.

'I'm glad you took my advice,' remarked my mother when she visited. I watched her cast an eye around our brand new three-bedroom house in a nice street, not far from the shopping centre. 'I'm proud of you.'

Never had she praised me like that before. I was so taken back that I didn't know what to say in return. But her words did make me feel better about myself.

That's not to say my life wasn't emotionally challenging, especially in those early years. Naturally, I took great care to put on a front before our son so he never guessed the truth. Sometimes friends asked why we hadn't had another child and I would say something vague like 'it just didn't happen'. Part of me still longed for a daughter but there was no way that I could ever let my husband touch me again.

Life went on. John Lennon died (it seemed impossible!) and we went to war with Argentina over the Falklands. ('Quite right too,' declared Jock.) As more years went by, the memories of that terrible time in Hackney began to fade and I began to experience moments of true happiness again, such as at school prize giving when Stuart got more trophies than anyone else. Jock and I clapped until our hands were sore and I had to stop my husband from whistling his excitement and pride. Those nightmares about Jane began to ease off, thank heavens. So too did my fantasies about Gary. Our son by now was growing up into a thoughtful young man. He had Jock's height but I made sure that he had none of his father's uncouth manners or gruff behaviour.

He was such a lovely boy, Poppy! So kind, and the way he would listen patiently before he spoke was completely unlike Jock. 'Quite a little gentleman, isn't he?' sniffed my mother, but not in a disapproving way.

By the time Stuart was doing his A levels, I actually began to feel reasonably content. And when he got accepted to read dentistry at Newcastle, Jock and I were over the moon.

'Fancy that,' said my husband. 'The first in our family to get into university!' He gave me a hug; the nearest we'd got to intimacy for years. And I found myself hugging him back.

Central Criminal Court, London

'I will ask the question again, Mrs Page. If, as you claim, you never wanted to see Matthew Gordon again, why did you agree to meet with him a third time?'

Poppy Page raises her head. Her eyes are red. Wild. She looks capable of almost anything in that moment.

'Because,' she says, as if through gritted teeth, 'that man hounded us. He refused to leave me or my family alone. He signed up as a patient at my husband's dental practice. He told Stuart that he was at drama school with me. He sent him a picture of us as students. He encouraged one of my clients to sue me. He told me he wouldn't stop unless I agreed to meet with him. So eventually I did. He told me to go to the Embankment Gardens. But . . .'

She stops.

'Please,' says the barrister silkily, 'continue.'

Poppy raises her chin defiantly. 'But before our meeting, I looked him up online to see if I could find anything on him.'

'Why did you do that, Mrs Page?'

'I was looking for a way to make him stop. Something to level the playing field. Then I checked out Facebook. And that's when I made the discovery about Sandra.'

She pauses again. The court seems to lean forward as one, waiting.

'Yes,' says the barrister, a trifle impatiently.

Poppy Page gives a hoarse laugh. 'You won't believe it.'

27

Poppy

The following morning, when Stuart is back in his surgery and Daisy is at home with a cold, I go back to Matthew's Facebook page.

A picture of a much younger Matthew beams out at me along with his profile. 'Title role in *Peter's Paradise* . . .'

The wording doesn't mention the fact that the show ended years ago. It's as if Matthew is still resting on his laurels. He hasn't put much up in the last two years, I notice, apart from a picture of him at the Association of Supporting Artistes and Agents' Christmas party, where he has one arm round Jennifer and another round Doris. 'Wonderful to meet stars in the making,' he gushes.

There's no mention of Sandra in his posts. Maybe I should search for her Facebook page instead. There's nothing under Sandra Gordon, so I look for her under her maiden name, Wright.

There she is! But goodness, she's changed. Poor thing looks like a shadow of her former self. So thin and gaunt. Almost angry too. Then I read the top post and gasp.

I can't believe what I'm seeing . . .

An RIP message. From someone called Tom. 'To the best sister in the world.'

Sandra is dead? I can scarcely believe it. That's awful. She was only my age. In fact, according to the date of this post (the last one on it), she'd died two years ago from 'complications' as a result of her MS. But not only was her early death tragic, it also showed Matthew in his true colours. All his 'sob stuff' about caring for his wife – not to mention the conversation I'd overheard on the staircase at the Christmas party – had been made up.

'I'm going to kill you, Matthew Gordon,' I say out loud. It's not the first time I've said or thought this. But this time, I mean it. 'Just wait until I see you again.'

Then I hear a scuffling outside my study door.

Quickly, I slam the laptop shut.

'Sorry,' says Betty, coming in as she knocked. 'I didn't mean to disturb you. I just wanted to say that I've made some nice onion soup. Just the thing for Daisy's sniffles. You might like some too.'

She's eying the laptop as she speaks. Had she seen me close it so fast? Could she have heard me? No. Or she wouldn't look so normal.

'I was just arranging to see a friend for lunch on Tuesday,' I say, trying to sound casual.

'Good for you. I'm always telling Stuart that the two of you work too hard and need to take more time out. How old are *her* children?'

I'd never actually said it was a female friend. Or that she had kids. Betty just assumed this was the case. In my mother-in-law's books, family is sacrosanct. And I'm grateful. I couldn't have run my business without her here. On top of that, Daisy and Melissa have learned so much from their grandmother.

Just as long as they don't learn from me.

By the time Tuesday comes, Daisy's much better. Meanwhile, I am champing at the bit to tell Matthew what I've found out.

'I can pick up the girls from school after my meditation class, if that's helpful,' Betty says before I set off. 'We'll drop off at a coffee shop on the way back.'

This is one of their treats. In fact, Betty often gets things out of the girls this way and then passes information onto me 'because I thought you ought to know, love'.

My mother-in-law would have made a great spy. Through her, I learned that Melissa definitely fancied Jonnie, that floppy-haired, slightly cocky boy from school. I only hoped that the intense happiness followed by the equally intense pain (both of which inevitably accompany a first love) wouldn't interfere with her school work. I'd already had various talks with her over the years about 'being careful when it comes to sex' and about making sure that she really cared for someone before 'getting too serious'.

I had been thinking, since Betty told me about this boy, that I should talk to Melissa again about using protection. I still cringe when I remind myself that Matthew and I hadn't used anything in the Worthing hotel. Talk about being a hypocrite. I really ought to get myself checked out, but then I could hardly go to our GP.

In the end I'd gone to one of those anonymous walk-in sexual health clinics near Tottenham Court Road last week, hoping, as I went in with my head bowed, that no one I knew had spotted me. London might be a big place but it's surprising how many people you can bump into.

There were three other women there, roughly my age at a guess. And two elderly men. None of us looked at each other. I got out my iPad to catch up on work emails, pretending that this was no more significant than, say, than a routine dental appointment. Inside, I felt dirty. How had it come to this? I'm a mother of two, for pity's sake.

But the nurse who did the vaginal swab was very matter of fact and told me that she wished more people 'of my age' were as sensible. If only she knew the full story. The good thing was that, to my relief, I was clear.

At least that's one thing I've been able to tick off my list of things to worry about.

'Don't hurry back,' Betty says as I now rush out of the door to meet Matthew. 'You enjoy your chin-wag. We need friends in this world, Poppy. Someone to share your troubles with.' For the briefest of moments, there's a look of sadness I have never seen before in her eyes. Then it's gone. 'Now have fun, won't you?'

What would my mother-in-law say if I told her the truth? I almost feel tempted. No. She'd be shocked. Horrified. Our relationship would be ruined for ever. So instead, I head into the crisp January sunshine – the type where the pale low sun almost blinds your eyes – towards the Tube station. I'm so wobbly with nerves that I drop my Oyster card on the ground after touching the scanner. 'Here you are,' says the man behind me.

'Thanks.'

He flashes me a smile. 'It's a pleasure.'

Going down the escalator, I feel him standing close. Is he anything to do with Matthew? I spend the whole ride

tensed up, ready to run, but at the bottom the man over-
takes me and takes the passageway going north instead of
south. I'm being neurotic. Matthew has made me doubt
everything. What exactly does he want to talk about? I
decide that I'll save my revelation about Sandra as a card
up my sleeve until I find out. It might convince him finally
to leave me alone.

As I emerge from Embankment station and walk past
the flower sellers with early daffodils in their buckets, I
can almost pretend that I really am going to see a friend
for a jolly lunch. I've always loved this part of London
with its view onto the Thames. When the children were
small, I would bring them here before a trip to the
National Gallery in Trafalgar Square. As they got bigger
and my business grew, these outings became fewer and
fewer. I realize too late that I should have done more with
the girls when they were growing up.

But then again, that's the least of my misdemeanours.
If they ever find out about Matthew, they'll never want to
see me again. I'm sure of it.

Once more, I cannot help running the future before
me. They won't want me at their weddings. They might
stop me from seeing my own grandchildren. I'll become
a pariah. The mother who wrecked their lives by having
an affair. I know this because that's exactly how I feel
about my own mother, hypocrite that I am.

'Pops,' says a voice. 'So you came!'

I almost didn't see him, but there he is. That high forehead. That dark swept-back hair. The nose, which might
look prominent on some men but which lends his face a
handsome, almost Grecian air. The firm jaw that juts out

at me arrogantly. (For some reason, he's stroking it.) The fact that, despite everything, I still feel a stirring inside when I look at him, makes me even angrier, not just with myself but with him.

'Did I have a choice?' I retort.

'Come on,' he says, holding out his arm as if suggesting I take it. 'We all have a choice. But you wanted to see me, didn't you?'

'You flatter yourself,' I retort, ignoring his arm.

'Well, I wanted to see *you*.' He rubs his jaw again and then takes a packet of pills out of his top pocket and swallows a couple without water.

'Everything all right?' I can't help asking out of natural politeness.

He grimaces. 'It's my wisdom teeth.'

'So it wasn't simply an excuse to see my husband, then,' I retort.

'No, it wasn't. They really are playing me up and I had to get them looked at, even though I get extremely nervous about seeing the dentist.'

'Who just happened to be Stuart.'

He gives me a wolfish grin. 'You could say it killed two birds with one stone. I needed my teeth looked at. And I was curious to see the kind of man you married, Pops. Not like me, is he?'

'That's precisely the point,' I snap back.

We fall into line, walking side by side in perfect sync, past the clusters of snowdrops and armies of purple crocuses beside the neatly clipped lawn edges. I'm so angry because of his lie about Sandra that it's tempting to confront him with it straight away. But I'm biding my time.

'How did you know Stuart and I were in Devon?' I say quietly. 'Did you follow us?'

Matthew gives a deep, rich, throaty laugh, which makes a woman – about my age, at a guess – shoot him a look of admiration as she passes by. She glances at me as if to check out the kind of companion who is walking with a man like this. 'Don't be so melodramatic, Pops. It was nothing like that. Your daughter told me. The older one.'

I go cold. 'Melissa? How? You've never met her!'

He touches my arm in an overfamiliar gesture. 'Darling, haven't you heard of Facebook? Melissa accepted my invitation weeks ago.'

I go cold. 'Why would she do that?'

'Because my profile says I am happy to pass on tips to aspiring actors, perhaps? It's a recent addition. I thought it might interest her. And our friendship has been most informative. I've learned so much about your family.'

In that moment, I could happily put my hands around his neck.

'Did you talk on the phone?' I demand.

'Only online. Stop panicking. It was all above board. I simply asked if acting was in the family and she said her mother had wanted to be an actress but ran an agency instead. She mentioned her grandmother – Betty, isn't it? – and her sister too. Oh – and she said that her dad was always working long hours. But most of our conversation consisted of me giving her advice on how to get into the profession. It's good that she's going to drama classes after school, isn't it? That might help.'

He's talking as if he knows my family. How dare he?

'I don't understand what it is that you want from me, Matthew,' I thunder. 'And don't give me any more of that crap about how unhappy you are with Sandra. I know she's dead. I checked out her Facebook page and saw her brother's eulogy.'

I wait for his surprise but he simply holds out his hands in a 'mea culpa' gesture. 'It's true. Took you long enough to find out, I must say. Mind you, if I'd still been a name, you might have read about it in some magazine or newspaper. But when you're no one any more, no one cares. Not even her so-called loving brother Tom, who refused to lend us any money when she was ill and won't even help me now.'

'You're disgusting!' I splutter. 'Why would you lie like that? I heard you on the phone to her – or so I thought – at the Christmas party.'

'I know you did,' he said. 'I saw you coming so I had a one-way conversation.'

He says all this without a hint of apology.

'Why? To make me think you were a good, kind man, who put his career second to look after his disabled wife?'

'Exactly! I knew you'd fall for it, Pops. You always were too kind for your own good.' He looks solemn for a moment. 'Although sometimes I do find myself having conversations with Sandra out loud in the house, especially when I'm lonely. It helps to feel I can still talk to her.'

He looks genuinely pained for a moment. But then Matthew always was a good actor.

'You really expect me to believe that?' I retort scornfully. 'You seemed to have no difficulty renouncing your love for her not so long ago in Worthing. In fact, I wouldn't be surprised if you were relieved she's dead.'

It's a terrible thing to say and I know it. But then a truly awful thought occurs to me. 'Please tell me you didn't kill her!'

'Don't be absurd, Poppy.' There's such genuine anger in his voice that I do believe him this time. 'It was pneumonia that got her in the end. That bloody MS had left her vulnerable. I'm certainly not a murderer.'

'But you *are* a liar! You said you were going to tell Sandra about us. You said I had to tell Stuart too so we could be together. Is this why you're trying to scare me?' I want to stamp my feet on the ground like a child, despite a man in a blue anorak staring at me as he walks by. 'If so, it's too late. You had your chance with me years ago and you threw it away.'

He shakes his head. 'You've got the wrong idea completely. It's not you I want, Pops. It's your money. Fifty thousand pounds, to be precise.'

'Fifty thousand?' I repeat, stunned. 'Are you mad?'

He sighs and sits down on a bench, motioning that I should do the same. Numb with shock, I do so.

'Come on, Pops. You can afford it. I read that write-up about you that said how well you were doing. It's what gave me the idea, actually. Otherwise I wouldn't have bothered going to the Christmas do. All that stuff about forming an agency myself was just an excuse. It was you I wanted. Why else would I have asked the receptionist to get me a room as close to yours as possible after the Christmas party? Good on you for resisting, mind – at least on that occasion. For a second there I really thought you *were* the devoted wife.'

296

I feel sick. 'But what about Worthing?'

He looks smug. 'You played right into my hands by telling me you couldn't find a hotel. Of course I wasn't really in the area by coincidence. I made a special trip down to see you. I couldn't believe my luck when you told me about Doris's accident and how you were worried in case your home insurance might not cover you.' He makes that wolfish grin again. 'And it *was* fun, wasn't it, Pops? You were pretty hot. Even more than in the old days. Consumed with desire, in fact.'

I burn with shame as I remember how much I'd wanted him only a few weeks ago. How he'd melted into me like we were one body. He was right, I *had* been consumed with desire. I hadn't just gone along with him. I had instigated it by suggesting we went upstairs.

'So you were playing with me the whole time?'

He shrugs. 'It was very enjoyable, I grant you that. But yes, I knew you'd feel guilty afterwards. Like I said just now, it's part of your sweet nature, Pops. So I thought that if I pretended that I wanted you to leave your husband and family there and then, you'd do anything to get me out of your life. Like paying me off. That piece in the magazine said you were a "highly successful" businesswoman. I've checked out your house. I know what it's worth. Yes, fifty thousand pounds is quite a tidy sum, but you shouldn't go leaving your bank statements in your handbag. I had a little look when you went to the bathroom.'

I can barely speak for rage. 'That's *all* our savings. We don't have any more. Besides, why do you need so much?'

He shrugs. 'I built up debts during Sandra's lifetime. The state gives you a certain amount of help, naturally. But you know me. I haven't changed. I like the best.'

I think back for a minute to the natty little open-top Ford Escort his father had given him for his nineteenth birthday – how all the other girls, including Sandra, had envied me when he'd driven me around in it! Then I recall Matthew's fashionable student wardrobe of clothes, bought with the big allowance he got every month.

'The parents left me without a penny,' he says, as if reading my thoughts. 'Too many step-siblings to provide for, I suppose. So I had to take out a loan to pay for private carers. My wife wasn't going to want for anything. I was determined about that.'

He sticks out his jaw defiantly, still rubbing it. 'I heard about a new treatment in the States. This MS consultant had made a breakthrough. Sandra was so excited when I told her. But then we found out the cost. She said it didn't matter and that she had faith in the hospital over here, where she was already a patient.'

There's a deep breath. I get the feeling that for once he isn't acting. 'But I was never going to let her go without that treatment. Not if there was the slightest chance it could have saved her.'

'You said you couldn't forget me,' I say in a small voice. 'You said Sandra knew that.'

'Well, she didn't,' Matthew said quietly. 'I *did* care for you, Pops, and over the years you did indeed come into my head every now and then. But the truth is that Sandra and I were made for each other. We were two of a kind. It's why I borrowed thousands of pounds. I'd have done anything to have saved her. I lost count of how many credit cards I maxed out. We were in America for two months and the bills kept racking up. Not just the medical ones but the hotel and all the other expenses.'

He pauses and I say nothing, waiting for him to continue. Matthew is so convincing. I simply don't know whether to believe one more word from his mouth.

'Anyway,' he says quietly, rubbing his eyes. 'The new treatment didn't work. We came back home and Sandra never knew about the credit cards. And then she got pneumonia. It was hell, watching her struggle for breath. Lying on the hospital bed with the life draining out of her.'

His brow furrows. 'After she died, it was a very black time for me. To make it worse, I was flat broke, living off baked beans and without heating in the winter. Of course, I tried to get work, but even the walk-on parts were drying up.'

His face is close to mine now. There is a fury in his eyes that sends shivers through me. 'I had to sell the mews cottage where Sandra and I lived but it still wasn't enough to pay off those loan sharks. Do you know where I am now, Poppy? In a tiny one-bedroom rented flat in Deptford, with kids who play music all night on the floor above me.' He gives a bitter laugh. Now I know he's telling the truth. 'I never thought I'd end up somewhere like that.'

And though I hate him more than anyone else in the world right now, there's a part of me that understands. I know how it feels to be disappointed with the way things turned out. And I can only imagine what it's like to watch a loved one die.

'Why are you telling me all this?' I ask.

He looks thoughtful for a moment. 'I need to share the pain in order for you to believe me. You see, I'm completely serious about you coughing up. I've invested a lot in this. You're my last chance.'

Any compassion I've had for Matthew is now disappearing fast. I can feel a large knot of terror and stress gathering at the base of my neck from where it leads into my shoulder. A sharp pain begins to throb in my temples. What an utter fool I've been.

'So anyway.' His tone is brisk, businesslike. 'What it all comes down to is that I need fifty grand to pay off my creditors. And you're going to give it to me, Pops.'

'And what,' I quiver, 'makes you think there's the slightest chance I am going to agree to that?'

'Well . . .' He reaches down to the flower bed next to him and plucks the head off one of the snowdrops. 'Because if you don't, I will tell your husband and your daughters we slept together in Worthing. I've got a feeling they won't like that at all. Then I'll tell everyone in the industry that you seduced me and that I was too overcome with grief to resist. On top of the trouble over poor Doris and your lack of care towards a client, it won't look good. Will it? People like their agents to be upfront and honest.' He tears the snowdrop petals into tiny little bits. 'I will destroy you Pops. Personally and professionally.'

I'm so stunned by his ruthlessness that I can barely move. Then a thought occurs to me, and I almost laugh.

'You're a fool, Matthew. I don't have insurance. If Doris sues me as you've encouraged her to, I'll have to pay her the money. There'll be nothing left for you.'

Matthew grins. 'Fifty grand for a fractured shoulder? Don't be ridiculous, Pops. Your reputation might be ruined, but you'd be able to afford to pay her out of what your husband earns in a month.'

That takes the wind out of my sails. I try another tack. 'How will I explain it to him when he discovers all our savings are gone?' I ask.

He shrugs. 'That's up to you. You didn't think of him in Worthing, did you?'

It's true. 'We're not made of money, you know,' I say desperately. 'I mean I know we look good on paper. But we have outgoings. Overheads. The girls. I've just had to get in carers for Dad too.'

'You have a house that's worth at least a million. Like I said before, I've checked it out online. I'm sure you'll find a way to manage. Meet me outside Waterloo mainline station at the bottom of the steps on the east side. Let's say 6 p.m. this Friday. And make sure it's in cash.'

He smiles at me. 'Otherwise you'll leave me no option but to send Stuart – and those sweet-looking daughters of yours – that picture of us curled up in bed.'

A potent mixture of anger and fear boils up inside me; scalding my insides. I stand up. I can't bear to be near him for a second longer. This man has ruined my life once before. He's not going to succeed a second time.

'I'm not doing it. And if you ever contact me again,' I spit, 'I'll go straight to the police.' Then I turn on my heel and storm off.

28

Betty

When Stuart left for university, everything changed. It's fashionable to talk of empty-nest syndrome now but as far as I knew, the phrase hadn't even been invented then. I kept finding myself laying the kitchen table for three instead of two. Jock and I struggled to think of things to say to each other.

How lonely I felt! There was so little to do without my son to fuss over. The long empty days stretched out before me without any obvious purpose ahead. There's a limit to how much housework you can do. If only I was qualified for a job! When I suggested to Jock that I did some kind of training, he looked disapproving. 'People will think I can't afford to support my wife. Anyway, you're too old to start a career.'

But I was only in my early forties. Magazines were full of articles about women who had led second lives after having children. I thought about getting voluntary work at a charity shop but once more, Jock vetoed it. 'I'm not having a wife of mine touching dirty old clothes that others have worn. What will people think?'

'They'll admire me for helping out,' I pointed out. 'Like many others.'

'Well, not my wife.'

At times, I thought about leaving Jock and starting a new life of my own. Once more, there were plenty of magazine features about that too. But I knew it would break Stuart's heart, despite the fact he was away at university. When he came back for 'the vacation' as he called it (such a fancy word!), he always gave us a big hug and seemed really pleased to be home. He was so tall by now that he towered over both of us. But, I reminded myself, even grown men need their parents.

Other women in my position filled their time by seeing friends, but I didn't have any. In fact, I went out of my way to avoid socializing, always turning down dinner invitations from neighbours or a suggestion from one particularly kind older woman in our road that I should join the local keep-fit class with her. I didn't deserve friends after what I had done to Jane.

Eventually, the same woman persuaded me to go to a 'hobbies' talk at the local Women's Institute. The speaker confided that she had taken up knitting when she'd lost 'someone close'. Her words caught my attention. So I started doing the same. Then I got bored so I went on to crocheting followed by tie-dyeing skirts, making papier mâché plates for my son's old Scout pack's bazaar and anything else that caught my eye. It didn't matter what it was. Just so long as it stopped me thinking about Jane. Since Stuart had left home, she'd started to appear in my dreams again almost every night, accusing me. I feared I would go mad. Maybe I had already.

'Got another craze, have we?' Jock remarked when he came home to find me making circular floral plaited rings out of salted dough for the town craft fair. I'd got the recipe from a woman's magazine. They were rather pretty, actually, and sold very well as decorations. I gave the profits to a local charity for bereaved families. Jock was in senior management now. It wasn't as though we needed the money any more.

When I'd had enough of salted dough, I did a class in making stained-glass panels. The year after that, I went on a botanical drawing course. I wasn't particularly good but it was a distraction.

'You never stop, Mum,' Stuart would say when he came home. By now he'd qualified and was working for a dental practice in London. Occasionally he brought home girl-friends. They were all perfectly pleasant but none of them lasted. 'Why doesn't he settle down?' Jock would grumble.

I wondered that as well. Yet at the same time I also wanted him to choose carefully. Not like I had.

Years passed in this way. Endless hobbies, all filling the gaps between Stuart's visits home.

But then you arrived, Poppy. I knew from the minute he first introduced you that you were different. For a start, you'd been hurt. I saw straight away that you were a sur-vivor. Initially, I thought it was because your mother had abandoned you and your father. This convinced me even more that I had done the right thing in staying with Jock. I couldn't have allowed my Stuart to be as bruised as you were. I felt the pain in your voice as though it belonged to me when you talked about your parents.

Poor Poppy. I wanted to cocoon you! Wrap you up in my arms. You were the daughter I'd never had. You were the woman my son had chosen and with whom he was madly, deeply in love.

But then I began to suspect that there was another side to your grief. A heavy burden you could not share. I could tell that, although you loved Stuart in your own way, it wasn't with that same intensity I knew he felt for you. When he reached for your hand, you often ignored it. When he padded across the corridor to your room at night, I heard you through the wall, telling him that it wasn't 'correct' under his parents' roof. True passion turns your mind upside down so it doesn't know the difference between right and wrong. I know that all too well.

My intuition told me – don't ask why – that you'd been in love with another man and that it hadn't worked out. I didn't know about the abortion then. And if I had, I would have understood. Of course I would have done. I might be from a different generation. But things like that went on in my day too, you know.

When Stuart announced that he was marrying you, I was elated but also scared for you both. Would you be happy with a sensible man like my boy? And would you hurt him down the line if (or when) you discovered that you needed the passion that I guessed you were missing? I suggested you asked your mother to the wedding but you were adamant. 'I don't want anything to do with her,' you said. 'But Dad will come.'

It seemed incredible when, a year later, you said you were pregnant. I'd never really thought too much about being a grandmother. But then when Melissa was born and we visited you in hospital, you asked if I wanted to hold her and I felt this rush of love and protection that I've never, ever felt for any other human being. Not even for Stuart. It's hard to explain. Perhaps it's because it felt magical knowing that my child had had a child of his own. I was also overawed that there was a little bit of me in this beautiful baby girl, even though she'd been conceived by two other people. One day, Poppy dear, if the girls have children, you'll understand.

'I'm always going to be here for you,' I promised her. 'You'll want for nothing.'

Even Jock got a tear in his eye. 'There were times when I never thought this would happen,' he said, squeezing my hand. 'We've come on a long way, haven't we, you and I?'

Yes we had. More than I could ever have imagined. It's why I knew, later, that you and Stuart still had a chance.

I felt the same outpouring of love when Daisy was born. To be truthful, I'd wondered whether I could ever love another grandchild as much as I adored Melissa. But I did. Was this how mothers with more than one child felt?

Jane would have made a good grandmother. She told me so in my dreams. '*If it wasn't for you,*' she would whisper, '*I might have had a chance.*'

Your girls, Poppy, reminded me of the children I had loved so much. What were Violet and Alice doing now? Had Gary married again? Sometimes I was tempted to look him up on the internet, but each time I stopped myself. What would be the point? I couldn't risk stirring up the past. It's the present that matters.

The grandchildren gave Jock and me a new lease of life. Milton Keynes isn't that far from London and we were always coming up to see you on the train, weren't we? You came to us too. Remember how we took them to Woburn Safari Park one day on our own to give you a

306

break? The girls did Jock and me a lot of good. They gave us a new common ground. We even started planning a cruise round the Med to celebrate his retirement, which was coming up.

Then Jock died. None of us expected it. I never knew pancreatic cancer could be so quick. He must have had it at Daisy's second birthday party but didn't even know.

'I'm sorry, my wee hen,' he said to me at the end. Those were his last words. I didn't have a chance to say that I was sorry too, for my part in it all.

At one point I would have longed to have had the house to myself. Instead it seemed empty. Cold.

You might have thought I'd feel relief now I could do what I wanted without a husband setting old-fashioned boundaries. But I didn't. Jock and I had been together for so long that I couldn't imagine life without him. We'd had some very bad times. Yet when all was said and done, Jock and I had reached an understanding. Besides, I'd spent the whole of my adult life with him. That counts for a lot.

If you and Stuart hadn't taken me in, I don't know what I'd have done. But waking up with Melissa and Daisy rushing into my room every morning and throwing their warm little arms around me brought a new meaning to my life. How I loved helping to bring them up; supervising their homework; taking them to school; playing French cricket in the garden. It suited me, to be honest, that you worked, Poppy. It meant I had something meaningful to do again.

And then you met that man.

29

Poppy

My mind is in such a whirl after leaving Matthew that I head off in the wrong direction and find myself walking along the Strand. Then I bump into someone, realize where I am and go back to Embankment Tube station. I take a moment to lean against the cold stone wall and attempt to clear my head. What have I done?

The more I think about it, the more I realize I can't go to the police. It would mean involving Stuart, and that's out of the question. The idea of me giving Matthew all of our savings is obviously ludicrous. How would I ever explain that to my husband? And the thought of giving in to blackmail makes me feel sick. But right now I'm struggling to see an alternative.

Suddenly I find myself unable to breathe with panic. I double over, my legs all wobbly, trying to draw in air like a runner who has just finished a marathon. Maybe I have. Perhaps this is the end of the road. Passers-by are staring at me. No one offers help. Once more I remind myself that London is a big place but you never know who is going to be walking past at any given moment. Someone might have seen me. Us. I'm in enough trouble already without that. So I head for home, still trying to breathe properly, checking my mobile constantly in case Matthew messages me again.

Perhaps I should have pretended to agree about giving him the money. That would at least have bought me some time and I wouldn't be worried sick about Matthew's next move. Whatever that might be.

As I walk up our garden path with its neatly planted wallflowers, I glimpse Betty's silver head and Daisy's auburn curls through the window, bending over a Ludo board. (My mother-in-law taught them to play 'good old-fashioned games' from an early age.) Coco is sitting beside them. Melissa is coming in through the door with a tray of something. She sits down on the sofa behind them. I watch them laugh. I'd like to tackle my daughter at some point about her online friendship with Matthew and the 'acting tips' he's been offering, but don't dare in case she smells a rat. Then Betty gets up to close the curtains – it's nearly dusk – and she sees me. Her face appears anxious until I remember myself. Swiftly, I smile and wave.

She waves back and then comes to the door as I'm fumbling for my key.

'Did you have a good time with your friend?' she asks as I slip past.

'Lovely, thanks,' I reply breezily, and then, after taking off my shoes, I go straight upstairs so I don't have to look her in the eye. 'I'll be down in a minute.'

Closing the bathroom door behind me, I perch on the edge of the tub, trying to order my thoughts. Yet again, a crazy part of me wants to confide in Betty, but what sympathy could I expect from the mother of the man I've cheated on? She might even tell Stuart. My mother-in-law is always declaring she loves me like a daughter but I'm sure that would quickly change if she knew what I've done to her son. The only course of action is to wait and see what Matthew does next.

Then my phone pings with a message. It's Sally.

Are you free to talk?

I call her immediately.

'Doris's lawyers have called. If we agree to give her £5,000, she will settle out of court.'

Compared with the ludicrous amount Matthew is demanding, this seems like nothing. Then again, Doris is only suing because Matthew put her up to it – something I don't feel able to share with Sally out of shame.

'Let's just do it,' I say.

'But we haven't got it. Not until next month anyway.'

Sally is the one with the head for figures. As anyone with their own business knows, keeping afloat is all a matter of cash flow. Although the Poppy Page agency is doing well, we're currently waiting for quite a lot of money that is owed to us from various production companies.

'I'll talk to Stuart about borrowing it from our personal account,' I say.

'Are you sure? It seems so unfair. I can't understand why Doris is suing us. I thought she was more loyal than that.'

'Let's just pay her off,' I say quickly. 'We need to insert a non-disclosure clause to say she can't discuss it with anyone. We don't want to get a bad name.'

'It might be too late for that,' says Sally quietly. 'Half an hour ago, I had a phone call from a production manager cancelling a booking. Apparently he's using someone from Sharon's agency instead. He said he'd heard 'through the grapevine' that we hadn't been insured at the time of the accident. I tried to get him to change his mind but he was insistent on switching.'

By the time I get to bed that night – after catching up on emails and finalizing details with Doris's lawyers, Stuart is already there. I hadn't even seen him over dinner because I'd stayed up in my office working. He reaches out an arm. 'Everything all right?'

'No,' I want to tell him. But I can't. Nor can I sleep. My head is all over the place. If Matthew calls again, I've decided, I'll declare that I've already told Stuart and that he's going to report him for harassment. It seems to make sense in the small hours but when I wake up the next morning, I've lost my nerve. Supposing Matthew calls my bluff?

I make the girls their packed lunches and drive them to school because they're running late. Betty has an early morning meditation session to go to. When I get home, I take Coco out for a walk, although Melissa did this first thing. I could do with the fresh air.

It's drizzling right now but it's doing me good to be away from my desktop.

Then I suddenly realize that with everything going on, it has been a good few days since I've spoken to Dad.

I scrabble in my pocket for my mobile and dial his number. But there's no answer.

He's probably at the social club, I tell myself. *Or maybe he's in the loo.* I call the carers' agency. 'One of our ladies called round today,' said the woman who picked up, 'but your father said he was busy and didn't need her.'

But of course he needs her. He can't do much with that ankle of his!

I ring again. I'm just about to put it down when he picks up. 'Dad?' I say.

'Hi, Poppy,' The lightness of his tone reassures me.

'The agency told me you'd cancelled the carer today.'

'Well, that's because I've got a visitor, isn't it?'

He says this as if I should already be aware.

'You didn't tell me.'

'He just called round, didn't he? I wasn't expecting him.'

'Who is it?' I ask.

But even as the words come out of my mouth, I instinctively know the answer.

'That young man of yours. The one you had before Stuart. Said he was in the area and thought he'd call round for old times' sake.'

'Matthew Gordon?' I try to keep my voice steady so as not to frighten Dad.

'That's the one!'

'He's there? With you now?'

'That's what I said, didn't I? You should listen more, Poppy. Then you wouldn't get into a muddle.'

'Let me speak to him,' I say tersely.

'He's in the kitchen, putting the kettle on. Ah, here he is.'

I can hear Matthew's voice now in the background. 'Poppy, is it? Great. Just the person I want to speak to.'

Then he comes on the line.

'What the fuck do you think you are doing?' I hiss.

'Lovely to hear from you too, Pops!'

'Have you told him anything?'

'Of course not!' Matthew's sounding falsely jovial. I'm beginning to know how he works now. 'Did your dad tell you that I was in the area and thought I'd pop in? I remembered how to find the bungalow. Not a bad memory after all these years, don't you think?'

'Get out,' I say.

Coco, hearing the tone of my voice, begins to growl.

'You're right,' he says. 'I'm looking forward to seeing you too.'

'I mean it, Matthew, I swear on your life that . . .'

'In case you've forgotten the details, it's Waterloo, the day after tomorrow,' he says. 'Six o'clock. That's what we agreed, wasn't it? Oh and remember your purse.' He laughs. 'Your dad tells me you're doing really well, so you can treat me to dinner if you like.'

Clearly this is code for bringing the cash. All £50,000 of it. There's no way I'm letting him get away with this. But the first thing I have to do is get him out of my father's house. I don't like him there. I run through the options in my head. Should I drive down? Maybe I should call Reg. And tell him what, though?

'By the way,' Matthew adds. 'I'm sorry to find your father's sprained his ankle. I was a bit surprised, frankly, not to see you here, looking after him.'

As if I don't feel guilty enough. 'It's none of your business,' I say tightly. 'Now just leave.'

'Don't worry,' he says in a reassuring voice that not only ignores my previous sentence but also sets my nerves on edge. 'I'll look after your dad for a short time, although I've got to get back to London to attend to some business.

Meanwhile, he needs to take care, don't you think? Otherwise he might have another accident.'

Beads of cold sweat trickle down my chest. 'Is that a threat, Matthew?' I say quietly.

'What's that, Pops? The line is breaking up.'

I know the signal is fine, I haven't moved. I think of Dad standing there, frail and vulnerable. Not long ago, it would have seemed impossible that Matthew would actually hurt my father. But now I am starting to think he's capable of anything. That he's mad. Unbalanced.

'OK,' I say tightly. 'I'll get you the money.'

30

Betty

If you want my opinion – and you won't like it, Poppy – I blame today's trend for 'disposable relationships' on the modern assumption that both parents can work while bringing up children. It might sound old-fashioned, but I reckon that the cracks in your marriage began when you and Stuart found your careers taking off at the same time.

'Thank goodness you're here, Betty,' you've always said. 'I don't know what we'd do without you.'

I was flattered, of course I was! But I was also worried. Yes – I was there for the children but they still needed you. I can't tell you how many times the girls would ask for 'Mummy cuddles' when you were at a meeting or upstairs in your office. They needed their father too. Not just at the weekend but during the week after work. Yet often they didn't see him from one day to the next because he'd come home so late.

It's not good for a couple either. My son would return tired and slightly fractious. You began to snap at each other, each feeling that the other didn't appreciate how hard they worked. Your worlds were so different. How could you begin to comprehend each other's pressures? I didn't get it at your age either, when Jock was working all hours and I was struggling with a small baby. But it takes time to understand certain things. And then, when you try to pass it on to the generation below you, they think you're out of date or that they know more than you do! I was the same with my own mother. Melissa and Daisy will probably be the same when they're grown up.

I tried to encourage you both to spend more time together. But as the years went by, I sensed that neither of you wanted that. Your businesses had taken over. You no longer had shared interests apart from the children. So I took Stuart to one side. 'You need to work on your marriage, son,' I told him.

He'd looked embarrassed. 'Don't be silly, Mum. Poppy and I are fine.'

My boy never was one to show his feelings. But I want you to see that doesn't mean he isn't sensitive on the inside.

I didn't think Stuart was the type to look at another woman. Yet you never know. Sometimes I'd pop into the surgery with the children 'just to say hello' but really to remind his attractive dental assistant that he had a family. I also got a bit concerned when I heard him talking to some woman he's writing a paper with.

'Janine!' I heard him say on more than one occasion when he picked up the phone. He said it in a way that sounded as though he was definitely pleased to hear from her. People can get very close to others in a working environment. Of course, you might wonder how I know that, since I gave up my last job years ago when Stuart was born. But we covered it in one of my OU psychology modules.

Work can be just as big a rival in marriage as another woman or man. And my Stuart is driven by the need to succeed. To make a name for himself. I blame Jock and myself for that. We'd encouraged him all through childhood to 'make something of himself'. We both wanted him to have the opportunities we hadn't had. But I think Stuart took this as an order to work, work, work.

You were the same, Poppy, if you don't mind me saying. I felt your pain when you told me that you had been desperate to be an actress but hadn't made it. Broken dreams are as sharp as broken glass. But then I read a magazine article about a woman who had made a career as a walk-on in films. Do you recall the conversation? 'Why don't you set up an agency helping extras to find jobs?' I said. I'm not bringing this up to take the credit. In fact, it's the opposite. All this is my fault. If I hadn't encouraged you to be a career woman, none of this would have happened. You and Stuart wouldn't have drifted apart.

And you might not have looked at someone else. Just look where that has got us.

My heart bled for you, Poppy, having to rake over the details of it all in court like that. I could have throttled that barrister. I wanted to take you by the hand and pull you off that stand. It simply wasn't fair.

I knew about your affair with Matthew Gordon long before you realized, Poppy. I suspected it the moment you came back from that work Christmas party. You had a look on your face, you see, which was just like mine when I'd glanced in the mirror after being with Gary.

317

You hadn't consummated it. At least I didn't think so. The guilt wasn't there at that stage. It was more like a vibrancy. A new life in your eyes. An excitement. That first flush of love. Addictive. All consuming. Reckless. Capable of doing anything.

And that's when I knew we were in real trouble.

31

Poppy

Why is Matthew at Dad's? To hurt him? No. Surely not. Or am I being naive? Maybe he's just trying to unsettle me. If so, he's succeeded.

Meanwhile, my mind is racing with my other problem. How do I pay him the money he's demanding without telling Stuart? There has to be a way.

Then it comes to me. I'll say I need to use our private account to settle Doris's claim. I'll pretend that she's demanding £50,000. It's a stretch, but you do hear of people asking for crazy amounts in compensation for the smallest things.

Of course, that leaves the question of how I will actually pay off Doris. But that can wait. It has to.

I spend a tortured hour at home (too jittery to even check my emails) while waiting for Betty to get home from her meditation class. 'I need to go down to see my father again,' I say, pouncing on her as soon as I hear her key in the lock. 'I've just been talking to him and he doesn't sound too good.'

'Oh dear.' Her sweet kind face wrinkles into concern. I used to think Betty was ageless with that lovely skin of hers. She swears by an avocado-and-yoghurt face mask, which she makes herself. But recently she seems to have developed worry wrinkles on her forehead.

'I should be back by the end of the day. Do you mind holding the fort as usual?'

I always feel I need to ask, even though it's what Betty does.

'Of course, love.'

'Thank you.' I give her a quick hug and grab my purse and phone from the kitchen table. That's when I see the text from Matthew.

> I hope you're not having second
> thoughts, Poppy. If I were you, I'd
> start getting your ducks in a row.
> You have two days left.

No 'Pops' this time. The 'Poppy' shows he means business.

I delete the message, say a quick goodbye to Betty and leap into the car. Before I switch on the engine I try Stuart's surgery. It's virtually impossible to get through to my husband when he's working. You can't simply drop everything when you're a dentist to take a call from the wife.

'You're lucky,' says the receptionist, as if she is doing me a favour. 'A patient has just cancelled so he's got a spare ten minutes. I'll put you through.'

'What's wrong?' he asks. Stuart knows I wouldn't bother him unless there was an emergency. My heart pounds. I'm going to have to be careful how I phrase this. 'I've got to go down to Dad,' I say. 'Nothing too serious, but I'm a bit worried. He doesn't sound right.'

'Oh, I'm sorry. Obviously, let me know if you need anything.'

I sense my husband's impatience. This isn't an emergency in his book.

'There's something else,' I say. 'That client of mine . . . Doris . . . the one who is suing the agency for a fractured shoulder. She . . . she wants fifty thousand pounds or she'll take me to court.'

'What? That's ridiculous.' Stuart doesn't normally get agitated but I can almost see him getting flushed with panic at the other end. 'She's trying it on.'

'The lawyer says that a court case could cost us much more – and will also damage the agency's reputation. He thinks we should pay her off.'

'But that's all our savings!'

'I know. I'm sorry.'

'We can't do that, Poppy. You've got professional liability insurance, haven't you?'

Now is the time to admit that it doesn't cover clients who visit the house and that neither does our house insurance. But I can't do it. It makes me feel stupid. Just like the old Poppy who couldn't make it as an actress. I might have made it big as an agent. But deep down, I still feel a failure. And I can't bear to go back to that again.

'Yes,' I hear myself say. 'Of course we have.'

'Well then. You'll just have to use it. I know it might affect your future premiums but that can't be helped.'

I hang up, my heart like lead.

There has to be some solution, I tell myself, threading my way through the London traffic. But what? How can I stop Matthew? Will he still be there when I get to Worthing? What if I find my father slumped on the ground . . .

I try calling Reg but it goes through to answerphone. I'm so distressed that I have to slam hard on the brakes at a red traffic light. *Concentrate*, I tell myself, *or you could be responsible, God forbid, for someone's death.* I used to wonder how someone could live with that. But that was before Matthew started to threaten me.

As I join the A24, I let my mind wander back. How can people change so much? Was Matthew always like this? We'd been together for three long years at drama school. I thought I'd known him. But then again, he'd chucked me for Sandra. So clearly I didn't.

I hadn't put him down as a blackmailer though. I sense he is hiding a lot of anger. He'd been angry with his mother, I remember. Maybe, deep down, he is angry with women in general.

I need time to find a way to get money. But I don't *have* time, unless I can convince Matthew to wait, and I don't think he'll do that. Stuart's savings and mine are in a joint account. Does that mean we both need to sign for any cash taken out? If so, withdrawing it without Stuart knowing would involve forging his signature. But I can't do that. Can I?

There's no car in the drive, I notice as I pull up. Then again, Matthew might have arrived by train and taken a taxi here from the station.

As soon as I get out, the woman from next door comes scurrying up.

It's the same beady-eyed neighbour who had told me about the police arriving when Dad had forgotten to pay for the petrol. 'Excuse me, do you have a moment?'

'Actually,' I say, glancing at those awful old grimy net curtains Dad refuses to let me wash because he's 'quite capable' of doing it himself, 'I'm afraid I'm in a bit of a rush. I need to check my father's all right.'

'He is, dear. I saw him just now through the back door. Getting himself a cup of tea, I think.'

That's something – but is Matthew still with him?

'The thing is,' she continues, 'that I couldn't help noticing your dad had a visitor today.'

Don't I know it? I want to say. *A visitor who might be hurting my father right now if you don't let me get a move on.*

'Actually, I've seen him here before. And I just thought it was odd, because I know your dad's always saying you're the only person who visits apart from that other friend of his. Reg, I believe.'

She has my full attention now. 'You've seen the other man here before? Sorry – when was that?'

'It was the day your father hurt his ankle during all that bad weather. I wondered at the time if I should have said something, but I thought that chap might have just been a door-to-door salesman. Then, when I saw him here again today . . . well, I thought you ought to know.'

My heart starts to race. Matthew was here the day Dad fell?

'Thank you,' I say to her. 'That is really good to know.'

'Well, you can't be too careful, can you? My daughter says I have an overactive imagination. Maybe she's right.

All these murder dramas on TV, they give you ideas, don't they? But there was something about that man's expression that I really didn't like, though he's good looking, I'll give him that.'

'I appreciate it.' Then I take out my business card and press it into her hand. 'If you're ever worried about my dad in the future, could you call me on this number please?'

The woman looks pleased. 'I certainly will. I know your father thinks I'm a bit of a busybody, but I like to keep an eye on people around here. It just seems the right thing to do, if you know what I mean.'

I walk down Dad's path, shaking with fear and anger as Matthew's words came back to me. *'I'll look after your dad for a short time but he needs to take care, don't you think? Otherwise he might have another accident.'*

Did Matthew push Dad in the first place?

If he did, I'll kill him.

'Poppy!'

Dad is at the front door.

'I thought I saw you out there, love. What are you doing here? If you came to see your friend, you've missed him.'

We make our way into the sitting room, where I help Dad sit down on the sofa.

'Your neighbour,' I say carefully, 'told me Matthew Gordon was here before today. You didn't tell me that.'

Dad hangs his head. Suddenly he's gone from being a grumpy old man to a child. 'He said I wasn't to tell you.'

'Why not?'

'Matthew said it was part of a surprise for you and that I'd ruin it if I said anything. Apparently it was something to do with your work.'

Dad looks up. 'We had a lovely chat. He asked how you were doing now and I told him all about how successful you are.' There is, touchingly, a discernible note of pride in his voice. 'He was really interested in that. Asking all sorts of questions about it, he was.'

'Like what?'

'Ooh, I can't remember. Stuff about your clients, I think, but I might be wrong there. I do remember we talked about the girls though.'

I can feel the hairs on the back of my neck standing up. 'What did he say?'

'He spent ages looking at their pictures.' Dad waved at the frames of my daughters on the mantelpiece, showing a series of Daisies and Melissas through the years in their school uniforms. Melissa looking more like twenty-one than seventeen in the latest. Daisy, with her puppy fat and her sweet, kind face. My blood boils. How dare Matthew try to wheedle his way into my family like this?

'He asked where they were at school. I said they were at different ones but couldn't remember the names.' Dad's forehead crinkled with worry. 'I told him it would come to me if I waited a bit, but it didn't. Then he said he had to go. I saw him to the door.'

'Was Matthew there when you fell, Dad?' I ask gently.

'Well, that's when it happened. He said he didn't want me coming to the door to see him off because it was cold. I told him that I might be old but I still had my manners. Matthew held my arm to stop me slipping on the ice. He was ever so upset when I fell over my slippers and hurt my ankle. Called the ambulance for me, he did. He couldn't actually come with me to the hospital because he had to

325

go back to look after his wife. She's in a wheelchair, you know.'

I go hot all over with fury. I almost tell Dad the truth about Sandra but I don't want to distract him. 'So why spin me that yarn about the kids knocking at your door and a passing stranger helping?'

'I've already explained. He said I wasn't to tell you he'd been here or it would ruin the surprise.' He looks worried. 'I hope I haven't spoiled it.'

I can hardly tell Dad that the 'surprise' was Matthew blackmailing me for every last penny of my savings.

'No, I'm sure you haven't,' I say lightly. 'It's fine.'

Sometimes I cannot believe my father can be both so stubborn and so remarkably gullible at the same time.

'Why did he visit you again today? What did he want?'

'What is this? Some kind of interrogation?' Dad speaks as though he's joking, but he looks disconcerted. 'He said he was passing through and that he just wanted to catch up on old times. A really pleasant chap, isn't he?'

'Very,' I say grimly. 'Now why don't you sit down and I'll make a cup of tea.'

I spend the rest of the day keeping Dad company, 'helping' him do his puzzles ('That piece doesn't go there, Poppy! Let me do it!') and making him a meal. But all the time I am wondering what to do.

I don't have any proof that Matthew hurt my father. But he might have done. And if I don't give him the money, he could be crazy enough to hurt him again or – I can't even bear to think of this – one of the girls. At the very least, he'll send that photograph of us in bed to Stuart. I am now fully convinced he'd do that.

I sneak off into the garden to use my banking phone app privately and discover that I can indeed, take out £50,000 from a main branch in two lots of withdrawals on separate days. I don't even need Stuart's signature. If I take the first tomorrow, I will just have time.

I don't like the idea but . . .

'Poppy!' thunders my father. 'Didn't you hear me? I said we're out of beans.'

'No you're not,' I say, forcing myself to sound reasonable, even though I literally feel at breaking point. It's not Dad's fault.

'Look.' I go into the kitchen and open a cupboard. There are rows and rows of beans, some with sausages and others without.

'That's all right then,' he says. Instantly, he is calm again.

'Would you like me to cook you some?'

'No. I'm not hungry. I just wanted to know they were there. I'm going to finish my puzzle now instead.'

He sits down at the dining room table. There's a 10,000-piece set there with a picture of the sea on the cover. How can he be so good at that when he gets confused about milk and baked beans?

I notice then how filthy his kitchen floor is. It's covered with dried egg yolk and something else that I can't identify. I find a mop in a cupboard and start to clean it. I feel calmer at once. There's something so soothing about the steady rhythm of the mop. The washing away of all the stains and the grime. It helps to make me feel I'm in control again. Then, while Dad is still occupied with his jigsaw, I tackle the bathroom, the loo and Dad's bedroom.

When my phone goes, I'm amazed to see that three hours have passed. Betty's name flashes up on the screen. She's probably wondering what time I'll be back. I should leave soon. I'm behind enough with my work as it is and I need to be with the girls. As for Matthew, my head is still in an impossible muddle.

'Poppy.'

Just as before, I instantly know something is wrong.

'What is it?'

'Coco.' Her voice is raw with grief. 'She's gone! Daisy was walking her in the park when she stopped to get her phone out of her bag. Her arm got twisted round the lead and a man walking past offered to hold Coco so she could take the call. Apparently they then both 'disappeared'.

I can hear Daisy's hysterical sobs in the background.

'I don't know what to do. The awful thing is that the identity disc on the lead broke off just before she took it out. So no one will know how to get her back to us. Daisy wants to call the police.'

'Did she say what this man looked like?'

'Apparently he had dark hair swept back from his face and a large nose. He actually introduced himself to her. Said his name was Matthew, although he'd probably made that up.'

His words come back to me. '*I'll look after your dad for a short time, although I've got to get back to London to attend to some business.*' He must have driven straight to London from Dad's. He knew where we lived. Maybe he saw Daisy coming out of the house. He'd paid close attention to the children's pictures from his previous visit, dad had said.

He'd have recognized her. Followed her into the park. The thought of him coming so close to my little girl makes me feel sick with rage and terror. He'd given his name purposely so she'd tell me and spook me out.

That's it. He's gone too far now. I have to do something about this. Once and for all.

32

Betty

I started to monitor your movements, Poppy. I know it sounds awful. But I had to. I couldn't let you risk your marriage as I had risked mine.

'*Too late for that*,' Jane whispered to me in my head. Sometimes I fancied I could actually smell her expensive floral perfume as if she was right next to me.

When you said you were staying at a hotel near your dad's, I had this weird premonition that you might be meeting someone there. You wrote down the number for the hotel. Remember? But you left out a digit and you didn't give the name. Your mobile was switched off. I wondered if you'd done all this on purpose. It was the sort of thing I might have done if we'd had technology like that, back in the day. Then I recalled you saying that that Sally had recommended the place where you were staying. So I rang her for the details. I thought I might talk to you. Update you on the girls. Remind you that you had a family at home just in case.

'I didn't suggest a hotel,' Sally told me.

My heart sank. So you'd lied.

'Sorry,' I said. 'It must have been someone else. It wasn't that important, anyway. I just wanted to check she'd got there safely but she's not picking up her mobile.

Please don't tell Poppy I rang, will you? I don't want her to think I'm fussing.'

'Don't worry,' she said. 'My mum's the same even though she's nearly ninety! It's natural to worry. But I'm sure she's OK.'

That morning, when you came back from Worthing, my worst fears were confirmed. You had slept with him this time. I just had to look at your face. This time, there wasn't that excitement I had seen before. It was guilt. Pure and utter guilt. You regretted it already. I just knew it.

Or did I? Maybe I was 'transposing' my own emotions onto you. That can happen. We covered that in one of my OU psychology modules too. *Perhaps*, I told myself, *you're just being suspicious because of your own experience.* So I did something terrible. I checked your phone when you were in the bathroom one night.

At first I thought there was nothing there. But then I remembered the part of my IT course that taught us how to hide texts and then open them again. And there they were. Horrible messages from this man called Matthew! But the worst was that picture of the two of you together in bed . . .

I can only imagine that you'd kept them in case you needed them as evidence of his behaviour. But as our tutor had warned us, it's a huge privacy risk. If my Stuart saw that picture, it would have broken his heart. He might even have filed for divorce.

Then Coco went missing. I rang you, if you remember. 'Did she say what this man looked like?' you asked.

You let out a little gasp when I gave you Daisy's description. I felt in my gut that this Matthew was responsible. I had to help you. I had to keep our family together.

I just didn't know how.

33

Poppy

Just as I'm about to leave Dad's, a terrible storm whips up followed by an amber weather warning on the radio. 'I don't want you driving in this,' says Dad as if I am a teenager. I can also see that he doesn't want me to go at all, but I am torn. The dog has gone missing. Daisy has been followed. I need to get back to my family to make sure this crazy maniac isn't going to do something worse.

'Sorry, Dad,' I say. 'I have to.'

But I don't even get as far as the outskirts of town. The roads are flooded and police are turning everyone back. There's no option but to return to Dad's.

We spend the evening watching some mindless television programme while I'm silently agonizing about what's going on at home. 'No sign of Coco yet,' texts Betty.

It takes until the following afternoon for the A24 to become passable. 'You will be back soon, won't you?' says Dad.

'Come with me,' I say.

'I'm not leaving my home,' he retorts. We've had this conversation before. He expects us to make the move down here. But it's simply not practical with the girls' education and our jobs.

When I finally get home after a terrible journey through floods, Daisy is hysterical. 'Coco will be cold and hungry,' she weeps, flying into my arms before I'm even through the front door. 'We have to find her, Mum. Please!'

I shoot a 'What are we going to do?' look at Betty. Stuart isn't back yet. According to the text I received on the drive back, my husband is having to work late because his assistant is off with flu.

'If you hadn't been on your phone, Daisy, it wouldn't have happened,' says Melissa. Pretty rich coming from her, I have to say. She's always on hers.

'I know,' weeps my youngest daughter. 'But I was taking a picture of something so I could sketch it afterwards.'

'Have you called the police?' I ask.

Betty nods. 'They say they'll keep an eye out. I've been emitting lots of positive thought waves too. So has the rest of my meditation class.'

Fat lot of good that will do, I think. But I bite my lip.

Then my mobile rings. 'Maybe that's the police,' says Daisy excitedly. 'We gave them your number too.'

But it's Sally. I run up to my study for some privacy.

'We've been given thirty-six hours to settle,' she says grimly.

I try to swallow the lump of panic that has stuck in my throat.

'The thing is, I might not have that five thousand now,' I say. 'Something's come up and I have to use it for something else.'

'I could use my divorce settlement to help,' Sally says slowly. 'But that will leave me with very little.'

'That's very kind, but no,' I say firmly. 'This is my mess. I'm not going to involve you.'

'The only problem is that there's something else.' Sally's voice – usually so calm and sensible – falters. 'An arts journalist rang me. His paper has got wind about Doris and the fact we weren't insured at the time. Someone tipped them off, apparently, and they're including it in an investigative piece about extras and the do's and don'ts of choosing the right agency. They want a quote from us.'

Someone tipped them off? No prizes for guessing who that was. 'Did you give them one?'

'The lawyer advised me not to. But not saying anything makes us look even worse, doesn't it? When you read things like this and someone says "no comment", they look underhand.'

She's right.

The doorbell goes as I put the phone down. What now? What else can life possibly throw at me? Then I hear Daisy cry out with happiness. 'Coco!'

I come tearing down the stairs. In the open doorway is that white ball of fluff, already in Daisy's arms, licking her mistress with such love that I want to cry.

And next to them is Matthew. He eyes me with an expression of triumph.

This is it, I tell myself. *It's over now. He will say something. In front of the children.*

'How dare you take my dog!' spits Daisy furiously. I've never seen my youngest so angry before.

Matthew crouches down to her level, a smile on his lips. It's all I can do not to grab her and slam the door in his face. But that might lead to more problems. 'I was worried you'd think that,' he says. 'The thing is that this little fellow ran off and I chased after him to get him back for you.'

'But you just disappeared,' snaps Daisy. 'And Coco's not a boy. She's a girl.'

He shrugs. 'Apologies. The thing is that your dog scampered into that woody part of the park. Eventually, I managed to catch him by his lead, which was trailing in the mud, but then I couldn't find you.' He wipes his face with his sleeve. 'I had to take it home with me for the night. Then I came back and have spent hours looking all over the place for you and asking people if they know anyone who owns a little white dog. Thankfully I struck lucky and bumped into one of your neighbours, who told me where you lived.'

He looks up at me. Now his eyes appear strained. Concerned. I almost feel like congratulating him on his performance. *Once an actor, always an actor,* I remind myself.

'Is this your mum? I hope I didn't scare you.'

'A bit,' sobs Daisy. 'But thank you for saving Coco. I'm so grateful.'

Our youngest daughter is now crying with relief, her face buried in the little dog's fur. Of course he meant to scare her, I realize. Not actually cause harm. But to put the pressure on. To make me give in to his blackmail.

'Take Coco into the kitchen,' I tell her. Betty is upstairs with Melissa, rehearsing her lines for the new school play.

Just to make sure she can't hear me, I go out onto the doorstep, check the door is on the latch and pull it shut behind me. 'What do you think you're playing at?' I hiss.

'First you push Dad down the front step and make him twist his ankle . . .'

'Pops! How could you think I'd do such a thing?'

'A neighbour saw you arguing.'

He actually laughs. 'I was trying to persuade him not to see me off at the door when I left and to stay sitting down. But he said it would be rude not to.'

'Then you kidnap my daughter's dog . . .'

'It ran off,' he protested. 'You were lucky I saved it before it got to a road.'

'I don't believe you. You took her home by your own admission. And then you came all the way back from your place to here, pretending you had found her.'

'What a vivid imagination you have!'

'You're trying to destroy my family.'

'I've no intention of doing so, Pops. Just as long as you hand over that fifty grand. In cash. I'll be outside Waterloo station at six p.m. tomorrow night. As soon as I have that money in my hand, I will delete that rather touching picture of you in my arms and get out of your life.'

'But how can I be certain you'll stick to your word?'

He takes my hands. 'You'll just have to trust me, Pops.'

I push him away. 'I hate you.'

He shakes his head. 'I don't think so, Pops. I think you still care, deep down. I was your first real love.'

'I was stupid then,' I say through gritted teeth.

'First love,' he continues, as if he hadn't heard me, 'never goes away. Does it, Pops? Seeing you again has reminded me of how much you meant to me too. I'm sorry. I really am. Believe me, I wouldn't be doing this if I had any other choice.'

Does he mean it? Of course not. And yet, his words still make me feel unsettled.

Then he's gone, heading down our path and disappearing behind the hedgerow.

'Why didn't you thank that man?' says Daisy when I go and find her in the kitchen. 'If it hadn't been for him, we wouldn't have got Coco back. Perhaps you should have given him a reward.'

'Nonsense,' I snap. 'And you shouldn't have spoken to a stranger in the park. I've told you how dangerous it is. If you see him again, you're to ignore him and come and find one of us. Do you hear me?'

Daisy gives me a strange look. 'You wish Coco had got lost, don't you? You've never wanted her.'

'That's not true,' I begin.

But her eyes swim with tears. 'Yes it is. I know when you're lying. Well, Coco means everything to me. More than my own family at the moment.' And then she stomps up the stairs.

At any other time, I'd have gone running after her. But I'm too exhausted. I can't take any more risks. I have to meet Matthew outside Waterloo tomorrow evening. My life has become like a piece of knitting which has started to unravel after a dropped stitch. Faster and faster.

Soon I fear there will be nothing – and maybe no one – left.

Unless I can think of something to save us all.

34
Betty

I overheard every word. I was helping Melissa learn her lines but had left my glasses in my bedroom. So I went to get them and that's when I heard you talking to someone on the doorstep below. I'd opened my bedroom window earlier to clear the incense smell. It's right above the front door.

'*You're trying to destroy my family.*'

My ears pricked up. Then I heard a deeper voice. I knew instinctively it must be him.

'*I've no intention of doing so, Pops. Just as long as you hand over that fifty grand. In cash. I'll be outside Waterloo station at six p.m. tomorrow night.*'

I could barely believe my ears. This man wanted your money? How dare he! Oh, what a fool you must have felt, Poppy. Briefly, I considered telling Stuart. But I knew he wouldn't see it the way I did. At least, as it turned out, Coco was safe.

It would have looked too obvious to have followed you. So I got to Waterloo early at 5.30 that Friday evening and tried to look inconspicuous. It wasn't difficult. There were loads of commuters and it was raining so I hid under my umbrella and hung around by the woman giving away free papers outside. Maybe, I hoped, you wouldn't turn up.

But you did. There you were, looking so pretty in that yellow spring coat of yours. With a package under your arm. Instinctively I knew it contained that money. Then this dark-haired man emerged through the crowd. You talked for a bit – I couldn't hear what you said – and I noticed he kept rubbing his jaw as though it irritated him. Then he snatched the package from you. Immediately, he marched away briskly, up the steps and into the station.

You stood and watched before bowing your head and walking slowly away. I wanted to shake you. Tell you what an idiot you'd been to fall for a man like Matthew Gordon. To be furious with you for threatening my son's happiness. He'd be devastated if he knew you'd had an affair. And where had the money come from? Of course, I'd no idea how much you had in savings. But I could only hope you hadn't taken it from the joint account without telling Stuart.

Yet even though I was cross, I also wanted to put my arms around you in comfort and love. I know I've said this before but it's important to me. You're the daughter I should have had. The child who was so close to making the same mistakes as me. Somehow I had to save you.

So I ran up the steps after this man and followed him into the main station, down the escalator and towards the Tube. Then he went through the barriers and down another escalator towards the Bakerloo Line.

I could almost touch him.

Central Criminal Court, London

It's taken its time but the case is nearly at its end now. The defendant is clearly exhausted. Witnesses have come and gone. The barristers have done all they can to persuade the jury one way or the other.

The jury is still out, deliberating. Everyone, including those in the public gallery, is fidgeting, as if wondering when it will return. The lawyers are noisily shuffling their papers. There's a general air of tight expectation, rather like waiting for exam results.

Then there is a stirring. The jury, puffed with self-importance, is re-entering. Have they reached a decision? 'We have, My Lord,' says the foreman.

Light glints from the judge's glasses.

'Do you find Betty Patricia Page guilty or not guilty of the murder of Matthew Gordon?'

The single word rings out.

'Guilty.'

There is a brief silence. Then everyone seems to shout at once.

From the *Daily Mail*

Grandmother-of-two pushed actor Matthew Gordon under Tube

Betty Page, a 70-year-old grandmother, has been found guilty of murdering actor Matthew Gordon by pushing him under a Tube train at Waterloo station.

Lengthy evidence was given during the trial by witness Poppy Page, who admitted that she had recently had a brief affair with the murdered man, an old flame, who then infiltrated his way into the lives of her husband and father. In addition, Gordon had lied about his wife being disabled to create sympathy when in fact she was already dead. Mrs Page is the daughter-in-law of the convicted killer.

Gordon's phone was found to contain pictures of him and Poppy Page in bed along with messages threatening to inform her husband of the affair. Gordon also kidnapped the family's dog before pretending to have found it.

The defence argued that Poppy Page's evidence showed that Matthew Gordon was a 'manipulative and possibly dangerous man'.

On the day of the murder, Betty Page watched her daughter-in-law hand over a package to Gordon outside Waterloo mainline station. This was said to contain £50,000 in cash, which he had demanded in order to keep quiet about the affair. She then followed her victim into the Underground, where she had an argument with him on the edge of the platform and snatched the package from him. The prosecution argued that Betty Page 'murdered Matthew Gordon in cold blood to stop him hurting her family'. The defence claimed that Betty's daughter-in-law knew nothing of her involvement – a claim substantiated in court by Poppy Page herself, who said, 'I wasn't even aware that Betty knew about the relationship between Matthew and me.'

Outside the court, several witnesses present at the time of the murder described the scene on the Underground platform. 'There was a real crush,' one woman told our reporter. 'Everyone surged forward to get close to the edge. Betty Page was still tussling with that poor man. That's when the train came.'

Matthew Gordon was married to Sandra Wright, a former actress who died two years ago. He leaves no children.

Sentencing will take place in six weeks' time.

PART TWO

35

Poppy

I've never been inside a prison before. I have no idea what to expect. A few years ago, I was on a set where some of my clients were inmates in a comedy.

But this is no joke, I tell myself, as I stare at the modern building in front of me. And this is no polystyrene mock jail on a set.

This is for real.

VISITS, says the board outside. There is also another notice, declaring that I will be given a lengthy sentence if I am found to have drugs or other prohibited substances on me.

Of course, I don't. I'm not that kind of woman. Just as Betty isn't the kind of woman to have pushed Matthew Gordon under a train. I simply don't believe it.

But there wasn't a chance to show my support before she was whisked off in a van to a remand jail, where she would, I was told by the barrister, stay until the sentencing hearing. 'Sometimes,' she told me, 'the accused is allowed to speak to family and relatives after the court case but I'm afraid Betty didn't want to see anyone.'

'Why?' cried the girls.

They didn't talk to me, of course. They addressed their anguished question to my husband. He wouldn't look at me either. I don't blame them. All three of them have had to hear terrible things about me in court. Just as I'd feared, they'll never have anything to do with me again. The sickening realization makes me want to curl up and die.

'How could you have cheated on Dad?' Melissa had yelled at me during one of the court breaks. She had her arm protectively round her little sister in a rare instance of sibling camaraderie. Stuart just looked at me as if he didn't know me. His silence was worse. I should have come clean with him about Matthew before the trial. Instead, he had to hear the sordid truth in public.

Now he has lost his mother and the children have lost their grandmother.

'I'll move out if you want,' I said when we got home.

'My mother's room is free,' he said shortly.

Since then, the girls have been pretending not to hear me. I don't blame them. I've tried talking to Melissa about the dangers of speaking to strangers online after her Facebook chat with Matthew. Again, she's ignored me.

Stuart has taken time off work to look after them, something he's never done before, not even for illness.

We have our meals separately, by unspoken agreement. Even Coco is ignoring me.

'I can't believe you could have had an affair,' said Stuart, as I was about to go into Betty's bedroom.

'I'm sorry,' I sobbed. 'And I'm sorry about the money too.'

The notes had scattered everywhere after the accident. About £18,000 was recovered but the rest, say the police, was either completely destroyed or stolen. Apparently it's not uncommon for spectators at the scene of an accident to help themselves to 'valuable goods'. Ironically, if the money had been in the new plastic £5 and £10 notes, they might have remained intact. But because of the amount, it had come in larger denominations Luckily, the bank was able to replace those notes that were still identifiable.

He gave me a scathing look. 'You're not the woman I thought you were.'

Those words hurt almost more than any others. Because they were true. In fact, I'm not the woman *I* thought I was, either. My mind goes back to the night of Matthew Gordon's death when the police knocked on our door.

'You're accusing my mother of killing one of my patients?' spluttered my husband when the officers interviewed us in our sitting room. 'She didn't even know him. Matthew Gordon was just a patient of mine who happened to be at drama school with my wife.'

I was as confused as he was to begin with. I'd only just returned from seeing Matthew all too alive and well. How could Betty – who was still out at one of her evening classes – be involved in his death? Now was the time to tell the police about the package; to confess that it was me who had met Matthew earlier that evening.

But I was too scared. Then while the officer was still there, Betty came home and – to our horror – was arrested and taken to the police station.

We found a defence lawyer who specialized in murder cases. Murder! It seemed completely unreal. But Betty wasn't even allowed bail. She was held on remand in a prison on the outskirts of London until the trial.

When we went to see her at visiting time, Betty told us what she'd told the police. 'I was on my way to my jewellery-making class and happened to be standing next to Matthew Gordon on the platform when he suddenly fell on the track. I didn't know him from Adam.'

It's possible, I suppose. When a platform is packed with so many people, you are bound to have a connection with one of them even if you aren't aware of it.

Then she burst into tears. She was shaking so much we could actually hear her teeth rattling. 'It was so awful when he went like that . . .'

'You're in shock, Mum,' said my husband. 'It was just a horrible accident.'

Then he awkwardly tried to give her a cuddle but one of the officers stepped in. 'No touching.'

When visiting time ended, she managed to whisper into my ear. 'Don't say you saw him too.'

That's when I realized. She had known about Matthew. But how? And there was still no way I could believe my wonderful mother-in-law was guilty of murder. There must have been some mistake. But I kept quiet, convinced she'd get off. After all, where was the evidence?

As for the money, it no longer seemed important. Not in the grand scheme of things.

Then everything really started falling apart. My husband's statement – which included the fact that Matthew had been a patient of his and that he'd been at drama school with me, led to further police investigations. The lawyer told me that staff at the hotel in Worthing came forward to say we'd shared a room. Guests at the Christmas work party were also contacted. Jennifer told them that she'd seen us go up to the fourth floor together. I swore that nothing had happened then, but I found that when I got to court I'd be quizzed about what went on between us after that.

'You will be asked to describe your relationship with Matthew,' warned the lawyer.

'Why?' I'd asked, panicking. 'What relevance does it have?'

'The prosecution might argue that this influenced Betty's motives and that she is indeed guilty.' She gave me a look that might or might not have been interpreted as sympathetic. 'Does your husband know about your affair?'

'No. Only . . . only that Matthew and I once knew each other years ago.'

'Stuart will find out when you give evidence. You might want to tell him first.'

But once more, I simply couldn't summon up the courage. Meanwhile, Betty refused to let any of us visit her again in prison. 'She's too upset,' said the lawyer. 'And she says it will only distress you all.'

When the case went to court, I wished I had followed the lawyer's advice about coming clean with Stuart. As she had warned me, the prosecution did call me as a witness to show what Matthew was like and the strain he had put me under. Then their barrister argued that Betty had killed Matthew in order to 'protect her family, including the daughter-in-law, whom she loved as a daughter'.

They forced me to reveal all the terrible things that Matthew had done: the stalking, the harassment, the blackmail. I hadn't expected such personal questions about Matthew and me. I hadn't realized I would be forced to go into intimate sexual detail.

Time and time again, I looked up at the public gallery, searching for Stuart and my daughters' faces. To tell them I was sorry. At one stage, after a particularly graphic confession, I saw Melissa and Daisy jumping up and leaving. That's when I knew it was all over. At least for me.

Later, the prosecution called another witness. A cellist who had been near Betty and Matthew on Platform 3. 'I saw them arguing over a package,' she claimed. 'There was a scuffle. He bumped right into me. I'm pretty sure she pushed him.' She shuddered. 'Then there was this terrible scream.'

Yet 'pretty sure' is no concrete proof, as the defence lawyer pointed out.

Sandra's brother Tom was also called as a witness to give a 'character reference'.

'Matthew was a bully,' he said. 'He fooled people – including my sister at first – by pretending to be charming. But in my opinion, he was a dangerous, obsessive man.'

When Betty was giving evidence, the argument changed.

'I put it to you that your daughter-in-law was indirectly responsible for Matthew Gordon's death. You murdered him because she asked you to, didn't you?'

'No! She wouldn't do that.'

'Are you sure?'

'Absolutely.'

'How well do you really know her?'

'Pretty well, I like to think.'

'Is it not true that you overheard her saying, "I'll kill you, Matthew Gordon," or words to that effect, in her study? Is that when you decided to do the job for her?'

'No. It wasn't like that.'

Betty's hands were gripping the edge of the stand.

'Are you certain? Because your youngest granddaughter, who was at home with a cold, was also outside the door at the time. She told us that you had advised her never to mention it again to anyone.'

'That's because it was just a turn of speech. Poppy didn't mean it. I know she didn't.'

'Then you did overhear her.'

'Well, yes. But like I said, she didn't mean it.'

'I see. My Lord, I seek leave to recall Poppy Page for further questioning.'

I gasped silently. *Please, no more!* As if sensing this, Betty's face turned to me. Our eyes locked. And suddenly I knew exactly what she was going to do.

'All right,' she cried out. 'I admit it. I did it. I pushed Matthew Gordon in front of that train, but it wasn't because Poppy told me to. My daughter-in-law had nothing to do with it. Shortly before it happened, I heard a conversation between them. That odious man was blackmailing her. He said she had to go to Waterloo on Friday evening with fifty thousand pounds. So I went there without her knowing and followed him down to the platform. That's when I did it. I had to stop that man from destroying us, not just financially but also mentally.'

There was a gasp that went through the courtroom like a wave. But at the end of the evidence, the judge addressed the jurors before they were sent out to make their decision. 'I should make it clear that the defendant's statement that she pushed Matthew Gordon under the train does not in itself constitute an admission to murder. The jury has to find that the necessary constituent elements of the offence of murder have been proven.'

In other words, all the other evidence had to be taken into account too.

It took the jury less than half an hour.

Their verdict was unanimous. I knew it would be. After all, Betty had been next to Matthew on the platform. A witness had seen them 'scuffling' and was 'pretty sure' Betty had pushed him. And although the judge had told the jury not to convict on the strength of Betty's admission of guilt alone, it had to have been a big factor.

The case was over. Betty would have to stay on remand before being sentenced. How long would she get? I couldn't bear to think of it. I ran around the court, frantically searching for my husband. But he had gone home with the girls, as I discovered when I came back myself, sick to the core. My daughters were upstairs in their bedrooms. Refusing to come out.

'I'm sorry,' I said to Stuart. 'I wanted to tell you about Matthew. But I was too scared. Our relationship didn't mean anything . . .'

'Stop,' he said. I have never seen him look so angry before. '*Didn't mean anything*? How can you say that? It's thanks to you that my mother is in prison. She was trying to save us.'

'Do you want me to leave?' I sobbed.

'No. The girls need you.'

'But they won't want anything to do with me either.'

'Not at the moment. They might, eventually.'

He was so cold. So clinical. My husband looked exhausted, as if all the life had been drained from him.

'What about you?' I whispered. 'Will you ever want me again?'

He gave me a hard stare. 'I don't know.'

I attempted to talk the girls round. 'Shall we write your grandmother a letter?'

Melissa stared at me blackly. 'You honestly think that's going to help?' she said, her voice laden with scorn.

She was right of course. Nothing could fix this.

My home was no longer my sanctuary. It was my prison now that everyone in it hates me. But still I tried. 'I understand that you had to tell the police what you overheard,' I assured Daisy. But she wouldn't meet my eyes.

'I heard you saying you wanted to kill that man,' she said. 'That's wrong. Granny said you didn't mean it. But I think you did. It's why I believe Granny killed him instead.'

'I didn't ask her to . . .' I started. But Daisy was walking away. I wanted to sink into the ground or go to sleep for ever. I don't deserve to be a parent.

Meanwhile, my initial relief that Matthew could no longer hurt us was becoming mixed with grief as the truth about his awful death sank in. No one deserves to die like that. I tried not to read the papers after the trial but in the end I couldn't stop myself.

'Grandmother Convicted for Pushing Man Under Train' screamed one headline. Then it went into grizzly detail – eagerly supplied by onlookers from the platform – which made me want to weep.

You read about people falling under trains all the time, but this was different. This wasn't just any man. This had been Matthew Gordon. I could see him as clearly as if he was standing in front of me. My first love with dark hair swept back from his face, revealing a strong forehead and a determined nose. Those lips, generous in their fullness. That squarish face. That manner of standing tall, as if assessing the rest of the world. An actor who enjoyed an audience.

That man was no more.

No wonder my husband and daughters hated me. I hated myself too.

I thought of the bruise Matthew had given me on my arm when I'd tried to get out of the hotel room. Had that been a sign of a violent nature? Or was he simply a desperate man? Did I believe what he'd said on my doorstep – that he took no pleasure in blackmailing me? I didn't know any more.

And now, two weeks after the trial, I am finally cleared to visit the one person who tried to save our family. The woman who had been my substitute mother is now facing years in prison because of me.

I am directed towards an officer behind a glass screen. I present my passport and my fingerprints are taken for visitor recognition with some clever infra-red device. 'Sign here, please,' she instructs. 'Leave your mobile phone and all personal possessions in the locker.'

The officer escorts me to a barrier, not unlike those in the Underground. I have to place my thumb on the pad. It opens. I am led down several corridors, conscious of her keys swinging from her belt. The walls are covered with posters offering help for families of those inside.

We are beyond that.

There's a burst of light as we emerge into a sunny courtyard. Some women in green uniforms are weeding. I don't expect this in a prison. They look up at me curiously and then down again. The officer accompanying me unlocks an outer door and then another. More corridors. Up a flight of steps. Women are sweeping the floors or just standing there, staring stonily. How would Betty cope with this, I wonder. She is too old for prison, surely? Yet there are other women here who look as though they could easily be over sixty.

The officer flings open a pair of double doors. 'This is the visitors' room,' she tells me. 'The inmates will be brought in shortly.'

I'm surprised. Pleasantly so. There's a coffee bar. Pictures on the wall. Tables. Chairs. Other people sitting there who look as confused and out of place as I do, while some seem more familiar with their setting. There are young children playing with toys in the corner and older ones sitting with their fathers.

I didn't tell Stuart or the girls I was coming here. I've no idea if Stuart has even applied to visit his mother. I don't know what he's thinking because he barely speaks to me. I only know that I need to talk to Betty on my own.

There's a stirring in the room. A line of women is filing in. They are wearing green prison uniform tabards like the women outside. One has sharp weasel features and long greasy hair scraped back from her forehead. Another looks as though she could be a model. One seems not much older than Melissa.

And there is Betty.

She looks the same and yet different, especially without her usual purple beret. Her face is still until she sees me and then it lights up. She straightens herself. 'Poppy, darling,' she says. 'I told them I didn't want visitors, but of course I made an exception for you.'

My mother-in-law is talking as if we are meeting in a coffee shop. 'Stuart applied to visit too with the girls but I asked them to wait until next week. It was you I needed first.'

She makes to clasp my hands but one of the officers stops her. 'No physical contact,' he says firmly.

'I'm so sorry,' she replies politely. 'You did tell us, but I'm afraid I completely forgot.'

Then she turns to me. 'You poor darling. They gave you such a hard time in the witness box. What is it like at home now?'

Her brow is furrowed. She is genuinely worried about me – not herself. 'They're ignoring me,' I say, choked. 'None of them wants anything to do with me.'

She nods as if it's what she expected. 'It's the shock. Children assume that adults shouldn't make mistakes. But we do.'

'You didn't,' I point out. 'Stuart had a happy childhood.'

Betty gives a smile that is almost sad. 'I hid quite a lot from him, you know. But that's all water under the bridge now.'

Is my mother-in-law implying that her marriage had had its problems too? To be honest, I'd never really cared for Jock and his brusque manner. There were occasions when I thought he was distinctly rude to Betty, even though she didn't seem to notice.

But I don't want to press my mother-in-law on that now. I need to ask her something else.

'They said at the trial that you followed . . .'

I hesitate. I can't say the name 'Matthew'. It makes him seem too real. I try again.

'That you followed him down to the Tube and tried to get the money off him,' I say.

She nods. 'Of course I did. Anyone else would have done the same.'

'But *why*? Why did you push him instead of reasoning with him?'

Betty says nothing. Instead, she is twisting her fingers. She always took great care with her hands. In fact, she and the girls would give each other manicures, giggling and sitting at the kitchen table with varnish and pads. But now I can see her nails are bitten to the quick.

I lean forward. 'Come on, Betty. You don't believe in aggression. You're always saying how important it is to forgive those who hurt you.'

She sits back in her chair, folding her arms. Her mouth is tight. This is a Betty I have never seen before. 'He tried to break us all up,' she said. 'I was furious. But at least now he's out of our lives. And we can carry on as a normal family.'

'But it hasn't helped,' I say desperately. 'It's made it worse. You're inside now. Goodness knows how long you'll get. And Matthew still succeeded in breaking us up. Stuart and the girls will never forgive me.'

Betty holds my eyes steadily. 'But do *you* forgive me?' she asks. 'I killed a man.'

I take a deep breath. I want to say yes. I sort of do. But murder . . . can that ever really be pardoned? Briefly I think back to when I truly wanted to kill Matthew myself. But each time I'd eventually calmed down and realized it wasn't the way to go about things.

'I know it was wrong,' she says with a tremor in her voice. 'Afterwards, I kept telling myself I hadn't done it. It was the only way I could cope.'

'Is that why you pleaded not guilty at the beginning of the trial?' I ask.

An odd look that I can't interpret flickers across her face. 'Yes,' she says.

'And did you then plead guilty to stop the court from recalling me and giving me more grief?'

I couldn't bear it if it had been my fault.

'No, although I didn't want you to be persecuted any more. The fact is that it was right that I should be imprisoned.' She almost looks relieved, as if a weight has been taken off her shoulders. 'The barrister says I'm probably looking at fifteen years.'

My eyes fill with tears.

'Don't get upset, darling,' she says, reaching out towards me and then stopping, as if remembering the no-touching rule. 'I'm looking forward to it. You see, I'm finally going to pay.'

36

Betty

I nearly gave myself away with that last sentence.

'What do you mean, "finally"?' Poppy asks, leaning forward as if confused.

'Well,' I say, hastily, 'it's been some time, hasn't it, since it happened. I was inside for five months until the trial, remember. But the barrister said I was lucky. You can actually be on remand for much longer apparently.'

Time is such a funny thing. It doesn't seem possible that Jane died all those years ago. Sometimes it feels like last week. I wonder, as I do almost every day, how little Violet and Alice are doing. They will be grown women now, perhaps with children of their own. Gary will have married again, I'm sure of that. A kind, charming, handsome widower doesn't stay single for long. I've seen the pattern in the groups I belong to. As soon as one of the women dies, the others flock around her bereaved man like bees to a honeypot.

'I'm a bit tired,' I say. 'Do you mind if we say goodbye for now, love?'

Poppy's disappointed. I can see that. But my mind is such a muddle! I need some time to myself. And if I can get back before my cellmate – who is still here in the visitor's room nattering away to her man as if he'd never beaten her up like she's told me – I might have some peace and quiet. I can't sleep in this place. I thought Jane and the smell of her floral perfume would stop visiting me after the accident. But she hasn't. On and on she goes, in my head, all night long. '*You think you've paid? Hah! You've only just begun, Betty. You don't know the first thing about suffering.*'

It's driving me mad. Maybe that's my real punishment – not just the long prison stretch looming before me. And like I said to Poppy, I deserve it.

I'm led back to my cell. I lie down on the hard blue plastic mattress and concentrate my mind on the cracks in the ceiling above. But it's no good. It's all coming back to me. Those heaving bodies on the platform at Waterloo. The perspiration. The pushing. The frustration radiating out from people coming back from work. The excitement of the travellers with their suitcases; the commuters; the mother with that sweet toddler in the pushchair; the woman with the Selfridges carrier bag. But it's Matthew Gordon's face, close to mine, that stands out. Furious. Sweating with desperation. His hands clutching that package, trying to stop me from grabbing it.

I'm not normally an angry person. But right now I am a lioness, protecting my cubs and my cubs' cubs. 'You are not having this money,' I hiss.

He grins wolfishly. 'Try to stop me.'

That's it. I give this odious man a little push. He falls backwards into a girl with a cello. 'Watch out,' she snaps, hugging her instrument protectively. 'This is extremely valuable.'

'I'm sorry,' I say.

And then it all starts to happen.

What follows next is the real story. No more lies. Honestly.

37

Poppy

I carry on working. It's the only thing I can do. Sally has been amazing, which makes me feel worse. Ironically, we are in even more demand after the court case. Every casting director in town is curious. 'It would make a great film,' says one. I don't comment. But silently I can't help feeling the irony that Matthew has finally achieved his desperate desire to return to stardom now he is dead. The world is talking about him.

As for the £50,000, I can't talk about it. It's a ticking time bomb waiting for the truth to explode. And it's also one more example – as if it's needed – of how I have let my family down.

Meanwhile, Doris has dropped her case against us after Matthew's death. The lawyer's letter simply said that she 'no longer wished to proceed'. I only hope she is feeling better but I don't dare approach her directly or ask through formal channels in case that gets misinterpreted like my flowers note did.

In other ways, things have carried on as normal. I visit Dad every week; spend more time cooking at home (never fish pie as that hurts too much) and doing all the other things that Betty used to do, like the cleaning. I like to think that our kitchen floor is almost up to my mother-in-law's standards. Is this why she was so house-proud, I wonder. Did she also do it to feel like she had control of her life, for whatever reason?

The children lay a place for their absent grandmother every evening at the table. We don't talk about her. They don't talk to me. I'm still sleeping in Betty's room. Stuart goes away one week for a conference, or so he claims. I feel I have no right to ask details. I'm too scared to mention the name 'Janine'. Mentally, I mark off each day until Betty's sentencing.

Then I receive a surprise call from Jennifer. 'Have you got time to talk face to face?' she asks. 'Don't worry. I'm not nagging you about work. But I've just heard a little snippet that might be interesting.'

We meet in a small restaurant off Marble Arch. Jennifer doesn't look so bouncy today. She doesn't speak in capital letters like she does when excited. In fact, her eyes won't quite meet mine. Maybe she's shocked like everyone else to find out that the woman she'd idolized (her word, not mine) had cheated on her husband.

'I'm sorry about telling the police that I saw you going up to the fourth floor with that . . . that man,' she says.

Like me, she seems to find it hard to say Matthew's name.

'I need you to know that I wasn't spying. It so happens that my room was on the same floor too. The police asked us all if we had seen anything at the party that might be relevant, so I . . .'

Her voice trails away.

'It's OK,' I said. 'I understand.'

She lifts her eyes now and looks at me. 'I might be able to make it up to you now.'

I want to laugh. Nothing can get me out of this mess I have created for myself.

'The thing is,' she continues, 'that I saw Doris the other day. Her shoulder is fine now.'

'Good,' I let out a breath of relief.

'But she confided in me about something.'

'Ah,' I say. 'I know what you're going to tell me. I received a letter from her lawyer. It's water under the bridge now.'

'Actually, I don't think it is.' Jennifer is twisting her napkin. 'Doris was too embarrassed to tell you the whole story at the time. But she was so shocked by what came out at the trial that she's asked me to do it instead. She thought it might help your mother-in-law.'

I sit forward. 'How?'

'Your . . . friend. I mean old friend . . . I mean . . .'

'Matthew Gordon,' I say, gritting my teeth.

She nods. 'Doris and Matthew got talking at the Christmas party apparently and swapped room numbers. She was on the fourth floor too.' She looks awkward. 'She told me they actually slept together after the party had ended.'

'Is that right?' I say slowly. A vision comes into my head of him saying goodnight to me so tenderly that I'd been tempted – oh so tempted – to ask him in.

Jennifer looks away again as if she can speak more easily when not facing me. 'They stayed in touch. After you told him about Doris falling on the carpet, he blackmailed her by saying that he would tell her husband about their affair if she didn't sue you.'

What? Just when I thought I knew the depths Matthew had sunk to, it seems he had plummeted further.

'She was so terrified that she agreed,' continued Jennifer, nervously picking at her short, squat nails. 'But she felt awful about it, especially when that woman Sharon began telling everyone that you were negligent in receiving clients at your home because you weren't insured. And then, when you gave evidence that Matthew Gordon had blackmailed you too, Doris felt even worse. She thinks that if she'd told you what he was doing at the time, none of this might have happened.'

It's not strictly true, although I might have been more on my guard.

'It's a bit late now, don't you think?'

Jennifer nods her head. 'I know. She was really scared to talk to you about it. However, she wants you to know that she didn't have a choice.'

'But we all have a choice,' I want to say. We simply persuade ourselves that we don't because we don't wish to admit responsibility for our actions.

'Anyway, how is this going to help my mother-in-law?' I ask irritably. 'The case has already been tried. Besides, as the barristers argued, Matthew might have been a blackmailer, but that's no excuse for Betty to have killed him.'

'I see. Oh dear. I'm sorry.'

Jennifer hangs her head. I want to cry. When she'd said that she had information that might help Betty, I'd felt hopeful for a minute.

'May I tell her that you forgive her?' she asks. 'Doris knows she was stupid and she's desperately sorry.'

I swallow the lump of mi...
worry about her suing us had driv...
tion at the time. But who am I t...
others? 'Yes,' I say shortly.

'Then can she return to your agency? ...
with Sharon.'

I push my chair back. 'No. I'm sorry. I don't ...
would work.'

'Why?'

Do I have to spell it out? 'How could I possibly have ...
client who would be a constant reminder of the man who
had slept with us both – and held us to ransom?'

'I see.'

Jennifer stands up. 'Then you'll have to terminate my
contract too, I'm afraid.'

'I don't understand.'

She is meeting my eyes now. 'Matthew took my number at the party as well, you see. I was flattered, of course I was. Not many men look at a big lump like me but he said he admired my curves.'

She flushes beetroot.

'We slept together a week later. He told me I was cuddly in bed. Afterwards, he asked if I could lend him two thousand pounds. He said he was in trouble over a debt and promised to pay it back when we saw each other the following week. I was so thrilled that he wanted to see me again that I gave him the money. And then . . .'

Jennifer starts to sob.

I can't help it. I reach out across the table and take her hand.

ne restaurant where we'd
ick up my calls and didn't

is cracked. 'I wish I'd given
But I was too embarrassed.'
'Then he di her potential witnesses had also
arranged or the same reason. 'Like I said, I
re ve made a difference but I'll ring

at

ny barrister, I discover I am right. It
would, apparently, be extremely unusual for further 'bad
character' evidence to overturn a murder conviction. 'It
only proves what a scumbag Matthew Gordon really was,'
she said.

During the trial, she and I had become almost friends.
I didn't feel she'd judged me for my affair. People, she told
me, do all kinds of things when they're under stress.

Then two days after we speak about Jennifer's revelation, my lawyer rings me. Her voice sounds hopeful.
Almost excited. 'Poppy? There's been a development.
Another witness has come forward. You're not going to
believe this.'

Right now, I'd believe almost anything if it might help
Betty. 'Try me.'

I hear her take a deep breath at the other end of the
line. 'Apparently there was a Japanese tourist on the platform at the time of the death. And he saw something you
need to know.'

38

Betty

'Do you understand what I've just said about the new witness evidence, Betty?' says the lawyer. She is sitting opposite me in the prison visits room, with an office-type desk between us. There are bars on the window and a poster on the wall. *It is a criminal offence to exchange items of any type without formal permission.* I turn back to the lawyer. I'm trying to listen but my mind is such a muddle.

'Betty,' says the lawyer again. 'I asked if you understood what I've just been saying.'

Once more, I attempt to concentrate. Poppy and my son are sitting at the side of the room on adjacent metal-framed chairs. There is a palpable coldness between them. I ache to feel their arms around me. To make them put their arms around each other too.

'Not really,' I mumble.

'A Japanese tourist on the platform at Waterloo Tube station was filming as part of his holiday portfolio,' says my son in his usual measured fashion. He's always spoken like that, ever since he was a little boy. 'And he caught on camera the argument between you and . . . that man.'

He can't say Matthew's name. No wonder. Jock had found it hard to say Gary's name too.

The lawyer takes over. 'Mr Takano didn't realize that someone had been accused of murder. Apparently, his son-in-law saw his holiday film some time later when he returned to Japan, but only put two and two together when reading about the trial on the internet after the verdict. He then got in touch with the British police. The film clearly shows that you stepped away from Matthew Gordon, who still had the package under his arm. Then he appeared to stumble and fall onto the track.'

She stops. 'It is very clear from the video that you did not push him. Matthew was responsible for his own death.'

39
Poppy

There are times when I wish Stuart would tell me to leave. On a few occasions, I've almost walked out myself. His silence when I speak and his refusal to look me in the eye are unbearable. But I can't abandon the girls, even though they've barely said a word to me since the trial. I also need to talk to Sally about something really big. But that will have to wait.

My – our – only priority is to get my mother-in-law out of jail.

There are, the lawyer has explained, two potential ways of dealing with this clear proof that Betty wasn't responsible.

There could be a retrial, which is a very long complicated procedure and might mean Betty stays in prison for months and maybe years while it goes through the different channels. Or there could be an appeal hearing in which the verdict might be overturned.

Three weeks later, the lawyer summons us to another meeting. 'A retrial or an appeal would generally only take place if the prosecution challenges the evidence,' she explains. 'They have, in fact, accepted it. So we are applying for Betty to be released as soon as possible.'

'That's amazing news!' says Stuart. For a minute, I think he is going to hug me. No. Of course he's not. Instead, we exchange glances of relief, which, for a few moments, unite us. Then it's back to the cold treatment again. Separate bedrooms. An offhand goodnight. Distance during the day, even when we're in the same room.

How much longer can this go on?

40

Betty

The video told the truth. It also revealed details that I had pushed to the back of my mind. I couldn't tell anyone about it after it happened. It was too impossibly horrendous. If I did talk, it would make it real.

But then they encouraged me to write my life story in our prison creative writing class. I did it in the form of letters to you, Poppy, because it felt more natural that way. How it all spilt out! It's strange how these things can appear on paper when you don't mean them to. Even if they aren't quite the same as the words I said under oath in court. I was flustered then. I forgot to say things. I said others that weren't quite accurate. I blanked out details that might have helped my case although the jury still might not have believed me. But my pen couldn't get the words out fast enough:

I can see those last few moments at Waterloo so clearly.

Matthew and I wrestle for the package, forced against each other by the crowds. He's a big man. For one awful moment, I fear he is going to push me onto the line. There is a hiss of air, indicating that a train is coming. He shoves his way towards me, his face red with rage. Scared, I move back.

'Push him,' urges Jane in my head. But I ignore her. I know it's wrong.

Then I notice something. The lace on his right shoe has come undone. My mouth starts to form the words to warn him.

It's too late.

One foot is already standing on the lace as he clasps the package to his chest. He seems to stumble. But I am frozen, unable to do anything. And then – I still can hardly bear to think about it – he just falls. Right in front of the train.

No! He can't have done. I must be imagining it. This hasn't happened. The rest of the platform is also frozen around me. But then someone screams.

And all I could think of was that, without meaning to, I had caused a man's death. Just as I had caused Jane's.

41

Poppy

I still don't understand why Betty had, at the end of her trial, declared that she was responsible when Matthew was, in fact, the author of his own misfortune. Or indeed why she didn't tell us the truth afterwards.

But here, in my hands, is the real account of what happened in black and white. The ending to her life story that the psychologist showed us when we arrived for our next visit.

'I thought you ought to see this,' she says quietly. 'I've just discovered it in your mother-in-law's creative writing folio. She said I could show you. Betty confirms that Matthew tripped – just as the tourist video shows. Of course, a written account can't be used as evidence. But it does confirm that she is now telling the truth.'

'Why did you lie about pushing him?' both Stuart and I say when Betty enters the visits room and sits down. She was still waiting for the Prison Service to agree to her release.

'Don't you see?' says my mother-in-law lifting up her face. 'It was because of Jane. All this was her idea.'

42

Betty

'Just tell the truth,' the barrister told me. So at first I did. But the prosecution made mincemeat of poor Poppy. It was like they were trying to incriminate her, even though I was the one on trial. It seemed obvious that they wanted me to say Poppy had told me to push Matthew Gordon.

I hadn't realized, until Poppy gave evidence, how evil that man really was. My poor daughter-in-law! Her life had such startling similarities to mine. When it was my turn to speak in court, Jane's voice came to me, right there. '*Tell them it was you,*' she suggested in a smooth, silky voice. '*It will pay for what you did to me. It can be your penance.*'

And then I saw Poppy watching me from the spectators' gallery. I was scared that in some way she might be blamed for what had happened because they knew Poppy had said she wanted to kill Matthew. My head was in a real mess by that point. So I thought I'd follow Jane's advice and take the blame.

'I did it,' I said suddenly. 'I pushed Matthew Gordon in front of that train.'

The jury then convicted me. It was a no-brainer, as my grandchildren might have said. I had admitted responsibility. Besides, there had already been one witness (that girl with the cello) who'd claimed we were 'tussling' and that she was 'pretty sure' I'd pushed Matthew. Of course, she was wrong but the truth was that there were so many people, all pressed up against each other, that no one could really see what had happened. I wasn't to know that the Japanese tourist's camera with its sophisticated equipment had caught a brief clear shot.

This was the chance I'd been waiting over forty years for to atone for Jane's death.

But she hasn't kept her part of the bargain. She is still tormenting my dreams. '*Did you honestly think I would let you go free?*' she laughs, night after night in my cell. '*You will never have peace, Betty. Ever.*'

43
Poppy

Stuart cried when the psychologist showed us Betty's letters to me. So did I, but I was surprised by my husband. I'd never seen tears on his face before. 'I didn't realize their marriage had been like that,' he said. 'I knew Dad could be tough but some of that stuff . . .'

He spread out his hands in an 'I can hardly believe it' way.

'I'm sorry,' I said, putting my hand on his shoulder. I'd hoped he might grasp it, or give me some sign that I could approach him. He didn't.

But my mother-in-law is the bigger issue right now. When we finally get her home, Betty's going to need a lot of help. The prison psychologist only has a limited amount of time. There are so many others for her to deal with. I've read about prison cutbacks of course, like everyone. Yet this is my first experience of how it truly affects staff and prisoners.

We're going to visit Betty again next week. With any luck, we'll be able to talk to her then about how to move forward. Perhaps we'll be able to make her see that she deserves forgiveness.

At some point I will need to address the problems in my marriage. I really ought to confront Stuart with my fears about Janine. Yet I'm too scared to have a frank conversation in case it breaks us up completely. It's like treading on eggshells.

How on earth are we going to function as a family, even when Betty is released? Stuart's declaration that we just have to carry on for the sake of the children will be a life sentence of misery if he is going to continue this stony wall of near-silence towards me.

There's also work to think about . . .

Something has to happen.

Then, a few days later, it does.

'You know,' says Dad when I phone to see how he is, 'I've been thinking. Let's do a bit of tidying up in the spare room. You could come down this weekend if you're able to.'

I've been trying to get him to clear his rubbish for ages. I suspect he's trying to distract me from my troubles. Dad's been amazingly supportive of me, given that my own mother had had an affair. 'No one is perfect, love,' he'd said to me after the trial.

'Why now?' I ask in reply to his 'tidying up' suggestion.

He shrugs. 'Just felt it might be time. That's all.'

So I drive down that weekend. When I survey the task ahead of us, my stomach sinks. This is going to take more than a weekend. Dad has kept everything! My old school reports, programmes from plays he and my mother had taken me to at the local theatre, photographs of me as a little girl on a beach somewhere, flanked by my parents. Then some of me as a teenager with Mum. We look more alike than I remember, apart from the hair.

'Blimey,' says Dad sheepishly after more than an hour of us sifting through it all. 'There's enough stuff there. I'd forgotten how much.'

Everything smells stale with age. 'I can see that.'

'Tell you what,' says Dad. 'Why don't you leave that lot and tackle that pile there?'

I look to where he's pointing. In the corner are a stack of battered cardboard boxes, sealed with heavy brown tape I usually save for Christmas parcels.

'We should probably finish this lot first,' I say. 'It'll be chaos otherwise.'

'Just look at those boxes, will you,' he says in a tight voice. 'I'm going out for a bit. We'll talk about their contents when I come back.'

What's got into him, I wonder. Then again, he was shocked like the rest of us by Matthew's death. It's changed all of us.

Once he leaves, it takes me ages to peel off all the tape, partly because it's stuck down so well and also because I am so scared of what I'm going to find. I can't help feeling it's something to do with my mother. Letters from her lover, perhaps? Photographs of them together? Evidence of years of infidelity?

Eventually I get the tape off and open up the cardboard flaps, choking on the swirl of dust. I was right. It does contain letters.

But they're addressed to me.

Stacks of them.

Unopened.

The letter on the top of the pile shows it was posted the day after Mum had left, when I'd just started drama school. Heart pounding, I slot a thumb under the seal and unfold the piece of paper inside.

Dear Poppy,

I can only imagine how hurt and angry you are with me right now. But I am hoping that when you are older, you will understand.

I married your father because he was there. That might sound crazy but things were different then. Some girls, like me, were worried that no one would ask us and that we'd end up on the shelf. In those days, you couldn't just live together like you all do. Besides, I wanted a baby. How we both adored you! We'd have liked another but it wasn't to be. Not because I couldn't have one — as we told you — but because I had, by then, fallen out of love with your father. In truth, I'd never been in love with him at all. He wasn't unkind to me. He was a good man. But there was no passion. He was also older than me. I still wanted to explore life. And, yes, I know that sounds selfish. But I'm being truthful.

Then, one day, I met a man. He was on holiday here with his wife and child. They were playing on the beach. You were with me, Poppy. You were eight. We began chatting and . . . what can I say? It was instant. Like a bolt of lightning. Of course, we couldn't tell anyone. Oh, how we felt guilty. We would see each other when we could, although it was hard because he lived so far away. Time after time, we broke it off because we didn't want to hurt our families. Time after time, one of us then called the other.

So we made a pact. We decided that when our girls — his was the same age as you, Poppy — got to eighteen and went to college, we would start our lives again with each other. I hoped, desperately, that you would be old enough to understand.

I do pray that you do, darling. Tony and I are renting a little house in the Isle of Wight. Here's a picture. I'd always wanted to draw before but there wasn't time. Now there's too much.

There's a little sketch below of a bay with hills rising above it. I hadn't realized Mum was so artistic. Was that where Daisy got it from?

Please come and stay with us when you come back from drama school at Christmas. We want you to meet Tony's daughter too. She understands.

I can't read any more. I want to rip the letter into shreds. But what if Daisy or Melissa were reading a letter from me in twenty-odd years' time? Wouldn't I want them to carry on?

The other letters continue in a similar vein. They ask how I am doing; express her disappointment that I haven't replied but say that she 'understands'.

I'm not sure if you know this, Poppy, but I wrote several times to you at your college address. You didn't reply. Perhaps you are still angry with me – I get that – so I left it a bit, hoping you'd change your mind. Then I wondered if you'd actually moved out of hall. I rang your department and found I was right!

So again I waited and sent them to the house instead. Perhaps your father didn't pass them on. Or maybe you still don't want anything to do with me. I only hope you receive this one. If you do, please try to see my side, Poppy. Just in case you didn't read my earlier letters, your dad and I simply weren't suited. I hung on for as long as I could with your father. But when you left for college, I couldn't cope any more.

I stop for a minute, unable to believe the words in front of me. I have a sudden memory of how my father would always be first to the door to gather the post when I came back for holidays. In those days, he was far more organized. Obsessive, almost, in keeping everything as neat as a pin. Yet how could he have kept this from me?

The letters get shorter after that but more desperate.

I almost wish I had never left now, Poppy. I miss you so much. Tony wants us to move to Australia. He says that if you won't have anything to do with us, it will be better to make a clean break. Please write back and tell me you don't want that.

There are also birthday cards. One for every year of my life since she left. Each has a little watercolour painting inside with her signature underneath. Some were posted on the same years that she'd sent envelopes to the PO Box address on my website. Envelopes that I had put in the bin unopened, not knowing about the earlier letters, thinking that these 'new ones' were too late. Clearly, she'd sent duplicates to try and persuade me to get in touch. I don't know exactly at what point I started to cry, but there are tears streaming down my face now. My breathing comes in racked sobs.

'You've read them, then.' Dad's voice is soft.

His voice from the door startles me. I hadn't heard him come back.

'Yes.' I stand up slowly and wipe my eyes on my sleeve.

'Are you angry with me, love?'

I don't say anything. I don't know what I feel right now.

'I was scared you might leave me and go and live with her, you see.'

Dad's voice sounds clearer and surer than it has for months. I still can't bring myself to look at him.

'And you never asked about her,' he continues, a note of fear in his voice. 'Not once. You didn't question where she was or how you could get in touch with her. So I told myself you wouldn't have cared anyway.'

He's right. But I hadn't talked about Mum because I didn't want to upset Dad. I was also angry with her. I wasn't ready to understand. Not until Matthew had walked back into my life at the Christmas party last year.

'When you got older,' he says, rubbing his chin in the way he sometimes does when upset, 'I knew I should tell you. But I was terrified you wouldn't want anything to do with me when you found out about the letters.'

He reaches across and takes my hand. 'I'm sorry, Poppy.' I still can't quite face him but I can tell from his voice that he's crying too. 'I'm so sorry.'

'I think,' I say, looking round the room, 'that we ought to get someone in and take all this stuff to the tip. Don't you? Then maybe we could put up a proper bed so I can come and stay.'

He holds out his arms and draws me to him. 'I'd like that, love. But shouldn't you go home now? You've got a husband waiting for you.'

'Stuart doesn't care,' I say quietly. 'Perhaps I should start again on my own somewhere. It will be easier for them without me.'

'No,' says Dad firmly. 'It won't. You've got to go back and give it time. That's the only way. The cuts won't heal overnight. But after a bit, they'll get better. You've got to learn from our mistakes. Families can still be fixed. It won't be easy. But you can do it.'

Just then my mobile goes. It's Stuart.

'Poppy?' There's an energy to his voice that I haven't heard in ages. A determination. My heart sinks. Is he calling to say he's leaving me? Is he running away with Janine? Just as my mother had run off with another man?

'Poppy,' he repeats. 'The lawyer called. The application to quash the conviction has been officially accepted. Mum's being released tomorrow.'

44
Betty

Even though I'm in my own bed after all these months, I wake up early at the usual prison time of 6.30 a.m. and wonder why my cellmate isn't sleeping on the other side of the room, curled up in her habitual foetal position because, as she told me, 'When my old man's around, I never know when he's going to clock me one.' I wait for the electronic bell. The queue for the crowded loos. The spitefulness of some women ('Don't mind if I eat your bread, do you?' my cellmate used to say at mealtimes and I didn't dare make a fuss in case she chewed my toothbrush like she had with my predecessor). The kindness of others ('Here, share mine,' said someone else).

It's still hard to accept that I'm free.

'We understand why you said you did it, Betty,' Poppy had said when they told me about my release. 'The prison psychologist told us. And we're so sorry you had to go through all that with Jock.'

But coming home was a shock. The atmosphere in this house is now almost as bad as it was in those early years with my husband. It's not until you 'try again' after an infidelity that you realize how tough it is. I'd forgotten until now how almost everything on television seems to be about someone having an affair. It makes it almost impossible to watch. Time and time again, I see either my son or daughter-in-law getting up and walking out of the room to 'make a cup of coffee' at an inconvenient moment on screen. I also suspect that Poppy was sleeping in my room when I was away because I keep finding small things like the odd hairband, which she always wears at night. Separate beds aren't good for a marriage in my opinion.

Yet there are also moments when I see her and Stuart talking to each other in a kinder voice than before. The other day they actually took the girls out bowling – just the four of them. But then Stuart went and ruined it all by having two 'late meetings' on successive nights for his 'research' with that woman I've heard him speak to on the phone. He even uses her name out loud – 'Oh, hi, Janine' – as if he doesn't care who hears. Can't he see what he's doing, silly boy? If he's playing tit for tat, it won't get him anywhere. Or does he really care for this other woman? Either way, he won't discuss her with me.

Still, the girls compensate for almost everything. 'I'm so glad you're back, Gran,' Daisy will say, snuggling up to me on the sofa. 'We missed you terribly. And Mum and Dad aren't arguing as much.'

Melissa says nothing but she holds my hand as though she is a little girl again, even though she acts all grown up when her parents are around.

Meanwhile, I've been getting help from the lady who used to run my meditation course. Poppy and Stuart wanted me to see a psychologist but I said that if I was going to go to anyone, it would be Brigid. She's a natural health therapist as well as a meditation coach. We're working through my guilt in all sorts of different ways, involving energy fields, herbs and chakras.

Jane still speaks to me, but now I am able to challenge her.

'I'm sorry,' I said to her the other day. 'But you can't change the past. You can only live with it.'

It's something Brigid has taught me.

Jane didn't have an answer for that one.

Brigid has also encouraged me to face the physical evidence of the past too. So I got out the old photograph albums. 'Are you sure you can't remember who that beautiful lady is with the little girl?' asked Daisy, leaning over my shoulder one day as I leafed through the pages.

This time I tell the truth. 'Her name was Jane,' I said. 'She was my best friend.' I swallowed the lump in my throat. 'But she died.'

Daisy's face fell. 'I'm sorry.'

'So am I.'

'What happened to the little girl?'

'I don't know. She's grown up now, I expect. So is her sister.'

Then I gave her a big cuddle. 'But I'm a very lucky person. I've got you two.'

'*Think of the positives.*' That's what Brigid keeps telling me. '*Every day, when you wake up, say "thank you" for everything. Forgive everyone, including Matthew Gordon. Forgive yourself.*' That's the toughest one.

I want to ask the girls if they forgive their mother, but it's too delicate right now. Maybe it will work out. Maybe not. Only time will tell.

The solicitor called again yesterday. It appears that there was something else that the Japanese tourist's camera picked up on. Matthew Gordon was extremely unsteady on his feet. I remembered noticing that at the time, but thought he had been drinking. It all fits in with the autopsy results, which had picked up excessive amounts of Valium in his blood. He had been prescribed it by his doctor for anxiety but must have taken too much. This, in turn, might have made him more likely to trip.

Or, as the police put it, it could have been 'one more contributing factor to a tragic accident'. Of course, if I hadn't followed Matthew down to the platform and argued over that package, he might not have died. Or maybe he would have fallen in front of a car instead, thanks to the Valium. Either way, it helps to know it wasn't all my fault.

'I'm so sorry you went through all that, Mum,' Stuart says to me when Poppy is out and the girls are in bed. 'You should never have spent nearly half a year in prison for a crime you didn't commit.'

'It was the right thing to do,' I say to him. 'Don't forget that I am responsible for a death, even if I wasn't totally to blame for Matthew's.'

'No!' The anger in my son's voice takes me by surprise. 'You've been poisoned by this needless guilt over your old friend which has tormented you all these years. You are entitled to happiness, Mum. You're a good woman. You just made a mistake.'

I'd hoped he would say this.

'If you're right,' I say quietly, 'why aren't you more understanding towards your wife? After all, she made a mistake too.'

45

Poppy

It's three months since Betty was released. She's been having therapy and seems less frenetic than she was before any of this happened. 'Brigid thinks I had to keep doing one hobby after another to try and block out Jane's voice,' she told me. 'The strange thing is that I haven't heard her for ages now.'

Melissa has, amazingly, passed her exams and is now at university. The house is so strange without her. She replies to my texts with one-word answers.

> How are you doing?
>
> > Fine.
>
> What's your accommodation like?
>
> > OK.

And so on.

She replies to my suggestions that I visit her for the day with equal brevity:

> > No.

Daisy seems just as distant on the surface, but I've overheard her talking to Coco, who insists on sleeping at the foot of her bed (I don't have the heart to say no).

'Remember that man who kidnapped you?' I over-heard her saying one evening when her door was ajar and I was on my way up to the bathroom. 'He was Mummy's boyfriend when she was younger. Then she started seeing him again. It's partly why Gran went to prison but I don't really understand the whole story. It's complicated.'

Her words broke my heart. In fact, they made me decide to talk to Sally about increasing her hours so I can spend a bit more time on family life. I'm still in the office during the day when Daisy's at school but I've been trying not to be at my desk every evening. I make a huge effort to ignore emails and, instead, to curl up on the sofa with my youngest daughter, watching some inane teenage pro-gramme, hoping that one day she might want to talk to me and not just the dog about 'the whole story'.

Stuart and I are politely distant. When I returned to our bedroom after Betty's release, he wanted to sleep on the floor but I'd persuaded him to stay in our bed. He keeps rigidly to his side, as far from me as possible.

And then there's work. After the trial, as I said, the agency enjoyed a surge of interest generated mainly by curiosity. But then one of our regular clients appointed a new CEO who wasn't so keen on our notoriety. Work we were relying on for cash flow was cancelled. Other com-panies followed suit. Sally and I both knew why. There's a lot of sheep-like behaviour and uncertainty in this busi-ness. People love you to bits one minute and turn tail on you the next. And even though I hadn't done anything wrong in the eyes of the law, the Poppy Page Agency was associated with *that* court case. When Betty was released, the headlines started all over again. It didn't matter that she was exonerated. The fact was that the business was once more mentioned in connection with a man's murder.

It's time for me to come clean.

I ask Sally round. We usually liaise through emails and telephone calls with occasional meetings. 'This feels very formal,' she says, sitting opposite me at my desk.

I stare out through the window at the garden. The rooftops. Then I force myself to look at Sally's open, trusting face. 'The truth is,' I say, 'that on the day that Matthew died, I went into the bank to beg for an emergency loan of fifty thousand pounds in cash against the agency.'

Her face blanches. 'Fifty thousand pounds?' she repeats. 'But isn't that the amount you gave to Matthew Gordon? The money that was lost in the accident?'

'Not all of it,' I say. 'We got about eighteen thousand back.'

'I thought that was your own money,' she splutters. 'That's what you said in court.'

'I did,' I admit. 'And in a way, it was true. The bank lent it to me on the strength of the agency's record. I didn't think we were going to lose business. And now they want their money back.' I swallow the lump in my throat. 'So the only way I can find the remainder is to sell the agency.'

I reach out to her. 'I'm so sorry, Sally. I can't afford to keep you on any more.'

She bites her lip. I hate myself. I've already let down my family. And now I've let down a woman who was not just the closest I had to a best friend but who also relied on me for work.

'I see,' she says. 'Have you got a buyer?'

'Not yet.'

'But why would anyone want to buy it?' she asks. 'Won't they just associate it with what's happened?'

'I was hoping to get something for goodwill,' I say weakly.

Sally gets up. 'I'm not sure that's going to happen.'

She's right. I'm kidding myself.

I wait a few more weeks but there's still no interest. So now I'm going to have to do something I never wanted to do. I tell myself that it doesn't compare with Matthew's death, which is in my head constantly. But it's still going to be a life-changer.

Of course, Stuart had asked after the trial where the money I'd given Matthew had come from. I'd explained I had borrowed it against the agency and that 'I'd be able to pay it back before long'. Now it's time to be open with my husband, just as I was with Sally.

I wait until Daisy is in bed and Betty is in her room. We're sitting in separate chairs in the sitting room. Facing each other. Then I explain my financial situation. I twist my hands. 'I don't know what to do.'

Stuart stands up, just as Sally had done earlier. He's going to walk away from me too. I don't blame either of them.

'All right,' he says. 'Use our savings to pay the bank off.'

I stare at him. 'Why?'

'Because what else can I do? You'll be declared bankrupt if I don't. I can't allow the girls or my mother to suffer any more grief.'

'Thank you,' I say. I reach out a hand to touch his shoulder but he moves away.

'I'm thinking of closing the agency anyway,' I say. 'My name has tainted it.'

He seems surprised. 'Surely people will forget.'

'Really?' I give him a sad smile. 'You can't. So why should they?'

46
Betty

Slowly, very slowly, we are all learning to put our lives back together. I have to admit that there were times when I wasn't sure this would happen. We've had our moments. I had to send several messages to Melissa, begging her to change her mind when she said she wasn't coming back for the Christmas holidays. My oldest granddaughter can express herself better in texts than on the phone, when she just clams up. She never used to be like that. I suspect she's too upset to speak.

> Why should I come back, after
> what Mum did?

she types.

> Because she's sorry. We all make
> mistakes.

> Not adults.

> Especially adults.

I can see from the dots that she's writing furiously.

But they're meant to know better.

> No one is perfect and that includes
> parents. Your mum might be
> closing the agency and she's
> really upset about it. Please come
> back. It would mean a lot to her.

I hold my breath. The reply takes a few minutes. But then it comes.

> OK.

Did I do the right thing or not? Perhaps an absent Melissa might be better than a sullen, hurt one who refuses to let her mother collect her from the station. But her reply, when I made the suggestion, is sharp and to the point.

> Just Dad.

When she's home, she spends most of her time at Jonnie's house. 'Young love,' I say to Poppy. 'There's nothing like it.' It's true. There isn't. It's only when you get older that you realize how special it was.

I can't pretend that Christmas was easy. 'Very nice,' said Stuart coolly when he opened Poppy's present, a navy-blue fountain pen. I happen to know she'd spent a long time choosing it.

'Thanks for the voucher,' she said to him in response.

He shrugged. 'I thought you could get what you wanted.'

In other words, he couldn't be bothered to choose something more personal. Or maybe I'm being old-fashioned. After all, it's what the girls always want.

'Hope you like this, Gran,' says Daisy shyly. 'We saved up to buy it, didn't we, Melissa? The lady in Selfridges said it was a "classic".'

'How lovely of you!' I begin unwrapping the pretty silver paper with the twirly bow. Then I stop. A lump sticks in my throat. It's perfume. Not just that. The floral fragrance is very like the one that Jane used to wear: the same one that haunted my nightmares afterwards. I can still picture the bottle that I would 'borrow' from her dressing table to smell nice for Gary . . .

Tears fill my eyes.

'What's wrong, Gran?' asks Melissa.

Everyone is looking at me. But I am waiting. Jane hasn't spoken to me for months now. Surely she'll have something to say about this? A caustic comment like '*I don't know how you can even think of wearing it!*'

But no. There's nothing. Maybe she really has well and truly gone.

'I'm just overwhelmed,' I say, holding both girls to me. 'Thank you.'

Of course, I can't spray it on me. It would bring back too many sad memories. But I will keep the pretty bottle on my dressing table because my grandchildren – my wonderful girls – gave it to me as a sign of love. The kind that can't ever be broken.

The rest of the day is pretty flat, to be honest. The girls watch a film and Stuart says he has some 'emails to catch up on'.

'At Christmas?' I question.

He shrugs. 'It's for research.'

Boxing Day is completely different, thanks to Coco. 'Come on,' says Daisy who doesn't seem to blame her mother as much as her sister. 'Let's take the dog out for a family walk.'

'Is Mum coming too?' asks Melissa sharply.

'Why wouldn't she?' says Stuart, who's just finished cooking bacon and eggs for everyone.

I watch Poppy flash a look of gratitude towards him. But my boy looks away.

We go to the park. Stuart is striding on ahead now on the crisp, icy grass with the girls and Coco. Poppy falls back and I do the same so we can walk side by side.

'You know,' I say, plunging my hands into my coat pockets to keep them warm. 'There's something I've been meaning to tell you about your husband. I wanted him to tell you himself but he won't.'

Her eyes widen. I suddenly realize she's scared. I wonder if she's going to ask me the question about him and Janine, which I've been wondering about myself. But she doesn't. So I continue.

'Stuart knew about your affair with Matthew long before the court case.'

'What?' Poppy gasps, running her fingers through that lovely auburn hair in the way she does when she's surprised or nervous. 'How? Who told him?'

'He isn't stupid,' I say, ignoring the last question. 'He wasn't fooled when you denied remembering Matthew from drama school. So he confided in me. He thought you might still have feelings for him.'

Then I stop briefly because this is the tricky bit. 'I agreed. I could tell something was up. It's why I began to keep tabs on you. But, like I said in court, I didn't tell anyone I was doing this. Then one day when you went down to see your dad, Stuart rang to get hold of you. You'd just left. But he got talking to your father, who told him how an "old boyfriend" of yours had recently visited him.'

Poppy gasps. 'No!'

I take her hands. She's wearing the red woolly mittens I knitted for her.

'Your poor husband was beside himself. "Do you think I'm imagining this, Mum?" he asked. I'd seen the picture he was blackmailing you with by then. I knew you'd slept together, although I couldn't tell my son that. I loved you too much. But I also had to be honest. "No," I said, "I don't think you are imagining it."

'"Then I'm going to punch his bloody lights out," said my boy.

'"Don't do that," I told him. "That's not going to help anyone. Just be calm. Let it run its course. Stay put and it will be fine in the end."'

Poppy was clutching my arm as I spoke. Her face was white. 'If he'd really cared, he'd have said something to me,' she said.

'No. It's exactly because he did care that he kept quiet. He was scared you might leave him. It's why I suggested you went down to the caravan.'

Poppy looks as though she's going to be sick. 'He asked me some questions about Matthew there.'

'That's because he was trying to give you a chance to tell him.'

Poppy looks awkward. 'Then he made love to me.'

'Maybe he wanted to see if you'd say no. Or perhaps he was trying to show who was boss.' I think back to Jock's behaviour in bed, even though I don't tell her this.

Poppy is puce red. Although we're close, we've never talked about sex openly like this before. 'So why is he showing his hurt now but not before it came out in the open?'

'Exactly because of that. After your confessions in court, he couldn't pretend it *didn't* happen. But it will work out. I know it will. I've seen the way he looks at you when you're not noticing. He loves you.'

Poppy doesn't say anything. Silently I pray that I'm right and that this Janine hasn't developed into something more than a research partner.

'Keep going,' I say. 'It's a new beginning. Look how Melissa is coming round. It will be all right.'

Poppy gives me a sad smile. 'I hope so.'

'Mum!' calls out Daisy. 'Come and throw the ball with us to Coco.'

She walks ahead. It gives me time to think. *It's a new beginning*, I had said to Poppy. And it's true. What has gone, has gone. You can't look back.

My fingers close around the small Christmas card in my coat pocket. I'd been holding it close to me ever since it had arrived via the lawyer.

Dear Betty, I read about you in the newspapers. The handwriting was old-fashioned and slightly smudged. People rarely use real ink any more. *I hope you are well. I want you to know that I still think of you.*

Gary had put his phone number at the bottom. But I'm not going to ring it. I'm not even going to keep the card. When Christmas is over, I will tear it into little pieces. Yet I can't quite bring myself to do that right now because it gives me a tiny bit of comfort. It's proof that someone once really did love me.

'Watch out!' calls Daisy.

A small rubber ball comes flying out of nowhere and catches Poppy on the face.

'Are you OK, Mum?'

It's Melissa, running up. 'I'm sorry. I meant to send it in the other direction.'

'It's all right,' she says. The beginnings of a big bruise are already forming on her right cheek. But it doesn't matter. Melissa has her hand on her mother's arm. Stuart is running up too.

'Are you sure?' he says. There's tenderness in his voice.

'I think so,' says Poppy. She seems a little dazed.

'I didn't mean to hurt you,' says Melissa.

'And I didn't mean to hurt you either,' says Poppy slowly. 'None of you.'

There's silence for a minute as we all look at each other. Then my youngest granddaughter breaks it.

'Group hug,' demands Daisy.

Somehow, we're all holding each other. Tightly. Determined not to let go.

But just as I tell myself it's going to be all right, Poppy's mobile rings. She breaks away to look at her phone.

And I watch her face go pale as she walks away to take the call.

47

Poppy

Reality kicks back in as I see the name of the caller. 'What's wrong?' Betty asks when I hang up and return to where they are standing. 'Is it your dad?'

I shake my head. 'No. It's Sally.'

Even Stuart looks up. So do the girls. They'd all liked my happy, chirpy assistant on the few occasions they'd met her.

'She wants to buy the agency off me using her divorce settlement,' I said. 'She can't give me more than five thousand pounds for the client base but she'd like to employ me as an assistant. It won't be my agency any more, of course. But it means I'll be back in the business.'

'You need that,' said Betty quickly. 'Doesn't she, Stuart?'

She shoots him a meaningful look and I wonder if they've been having words about me. Sometimes I think that the only person who has any influence on my husband is his mother.

'It will be better than you hanging around the house, waiting for the phone to ring,' he said.

I hadn't realized he'd noticed. Even though Stuart had insisted on using our joint savings to make up the balance of my bank debt, bookings had been painfully slow.

A new name – unassociated with mine – might make all the difference. And our regulars like Jennifer, Doris, Ronnie and Karen (with the tattoo) have all pledged their loyalty.

'I'd put Sally's money straight into our account,' I say quickly. 'And as her assistant, I wouldn't be responsible for any financial liabilities.'

'Won't you mind not being the boss any more?' asks Melissa.

'No.' I never thought I'd say it, but it's true. 'It will give me more time for all of you.'

Stuart says nothing, but Betty takes my hand and gives it a gentle squeeze. 'It will all come right in the end,' she says softly. 'You'll see.'

It's the New Year. The snowdrops and crocuses have burst through the winter soil. They remind me of the flowers in the Embankment Gardens. And of Matthew. I'd like to say that I don't think of him, but every now and then he comes back into my head. Yes, he caused me terrible pain. To say he acted badly is an understatement. Yet he might be alive if it wasn't for me and I can't forget that.

But there's another reason I can never block him out. Matthew Gordon is inextricably tied up with my younger self. Little dumpy Poppy Smith with the bright smile and auburn curls who had fallen madly in love with a man, unaware that he was going to break her heart. An eighteen-year-old girl – the same age as my Melissa – who had had such high hopes of being an actress but whose hitherto happy-go-lucky approach to life had been smashed by her parents' breakup.

I used to think back on that 'me' with sadness and disappointment. I don't any more. Now I look back with acceptance. The past is the past. It is time to move forward. No more secrets. No more lies.

Which is why I needed to have another talk to Stuart. Every day over the Christmas holidays I'd braced myself, and every night I'd failed to say something. The words wouldn't come. Despite that group hug – and Sally's unexpected offer – everything was still so strained. We limped on through January and half of February, while at the same time attempting to put on a united front for Daisy. At least now Melissa has just started to send me the odd two-line text from university instead of one word.

If it wasn't for work, I'd go mad. Sally's Agency, as she's named it, is doing surprisingly well. At first I was worried that my presence even as an assistant might deter potential clients. After all, hadn't people shunned us because of my ruined reputation?

'Memories are short,' Sally told me. 'New casting directors are coming in all the time. Besides, I need you. You have far more experience than I do.'

'Are you sure you're not taking me on out of pity?' I asked.

'You did the same for me when I came to you after my divorce,' she pointed out. 'Just call it quits.'

It helped that our regulars kept their promise to stick with us. Doris was thrilled when I got her a one-line role in an ad featuring Hollywood lookalikes to promote skin care. Ronnie the vicar is going from strength to strength, constantly singing our praises. And Jennifer has found her feet (or should I say paws?) in an animal television commercial where everyone is in costume. 'THANK you!' she said, flinging her arms around us both.

I've found to my surprise that I'm enjoying my work more now than when I was in charge. I've learned to shut down my computer and put my mobile on silent at 6 p.m. every evening so I can have 'quality time' with Daisy.

But I'd happily lose the agency a second time, to get my marriage back on track.

Then, one evening when it was just Betty and me at home (Stuart was working late again and Daisy was at a friend's), my mother-in-law came up with her idea.

'Why don't you go down to Devon again, love? You know, I wasn't too keen on the place at first because of Jock's behaviour on our honeymoon.' She faltered for a minute and I put a hand on her arm in comfort, remembering how she'd described his brutality in her prison creative-writing sessions.

'But later,' she continued, 'when things improved in our marriage and we started to take Stuart down as a young lad, I found the sea so relaxing. It helped me to think clearly. It's why we bought a caravan of our own. Give it a go.'

'Our last visit didn't help,' I pointed out, thinking how it was there that Stuart had shown me the picture of Matthew and me at drama school. Besides, the sea had lost its charm for me when Mum had left home, staining all those childhood memories of us finding shells on the beach.

'Like I said,' whispered Betty, giving me a cuddle, 'things change. And it will give the two of you time on your own.'

406

'Stuart would never agree to that!' I said. But, astoundingly, he did. Maybe Betty twisted his arm. It wouldn't surprise me.

Even so, we drive down almost in silence. *This isn't going to work*, I tell myself, glancing sideways at his set expression every now and then with a sinking heart. Then we go up a steep hill in first gear and down again. There in front of us are those huge rocks rising magnificently out of the sea that I remember from before. Fields stretch out around us.

'Beautiful,' we both say as one.

For a minute we are joined together by stunned admiration. Then Stuart and I go back to polite practicalities as we unload the car and open up the caravan. This time we'd arranged for someone on site to air it and put on clean sheets. There's a bunch of pink spring blossom on the side along with a pot of local honey, but even so, I'm beginning to have doubts about coming here. Marriages can't be saved simply by a change of scene. Can they?

'Shall we go for a walk before we unpack?' says Stuart in a flat voice.

'I'd like that,' I reply, trying to sound enthusiastic.

We go down the slope towards the beach. A fisherman is hauling his boat across the sand. 'Afternoon,' he says in a friendly way. If a stranger greeted us like that at home, we'd be suspicious. But here it seems warm and welcoming.

The sun is dipping. The sky is a blend of orange and yellow streaks. Stuart and I walk side by side. Still we say nothing.

But something odd is happening. That breathlessness which has been inside me for so long is beginning to subside. Betty was right about the sea. It *is* calming, with that gentle rhythm of the waves, lapping onto the sand like a persistent heartbeat that says, 'I'm still here. Don't give up on me.' I'm beginning to feel like a different person away from all the memories of court and the terrible things that have happened.

For a while, we stand in silence. Watching.

'You know,' says Stuart eventually, 'what I love about the sea is that it's angry sometimes and calm the next. A bit like life.'

I am amazed. My husband isn't usually the philosophical type.

I want to tell him once more that I'm sorry. But it might spoil things, so we carry on, crunching over the pebbles in silence. Yet, I realize slowly, it has become a comfortable silence. Not a tight one.

That evening we drive down to a pretty Regency seaside town along the coast and buy fish and chips. We munch them sitting side by side on the low wall on the promenade. The sea stretches out as far as the eye can see. Behind us, the line of historic hotels with their blue plaques glow with the warm, welcoming light from their windows. One of the bars has an open courtyard with pretty fairy lights. Maybe we could go there tomorrow evening.

'Sure you're happy eating here?' he says.

I nod, thinking of all those London restaurant meals where we had sat stiffly over the years. Here, we can listen to the sound of the water gently slapping against the shoreline. 'Definitely.'

'Me too.'

There's something between us. I can feel it. But still he doesn't take my hand. And I don't dare make the first step in case he rebuffs me. 'Let's go,' he says after a bit. We drive back to the caravan, each wrapped up in our own thoughts.

The bed, which unfolds down from the wall, is small. It's not so easy to lie apart like we do at home. It's also cold.

I shiver.

'Do you want another blanket?' he asks.

'No,' I find myself saying. 'I want to know where we are.'

He turns on the light. We both sit up, looking at each other.

Stuart rubs his eyes. There are bags underneath. He's aged in the last few months, I realize. 'We've been through all this before, Poppy. I'm trying to come to terms with everything but it's hard.'

'I know it is. But you haven't been truthful with me either, have you?'

A look of alarm flits over his face. 'How do you know . . . ?'

I feel sick. 'So you are having an affair, then?'

His face clears. He lets out a snort as if this was actually funny. 'Of course I'm not.'

'Then why have you been turning away from me at night for ages? Long before . . .'

I stop, unable to say the words 'before I slept with Matthew'.

I can see him looking awkward. 'I don't know. I suppose it's because I'm always tired. And . . . well, that does affect the way we men work. I can't always . . . you know.'

'What?'

He looks away. 'I can't always do it.'

For a moment I don't know what to say. That possibility had never even crossed my mind. 'It's not because you fancy Janine?' I ask doubtfully after a minute or two.

'What? No!' Stuart shakes his head in disbelief. 'Is that what you've been thinking? Poppy, she's a colleague. We're writing a paper together. There's absolutely nothing between us, I swear to you.'

He is so indignant that, for a minute, I'm scared he's going to get up and leave.

'But you made love to me the last time we were in the caravan,' I point out.

'I was scared you were going to walk out on me for *him*,' he says. 'It did something to my body.' He rubs his eyes. 'It's difficult to explain. Maybe it's a man thing.'

But I think I get it.

'About Janine,' he says, more slowly now.

My heart catches in my throat.

'We're going to be presenting our paper at a conference next month. Would you like to come along?'

I'm so taken aback that I hardly know what to say. 'Wow. I mean, OK. I mean, yes, I'd love to.'

'Good.' He opens his arms. 'Cuddle up.'

We don't do anything else. But it feels warm. Comforting. Yet I still can't help feeling that something isn't right.

I dress with particular care for the conference. Leaning forward towards the mirror, I check my reflection, wondering if the eyeliner is too much. I do believe him about Janine, but still, I want to look my best.

'You look very nice,' says Stuart. He himself looks pretty good in his dark woollen suit and pale yellow tie. But I sense he is on edge.

He's still nervous as we approach the conference centre, taking his hands in and out of his pockets.

'This research paper is a big thing for me,' he replies when I ask if everything is OK. 'There will be some important people here.'

I give his arm a squeeze. 'I'm sure it will be fine.'

He doesn't respond. Once more I feel that old flatness coming back. Why can't he show his feelings more?

We go through the big glass doors into the foyer.

'Stuart!'

The most glamorous woman I have ever seen is suddenly at our side and kissing my husband on both cheeks. She is blonde, impossibly slender and dressed in a sleek blue suit. I feel my cheeks grow hot. So this is my husband's 'colleague'?

'Poppy,' she says, turning away from Stuart and extending a hand to me. 'I'm Janine. Lovely to meet you at last.'

Really?

'This is Amanda, my partner,' she continues.

Another woman, equally beautiful, her short brown hair swinging around her ears, sidles up and takes Janine's arm.

'We're so excited about the paper,' Amanda says, her green eyes sparkling. Those eyelashes are incredible. Can they actually be real? 'Now hurry up, Janine. You too, Stuart. It's about to start.'

Amanda and I take our seats. 'Do you understand what they've been working on?' she whispers in a confidential little-girl tone as though we've known each other for years.

'Not really,' I confess.

'Nor me. It's not my field.' Then she drops her voice. 'Actually, this is a big day for Janine and me. It's the first time I've met any of her colleagues. She was worried about what some of the stuffier ones would think.'

I'm not sure what to say. What a relief! But why hadn't Stuart said? It would have been so much simpler.

'That's brave,' I manage.

'Just what your husband said. I wondered if he'd told you.'

'No,' I say.

Then an idea comes to me. Had Stuart wanted to make me jealous out of wounded male pride? What better way than to have regular assignations and phone calls with another woman? After all, he'd suspected me of having an affair. So I can't blame him for making me think he was doing the same. I'm beginning to wonder if there's more to my 'serious' husband than meets the eye.

'Janine confided in him, you see,' continues Amanda. 'It was him who encouraged her to be open about her sexuality. You've got a good man there.'

The person in the row directly in front of us turns round and shushes us. I flush. Amanda nudges me in the ribs. 'Here they are.'

Usually I tune out when Stuart goes into what I call dental-speak. But this time, I try hard to listen. There are a lot of complicated diagrams and phrases and figures. Amanda rolls her eyes every now and then, which makes me want to giggle. Then the audience is invited to ask questions. It's all too complicated for me! A man near the front puts his hand up.

'Yes?' says Stuart.

'My question is not directly related to your research, but I would be grateful for your advice. I have a patient who is so terrified of dental treatment that I have been injecting him in the mouth with a sedative that is a member of the same drug family as Valium. Could this interfere with the pain relief methods you have been discussing?'

Valium? I stiffen. Sit up straight. Stuart looks unnerved. It doesn't happen often, but after all these years together, I can tell the signs. His right eye flickers very slightly and the edge of his upper lip goes up on one side.

'That isn't something I've had much experience of,' he retorts tightly.

He is fiddling with his cuffs as he speaks. My husband is usually honest. It's one of the reasons I married him. But my instinct tells me that this time, he is lying.

My mind shoots back to the autopsy. No further questions had been asked about the large quantity of Valium in Matthew's blood. The doctor had given him the tablets for anxiety. The report had made that clear. But he was also in pain with his teeth. He'd said so in the

Embankment Gardens. '*They really are playing me up and I had to get them looked at even though I get really nervous about see-ing the dentist.*'

But that was on the Tuesday. The accident had hap-pened on the Friday. A strange buzzing starts in my head. If my husband had given him Valium, surely it wouldn't have still been in his bloodstream by then? Only the amount prescribed by the doctor unless, as had been suggested by the autopsy, Mathew had taken more than the recommended dose. Hadn't he been rubbing his jaw just before he'd snatched the package of money from me at Waterloo? Was it possible that he'd been back to see Stuart earlier that day? Even if this was the case, why would my husband have given him extra Valium? To calm him down as suggested by the ques-tioner in the audience? Or to deliberately make him woozy? Even then, Stuart wasn't to know that this might cause an accident. Although perhaps he'd hoped it would make him unsteady on his feet.

Maybe it was his way of inflicting a 'wound' on a man who had tried to take his wife.

So many ifs. So many buts.

I could of course just ask him now. Perhaps there is a perfectly reasonable explanation. But how do I know my husband will tell the truth? Still, I can but try.

'Well done,' I say to Stuart during the coffee break before the next speaker. Amanda and Janine are talking to other people. Every now and then, one will touch the other on the arm. No one seems to bat an eyelid. Nor should they. I can't help envying them for their obvious love and commitment.

'Your research seemed to go down very well,' I say.

Stuart nods in acknowledgment of the compliment. 'Thank you.'

'I didn't know that a form of Valium could be injected into the mouth,' I continue.

Stuart fiddles with his cuffs again. 'It's not standard practice.'

'Especially,' I say quietly, 'if someone has already been prescribed Valium by the doctor. That would be dangerous, wouldn't it?'

'Yes,' says Stuart carefully, meeting my gaze. 'It could cause an overdose. But, of course, that would rely on the patient disclosing to his or her dentist that they were on Valium already. And some people don't always tell the truth because of embarrassment.'

Some people don't always tell the truth. Would Matthew have? Would Stuart?

I go to question my husband further. Then I stop. What would it achieve? We've reached a better place than we were in before. I don't want to jeopardize it. Not just for the sake of the children but for my sake too. And Betty's.

Stuart puts his arm round me. 'Shall we skip the rest of the conference? I think we could do with a couple of hours to ourselves.'

I put the thought to the back of my head. *There comes a point,* I tell myself, *when you just have to trust the person you love.*

Epilogue

Poppy

'Why don't we move to Devon?' my husband suggests when we come back from the conference. We're sitting next to each other on the sofa. Betty is in bed. Those days when I slept in her room seem so far away now.

I look at Stuart as if he'd suggested emigrating to the moon. 'But what about your work? My work? Daisy's school?'

'One of my old lecturers was there today,' he says. 'Did you see him? A very tall chap in a brown dogstooth suit.'

I did, as a matter of fact. He and Stuart had been deep in conversation at the bar while I'd chatted to Amanda.

'He wanted to know if I'd be interested in joining his practice in Exeter,' continues my husband. 'He's retiring and thought it might suit me. As for your work, you can do it anywhere. You've always said that. There are some great sixth-form colleges for Daisy. Melissa will love the beach life in the holidays and I'm pretty sure that Mum will be up for it too.'

He's right. They are. And once I agree, it only takes a bit of persuasion on my part to get Stuart to see the doctor. That funny ad on television helped! The one with the hunky middle-aged man who dances down the stairs in the morning with his woman after taking Viagra. To our surprise, we'd both found ourselves laughing when we saw it during a commercial break. 'See,' I said. 'There's nothing shameful about it.'

It's amazing how regular sex can bring you together. It's not the act itself. Or just the feeling of being wanted. It's both those things, combined with a large dollop of love and the family cement that comes from having two children, a granny and a dog to unite us.

But right now there's another type of new start I'm trying to make. In fact, I've been agonizing over it for months. I could have asked Betty for her advice. I could even have asked Dad. But in the end, it's Stuart who helps me make the final decision.

'I think you should go ahead,' he says. We're lying in the semi-dark, our naked bodies entwined. 'I know it's scary. But it's the right thing.'

He holds out his mobile phone to me. 'You could do it now, if you want. It will be daytime there.'

My fingers shake as I ring the number my mother had put at the bottom of those letters. Every single one. The phone rings five times. My heart is beating so fast that it feels as though it's in my mouth. I'm not going to be able to speak to her like this. I press Cancel.

'Why don't you do your pillow thing?' says my husband.

What? He's always laughed at me about my childish habit of turning it over three times for luck. My mother had done the same when she'd been young and she'd passed on the superstition to me. Daisy still does it, though Melissa now declares it to be 'stupid'. Maybe she's right.

'That's just silly,' I say, a little embarrassed.

'Not if it works for you,' says my husband gently.

I turn my pillow over – one, two, three times.

Then I press redial. One ring. Two. Three. Four. Five. Six. Seven . . .

'Hello?' Her voice is breathless, as if she has just come running into the house. From the garden maybe. There is no Australian twang. It is exactly as I remember. It sings of summer in the Welsh valleys where my mother had lived before marrying my father. Of love. Of hope. Of a childhood when I thought everyone was always happy. Of a future that can still be rescued.

'Hello?' she repeats.

There is a silence. I want to speak but I can't.

'Who is that?' she asks. There's a slight tremor to her voice as if she thinks she knows but doesn't dare hope.

I struggle for the right words. What do you say to the mother you rejected all those years ago?

Keep it simple, Stuart had advised.

I take a deep breath.

'Mum?' I say. 'It's me.'

Acknowledgements

Huge thanks to the following:

My family for putting up with me when I disappear into my study and my own fictional world. (I'll be downstairs in an hour. Promise!)

My amazing editor, Katy Loftus. Her talent is awesome. I bless the day we met.

Rosanna Forte and Victoria Moynes for their clever suggestions.

Natalie Wall for guiding the book through pre-production; Georgia Taylor and Ellie Hudson and Jane Gentle for their amazing work on the campaign; the whole Penguin Adult sales team who worked miracles; and DeadGood and Pageturners, who are always brilliantly supportive online.

My incredible agent, Kate Hordern, who, together with Katy, has changed my life.

The professionals who advised me on dentistry issues, including Richard Davies, Professor Damien Walmsley and the British Dental Association. They all helped me get my gnashers into the subject!

Countless agencies for extras/supporting artistes, including Ray Knight, Alan Sharman, Casting Collective and Universal Extras. As always, any mistakes are my own. Sounds like a great career.

Bectu, the union for creative ambition.